CRIMSON SNOW

JASON R VOWLES

Also by Jason R Vowles:

The DC Daniel Hudson Prequels
The Long Night

The DC Daniel Hudson Series
Crimson Snow
Haunted Mind
Dark Promise *Coming Soon*

First independently published in the UK by Jason R Vowles, 2020
Official third edition, independently published, 2021

Copyright © Jason R Vowles 2020

Cover Design Copyright © Nick Castle, 2021

The moral right of the author has been asserted.

All characters and events in this publication, other than those clearly in the public
domain, are fictitious and any resemblance to real persons, living or dead, is purely
coincidental.

All rights reserved.
No part of this publication may be reproduced, stored in a retrieval system, or
transmitted, in any form or by any means, without the prior permission in writing of
the publisher, nor be otherwise circulated in any form of binding or cover other than
that in which it is published and without a similar condition including this condition
being imposed on the subsequent purchaser.

ISBN 979-8-664461534

Independently published by Jason R Vowles

www.jasonrvowles.com

For you, Nan, as promised. I finally did it. Love you always.

Monday, 4th February, 2019
20:14

Outside the office, in the bustling streets of Tower Hill, thick grey snow and gridlock traffic filled the space between canyons of glass and stone, frosted pale from the winter freeze. I flipped my hood up and fell into step with the rush hour crowds, feet kicking through the slush, my breath rolling clouds of steam. My weary feet led me down Crosswall road past American Square. I was heading toward the Overground. But, after a furtive look over the shoulder, I decided on a sharp left heading south along Cooper's Row and then the underground for the district and circle line.

Hands stuffed into a thick pea-coat I'd worn just twice, I weaved my way past commuters, huddled within the shadowy confines of tall buildings. Here, storeys of Georgian rows blocked the onslaught of snow, sheltering the city ants and me. It allowed for a slightly drier walk to the station. Allowing me to remain hidden.

Something touched me then. Not physically. Not a hand at my backpack or perversely on the wrist. Instead, I felt something creep along the edge of my mind, pacing to and fro and caught a reflection in the tall windowed fronts of a lavish Thames side hotel.

My pale and cold complexion.

A shiver scuttled the length of my neck, burrowing deep into the nape. Was that me? Was that me staring back, eyes black as glass? Looking closer, I fixed my coat and checked my teeth.

Halting for a little longer in the doorway, I pulled out my phone and checked the time. A single snowflake drifted past and landed on the screen, melting slowly into a bubble of water. It beaded quickly, then rolled off completely.

A few more drips followed. One after the other. And it began to snow.

The commute by tube was as expected; busy, hot, with slush from outside having slicked the dirty tiled floors. I sent a quick message to the bloke I was due to meet for business purposes back in the open air, before making a short detour ten minutes from Hyde Park.

I turned off into a small side street, leading me into a mews. A tucked-away haven of incredibly expensive cottages, blocked by the taller buildings and out of sight. Ultimately, it provided me with perfect privacy.

Perfect, quick opportunity.

I fished through my backpack and pulled out a tiny little plastic pouch. Cold fingers fumbling, I peeled open the clips and leaned forward, sniffing the powdered contents with sudden hunger. Almost immediately, I felt the sharp metallic feeling against the back of my throat, the kick almost instant as my pupils no doubt dilated.

I was whole. Calm and composed. And now, ready for my evening appointment. Work like this always required a little something more potent.

Conscious of time, I used some snow to melt against my face and clean up, tossing the bag into a bush on the street. Now feeling so much more confident and in control.

Next to a small café at the very entrance to the park, a tall, well-built man with a slick comb-over and a long black parka stood waiting. His head turned left and right. Searching. I didn't wave or draw attention. Discretion was the name of the game.

'Evening, nice to finally catch up,' he said as I crossed the road. 'How're you?'

He held out his hand, and I shook it.

'Care to lead the way?'

'Bit of an odd location to talk, don't you think?'

'It is, Robert,' I said. 'Which is why it offers us perfect discretion to discuss what we need to discuss. I also have a soft spot for the place.'

Robert shrugged. 'Fair enough.'

We turned, walked around the café and onward into the park.

I was quite tall already. About six foot and yet was markedly dwarfed by Robert's much broader and taller frame. He didn't intimidate me, though. No. The ball was in my court this evening. It had been planned for weeks. Months. Now the time had come to really kick things off and put things in motion.

I had to commit. Which may explain why I was so forthright in submission, something that was not atypical of my character at all. But I had to sell this just right. I couldn't miss a beat, or all of this work would have been for nothing.

'So, how long have you really worked investment banking?' I asked, firing up the conversation as we walked deeper into the park.

'Told you before. About twelve years now. Time flies. You?'

'I'm not directly in investments. More of a consultant by trade, but dabble in investment when needs must. Diversify income and whatnot.' I changed the topic. 'Shame about the bloody snow, been murder trying to get here. Tubes are still running, though. For now, anyway.'

'Oh, I dunno 'bout that,' Robert said, his eyes wandering across the park between lines of oak trees. The grass hidden beneath inches of untouched snow and away from the bustle and scurry of London feet. A bubble of solitude and muffled sound in the dark, highlighted by the luminous lamplights. 'I rather like the snow. Still, we're here. As weird as it is. It'd be a shame not to savour it whilst it lasts.'

I laughed. 'Didn't take you for a softie?'

'Fuck off.'

We carried on our walk a little further, heading west toward the lake. The scene was beautiful, the palace lights in the distance catching the park in a beautiful orange glow.

Stirring the silence, Robert pointed toward my back. 'So, what's in the bag?'

'Just work stuff, really,' I lied. 'Couldn't drop it off anywhere before I came here.'

He frowned, shoving his hands into his pockets. 'But you knew you were coming tonight. In advance.'

'It was a last-minute thing. Anyway, let's discuss the accounts. Where do you want to begin?'

'Right. Let's start off with the Saudi accounts. Those are a nightmare. Let's take a look.' Robert pulled out his phone and walked closer to me. He tapped away quickly, bringing up figures. 'I think the strategy here is perfect, but the implementation is off. I've kept this all in house, just me. No one knows, so I've not had the man-hours to move bits and pieces around. Have a look at this, tell me what you think.'

I leaned in next to him and surveyed the data on his phone. But it wasn't what I was paying attention to.

'I'm sorry, what does this bit mean?' I calmly asked, plunging the hidden knife from my jacket repeatedly into his chest and abdomen with sickening thuds.

His eyes flew open in shock, dropping his phone into the snow. Blood dribbling out from his mouth and down his chin. My methodical attack continued, my voice remaining steady. It was all too easy. 'I'd say the data looks just fine, Robert.'

The man collapsed to his knees, the onslaught of my attack absorbed by his large mass. Shorter, vulnerable and now exposed, I turned the knife to his face, tearing the flesh, eyes to dribbled jelly, his screams caught in a gurgle of blood. I made the final stroke.

And Robert collapsed dead in Hyde Park, his body and face mutilated beyond recognition and the snow soaked in thick, hot blood. A dash of it catching my face and coat in the process. Tendrils of steam escaping the wounds.

Panting, arm aching a little from the activity, I looked both ways, ensuring no one was around. Most in cabs, cars or buses on the way home, or already there, tucked up on a warm sofa. But I worked overtime; by day, a city worker, by night a butcher in the dark.

Thinking quick then, my chaotic mind whirring, I slid my arms under Robert's armpits and pulled. And pulled again. And again. Then again, heaving, aiming for the bush beside us, a growth around a large tree opposite the lake.

Wincing from the struggle, I stretched my arms out. Arms that were toned and used to the weight. The years in the gym. The decades of being in peak physical condition. You had to be. I had to be, to always come out on top. The skills were still… transferable.

A loud popping sound echoed; one of Robert's arms escaping from the socket, and I came colliding with the ground, coat drenched.

'Shit!' I cried. 'Move!'

Wiping the cold sweat with the back of a bloodless sleeve, I took out a set of goggles, a hat and a hammer. Ready, I swung the hammer up and struck Robert hard just above the forehead. There was a loud crack and a squirt of blood. I went at it again. And again. And again, until I was almost exhausted. I worked at it until I could remove the top of his skull following a quick scalping. There, his brain sat. Dead. Exposed and yet magnificent in design. I reached in and spent a while wiggling it out, cutting the top of the spinal cord with a knife, before placing it down on the snow as far as I could.

Satisfied with my amateur efforts a few minutes later, I thanked fortune the weather would save me this time and, wasting none to fantasise at the moment, took off my bag, coat and shoes and swapped them for a thick jacket and a set of boots. Shoving the blood-stained clothes into the backpack.

Now a little more comfortable, wearing thick walking boots and a coat with a hood, adding at least a few stone to my frame, I threw on the backpack, double-checked my efforts and then the time. A strange laugh tumbled out of my mouth.

When I finally arrived beneath Albert Bridge, forty minutes later, hidden in darkness permeated faintly by the distant glow of the moon, the numbness had begun to seep its way throughout my entire body and all but robbed my sense of touch. As I approached the pavement wall, I placed my bare palm on the powdered cropping and peered down into the dark ooze below.

'Right...' I whispered, taking the bag off and resting it on the wall, heart-pumping steadily and rhythmically. A gust of snow, my eyes glazed over, and I was back at the park, covered in blood, staring at the devastating remains of his face and body.

Push it over.

His eyes peeled open, the hole where his mouth was gaping wide, sucking at the air.

He's dead. It's over. Push it over the edge.

But Robert reached out to me, fingers trying to find purchase and a silent scream never escaping his ruptured throat.

Finish it!

Robert lunged at me, blood erupting from his chest... And with a little nudge, the backpack went tumbling over into the icy depths, splashing as it hit and sinking quickly with the weight.

And Robert was gone. And so was I.

My eyes lit up then as I smiled. Nausea all but vanished along with the contents of the bag. Now, at the edge of the river, my senses heightened. All I could picture was his beautiful brain. Exposed. Revealing everything. Removing the lies.

My smile broadened.

'It's time for you all to know the truth.'

Tuesday, 5th February
06:18

From the steamy confines of the bathroom, a distant cry told Daniel Hudson his flatmate, Eisa, was wide awake and urgently in need of a piss. Rinsing the shampoo from his hair, he fumbled out, towel around his waist, soaking the tiled floor behind him.

'Sorry, lost track of time.' Hudson mumbled, still weary.

Eisa, only a little shorter, sporting a Super Mario dressing gown and a skull earring, flapped her arms and stormed in, slamming the door shut behind her. Hudson chuckled and quickly got himself dressed. He dismissed the odd assortment of candles in the living room and a stack of hardbacks on the kitchen counter, teetering and threatening to fall. Eisa co-ran a bookshop with an old University friend on the ground floor below the flat in question. They barely broke even, but her unprecedented, slightly pretentious love affair with books kept her going. Kept the roof over their heads. That and selling acrylic paintings on eBay.

Before Hudson had moved down to London in the new year, he'd struck gold on Gumtree finding this flatshare. There were plenty of pedantic and ludicrous requirements to satisfy her vetting needs, such as a healthy respect for literature, prompt cleanliness, and his favourite, no alt-right *flat earthers* who never vaccinate. Either way, it was an easy decision considering the asking price in the area.

He hummed along to some Bellrays whilst finishing the dishes, a filter coffee behind him rumbling. Eisa re-appeared, took first dibs on the sludge and watched with mild interest at Hudson being vaguely domesticated.

'Well, I'm rather glad to see this is still consistent,' she said.

Hudson laughed.

'Oh no, this is it. Last wash. It's all downhill from here.'

The gurgle of the sink draining failed to drown out Eisa's indignant scoffing. 'Hilarious.'

'Quite.'

Hudson finished up, got dressed and took a few moments to sort through some crap on his bedside table. A furniture selection also found online. A mismatch of wood types and shitty shelving. But it worked.

On top of the pile of papers, he took up a leaflet for a nearby Brazilian Jujitsu dojo, classes every Wednesday and Friday. At the moment, despite curiosity to follow up, he just didn't have any time. Since moving down from Gotham in Nottinghamshire, things had gotten busy. Very busy. But that was the price of his most significant career move yet. The chance for more substantial cases and a better chance at promotion. It also meant he could be closer to people that mattered to him.

His sister.

Since they were young, when his mother had chosen to adopt her from an abusive Polish family, Hudson had always admired her and feared her in equal measure. It wasn't until he was older that he grew more protective of her—when the mental breakdowns and trips to therapy grew more regular.

No family was perfect, least of all his, but having not seen her for several years, he was keen to change that. Make amends if he could. She deserved that much.

Sliding his feet into a pair of weather-proof boots, Hudson noticed a text from her and decided to reply straight away with a quick call. It was just easier that way.

'Hey, y'alright?'

No reply at first. Hudson busied himself with the laces until she finally answered.

'Just another day, thought I would see where you are.'

'I'm in my new flat, just getting ready for work. You OK?'

'Why're you asking me that?' Her voice was immediately standoffish. And Hudson was used to it.

Just his coat to grab, he made the last of his call by the front door, pissing off Eisa, who looked busy in an accounts book. 'It's just a question, Krystina. How are things? When are you next free?'

Another moment of silence. Some rustling in the background.

'Chat to you later, Danny.' And she hung up.

Confused, staring at his phone, Hudson pocketed it and got his coat on. Thinking what on earth that could have been about? But, as was expected, he would soon find out, usually in a dramatic fashion that ended up getting someone hurt. That was her curse, and Hudson had tried his best throughout their childhood to be there for her. At least in a better way than their Mother had been. It had never been enough, and ultimately it had cost them. Which is why, Hudson reassured himself as he locked the flat door behind him, he had jumped at this promotion to the Met. Policing and making the world a better place wasn't just about the strangers around you but sometimes the people closest to home. Family.

And that was Hudson's first priority.

Tuesday, 5th February

06:45

Hudson's phone buzzed as he left the flat via the stairwell. Thought it might be Krystina abut noticed the unknown number.

'Hello, Daniel speaking?'

'Morning sunshine, it's Hiraoka. Add me to your damn contacts.'

Hudson fumbled his phone leaving the building and started crunching through the early morning snow. 'Sorry sir, what is it?'

'First case is in. You can forget all that training bollocks you've been running through. Get washed and dressed.'

'Really? Excellent, well, I'm already jumping into my car. Much parking at the station?'

A deep laugh met him on the other end. 'You ain't going to the station Hudson. Meet me at the south gate, Hyde Park.'

Hudson slammed the car door of his Renault Clio, chunks of ice falling from the windscreen.

'Hyde Park?'

'Yeah, is the line breaking up?'

'No, but wh—' And then it dawned on him in slow, horrible realisation. 'Already?'

There was a pause on the other end. 'Get here, asap. Hope you didn't eat breakfast.'

The cold slush of morning snow sprayed the curbs as Detective

Constable Hudson made his way through the packed streets of central London. The grey of it all contrasted with the white fluff on the tops of cars and pavements. Untouched for the time being, until kids got their hands on it to make snowballs or giant snow dicks. But right now, the city was hibernating.

When Hudson pulled up outside Hyde Park, a few police vans sat parked up on the pavement, blocking the main gate. He climbed out, zipped up his coat and marched over to the uniformed officers standing guard.

'Detective Constable Hudson,' he shivered, flashing his badge.

The park looked serene and picturesque. Like a Christmas postcard where snow clung to tree branches by inches, only bird prints marking the top. Except this image betrayed what lurked further in the grounds. Something he knew deep in his gut would look horrifying, and no amount of mental preparation could ready him for it. The real fieldwork.

His first homicide.

Only last year, Hudson had been given the transfer of a lifetime to a London Met position from Gotham. Comfortable in his tiny office and small-town crimes, he felt the move was a sign for new challenges. A new life. But until this morning, he didn't really know what he'd gotten himself in for. Setting aside his doubts, Hudson took in a deep breath and readied the cogs of his talented investigative mind.

After a short walk through the park, milling around just off the path by a small grove, the SOCO team looked busy, their work area now a muddy slush. Stood next to them, the broad figure of DCI Hiraoka, hunched forward, puffing away at a cigarette. As if sensing his presence, or merely hearing his approach up across the snow, Hiraoka turned to him.

'Nice of you to turn up, detective,' he barked.

DCI Hiraoka was a large man, just a nudge taller than Hudson. He wore a long dark parker coat, black jeans and boots. Around his neck, a dark red scarf. His hair hung loose, parting naturally down the middle, falling low over the ears. At a glance, he looked menacing and up closer, even more so. His dark eyes and hardened features hinted at a tough-working life.

Hudson rose a hand up apologetically and jogged the rest of the distance. He stopped relatively quickly, catching sight of the mess behind his senior and to the left of a large crime scene tent.

'Jesus. Who found it?'

'Royal Parks OCU weren't on shift. Pair of uniforms found this little treat taking a short cut. Nasty one isn't it?'

The voice hadn't come from the inspector, but from one of the guys down in the slush, a portly man in white overalls and a gloved hand gingerly inspecting the shredded face of their male victim. Hudson had heard rumours about the iron cast stomachs of the London SOCO teams. Coming across some of the country's most gruesome murders and carrying on with their work like it was spilt milk. But of course, it wasn't. They all felt it in their own way, but none of them showed it. They were all hard as nails and as the fat one stood up, side-stepping from the corpse, exuberating nonchalance, Hudson felt a wave of respect for the man. Then he noticed something else. Something pink, the size of a grapefruit in the snow beside the head.

'Just a bit. Is that… is that a…' Hudson paused, feeling his stomach churn. Hiraoka and the SOCO guy eyed him cautiously.

The inspector pulled out a fresh cigarette. 'TOD?'

'Hard to say. Rigour's set in. Temp will skew the time, but I'd say late last night, possibly midnight.'

'Eight or nine to midnight then?'

'Yup. No wallet, phone or possessions found either. Likely taken.'

'What's the song then, Petridis?'

Hudson had regained himself a little and frowned at this. Song? Some new London copper lingo he'd need to learn? Or maybe he had misheard?

'Heavy Metal. Screamo even. It started extremely quick and sudden, full of rage and passion. The angle of the knife wounds, of which there are many and still counting, came in almost level with the victim, suggesting someone of similar height.'

'Height of victim?'

'Six-three, six-four. He's a big bastard. All conjecture, of course.'

Hiraoka lit his cigarette and took a quick puff. 'Someone, or something big, came along and knifed this one to bits, then lobotomised them? Did it discrete at night, in the park with no one around to see shit, used his strength to dump him here?'

Petridis shrugged. Hudson hurried to take out his notepad when the inspector shot him a furtive glance.

Take some bloody notes.

'True. The murder was done just along here. There's some hardened ice beneath the snow around the left of this bush, some blood. We think he was killed just off the path then dragged a few feet round here. Would have required some strength, so a large man does fit the MO but let's not rule anything out just yet. It's not a lobotomy, by the way. Commonly confused in media and on the telly. But the medical term for full removal of the brain is called an Encephalectomy. I've never come across this in my career. Ever. Don't envy you being made senior investigator of this mess. You always seem to catch the weird ones, John.'

'It's just my brand,' he said. 'So, passionate then? What type of knife are we thinking? Small, easily concealed?'

Petridis nodded again. 'Yup. Small sharp object to puncture the body, sever the brain from the spinal cord, but the most interesting part is the face. Here, I'll show you.'

Hiraoka knelt down beside him and looked to the face of the victim, the flaps of skin hanging frozen by blood and ice.

'Fuckin' hell. Why the need?' Hiraoka took a longer drag this time, Hudson waiting from a comfortable distance, stomach still squealing.

'Indeed,' said Petridis. 'Hey, Rick, what was the wording you used?'

The other SOCO bloke there smiled at Hiraoka almost proudly. 'Like pulled pork.'

The chief inspector frowned, cigarette hanging off his lip. He looked between the two men in disgust. 'You two are fucking unhinged. What about the brain then? Not seen anything remotely like this since I was back home.'

'Hammer. Something similar. The blows around the skull are varying in-depth and damage, so it looks as frenzied as the knife wounds. Very passionate. Angry. But the display is, well, artistic. Don't you think?'

'That is my job, yes. Thank you for the thought.'

Petridis chuckled. 'Right, well, the attacks to the centre mass, though frenzied and deep, are measured. They go in and come out fairly clean. They weren't a hack job. But if you take a look at the cheeks here, and across the nose, well, where the nose used to be, you can see the tears on the flesh. Here and here.' He pointed.

'So, stabbed to death, dragged here, then the guy's gone to work on him afterwards for good measure? Then cracked him open and removed the brain for display?'

'Yup.'

Hudson's pen was working away, his curiosity piqued. Why had the killer done that? What did they get from pulling them a few feet and then mutilating the face? Was it to do with displaying the brain? The guys had mentioned *passion,* but to him, it looked a lot like rage. Someone deranged. Someone who wasn't in their right mind. What's more, why was a member of the SOCO so forensically liberal? Surely, someone such as a medical examiner would be best trained to give out such preliminary findings?

'Maybe to conceal their identity?' Hudson mumbled.

No one heard him.

'Post-mortem?' Hiraoka enquired.

'Yup. Well, we'll find out properly when we get the body back to the morgue, but I think so. Done this long enough, couldn't really pull off these stabs halfway through the killing, could you? There'd be glance off marks on the neck or the victim's hands. Signs of struggle.' He paused. 'What's got you out of the office? Not like a DCI to come out into the field and get mucky. Grown bored of your old detective's clubhouse?'

Hiraoka took a long drag, puffed out the smoke toward Petridis who coughed and waved a hand.

'An ethos of mine. I like to see the crime scenes my team are working on when I can,' he said. 'Also, it ain't no clubhouse, contrary to your dirty rumours about the donations. That and I've got this one under the fucking wing. Oi, *Kabu.*'

Something Japanese Hudson would have to look up later.

Hudson finished a quick scribble, the final notes from their discussion when he looked up, his face whiter than his surroundings.

'Sorry?'

The chief inspector grumbled. 'If you've got your notes we can leave if you want, you need to do a little canvassing and chat to the uniforms who first called it in. Just so I get a feel of you and then we're done.'

'Right, OK. I have everything here. Sir, I've never seen anything so…'

'So, unnatural?'

Hudson shook his head, but not to disagree. 'Crime scene photos have not prepared me for the close-up, sir. Nothing like that ever popped up in Notts. A few violent assaults and accidental manslaughter cases in the city but, never this. Don't think it ever has on our records. What the hell drives a person to do that to another? It's not human.'

The pair made their way back out of Hyde Park, walking toward a couple of uniformed officers at the gate, one of them looking almost as nauseous as Hudson. Hiraoka clapped a large hand on Hudson's shoulder. Regarding the buildings that wrapped themselves around the park. A small, green jewel in the heart of the city.

'You're a London copper now Hudson. More places for scum to hide in bigger cities. They tend to do a whole lot of nastier shit, too. Where is it you were part of? West M—'

'East Mids, sir.'

Hiraoka slapped him hard on the shoulder again, shaking him a little. 'I understand it'll take some adjustment, but I don't want you vomiting on my crime scenes. It'll make for some paperwork and a few extra meetings I could do without. You're also under my wing, so when you shit, I wipe. But we both know that's not how things will go, crystal?'

'Yes, sir. I've only got five years of investigative experience, but in getting this position, I'm sure I can contribute.' He forced an obliging smile.

The detectives reached the road that ran the length of the park. Hiraoka slapped Hudson on the back and chucked his cigarette into the snow beside him.

'You can lead here, I want to see you in action.'

Hudson frowned. 'Sorry?'

The inspector nodded at the officers, the pair introducing themselves rigidly to the plainclothes investigators. Frozen stiff from standing about for hours.

'Right, yes, sir.' Hudson shuffled forward, drew out his notepad, smiled at the uniforms who returned it somewhat coldly.

The male uniform, tall, thick black eyebrows and a sharp chin, gave Hudson's senior a questionable look before waiting for him to collect himself. Hudson did so awkwardly, making a mess of his notes.

'Morning both, I'm DC Daniel Hudson. I need to establish which, er, which one of you were on the s—'

'Myself and Officer Milsom were. I'm Officer Price, for the record.'

'Milton and Price.'

'Milsom.' The other officer corrected.

Hiraoka turned around and pretended to survey a brick wall.

'OK. And what t—'

'We arrived on the scene at 5:46am this morning sir. No one called it in, we were the first to discover the body, which struck me as a little odd, but considering the weather sir, the park has seen a lot fewer visitors.'

Hudson felt a little relieved Officer Price was confident of picking up from his clumsiness. 'Yeah, the weather has been awful. Thank you, Officer Price, Milt— Milsom. End of a night shift was it?'

They nodded. Hudson made a note. The pair looked exhausted, ready to clock off and hit the sack.

'Your typical route round by here? What made you two venture out into the park?'

The two PC's glanced at each other. 'We er… we wanted to walk around the lake.'

Milsom flushed.

Hiraoka smirked. Hudson scribbled some more.

Still thoroughly awkward, Hudson feeling the impostor, Officer Milsom made to speak before the inspector or Hudson could interrupt for another question.

'Hudson,' she said. 'We don't want to waste your time, but there really wasn't anything else. We saw no one around, and we've spoken to a few people, no witnesses as of yet.'

'That'll leave us with CCTV then, thank you both.' Hiraoka had turned back from the wall, taking a long drag from his cigarette and looked out across the street over Officer Milsom's head. Hudson hadn't thought about CCTV. Gotham wasn't known for its anti-criminal measures, least of all that London was one of, if not the most heavily CCTV'd cities in the world. It proved valuable and often invaluable in numerous criminal cases.

Hiraoka smiled. 'Milsom, Price, make sure to send across the notations when you can get copies drawn up, and we'll take it from here. Who do you report to again, is it Inspector Hayfield or Patel?'

'Patel, sir,' said Officer Price, trying to retake command in the presence of authority.

'Excellent bloke, OK, well I'll be sure this gets done, I don't want to sit on my arse later today twiddling my thumbs if we don't come good with any tapes, are we good?'

The officers nodded, and the two detectives left. Once out of earshot and over the road near a newsagent, Hiraoka turned to his new constable.

'So, ideas?'

Too busy freezing his tits off, Hudson hadn't begun to really sober his ideas on the crime. Only that one thing was bothering him a little bit.

'Well, witnesses. I'd expect at least one person to have seen something that night, even with the weather.'

The chief inspector crossed his arms, inclining his head to suggest he kept speaking.

'And...' Hudson continued. 'That brain. More than just a passionate, frenzied kill. It was displayed out deliberately not by accident. So could this have been planned and not spur of the moment?'

'Not bad,' Hiraoka replied, winking. 'We can't rule out spur of the moment, but that's my takeaway too. Premeditated. Best you write that up after our canvass. Now, how about you nip in, grab me a Dr Pepper and see if we have any tapes or CCTV footage?'

Tuesday, 5th February

12:14

The two detectives left for Charing Cross police station a few hours later, having visited the numerous array of properties facing Hyde Park. Hotels, law firms, museums, but knew they'd be hard-pressed to waltz into the French Embassy, if not for all the bloody trees which blocked a line of sight to the park. Though as luck would have it, a small café pavilion inside the park just so happened to hold real CCTV cameras, accompanied with real, saved taped footage. Something like gold dust in the real world.

The owner recognised Hiraoka immediately and after a quick chat, felt happy to oblige their request and returned with a bag full of tapes. A few chuckles were had, and the two were back outside in the cold winter air, zipping up their jackets and swearing the morning away.

After grabbing a bag of fresh pastries and a couple of coffees, he stood a few feet from his car, gazing down one of the wide-open avenues leading off of Knightsbridge. Out there, in the depths of the city, a monster beneath a human facade, consuming breakfast like anyone else. Perhaps a fry up, with some tea or a glass of orange.

Just going about their day as usual.

Happy, possibly even excited that they'd gotten away with murder. The thought angered Hudson, almost squashing the croissant he'd bought. Hiraoka leaned over in the car, beeped the Clio's horn, and

Hudson came to.

On the drive back to the station, Hudson's mind was whirring. Troubled. Uneasy. The biggest problem wasn't just seeing his first serious murder, or that London was in chaos from heavy snowfall, but that his new partner, Chief Inspector Hiraoka, was a complete dickhead. The man seemed hell-bent on hurling his arrogance and big-city expertise around as much as he could, trying to throw him off. Hudson already sensed from this morning's charade and theatrics that he'd be a bit of a nightmare to work with. Always wanting to make a show. Always wanting to put him down. But he'd handled bullies before. Whether that be subordinates, fellow colleagues or seniors. You just kept your head down, did your work and took no one's shit. That way, in the event it kicked off between the two, at least he'd crossed his t's and dotted his i's. And with a case like this, he'd have to be extra careful with so many eyes on them.

A large hand came thundering down onto his back, and Hudson jerked awake, almost spilling his machine coffee. 'Wakey wakey, how's he been treating you?'

A heavyset looking man, hair thinning with a small white beard on his broad chin, stepped into his path. The drive back had been a blur. They were already inside the station. His grey eyes squinted up at his own, peering for an answer. 'Not been grilling you too much?'

'What's this, opening up an enquiry on me Rich?!'

Hiraoka came around the corner, carrying his own cup of steaming coffee. 'We've been doing just fine.'

Haskell laughed and crossed his arms, threatening to tear his suit jacket at the shoulders. Though on the shorter side and a bit chubby, he was built thick beneath it all and looked like a man who could handle his own. Hudson made a mental note never to bump into him on a bad day.

'Yes sir, I'm sorry, we've not met,' said Hudson.

'Of course, I'm sorry, know you only by rumour. Been on leave. Chief Superintendent Haskell.'

Hiraoka grimaced. 'Don't scare the boy, sir.'

The pair of them laughed. Good old man wheezes and Hudson stood rooted, awkward and feeling like he was on work experience. All those years of work back home washing away. He was eighteen again, standing between the two big boys who ran the show.

'Right, so I'm sure you're both well underway then with this Hyde Park business? Lucky for you, winter has taken a great big shit over the city, buying you some time from the media.'

A *big shit* over the city was understating things, Hudson thought. Headlines, social media noise, including a selection of celebrity tweets, were reporting the snowstorm as something biblical. That London had not seen weather so severe in decades. Some news sites are reporting snowdrifts as high as three feet in some boroughs and several overground trains being cancelled altogether, plummeting the city in even more disruption.

'Hmm,' Hiraoka sounded unconvinced. 'Gives us time on getting the ID.'

'Elba working on that one?'

'Should be, might take a bit of time mind, the face was in ribbons.'

Hudson contained his flinch just enough, but couldn't shake the gruesome image from his mind. The cold, mangled corpse chucked mercilessly behind a bush, chest yawning open from the barrage of knife attacks. Face destroyed from eyes to chin, a horrible, gory state. And the brain… totally removed. Like something straight out of a Stephen King novel.

Haskell shook his head, then smiled. 'Nasty. Keep me informed John, I want the usual close of play and of course, especially on this one. Nasty MO. And Hudson, let me know how things are going as well. I've signed off on workplace counselling if you need it. Dr Podelcki is a good chap. Anyway, I'm sure I'll see you back at the base later this evening. I'm here for a bit, duty calls. Don't ever get promoted too high, Hudson, it turns into bureaucratic bullshit.'

Haskell wandered off down the corridor. The young detective couldn't ignore his swagger, nor the broad back that a history in the gym would have earned him. That or hard labour. Hiraoka slapped Hudson again on the shoulder. 'Give us a mo' and grab me another one as well.

No sugar.' And went off after him.

Busying himself with a noticeboard in the hallway, a small, niggling little thought crept into his mind—amongst the images of torn faces.

Haskell, sir, I don't think he's quite what we were looking for in terms of a replacement. He's a village boy, he hasn't dealt with homicides like this. Let's toss him back and re-hire. Plenty of lads wanting a punt, I'm sure of it.

Hiraoka's voice was easy to imagine. A deep, London grumble slurred with the odd hint of his Japanese heritage; a few slips here and there.

Stirring the coffees, he chucked the plastic spoon into a nearby bin and watched the corridor, waiting for Hiraoka to reappear. After a few minutes, beginning to worry, he came striding back with a hand in his pocket, nodding to a few officers on his way.

The chief inspector took his coffee. 'Sugar?'

'Nope.'

'Perfect. Right, let's get a move on. I don't think you've actually seen our Fitzrovia office, have you? We'll walk, only take a few mins. I'll direct you.'

'Discreet location, sir?'

Hiraoka's face darkened. 'Do I really need to confirm that, constable?'

As it was, the location was rather discreet. Huddled out of sight down a mews in Fitzrovia, Haskell's Central West Murder Investigation Team's operating headquarters was ideal. Not only for the locale but as Hudson soon found out after cautiously navigating the icy cobbled way, the headquarters windows revealed old Georgian sized rooms, converted for office purposes. Apparently, an investment made some years ago following the new threats of terrorism. They weren't too far from Central North, either.

Hiraoka led Hudson inside, and he was thankful for the warmth again. The walk had been more than a few minutes. Closer to half an hour. For two flights, oak bannisters rose up to the top of the stairs, the spaces filled by stained carpets. Once Hiraoka had got them through a securely coded set of doors, the top floor opened out into an open plan office filled with the browns of old Victorian furnishings and the deep greens and reds so favoured then. Had it not been for the file cabinets and computer monitors, Hudson would have felt like he'd travelled back in time.

Before the chief inspector introduced him properly to the team, he waved a hand, gesturing to the desks.

'Unfortunately, the tech the Met can afford is just as old as the interior design. Bonus, we work out of a beautiful building. The downside, we're making do with Windows 7. Most of our fancy tech is sat at Charing Cross or Scotland Yard.'

Hiraoka took his coat off, threw it over the chair of a large desk furthest from the windows and slapped his hands together.

'Er, where are the team?'

'Out. Other cases. Haskell tries to promote as little desk time as possible. A lot of police work is done on the databases, but it's also done speaking to people. With cuts from the glorious Home Secretary, it's more important than ever to show a presence, rather than working from the shadows. But it's never that easy. Patel is tied up in court at the moment, so we won't be seeing him for a while. Some of his DC's are on holiday, and I believe DS Campbell left recently. We're running thin, but we have some of the best at our disposal. Let's hope that will include you over time.'

Hudson grinned sheepishly. He'd definitely expected a bigger team. Closer to fifteen. The cuts were hitting everyone, that much was true.

But one thing piqued his curiosity. As he took a seat at his new desk, middle of the room, Hudson rapped his fingers along the chipped oak, pondering.

'Sir, back at the crime scene, I heard you say something in Japanese. When you were looking down at the body. What does it mean, Hoshoshu-ka?'

The chief inspector looked grimly at Hudson for a moment, swirled a coffee he'd rudely poured himself and corrected him.

'It's pronounced, *Hoshoku-sha*,' he said, taking a sip. 'It means predator.'

Despite recent events, a bit of snow, murder and a wind chill driving most sane people back inside, the gaggle of idiots Daniel Hudson had once called his mates from Uni, were still stupid enough to brave it out for a few pints. The blessing was that they all had to leave early and he'd get to enjoy the real purpose for this night out.

Then there she stood. Jessica Meyer. Athletically built, comfortably postured and exuding wit. An expensive-looking long coat hugged her form, adorned with a thick scarf bunched at the neck and a set of leather gloves. She caught Hudson's eye and shot him a wink. He raised his eyebrows in mock dismissal, sat back and called over.

'You look like shit, Jess.'

She laughed, threading her way through a few confused pub-goers, obviously not the atypical way to greet old friends.

It'd been years since he'd last seen Jess. Perhaps since the last Uni reunion back in Nottingham. Hudson had the fortune of sharing many of the same friends, so had gotten quite close. Typical of his age and naivety, he just couldn't ask her out for a drink. It seemed like a plan that required a good solid decade to come to fruition.

'Hiya. What're you drinking?'

'Just a beer. Want me to grab a round? How's this procurement gig then?'

'Not bad,' she said, placing her handbag on the counter. 'It's been quite good actually. Focusing on I.T contracts mostly. That's where the money is in procurement.'

'Ah, right, right. Yeah.' Hudson managed to catch someone to order the drinks.

'Said you'd moved in recently too. Not far? Brixton is it?'

'Yeah, Brixton. It's just above an old book shop. Live-in-landlord. Still decided to keep the old banger as well, despite my warnings of London traffic. I think this weather,' he said, gesturing to the snow outside. 'Has also tried convincing me to sell it.'

'Oh, nice. How's the landlord? And, old banger? Surely you don't mean the Clio?'

'Yup,' he laughed. 'The very same. And no, her name is still not Betty. I can see by your face you're disappointed but, god damn, Jess. It's been a while.'

'It has. It's so good to see you again. You're looking rather well. This new location must be agreeing with you.'

The irony in her compliment side-tracked him. Instead of blushing, he laughed loudly, which confused her a little. 'Well, not really. It's a bit of a nightmare but being here closer to people is what I did it for. That and I'm more in con... well, I'm more involved.' He decided against mentioning his sister Krystina. This night was for them.

'Oh, is that right? How so? If you don't mind me asking?'

'The police work, which I can't really go into. The usual.' Hudson adjusted his collar. He suddenly felt stuffy. Wanted to get out. 'How about we get some proper room, grab a table outside?'

Expecting protest, Hudson was happy to see she was just as claustrophobic as he was.

They both left the bar and took a seat under an awning outside. Sat with their coats done up, drinks close to the chest. A sizeable outdoor heater just next to them, ensuring they were good and toasty.

'It's fine,' he continued. 'Just a case, as you might expect.'

'What kind of case? Gang violence? There's a lot of that going on lately. Murder maybe? Sorry, I'm prying too much. By the look on your face, I'm guessing it's something quite awful. It is exciting to hear first hand, though, rather than from the media.'

Hudson grinned, enjoying her voice. The lingering smell of her perfume. 'No, no, it's fine. Obviously, I can't reveal anything, but it's just a tough one is all. A murder case. Nothing to go on at the moment, and frankly, that's all I'd want to tell you. It's pretty grim.'

'Bloody hell, sounds exhausting. Maybe the killer was extra careful? They sound like they know what they're doing if you can't find a lead.'

'Well actually,' he countered. 'It's not definitive yet. You can't close off all avenues so fast. There's always more to look at, and I'm confident. Well, we have to be. It's only day one.'

She paused for a moment, regarding him and then grinned broadly. 'It is good to see you again. Grown into a man! So many years!'

'I know! It's what life does, though. Wraps you up and sends you down the road, often without time to stop and get off.'

'Indeed,' she said. 'But isn't that part of the fun? A rush? A bit of a challenge? My job has provided me with that. It's why so many of us moved here to pursue work. Not just for the location but actually obtaining the positions in London are very fucking hard. We love that. We all do.'

'Hmm, perhaps.'

'Managed to get your old pal James to move yet?'

'Nah, he loves the country too much.'

Jessica laughed. 'You were both such country dorks. Always out hiking or fishing. Absolute ramblers.'

They sat and drank their drinks. Looking across the road, fresh snow started to fall once more. Confetti in slow-motion, disappearing into the snow piles all around them.

'Think the world is ending? What with all this?'

'Nah,' Hudson said, turning to face her. 'Not looking too bad if this is judgement day though. Romantic, even. Can I get you another round?'

She met his eyes, a hint of mischief in them. 'Obviously.'

Wednesday, 6th February
05:01

Not a fistful of paracetamol and his favourite Bellrays album would have prepared his throbbing head for the ear-splitting scream of his alarm. Dribbling into his pillow, Hudson fumbled for his phone on the floor, hidden amongst his clothes, wanting to turn the bloody thing off.

A thumb found its mark, and he tossed it. The time registered slowly, realising it was five am already, and he'd made a pact to get up on the dot. Make an early start.

'Fuck.'

A few minutes later, Hudson swayed in front of the bathroom mirror.

'You wanted this, Daniel. You wanted this.'

A thud on the door roused him, and he coughed, toothbrush hanging over his bottom lip. Déjà vu.

'Excuse me? Excuse me? Are you quite aware of the time? Considering the infancy of your tenancy, I shall overlook this, on the condition you must remain quiet at such ungodly hours as these.' There was a pause. 'It's Wednesday, Daniel! Some of us need to sleep at normal hours!'

Hudson stifled a laugh despite himself, coughing Colgate into the sink.

'Not for me, Eisa, sorry!'

The sweet tang of toothpaste was swapped for the bitter, merciless exchange of coffee only half an hour later. The hot beverage was warmly welcomed. Around him, the last nights second snowfall only adding to the chaos that had ensued a few days previously, producing fields of hidden black ice, waiting to ensnare unwary passers-by or careless drivers. Flicking through the morning news had alerted Hudson to several problems plaguing various industries and transport systems in London. Logistics were suffering from the snowfall on roads, delayed in getting food to supermarkets. Snow on the tracks had cancelled a variety of overground and underground lines. As a result, some companies were being flexible with working from home schemes. Others not so much. So roads were still congested.

Hudson had made a bright decision to leave the Clio parked for the foreseeable. Safer on foot. He walked the half dozen miles through the ice and slush, not a wink of sunlight to be seen, with the hot paper cup of black sludge slowly warming his digits. It was all his Mum's fault, impressing upon him this work ethic. But as he took another sip, turning right toward the next set of traffic lights, presumed that she'd likely seen a lot of people during her line of work. Not just a mother's instincts, but as a psychologist, she was quite literally a pro. His half a decade and more on the East Mids Police wasn't to be sniffed at either.

So pull your finger out, Hudson. Get some guts now before you're arse over tits in new systems, files and corpses. He could picture it still, Hiraoka's embarrassment, declaring his incompetence to the entire squad, sending him back up north. This idea alone spurred him on, and he soon found his own pace quickening, churning up the grey snow beneath him.

Fumbling only for a few minutes at the key-coded door, Hudson was soon inside and busy setting up shop to do some CCTV run-throughs. Looking around at the rows of old new pinewood desks; a reminder of public service cuts, he eyed the computers, paperwork trays, and the crime board. The whole lot. The gig he'd gotten tickets for. This was it. Windows 7 and telephones a quarter his age. Had volume crime sucked up the vanishing budgets?

Hudson recalled as he took a seat at his own desk, booting up the computer. His first stage of the application. Wheeling the mouse around, he navigated the folders and popped up his emails. Sat in his inbox, then typed up notes from the two uniformed officers first on the scene at Hyde Park. He printed them off, grabbed them from the printer (knocking himself in the dark), and rifled through them several times.

No witnesses. Not a single one. And because of the snow, not even the homeless were around, loitering, waiting to spill gossip on a murder. Likely hunkering down in various underground tunnels and the circle line. No, by the looks of things, and until the forensics were processed, he would have to dig through the large pile of CCTV footage. Hours and hours of it. And the notes weren't that thorough either. He had a mind to re-question the officers, but that would require a sign off from Hiraoka.

'Let's hope people invest more in CCTV here than back home.' He yawned, standing up, re-tucking in his shirt and making his way, with a key, to the evidence locker. A temporary, secure holding for about a two dozen items. It saved them running up and down London to Charing Cross for any little bit of evidence they needed, apparently. Hudson couldn't complain. Though for any interviewing, official meetings and general storage, they would have to make the trek.

Once back, he went into the side room, a shit little TV from the '90s perched on a wobbly steel shelf-on-wheels. The sort your maths teacher pulled in to calm the kids on the last day of term. A loud clatter echoed between the peeled plaster walls and windows locked shut with black bars. Hudson sat, stuck his hand into the first box and pulled out a tape, shoved it in and clicked play.

Static. Bollocks.

Leaning back into the box, he grabbed a second, shoved it home and clicked play again.

Only a few hours passed before a few noises downstairs hinted at other detectives creeping to work. A knock on the door to the interview room he was using jolted him awake. A tall, grumpy looking man appeared in the way.

'The hell are you?'

Hudson coughed. 'Sorry, I'm DC Hud—'

'Oh fuck, yeah, Hudson, David Hudson, right?'

'Daniel.'

'Daniel,' he corrected. 'Yes, right well you're in a bit early aren't you? Didn't know you were on earlies?' His heavy brow over blue eyes turned to the TV, hands shuffling in the pockets of his overly large puffer jacket. 'Tapes of that Hyde Park job is it?' Taking a closer nose.

Hudson nodded, dramatically pulling at his face. 'Yup. Loads of 'em. Thought I'd come in, had nothing on.'

'Fair enough. Any Friar?'

'Er... Friar? Sorry, what?'

The detective suddenly looked a bit annoyed, shook his head and slapped the door frame.

'So Hudson, you're the one from East Mids, is it? Jesus, didn't get the cockney dictionary, did you? It means luck. Friar Tuck. Fuck me even the Jap knows that.'

He shuffled uncomfortably at the comment on Hiraoka. Despite his generally negative first impressions of his chief inspector, he didn't take well to from-the-hip racism. Very quickly Hudson wasn't a big fan of this guy either.

'Right. Well, no, quality is terrible. Worth combing through though.' He paused, thinking. 'Is he in today?'

'What, Hiraoka?'

'Yeah.'

The big prick pivoted out the doorway and peered into the office. Shouted, laughed and then looked back in. 'I forget being the fresh meat. He's always in bruv.'

A few minutes later, slamming in another tape and placing the other neatly on the table, the doorway was filled this time with the imposing shape of DCI John Hiraoka. His face quickly looked far more inviting and professional in comparison to its previous neighbour. Hudson leapt at him first before he could speak.

'Sir, who was that?'

'DS Hunt.'

'Hmm, right.'

The chief inspector looked amused, walking in and shutting the door. Not a single glance at the TV or the tapes. 'Why's that?'

Hudson shrugged, hitting the play button. 'Just getting the name's down, sir. Never been too good with names. Better with faces.'

'Is that right?' Hiraoka pulled up a chair beside him. Leaned on his elbows and watched the TV for a little while.

'Enjoying spending your unpaid, unauthorised overtime staring at static? Is this what good policing over in West Mids looks like?' He waved a hand at the screen.

'It's East Mids, sir.'

Hiraoka's face suggested he wasn't impressed with his tone.

'Want to try that again, son?'

'Sorry,' he said. 'I'm just not getting much of anything on these tapes. So far I've gone through the immediate; the tapes covering the early evening. I'm yet to check the few video files emailed through. Most of it's on archaic VHS. I'm also yet to reach the time of death, but I should do by lunch. Some of the tapes are ruined but, the others show barely anything. The snow and general quality means I can't read even a number plate, never mind a face. The quality is awful even by CCTV standards.'

Hiraoka made a deep humming sound in the back of his throat and sat back. 'It's from a shitty little café. Ideas?'

'Erm... well, I don't want to rule out eyewitnesses at the park. I know Hyde Park is popular, maybe even in this weather? Maybe someone homeless saw something? Sooner I get back out there the better but, it looks like a large male did this. Someone with experience in autopsy work? Medical background?'

'Don't leap so far ahead.' The DCI warned. 'Just because it looks like someone strong did it, doesn't mean someone tall, or male, or with autopsy skills made the kill. It's easy to see it but let's see what a witness might give us. Could be a group of people who killed this man, for all we know.'

'Right.'

Hudson knew he was right. Maybe he was too eager to leap to the most probable profile of the killer. Ultimately, they had nothing to go on.

After he followed him out of the small room and back into the open-plan office, the large Japanese detective slumped down into his chair, rubbing his hands and peering angrily at the frosted windows. 'Fucking place is almost as cold as the house I grew up in, in Takayama. Well, do what you can with the tapes. But I want some witness reports by the end of the day. I'm assigning you to DC Kukua Leigh. Help support. She doesn't know yet. You'll find her outside smoking. Go introduce yourself.'

Hudson nodded, eager to get away from the dull, surveillance work. 'Yes, sir.'

Blue, gentle wisps of smoke unfurled their way up into the cool air. Mingled with the rolling cloud of hot breath. Detective Constable Kukua Leigh let out a long, exasperated sigh and flicked a bit of ash toward the car park drain. London looked frostier than ever. Steel grey, cold snow, unmelted on cars and across wall tops. Pavements turned to canals of slush and ice.

The city took on a disguise. A white cloak clinging about its architecture, bringing on new characteristics. New personality. In winter, Hudson thought London appeared almost charming. Soft and unspoilt. Hiding all the filthy holes and corners the city had to offer. Regardless of how picturesque the metropolis now looked, with its cathedral overhangs glazed like the front of a Christmas card or the corners of cream-stone buildings piled high with snowdrift, a criminal's paradise it still remained. Beneath it all, rivers of blood still ran. He'd learnt that much already; crime statistics merely reinforcing the fact.

DC Leigh, a true Londoner, had known this all her life.

Her second drag was longer than the first, blowing it accidentally into Hudson's unassuming face. Did the whole team smoke?

'Shit, sorry. The hell did you come from?'

Hudson coughed, trying to be polite and zipping up his coat. 'Sorry, just came out for some air. Hiraoka said I should pop out and introduce myself.' Then looked down at who he was speaking to.

Plainclothes, dressed far more casual than him. Leigh's hair was short, a cropped afro. Donning a long navy overcoat and a cream scarf to boot, she also came across as incredibly stylish.

She looked him up and down. 'Think I saw you at Charing Cross? Inductions?'

'Oh, I didn't see you.'

'Erm... OK?'

'I mean, I don't recognise you, sorry. Was a bit of a crazy day.'

She rolled her eyes. 'I know what you meant. Christ, don't shit yourself.'

For the second time today, Hudson found himself making a poor impression.

'Can't promise anything.'

They both laughed, and Hudson held out a hand. 'Let's start again, I'm DC Hudson. Daniel Hudson. I'm just in, working the Hyde Park case with Chief Inspector Hiraoka. Well, doing the admin for now.'

Her eyes widened at that. 'Oh, really? First case in Serious Crimes?'

'Yup.'

'Well, pleased to meet you. I'm DC Leigh.' She paused for dramatic effect. A glint in her eye. 'Kukua Leigh. I'll no doubt be supporting you on this bloody Hyde Park case if Hiraoka has anything to say about it.'

They shook hands, and DC Leigh took a third, long and satisfying smoke. Hudson watched the wisps for a little while, enjoying the mood. Savouring a sense of calm he gambled would be rare here. No one joined the police for peace and quiet and risk-free day-to-day.

'That's exactly what he said, actually. So, what other cases are you working?'

'John then. What do you make of him?' she asked, ignoring his own question.

Hudson provided his signature shrug of the day. 'He's OK. A bit unorthodox and a… well, he's a great detective. He's showing me the ropes well enough, and I could learn a lot from him.'

He made sure to kiss as much arse as possible. Didn't know the gossip culture here just yet, but John had learnt one thing from back home. Those in small groups and teams loved to talk, whatever the reason. Offices especially. As his psychologist mother once explained, gossip between people was simply a form of social bonding and nothing to do with the negative repercussions.

Though, of course, there always were. Sooner or later. The wrong words could kill just as effectively as a knife or a gun.

'Great detective? Oh, he'd love to hear you say that, good ol' John. Loves it.'

'Sorry?' He did it again.

Leigh took a couple of short pulls of her cigarette and chucked it, crushed it into the slush. 'Likes the image. Likes theatre and jazz, just so you know. Not to say he's unprofessional. So it'd do you well to polish his ego now and then. Would probably let you polish his cock off as well, to be quite honest.'

Hudson stared back at such an outlandish statement. 'I beg your pardon?' He came out a bit too posh than he wanted.

She laughed. 'I'm pulling your leg. He is great but, listen, there's, of course, a lot of back story to the bloke. When is the last time someone Japanese helped run a unit? There will be gossip, and you'll want to know the shit from the sugar.'

'Right, so baggage then?'

'Oh, so you've noticed?'

He had. With a swift induction, spending his time mucking about at Charing Cross station, his introduction to Hiraoka shortly after had been memorable. Though perhaps only for Hudson. Now, this case. The way he stands, speaks and smokes.

'Well,' he said. 'How does that sit with the Met? Are they happy with that?'

'I hear it didn't back in the day, but Haskell has been snug with Hiraoka for years. He's a bit twatty but what senior isn't? He works well, and we work well too. Regardless of what you'll hear from other teams. Always going to get the white guy bashing the minority. No offence.' She pulled out another cigarette.

Hudson nodded. 'None taken.'

'So when did he transfer to the Met from Japan?'

'Oh. Years ago. He's been a British Citizen for ages. No, he... he, er,' she paused to light it up. 'He worked narcotics in Kyoto. Started quite young as I remember. Well, his team tackled a case which blew up, got him the stars and merits the man deserved and bumped him to murder.'

'Sounds beautiful.'

'Didn't let me finish,' she said. 'This was at the age of twenty-four.'

Hudson scoffed. 'Made an investigative officer at twenty-four? I'm not that fuckin' new...'

Leigh rounded on him a little, resting her smoking arm against the other, crooked beneath at the elbow. 'Bloody Japan, Daniel. And not an investigative officer but a fully-fledged detective. He met a diplomat, British and moved over here soon after. Been working murder since. Fluent as hell, isn't he?'

'Yeah. Yeah, he is. Only noticed the odd twang on a few words. Bloody hell, fair play to him. Great record. Didn't know he was married though. Not that it makes a difference.'

DC Leigh laughed, flicking ash again toward the drain. 'That's for next time. It's very cliché. How old did you think he was?'

'Late forties?'

'Add another decade.'

Hudson laughed and ran his fingers through his hair. 'Really? Fucking hell. What does he drink?'

'Everything,' she replied, with not a note of humour. 'Right, enough of the romance, Daniel, I hope we get along well as I'm sure we'll work very closely. I'm currently finalising my own casework so, don't be surprised if Hiraoka or his club drag a few of us others into this Hyde Park shit storm.'

'Shit storm?' he said, the pair now walking back into the station.

'Oh yes,' she replied. 'This one will be a cruncher.'

As fate would allow, Leigh and Hudson were already in tow, just a few hours later. Coats up to the chin, scarves wrapped around their faces, the two detectives walked on through Hyde Park. In search of someone to talk to. Anyone.

After a second lap, a few quick chats with the public outside the cordoned-off area, they'd gotten nothing. The sun was already setting at half four. Long, eerie shadows stretched out over the snow. Hudson was losing any hope or positive thought.

'Don't look so beat up,' Leigh grumbled. 'It takes a bit of time.'

'I know,' he said, breathing hot air into his hands. 'Still doesn't make it any more glamorous. What we need is some peeping tom or bird watcher to come jumping out to tell us everything.'

'Mhmm, yeah alright, then.'

'But in the meantime,' she offered, nudging snow off a tree branch. 'How about our mate over there by the wall?'

Hudson followed her line of sight to a homeless man wrapped in several thick layers, bumbling about aimlessly. He looked sad, and Hudson knew despite his feelings about them, would have to ask him to move on if he was loitering. As they approached, the man revealed himself to be much older than first thought. And scared.

'Afternoon sir, mind if we have a quick chat?' Hudson started, rummaging for his notepad.

The old man made a hacking sound and started shaking his head.

'No? No chat?' Hudson looked at Leigh for guidance, but she just smiled, waiting patiently.

'I'll cha'. Wha' you wanna know mate? I know it all, curse of it, innit?'

Hudson then ran through the usual. Name, age, and origin. What he was doing in Hyde Park and how long he'd been homeless. A fifty-seven-year-old, originally from Watford, who no longer has family and a bad run of redundancies left him out to dry. It hit home how close anyone could be a months wage away from the same situation. He'd heard that statistically, most people were just one away from being out on the streets.

The man seemed a bit at ease now, talking, so Hudson decided to probe about the night before.

'Benjamin, were you about the park two nights ago?'

'Er… yeah.' He thought for a moment longer. 'Yeah. Been here for three or so days I have. Snow's go' me pinned mate.'

'See anything suspicious at all? Anyone hanging around? Anything that would have stood out?'

The man's face paled visibly, matching their surroundings. His hacking cough returned, and he started to shake. Benjamin's eyes looked at the ground, and Leigh jumped in.

'Benjamin, we don't need names or faces. Just a little hint and we won't bother you. Only something for us to go on? We're worried about the safety of people here and anything you can do to help me would go along way to help keep you safe too.'

Hudson smiled. Impressed with her measured tone and approach. It worked on Ben, and though he still looked shit scared, he mentioned one thing.

'Fuckin' big thing it was. Bigger than me, anyhow. Bigger than you two. Saw it shape-shift righ' over by the lake. So I fuckin' hid and…' He couldn't stop shaking. Leigh gave him a quick hug and set him on his way.

As the pair made their route back, Hudson had almost forgotten to finish his notes.

Debated on whether to jot down *a shape-shifting murderer.*

'So, what do you think?' Hudson asked, shoving his notepad away and surveying the distant city skyline beyond the trees.

'I think I was right,' she replied, taking out her phone. 'This is going to be a nightmare.'

Thursday, 7th February

08:30

The following day, Hudson arrived at the station and parked up. Well over an hour late due to the snow and various road closures. About to set the car in neutral, Hiraoka climbed in from out of nowhere and cranked on the heating.

'Sir?'

'I've just had a call from the coroner's office, we've got a green light. So, I'm going to introduce you to the Queen herself.'

Hudson frowned. It could only mean one thing. 'We haven't even ID'd the vic yet? Taking it as a special case?'

'Very, special case. Do I need to expl—'

'No sir,' he said, hand to his mouth. He saw the body swim before his eyes again. The brain exposed. Face torn apart. Most of the skull wholly obliterated. What sort of monster was capable of such violence? And right out in the open?

'Don't think you need to. Doubt we'll forget that any time soon.'

Hiraoka's huff was the sound of a man who both agreed on the notion but had also seen his fair share of gruesome murders. That made Hudson think, as he glanced across at the chief inspector, just how much had this man seen?

With no further sweet nothings or so much as a good morning, the pair sat silent and grumpy, working a frigid and miserable Monday. Hudson drove slowly, careful of the ice and kept an ear to his chief inspector's very abrupt directions before any sudden turns.

'Shit, sorry, is it this right? Is this it?' he asked Hiraoko, pulling up to a car park sign for the Westminster Mortuary. It was here, as the pair jumbled out of the car, zipping up their coats to their chins and shoving hands into their pockets, that they would get to meet this so-called *badass* and Queen of the morgue. According to Hiraoka, as they approached the building's front, she was revered all around Scotland Yard. This only made Hudson more nervous

They signed in at the front, Hiraoka saying a few hellos and promising to keep out the way before a very short Indian lady walked up to them, grinning from ear to ear, her eyes alight with absolute joy.

'John! Hello, hello, it's been a while! What have you brought me?'

He laughed deep and flirty, bending down to kiss her on the cheek. Hudson stared on, shocked to see his softer side so soon. 'A terrible one, I'm sorry. We're here to see him now, show this one how it's done.'

'Dickhead, it's this handsome one I'm on about. Where did you pluck him from?'

'Oi. You only have eyes for one man. This is DC Hudson. East Mids. Hudson, please meet...'

The short mortician stepped forward confidently. 'I can introduce myself, John. Daniel Hudson, is it? I've heard about you, John's new sidekick? How's training? Well, I'm Nita Arora, pleased to meet you. No doubt we will get to know each other well. Fingers crossed not all your little friends end up in my freezer!'

Nita and Hiraoka shared a moment. Hudson carried on staring awkwardly, shuffling on his feet, waiting for the next move. 'Nice to meet you, Nita.'

'Excellent. Have you both signed in? Yes? OK well, let's go have a little poke about shall we?'

She led the two; Hiraoka throwing Hudson a look of deep amusement, down a series of stairs into the deep depths of the mortuary. A subterranean level from the nineteenth century. It grew dark, cold and they found themselves navigating a long, wide corridor with exposed piping on the left wall and ceiling.

'Bit grim down here, isn't it?'

'You may so say,' Nita echoed back, having heard Hudson's small whisper. 'But I prefer it. Many of the old stations and even buildings like this around London have a mortuary deep below. I suppose it serves a purpose, however you look at it. Saves clogging up hospitals. And here we are gentleman, as always.'

She motioned them in through a door.

Cool, dim, fluorescent lights illuminated the eerie chambers of the Westminster Mortuary. The oxymoron of it all was glaring, the way Nita pranced across the room with ease and comfort, toward a series of metal doors holding the bodies of the dead. A green folder labelled log notes with a few pens on the side on the desk to the right. A laptop next to it also. Apprehensively, Hudson looked around. Poised. Waiting for a door to swing open and a long, white, motionless corpse to come flying out. Screaming.

Instead, Nita and Hiraoka lead the way into a second room. The autopsy room.

'Welcome, Detective Constable Hudson, to my lab of wonder. Here I shall perform minor miracles, least of all the one you'll see today.'

Nita flamboyantly motioned them to a table in the centre of the room. Silver tables on each side, with trays of tools and other instruments. Nothing of detail Hudson had seen up in Notts. Even the hospital morgues weren't this well kitted out.

'Bloody hell,' he whispered.

'Quite the hideaway. I'm praying for a miracle here Neets,' said Hiraoka, following her closely, arms crossed, to the corpse shaped lump on the table, covered with a large cloth. 'Put it in the bag, so junior, and I can walk away heroes. Haskell and the lords above are putting some pressure on this one.'

She raised an eyebrow.

'Where credit is due, obviously.'

A smirk was all he got. Away came the cloth, and up came some more bile from Hudson. He managed to swallow it back, coughing and gagging behind his hand.

'I'm so sorry.' And he really was. 'It's just the face. Jesus fuck, it's that damn face. Why the hell has the killer gone and done that?'

Done laughing, Nita composed herself and tiny as she was, commanded a grand stage as she went to work. Did her thing. Hiraoka saw it coming and stepped back, leaning against a pillar holding up the entire building above.

'Well, DC Hudson, I'm glad you've asked. I was ever so intrigued when the coroner gave me a ring about the murder, that I immediately jumped on board and took a look. I understand the type of SLAs you chaps deal with and, naturally, I don't give a toss, but I was just so intrigued. It'll speed things along for you anyway.'

Both men's ears perked up at that.

'So, apologies for the er... grisliness of this Hudson but, if you look here, I've artistically put most of the flaps of the face back together. Some of it was beyond repair, ruined by the frost but I managed to construct it. Now, the guys took the bloods, and I'm expecting them this morning. It got whizzed through, so I'll wager Haskell had something to do with that. Anyway, bloods should confirm the identity, but so far the victim was male, in his late thirties and... well... he was very healthy.'

'How so?' Hiraoka and Hudson both asked.

'Well,' she said, pulling the sheet back further, revealing his stomach, genitals and legs. 'The sample for the toxicology testing has been sent but will take a good few weeks to come back even with escalations. From my own analysis though, body fat levels are just below what you'd want in a healthy male, excellent muscle mass, his nails are groomed, his lungs are clear, so he wasn't a smoker. Barely any fillings. Just a very healthy chap. But as I said, we'll have to wait for the toxicology report. There will be an inquest, of course.'

He wanted to address the elephant in the room. The reason whispers rippled through the Met.

'What about the brain? SOCO on the scene said they'd never seen a... brain removal before. Sorry, I forget the word. How did they manage it?'

The chief inspector seemed resigned to let the constable question.

Nita looked disturbed.

'Encephalectomy. Nor have I. Typically something done in a lab, by myself. So, as you can imagine, it was a little strange to hear of someone doing that for me. And shoddily, too. It's off for tests. It wouldn't have been too challenging to remove once the victim was scalped and the skull broken. The brain is very, very delicate. Very soft, especially not long after death. Just below, where the spinal cord is attached to the medulla, part of the brain stem, a sharp tool like a cerated knife from any store could cut through it with great force. Once severed, the brain can be lifted out. I did, however, notice impressions along the medial surface. It's off for testing, currently, along with some other pieces. Again, I saw abnormalities with it, so until more tests are back, my assumption thus far is a healthy adult male.'

Hudson took a while to mentally digest all of that. Someone experienced had to have done the murder.

Someone with a medical education.

'Right,' Hiraoka interjected, resting an index finger on his chin. The blue haze of the basement lights oddly illuminating him from where Hudson was standing. He hadn't noticed the wrinkles before. So many hard lines. So much life. 'But what does that tell us exactly?'

'Perhaps not much. Perhaps a lot.' Nita began. 'The fact he looked so healthy got me thinking, so I had a further poke around.'

She laughed a little, and pulled off the rest of the blanket, motioning for the detectives to come and have a look at the cadavers feet. 'See here, the level of an impression on the heel and ball of the feet? Well, everyone gets it, especially those who walk a lot but, this is typical of a very regular runner. This chap not only ate and drank well, but he also maintained a very physical lifestyle.'

A pause followed. Nita swallowed and nodded over toward the face she'd put back together. 'If you can get an artist to reconstruct that face...'

'Running clubs,' Hudson blurted.

The chief inspector looked pissed, but Nita clapped her hands joyously. 'Bingo baby! Well, maybe not bingo but it's a fine start, don't you think? John?'

Hiraoka looked at the body. The face. The feet. Then thought for a moment. 'What about the brain?'

'Very amateur,' Nita said with a hint of disdain. 'The skull fragments reveal a frenzied attack, haphazard. No knowledge at all of removing it but clearly wanted to get at the brain. But no other damage. No damage to the brain or sign of it being properly removed. Odd, really.'

'Not really,' Hiraoka grunted, shifting for a lighter, his mind already made up. 'Killer's mistake. Didn't know how to remove it, or didn't have enough time to.'

Hudson listened to the pair exchange ideas, walking around and inspecting the body a little more. Hiraoka's phone rang then, interrupting the discussion and the chief inspector's gaze hovered over Hudson. A call had come in. They had to get going. Hudson gave Nita another smile and nod before the two detectives hurried out.

Fumbling with his car keys, almost breaking his neck on a little black ice, Hudson took a call from Charing Cross.

An eye witness. Hyde Park. This time, not the homeless old drunk.

'There now?' he asked, getting into his car, Hiraoka tossing his cigarette into the drain. 'A teenager? Right, on the way.'

Hudson chucked his phone into the door shelf and grinned at his inspector. 'We've got another set of eyes. Waiting at the station.'

They had just turned twenty. Still at University. Royal Holloway, studying History. It seemed, apparently, like a good idea to be out in the snow. Hyde Park. Have an explore, soak up the postcard richness. Maybe even make a snowman.

'I don't have many friends,' she said from beneath a long, purple fringe. 'Some. Few. I often go out for walks on my own. I like my own space sometimes.'

Leigh and Hudson were sat opposite, coffee cups for three. Hudson had the tape whirring and a notepad in front of him. Leigh stretched across the table, warming her hands, an empathetic smile on her face.

'We really appreciate you calling in. Any detail we can have of what you might have seen will be great.' She skipped a beat. 'What prompted your call in? Desk staff told us you saw a scuffle break out?'

She nodded, tucking some of her purple hair up under her beanie. 'Shadows. Looked like they were arguing, maybe. I'm not sure I was quite away from them. Across the lake.'

Hudson had already started making notes, a few scribbles despite the recording. Maybe just to make the transcribing easier on them. Or to keep his hands busy. He took a sip of coffee, winced at the taste, and quickly returned it.

'Anything else about the figures, Lucy?'

Another tentative nod. Hudson could tell she was nervous, knew this murder was a nasty one. The media had been suppressed so far, but not for long. Rumours were spreading about the police tape and tents in Hyde Park. Whispers that more knife crime had plagued the city. So, for now, no one was lifting an eye. Hudson, indeed, the entire squad wanted it that way. Left them with room to breathe.

'Tall. I remember they seemed quite large. Both of them. I don't want to say for sure but probably two men. Fighting. Both wearing hats, maybe? Thick coats if I had to make a guess.'

'I appreciate it was dark, but no need to guess. If you're not sure, that's fine but—'

'Sorry,' she said, gulping her coffee down suddenly. 'Sorry. I mean. Yes, both dressed for the weather. I saw one of them go down and, I… I just ran. I'm so sorry I just, yeah. Just ran. I didn't even think I would in such a situation, you know. A murder. I thought I… w-well, bystander effect and… shit…' Her tears started rolling now, hands shaking as they gripped her drink.

Leigh reached over instinctively. Placed a hand on hers.

'We can take a break if you want? You're doing great.'

To Hudson's surprise, she shook her head. Took a deep breath.

'No. I need to help, don't I?'

Leigh let out a sigh, tapped the table twice, and rose up. 'No. Let's take a few minutes.'

Hudson pulled Leigh aside by a water dispenser when they left the interview room. Concerned about her reaction.

'Alright?' he said.

She sipped her water, paused a moment. 'Yeah, but I'm not so sure about this witness.'

Not the answer he anticipated. He waited for a few officers to walk by before speaking again.

'I'm sorry, what part of a credible witness that matches the notes we have from the homeless guy sounds like an issue?'

'Well, they're not, are they?'

'Credible?' he asked, pointing to the room behind him. 'She's one of the best leads we've got so far. How are we going to take the word of some fucking homeless pisshead? Shapeshifter? Seriously, this is a good lead, Leigh.'

'No, Hudders, she's some scared little girl who barely saw a shadow. At best, we can use it for timestamps, build a time-line. We can't ID off that.'

He felt she was right but hated to admit it to himself. He'd felt too optimistic about the interview, getting a second potential witness on this level of case. His first murder just a few months into the Met. This would be a good time for Hudson to take it back a notch and regroup. Not let things get ahead of him. Stay focused. Stay rational. He scolded himself.

'So what's the mo—'

His phone started ringing. Checking the caller ID, he saw it was Krystina. Leigh motioned to him to be quick as she finished her water.

Officers were bustling through the main hallways towards the front of the station. Water slicking the floors, voices raised. Cold wind rolling in from the doors. The chaos was too much for Hudson to hear his sister on the other end, so he dashed outside, braving the snow.

'Hello? Sorry, couldn't hear you before. Alright?'

'I'm inundated right now. You wouldn't believe these fucking clients of mine. Honestly. I mean, God!'

He waited for something else. Knew what his sister was like when it came to random call-ins. To having a good old rant.

'So,' she continued. 'When are we meeting up? You did promise me, Danny, you did promise!'

'I know, I know. Well, I'm also up to my proverbial tits with work. Got a case of my own. Can we do it this weekend?'

Swearing on the other end. Hudson jostled on the spot, trying to keep warm. He'd only wrapped a cardigan around himself on the way out. Coat still on the chair of the interview room. For a second, he started daydreaming about the warm inner-lining.

'Next weekend?!'

'No, no no,' he said. 'This weekend. This weekend.'

'This weekend? Not next? You did promise me, Danny.'

A small breath rolled out. Hudson tried to keep it quiet. Knowing how critical she could be of human emotion.

'This weekend. I promise. Look, sis, I really have to go. Are you going to be alright?'

But she'd already hung up. A short text followed immediately, all sweet and roses. *Love you, bro!* Hudson shook his head, still dizzy. Still never quite used to her behaviour. The way it seemed to control not only her life but his too.

Only his mother would say that's his choice. The rest of the family had paid their price. Parted ways. And in his honest opinion, that's what had done the most damage. He was here to pick up the pieces. With a brainless corpse in the morgue and two shitty witnesses, he couldn't make heads or tails of anything yet. His only lead now was working the CCTV tapes and researching running clubs until the ID came back. Which, hopefully, would arrive by tomorrow morning.

Friday, 8th February

09:00

The doorbell rang. No answer.

'Sure it's this one? It looked like a seven,' Hudson asked.

Hiraoka shook his head. 'It was a one. Back up, son. Where're those good spirits from earlier?'

Truth be told, he was feeling anxious to question the family given how he'd been found. Like Nita had predicted, early bloods had come back to match up with a man named Robert Short. His details were in the system for a minor offence quite some time ago. They immediately tracked down next of kin and discovered, with more searches, she was divorced and currently lived alone. Deciding to skip on the empty flat treatment, they chose instead to visit his ex-wife. Dig in deep before the week ended. And perhaps Hudson and Leigh could team up to go over the victim's abode.

'Sorry, sir.'

'Don't be,' he assured. 'Though let's not fuck it up.'

Another ring of the doorbell conjured a face behind the frosted glass. The knob turned, a lock slid away from its latch, and a tender, heart-shaped face appeared. Eyes inquisitive.

'Hello?'

'Hello there, er... Mrs Short. Sorry. Erm, Miss Russell. DCI John Hiraoka and I are here to ask you a few questions about Robert.' The sheer pain and agony of reeling it out glaringly evident for the whole party; only Miss Russell looked exasperated more so than Hiraoka.

'Oh god, what has he said and done now?'

Hudson looked at Hiraoka then back at Miss Russell. She didn't know. 'Nothing. Actually, it's to do with him exclusively. Do you mind if we come in?'

'Of course, yes, sorry, where are my manners? Tea? Coffee?'

'Tea yes,' Hiraoka jumped in. 'Two for us.'

'Ok. Er, this way, the room is just there. Take a seat. I'll just grab the drinks now.'

The house was lovely. Very nice indeed. The leading hallway was panelled deep oak, walls washed a lilac white, and the living room; enormous, contained dark green chesterfield furniture, antique tables, and a wall-mounted flat-screen TV with inbuilt speakers. The full works.

Hudson sat down slowly, admiring the finer details of the architecture and design when Miss Russell appeared again, holding two cups of steaming brilliance.

'Thanks,' said Hudson, taking a cue from the DCI to go on. 'Now, Miss Russell, I shan't dance around this. We've unfortunately ID'd the body of a man found four nights ago in Hyde Park, and it's your ex-husband. I'm really very sorry to be the one to tell you this, Miss Russell, but he was murdered. And awfully, too, so we're eager to learn as much as we can to catch them.' And then he braced himself. Waited for the response.

But the tears never came. Had he said it took quick?

Miss Russell went wide-eyed, put a hand to her chest, and looked between the two. 'No. Are you sure? I saw him not long ago, he was fine. What do you mean?'

Hudson wanted a bit of guidance but decided to plough ahead. 'We did make a positive ID. We used the blood on record and matched it. I'm really very sorry,' he repeated. 'We have a lot of people on hand to help you during this time of—'

'Good-fucking-riddance,' she spat, taking a sip of her tea.

Hiraoka choked on his, then took back the line of questioning.

'Miss Russell, I'm not sure I understand. Your ex-husband has just been brutally murdered and left to freeze overnight. Are you not at all bothered by this?'

'You obviously didn't know my ex-husband. The man was a horror. If you'd done your job, you might see he has a record of harassment and stalking to his name. The divorce was awful. I won't pretend I'm upset over his passing but know that I do have an alibi. A solid fucking alibi. I can see how your lap dog is looking at me.' The last bit was directed at Hudson.

'Well, that is for us to deduce, Miss Russell. Of course, you know we'll make a note of how you reacted to this news. So I'll ask you right off the bat. Where were you between the hours of six and midnight, Monday evening?'

Miss Russell sat back, holding her tea very proudly now, and smiled between the two detectives. Brilliant white teeth appearing between her lipstick lips. 'At my son's school production in Crayford, if you must know. Then I hung about with the parents for a few hours afterwards for drinks. I was home at midnight.'

'What school is that?'

'Crayford Comprehensive.'

'Excellent,' he grunted, not sensing a lie. 'We'll make the necessary calls to corroborate your alibi, of course. Friends, family, colleagues.'

Miss Russell stood up then. 'Right,' she said. 'If that's all, I'm sure—'

Hudson jumped in. 'Actually, it isn't, Miss Russell. We need a bit more than that. Given our information on your ex-husband is very limited, we need to understand his character. What he did for a living, who his friends were? That sort of thing. We need to establish who may have wanted to murder him.'

She sighed and sat. Picked up her cup of tea again and fingered it with a long, manicured nail. 'Right. Sorry, well, there's plenty to say. We didn't divorce because he was funny, charming, and sensitive.'

'I imagine, but try to be unbiased. Gossip and scorned afterthought won't paint a good picture for yourself.' Hudson regretted his idiotic outburst immediately.

Hiraoka put a hand to his face. Miss Russell's eyes bulged, mouth falling open. 'I beg your pardon, detective?'

Hudson made to jump in, fix the mistake, found himself flaring because of her very comfortable reaction to the murder that had been churning his gut all weekend, but Hiraoka beat him to it. Added a level of expertise and calmness.

'Sorry, Miss Russell, excuse my partner. It's been a bit of a long week already, and we just want to wrap this up, given the nature of the murder. Get out of your hair as soon as possible. I'm sure you can understand that?'

She looked again between them both, sipping her tea furiously before placing it down in her lap and letting out a long, deep breath. 'Fine. Let's get this over with before I file a complaint. What do you want to know about the prick?'

'Well, that didn't go as expected,' said Hiraoka, taking out a smoke. 'Hit the gas, Miss Daisy.'

Hudson jammed the keys in and set off down the road, leaving Croydon for London's centre. 'Bit underwhelming, sir.'

'Well, most of them are. I'm sure the civvies up in West Mids were just as beige.'

'East Mids,' Hudson corrected, squeezing through an amber. 'Just doesn't seem like someone to murder. She's definitely not got the stature to pull anything off like that. Hasn't got the build and her records have her down as a manager for a catering company, not a brain surgeon.'

The chief inspector shifted in his seat. Ran a hand through his long, curtained hair. It looked like a vein somewhere by his eye was twitching. 'Is this an act? Please tell me it is. Please tell me you're not this fucking dense?'

Hudson went quiet. Hands cold on the wheel, chewing the inside of his cheek to keep himself from biting back. What was this bloody Training Day?

'Are you aware of very standard process? CID process, everything from interviews to CPS submissions. The fucking lot.'

A beat. 'Yes, sir.'

'Brilliant. Glad that's cleared up. How about the notion that, regardless of alibi, regardless of his supposed background, someone saw it fit to slice his face up into pork cutlets. I want you on HOLMES2 and filing up all documentation write-ups from this interview. The lot. I want you administrating the case file on this. You know, actual policing rather than churning through half-concocted assumptions. I'm going to need a show of competence after that theatrical.'

'Sir, I'm sorry if I stepped out of line back there...' He forgot to indicate, getting a few beeps from a taxi behind him.

Hiraoka tutted, muttered some Japanese under his breath, and when he started talking again, the faint twang of his accent stood out for a bit more. 'Look, Hudson, I don't want apologies. Let's just keep that head of yours working. Write up what we have today. I'll take a stronger lead on this now. Leigh, Nguyen, Hunt etcetera will run further leads. You sit back and try not to trip over. You'll meet the rest of the team shortly.'

Hudson looked over at him, stopping at a red light behind a large stagecoach. 'Hang on, sir, are you benching me?'

'I shouldn't have to answer that, constable. Don't come waltzing into my murder squad and expect to be galloping around central like you're John fucking Wayne. Run. The. Admin. Keep this case in check, report to me.'

'Right.'

'And Hudson...'

'Yes, sir?'

He pointed out the window. 'Light's green.'

The rest of the day went just how the DCI had planned. Interview follow-ups were picked up by the rest of the team, with Hudson relegated to temporary desk duty. The operations base in Fitzrovia had much older central heating systems than the station, so by late afternoon, the windows had already frosted, and Hudson was shivering.

Exhausted, fed up, and finally glad to see the last few minutes of his shift tick by, he grabbed his coat and left with only a few nods and goodbyes. Once outside, Hudson noticed his car jammed in by the further snowfall. Not wishing to add misery to his day, he decided against digging for hours and made a move on foot. Blustery winds choking and freezing any exposed skin. The merciless trudge was a long one. Over an hour at least, because when he crept, Eisa had already finished dinner, stacking away the dirtied utensils.

'A little late of hour, wouldn't you say, dear Daniel?'

He huffed, wriggling out of his coat and slumped down on the sofa, almost squashing her scattered accounting books for the shop. 'Shit.'

Eisa's protests were drowned momentarily when he spotted another text from his sister and a few idiotic texts from his mate Andrew, who also lived in London. Maybe he'd get around to a pint or two. Maybe.

'Got any wine knocking around?' Hudson asked optimistically.

She scoffed at such a request. 'No. But I have a fine array of pale ales. American by brand and almost offensively delicious in taste. And what about my demeanour and tone prior to this circumstance, pray tell, hinted toward any sort of willingness to part with my best stock? You've hardly presented yourself as the model tenant.'

Hudson slowly turned his head, dark patches visible beneath his eyes.

'The victim of our case was slashed to pieces, his next-of-kin doesn't give a shit, our witnesses are idiots, and following a shitty day, I've been shoved to admin tasks. I'm cold, tired and could really do with a fucking beer if I'm honest.'

'That,' she concurred. 'Is why I'll introduce you to my seven percent stock. Fire up the Switch. I know just how to unwind.'

Sunday, 10th February

01:27

The slow, pulsing, methodical throb of ethereal purples and greens hypnotised me. I liked to watch them late at night, the shining lights of Soho. And with blankets of snow on roofs and chimney stacks, the lights glowed against the canvas, allowing the whole of the city to shine and shimmer like a living room at Christmas. Or hundreds and thousands melted in ice cream. I licked my lips at the thought and turned back to the cashier. I paid the man and left, shouldering my backpack and guiding my feet through the slush.

Falling in step with the small Saturday night crowd, I jostled my way along, closer toward Chinatown. I could feel a sense of excitement building this time, instead of the last rush of anxiety, like before. Only now, I was also strangely angry. Livid, even. For several days now, not a single thing had appeared in the news about my first escapade in Hyde Park. Not a single slot. Not fifteen minutes. Not that, of course, it was all in aid of fame and the spotlight. There were bigger plans at hand now. Plans more significant than myself. A message to be seen by all.

After a slow fifteen minutes strolling, I took a right down an alley between two parallel streets. The cobbles beneath the snow, dangerous and slippery. I took another right beneath an overhang, out of sight of CCTV cameras, and took off my backpack. Inside, a change of gear. I swapped my attire for the more generic boots and thicker coat from the park. Placing a beanie over my hair, I now looked that much different. That was key. Change the shape, change the size. Having shown my face around a few shops, I felt confident of my objective to blend in and scout.

Now all I had to do was pick the right one. The right person to deliver my message. Tonight, things would evolve. The recipe would need to be adjusted to produce something tastier. Something rich for the detectives to feast on. This wasn't just about ensuring the purpose of my mission. At every step, I had to make sure I confused the police enough to allow my plans to go unencumbered. If they caught on too quickly, it would all amount to nothing.

A few minutes ticked away, the sound of giggling and swearing from nearby bars rang out, and a gaggle of drunks came tumbling by. Tugging out a glass bottle of water, I took a swig, and stepping backwards, stumbled a little, fumbling the bottle dramatically to get their attention.

'Shit!' I shouted.

The group laughed, which made me smile, happy to have momentarily disarmed them. Before they got closer, to see if I was OK, I took a quick left out the alley into the next road, almost colliding with a little lady. Our eyes met briefly. My sinister motives must have flashed across my eyes because the young lady gasped, jumping out of the way immediately.

'Sorry! Sorry!' she said in a strong accent I took to be Italian.

Frustrated and growing impatient, I skulked around a bit more, widening my circuit, making sure to keep my wandering by the CCTV as irregular as possible. Cautious, my activity would look odd. The up-side was the snow, the low quality, and my rough shape. But I needed to deliver something tonight so that it could all continue to tick over. The message had to remain potent.

Taking a quick piss in a McDonald's, I heard a few of the girls giggling outside about having a sniff. Most of them didn't want to, told her to shut it, but one of them, a student-type with a young, girly little voice, was entirely up for the lark. Coming out of the toilet, I washed and left.

Leaning against the brick, I poised and waited until the group of gigglers tumbled out, holding burgers and milkshakes. Hanging back a good few dozen feet or so, I followed them down the street, agonisingly slow as they struggled with their heels. Moving between thinning groups of club-goers. Vomiting idiots tripping over their own feet. I also noticed how slutty and pathetic they looked, wearing short, cheap skirts, vest tops, and nothing else but a cardigan between them all. Not a bit of class or sense amongst the lot. This odd thought invigorated my motivation.

Kept me following.

Kept me hunting.

The snow began to melt now, despite the bitter night, another half hour passing as I meandered around Soho, following the group. But eventually, as chance would have it, the young student wanting a bit of coke broke off. The others, drunk and barely upright, stumbled on in the other direction.

I knew all about that urge. That wet kick. That hunger to dart off and take a hit. It's what made you vulnerable now.

I stormed across the street, after a few moments of waiting, and followed her. Crossing my fingers beneath my coat, checking the beanie was on securely. I moved down into an adjacent alley, breath steady. Eyes pinched.

Hidden in the dark, I saw the young woman diving between two large bins, shifting through her bag for something small. I shook my head, the sense of irony in it. How cyclical life could be. But now, I didn't feel the same dread as before. It felt, instead, like a sort of calm. Like I was where I needed to be.

She didn't hear me coming. Grabbing the sides of her head, I picked the little thing up, pulled her further back behind the bins, and snapped her neck in a neat twist. A puff of cocaine exploding from her nose as she fell.

The neck had been much easier to go than I had thought. Her body lay crumpled against the brickwork, arms splayed across some bin bags wet with slush. It looked pitiful, but I knew what it was leading to. I smiled.

Acting quick now, I took out a knife and plunged it furiously into her tiny, plump flesh. White as ice even against the snow. Her eyes stared dead back at me, glazed over, blood slowly dribbling black down her chin. And I continued my work, destroying her face. I cut and tore away at the nose and lips with my small and concealed blade. Within moments the face was unrecognisable, the almost naked body of this creature a mess and memory of what she had been only a night before.

I stood away from my artwork and hid the blade. Taking the rucksack off, I removed a hammer and took it to her head, cracking the skull much more quickly than the last one. The brain matter flew out just like before but matted in her long hair. Using a different knife, I peeled the scalp back and broke away more of the skull. Soon, the brain was entirely exposed, and I worked it out as best I could. More prepared, I hacked at the brain stem, or what I thought was the brain stem. No sirens. Not yet.

After a few minutes, nothing seemed to work. Frustrated with the sloppiness, I left it as it was, almost like the first.

A slither of rage ran up inside. Penetrated me. Gave me a chill. A cold fury which spoilt the whole evening. This wasn't how I would want this. But there was still time. In a location like this, as I had planned, as I had adjusted from the last kill, it would be found. And soon. Much sooner. Then things would escalate. And I would only get better with practice. To present the greatest exhibition.

Looking down at the body again, I stood hypnotised as the blood pooled quickly beneath the girl, flushing the snow around her pink.

If there was one sin, I succumbed to most frequently, it was impatience. There would be no loitering for months or years for the perfect kill. There would be no pandering about to satisfy a fetish. This was artistic and powerful. This was the ultimate challenge. To finally and truly test me and see where I measured up in the city of smoke and ash. A city filled to the brim with killers and paedophiles and rapists. All loaded and enjoying the high life. All rising up like cream in the coffee.

I turned suddenly, noticing a glint in the window, only for it to be the reflection from some neon lighting.

Time to go. Let's see what they make of this.

Come and get me.

Saturday, 9th February
14:04

Late shifts meant films for Hudson. And extra long lie-ins. Regularly exhausted from the job's mental and sometimes physical strains, he often found a good film marathon at the local cinema a great way to unwind. Comedy, drama, maybe even a bit of romance. It meant he could escape into another world. Just for a time, at least.

It lasted for as long as he needed. Meant he could wash away some of the tar in his mind. Unstick himself from it. He could do it too with his music. Back home in Gotham, it would be his hiking trips. Out in nature, in yet another world away from crime. But London was painfully concrete, and he'd found it harder to obtain solace. To discover that bastion of safety and refuge.

Not quite here, Hudson thought, hands stuffed in his coat pocket just outside Hyde Park. Friday's shift had been a long one, so his weekend off was being savoured as much as possible. He watched the rotation of PCs on the beat. The slight increase in police presence since the murder. Birds fluttering between the snowy branches. Smelt the car fumes and the melting ice.

After a late morning of Scorsese films and walking around London to get more familiar with the streets and roads, a directive his seniors in the Met had recommended since day one of his promotion, he ambled his way back toward Brixton. Deciding against a direct route favouring some more time in the air, rather than stuffed inside the underground's metal coffins. That and his damn Clio sat wedged, still, in heaps of frozen snow and ice in Fitzrovia.

A coffee at some trendy bar served as a refuge from the cold. A warm cave from the frigid temperatures outside. At least for now, something Hudson was happy with. He noticed the flurry of flakes outside the building and the customers growing. The noise was oddly comforting. Groups of friends, couples, people taking a liquid lunch. It felt nice to play voyeur. Detached. Removed from the chaos.

Not responsible for what was happening.

Which is precisely why Hudson practically shit himself when Leigh thumped him on the shoulder from behind.

'Alright, Hudders?'

She immediately took a seat, chuckling at his expression. She had a yellow puffer jacket in her hands, and her hair looked shorter.

'You absolute ninja. Where the hell did you come from?'

'Just got here. Late shift later? Didn't think Hiraoka would sign off more weekend work so soon.'

Hudson nodded, checking his coffee and feeling like he might go for another. 'I am indeed. Looks like they're rotating to keep as much resource on this as possible. Toxicology on our vic is going to take some time, so a bit stuck at the moment. Decided I'd do an extra shift. How did the house search go, by the way?'

'Not bad,' she said. 'Nguyen and I went. A nice studio apartment in Shepherd's Bush. He had a laptop, and that was it. Nothing out of place, no forced entries, no sign of violence. Came up empty, but we have the laptop bagged in evidence now. That's about it.'

'Bugger.' Hudson noticed something different about her. 'New haircut, by the way?'

She feigned a flutter, cupping her afro a little and grinning. 'Yeah! Had it tidied.'

'Very nice. You usually come here?'

'I do actually,' she said, flagging a member of staff and requesting two americanos. 'Surprised to see you here. What's up? You doing much?

60

How're you fitting into London living an all that?'

Hudson and Leigh fell into it pretty quickly. Chin wagged about anything but work. Then spoke a little about work too. What would be waiting for them later. The conversation wandered to Hiraoka when the noise grew louder, and a different kind of customer busied the staff. Under the safety of noise, Hudson voiced his thoughts a touch more frankly.

'How has he been to work under? Since you've been in the Met?' he said, gripping his cup anxiously. Having to lean forward a little to make sure Leigh heard him.

She seemed to consider it for a bit. 'Just.'

'Just?'

'Yeah,' she said. 'Just. Hiraoka is a classic. Don't let his act fool you. He brings some habits over from home. Get me?'

Just a nod and a pensive sip. 'Get you.'

'What do you think of him? If you don't mind me asking the newbie?'

'Can't really say. Don't think I've known him long enough to make a decent judgement. But, he's an entirely different calibre to what I worked within Notts. Plus, I was only milling about doing some investigative stuff. This is a bigger jump up for me.'

She laughed. All her white teeth on show. Hudson noticed that and felt his tongue in his own mouth feel out the gap at the back. Another story for another time.

'That's far too fucking diplomatic, Hudders, but we'll let you off.' She checked her phone, pursing her lips. 'Best we get going.'

Hudson had frozen, staring at the phone in his hand, and swore. 'Fuck.'

'What's wrong?'

'Fuck fuck fuck. Er, nothing. It's… it's just I promised to meet my sister this weekend. Completely forgot with everything going on.'

'Hey, don't worry about it. It's one weekend. She'll get over it. Now, have you eaten?'

He wasn't convinced. Knew Krystina wouldn't react like any regular person might do. And that worried him. 'No. Place in mind?'

They both got up and headed out the door. The sun had set already. It threw Hudson off a bit as they'd obviously gotten carried away. He zipped up his coat and silently swore to buy himself a scarf. 'What're we eating then?' he prodded impatiently. Stomach rumbling.

'Curry, obviously. Never done a night shift?'

Hudson frowned, surely mishearing her. 'Curry? Are you serious?'

They both laughed and started their trek to their bus stop. Both in tow. Ready for whatever the night threw at them. Ready for some answers. Ready for that dark, growling shadow that came out at night. With full intentions to not let the snow get the better of them. The detectives had enough obstacles to contend with.

Sunday, 10th February

04:20

Nguyen was working a double. He was known for it. Known for his work ethic, and apparently, he was sniffing for promotion to DS. Hudson grew to like him quickly. Always light-hearted but no bullshit. Everything Leigh had mentioned about him overwork had been glowing in praise and admiration. So when he saw him charging across the office at four in the morning, moonlight and amber neon from the windows illuminating his shocked face, Hudson knew something was wrong.

'Chief inspector on the phone. Grab your shit.' And passed it over to Hudson. Leigh came over from her desk, hands-on-hips.

'Morning, sir. Nguyen just—'

'Get here, asap. I've texted the postcode. It's by that new Thai food place in Soho.'

'Yes, sir. Lead?'

Hiraoka went quiet, speaking to another officer in the distance. It sounded like he was outside. Making out background chatter and a slight wind. 'No. We've got another body.'

That immediate sensation of having cold water thrown over you was both exhilarating and shocking at the same time. Not always in equal measures, but still a great big bloody wake-up. The chill as it enveloped you, seeped into your pores and drenched you. Cooling your core and freezing you solid. Your arms and legs stiff. Eyes wide. Mouth open, the breath knocked from you.

That's how Hudson had felt when he heard the news.

With the car heaters on full blast, the dull drone of Radio 1 barely audible, he gripped the steering wheel and clenched his teeth. Willing himself to remain calm and composed. But he couldn't stop shaking.

Maybe this time it would get easier? Is that how it worked?

Probably not, he thought.

Thirty minutes later, Hudson gagged at the sight of their newly discovered victim, having to step away and put a glove to his mouth. Earned a few awkward looks from the veteran detectives. Who was this kid?

The place was sprawling. Tents up, cars everywhere, and tape holding back the looky-loos. No time for Hudson to be mincing his guts out. Had to get a grip of himself.

When Hudson rose, he caught the attention of a PC, who stood rocking on the spot, breathing into his hands. Had probably been here a fair while. Introduced himself briefly.

'How long has this been up?' he asked.

'A good few hours. I'm told since about three in the morning.'

'Jesus Christ. Who found them?'

'Some club-goers this morning. Caused a bit of a scene, I hear, before anyone called it in. They're over there with some officers now being spoken to.'

Hudson followed the officer's finger to a group of young men and women, wrapped in silver foil insulators, talking to another pair of uniforms. Considered the potential of crime scene contamination from them before anyone had arrived at the scene. Groaned a little as he noticed Hiraoka was not with them. Hiraoka was with the body. Where he looked far more comfortable.

'Right. Thank you...'

'PC Hristov. And yours?'

'Hudson. Thanks.'

He scrunched up his nose, gave him a nod, and returned to the alley, a little more cautiously this time. His pace steadier.

'Sorry, sir, might be a stomach bug.'

'I have a philosophy, Hudson,' the chief inspector said, standing up from the scene, hands dropping to his pockets to find a pack of cigarettes. 'If you can't buy your own bullshit, no one else will.'

He didn't say a thing, only sidestepping the remaining SOCO team members to get to the body.

'Done already?' Hudson asked, checking his watch.

Hiraoka dropped to his haunches, playing a cigarette between his long fingers. A few feet from him, the corpse, a young woman, splayed out in the snow, blood turned black, a great pool of it spreading for metres in all directions. Cuts weren't evident anywhere on her arms or legs. Just the chest.

But it was her face that had been dealt the blow.

'They've been here for hours. Time for us to work. So, Hudson. What're your first thoughts?'

'Same MO as Hyde Park. Secluded environment. Hidden. Multiple stab wounds and the face has been… has been torn apart. Jesus fucking christ and the brain has been removed like last time. What is that? Who the hell has the sheer balls to pull off something like this so close to the populace?' he mused, then added. 'Same killer? Are we looking at a double killing?'

'Connections.' Hiraoka pointed to the victim's face.

Hudson moved closer to him, hands in pockets, and breathed out a long, steamy cloud. 'What connections?'

'No one kills this quickly, in this fashion, without a strong motive and connection. The two murders are absolutely linked.'

Hudson could sense the inspector had snagged a hunch. It happened to them all. When something on the case seemed to resonate, it seemed to sing something back. Not wanting to vomit, he focused on his voice. He wanted to know his theories.

'How will we know? The last scene hasn't brought back anything yet, will take ages to profile this one. Another several weeks on toxicology and reports. More time until we can compare those with our first vic. Are we going to get a profiler in?'

Hiraoka grunted. 'Maybe. Also, all her possessions are gone too. The killer wants to stall our investigation. He's a smart one and knows damn well what he's doing. We're not dealing with an amateur with a kink.'

'Nothing for us to trace,' Hudson added. 'It doesn't stop us for long, but it sort of gives him time. How long ago was the last murder? Four days? Five?'

'Mhmm.'

'So, we're being stalled long enough for him to plan his next big murder. Occupying us, so we're looking the other way? Fuck. Look at this... This is psychotic. But if it's careful and planned, are we dealing with something far more dangerous? A psychopath maybe?'

'There's a theory in there, Hudson, I wouldn't lose that. But I wouldn't start classifying so quickly based on this. Remember what I said about assumptions.'

He left him there with the body, passing the SOCO who had returned with cameras and a body bag. Just as they were setting things up, Hudson had a quick word with one of them, asking for a moment or two to have his own little look at the body. Obliging Hudson, they stood aside, taking a few photos of the surrounding area.

The young detective knelt down, ankle-deep in slush, snow chill hitting the nape above the collar.

His eyes fell across the wounds. Looked over her legs. Her arms. Splayed outward, toward the alley wall and some bin bags. Her feet were curled up to the left as if she had crumpled. At the wrists, a purple tinge. Bruising of some sort. Snapping on the gloves provided at the tape, Hudson leaned in closer, holding up the arm. There, a row of purple like sausage shapes. Finger marks.

Calling over one of the SOCO boys, Hudson asked for a quick snap just in case they hadn't seen it. It had been well hidden.

'Good spot, the sleeve was partially covering it.' The man in overalls stepped forward, tugged the sleeve up with a gloved hand, and stepped back to take a shot. The flash illuminated the crime scene. The gore in vivid detail.

'That's good. Might get something from it. But Jesus Christ, I can't get used to this.'

The SOCO guy pointed at the body, sighing heavily. 'This is the stuff of fucking nightmares. It will haunt you and kill you if you let it. It can do a lot of things to us. Do things behind closed doors, in the deeper parts of our mind. You have to be careful doing this job. This line of work. So, call me a prick or a twat. Whatever, just don't bottle it up for a counsellor twenty years down the line. Making sense?'

'Don't call him a cunt though,' piped up another member, quietly unzipping a body bag.

They all laughed.

'Well, enough of that. Fact is fact, whether or not you like it. You have bugger all to work with here. Lab will confirm, so fingers crossed.'

Hudson felt scolded. Like a child. But he knew the words; had heard them in some way, shape, or form before. It did him a bit of good to listen to them again; from someone who lived with the dead.

'Where's Petridus?'

'Day off,' he said. 'Name's Nimo. Like the clownfish. He wouldn't help you either.'

Hiraoka had returned, maybe the same smoke in his hand, and nodded at Hudson.

'Getting your fortune read?'

'No sir, just a bit of speculation.'

The body was bagged, picked up and walked away from the scene to the ambulance. Police officers waving away onlookers.

Hiraoka finished his smoky breakfast as the pair approached a group of students still being held by officers. Crime scene floodlights illuminated the street in a whitewash, fighting back the early morning darkness. Snow on the surrounding cars lit up like beacons.

'Excuse me all,' Hiraoka interjected, causing them all to turn his way. 'If we could have a few moments with these lot, myself and Detective Constable Hudson?'

They all dispersed rather quickly, leaving Hudson startling aware of his command with others once more.

'Right, names?'

Three young guys and two young girls, all about university age, looked a bit pissed to be going through the questioning process again but one of them still looked visibly shaken. Wrapped in silver sheets from the medics to keep themselves warm. Only dressed in light clothing.

Hiraoka cut them off quickly, giving Hudson a bit of time to pull out his notepad.

'I needn't remind your friend here, the severity of this. No one is leaving until we can get a full account.'

They nodded in unison and started handing out names. Too tired to protest. Hudson made a note, adding a few scribbles about how they responded.

Hiraoka led the questioning, asking what time they found the body, where they were precisely, and how they saw it. Did they see or hear anything suspicious? Where they were previously and what clubs. Hudson knew they'd have to verify that all with alibis and timelines to match. But more so, he was impressed by how much leg work the DCI was doing. This was the grunt work usually palmed off to constables. Maybe they worked differently down here? Or perhaps Hiraoka needed to grasp onto this case with both hands.

Hudson whizzed his eyes over his scribbles, then over at the kids, now visibly tired and gaunt in the eyes. None of them ready for what they saw. You could see that. It had sapped everything from them. No witty remarks or jokes.

He took the initiative to ask. 'Kids got a way home? Is that all sorted?'

They all nodded, and Hiraoka chopped in. 'Great. We have liaison officers here to speak with you further, take you all back to the station for some food, coffee that sort of—'

A loud shout interrupted him.

'If we need—'

The shouts came again, and the chief inspector growled, seeing the journalists hanging like flies on shit at the police tape.

'Hudson, would you? The uniforms seem to be struggling.'

The detective tapped his legs with his palms. There it was. Shepherding the sheep to work. 'Sure.'

Feeling oddly commanding, happy to be given something to do rather than scrawl down the teacher's notes, he walked on over to the journo, his teeth set.

'I'd like to remind you this is a live crime scene, and we are still conducting initial investigations, so if you could—'

'Detective! Detective!' She was tall. Very tall. Heels adding to the effect. Very straight blonde hair. Grey eyes piercing, lips set firm. She looked ready for business. No bullshit. 'This is extremely significant, don't you think?'

Hudson frowned. 'I'm sorry, I don't know what you mean? Could you please step away from the ta—'

'A second killing of this level of brutality in just a week! Could this be the emergence of a serial killer? Maybe like the Ripper? Is this because of all the gang violence we're seeing?'

A few nearby journalists and *looky-loos* perked their ears up. Hudson was suddenly caught off guard. How did she know? Nothing had been released to the press.

'I... er... we're not treating this as suspicious as yet. We are still undergoing investi—'

She interrupted him for the third time. 'So you're not denying the first stabbing? I knew it. Excellent. Thank you, detective. Could you, for the Mail, let us know what your theories are thus far? What's your name?'

Hudson waved a gloved hand, zipped up his overcoat in defiance, and huffed at her. 'Listen to me. We are not giving out anything at this present time. If you could please just step away—'

The journo was making a habit of butting in. Hudson grew impatient. 'Your name, detective, for the record? I don't seem to know of you. New to the force? You look fresh out of school.'

Hudson ignored her attempts to get a name for her story. 'Just get lost? There's a dead girl here.'

'There's no need for that! Well, I've got what I need. Say hello to John for me.' And the lanky woman marched off, leaving a few of the other journalists to puzzle at what she'd somehow obtained from virtually nothing.

But it wasn't nothing. A scratch somewhere in the back of his head. She had obtained information from someone quite close to the case. How else had she'd known about the murder? Learned that there had already been two within a week? Sure, for a detective from a small town, this was all giving him whiplash and nausea, but still, perhaps it was a bit of a leap? Perhaps these London nutters truly did get turned on by the most absurd things. A fetish for the crazy?

He walked back in, Hiraoka done with the questioning.

'Good work. How the fuck did you get her to go so quickly?'

He shrugged, swallowing a sense of guilt. Like he'd revealed a dirty secret about his chief inspector, and now she had rushed along to spread the word. 'Just said my part, sir. She got the message. Seemed to know you, though.'

Out came another cigarette.

'She's always been a pain in my arse. It's not just her. Fucking Daily Mail.'

'She said *hello*, by the way,' he grinned, folding up his notepad and shoving it inside his coat.

'Right, that's enough of that. What else do you suppose we do?'

Hudson pondered, looking around. 'Sir, really?'

'Yes?'

'Are you suggesting we...?'

'Yes?'

'How much does the Met subsidise glasses?'

'Twenty-five quid, why?'

'Because,' Hudson declared. 'If I look at another hour of CCTV, I'll go blind. Is London really that...'

'Yup. Most heavily CCTV'd city in the world.' He paused to light up his cigarette. 'But you're in luck. This is a bit of a blind spot unless we pop around the corner. So not many tapes. We will have to do it the old fashioned way now. Then the tapes.'

From across the street, a few hours into the early morning, in a twenty-four-hour café, I sat drinking hot coffee. Police officers coming in and out to get theirs, too. Oblivious to me. Unaware of what I had just done. I absorbed the production, savouring the theatrics of my message.

Well, it wasn't really that: Theatre. But I had pulled it off. The hysteria and drama of it all was very tantalising. I could still taste it in the air. Iron on the tip of my tongue. I continued to sip my coffee, pooling the brown liquid at the lip of the china cup.

I'd been watching them for a while now. The detectives running the case of my excellent murders. Both tall. Both looking like they meant business. I watched the Japanese one smoke cigarette after cigarette whilst the young, quirky looking one arrived. Spent quite a bit of time with the body. He was a curious one. So I hung about and took a seat front row.

They weren't going to find anything, of course. I was conscientious. Meticulous in my rage and artistry. The message couldn't and wouldn't be sullied by error and mess.

I watched them roam about conducting their police work. Trying to make sense of it all, and for a fleeting moment, I hoped they would. Despite the preparations. The effort. My design. My hunger and thirst for the purpose, I wanted them to be included. To add a new recipe to it all.

Perhaps I could include them. Have them trip and fall in the wake of more destruction. Not only surpassing my peers and the scum of London but also the Met itself. It was perfect. The idea had me lick my lips, imagining the work I would do. Conducting them like puppets. Which only made me want to kill again, that much sooner.

Emptying my cup, I tidied myself, wrapped a scarf around my neck, and left the café. Walking down the street, I shoved on some sunglasses and approached one of the journalists. One that seemed in a rush to reach the tape. Very good looking. I took out a phone and a note pad and gave her a nudge.

'Hey, er, heads up, no sources but, you know this is supposed to be one of a few?'

'Excuse me?' said the journalist, frowning at me. A bit taken aback by my presence, no doubt.

'The murder. I'm also investigating it. Privately, of course.'

'Oh? PI?'

'Something like that,' I said, laughing inside. 'There was a murder in Hyde Park earlier this week. I don't know much else, except this looks like a serial killing. Big bloke doing the work too. Trying to send a message.'

The journalist raised an eyebrow, flapping her long, blonde hair across her shoulder. 'This seems a bit convenient.'

'Convenient or not, I fucking hate it when the police keep things hidden. This leftist pandering is choking the media. The quicker they expose it to the public, the quicker people like you and I can help. Often suspects are found when the public jumps in. The police. The Met are often a liability to their own cause.'

She laughed. Looking over toward the tape.

'Bloody hell, OK, fuck it. Want a reference?'

I shook my head, acting casual. 'No, I just need this in the papers. It'll help us both.'

'Fair enough. Name?'

'No can do. Nice meeting you, though.' And I took off quickly, ensuring my back was to the crowd.

I couldn't believe how easy that had been. How simple and disruptive that little play would prove to be. Now, the media would descend into a frenzy and pile on the pressure for these detectives. Not only making their lives more difficult, prone to mistakes but making mine that much more manageable. Easier to plan my third act.

Canvassing was a surprisingly exhausting job. Moving from location to location, speaking to people of all ages, genders, ethnicities, and class. It meant the constant shift of approach to each conversation depending on personality. Everything was by the book, but some people required different tones or different body language. After an hour or two, it could take its toll.

And all of it to be documented with every detail.

The first thing Hudson and the team tackled were any residential properties in the area. Numerous flats above shops, pubs, restaurants, small firms, and offices. And then, once the sun had risen and businesses opened, detectives and police officers coordinated to clean up as much CCTV as possible. Which meant even more paperwork and cataloguing. It would prove to be an administrative black hole, and one Hiraoka wouldn't think twice of throwing Hudson into if only so he could spend more time questioning the family they had all too recently visited.

Apparently, they'd been calling in on the hour wanting updates. Of course, they had no idea yet about the murder they'd just uncovered. None of the team were keen on them finding out. Efforts had been made to limit the leaks to the media, but it was only a matter of time. Investigations only got tougher with the news breathing down their neck. Scrutinising their every move, hanging around their crime scenes like pigeons to bread crumbs. Like flies to shit.

'I give it a day,' DC Leigh said after another flat door closed with a snap.

'Til what? Let me grab a sausage roll quickly. I'm starving. Coffee as well, want one?'

'Yeah, go on,' she said, tucking her own notebook into her coat pocket. 'I mean until the papers are fucking wild with this. It's been a week now, so we've been lucky as it is.'

'How d'ya mean?' Hudson asked, crossing the street towards a bakery.

Noticeable concern came with the increase in police presence. Heads turned to watch the two detectives as they walked the street. Some chatting amongst themselves, others with their faces buried into their phones just as always.

Snow and ice had begun to melt and turn grey all too quickly. Hudson worked his way towards a bakery, for his sins, thinking about the journalist from earlier. Leigh was right. It wouldn't be long.

'The weather. Had we not had snow, there would have been more footfall. More eyes and probably more media craziness. I don't suppose you're a fan of winter, are you?' she asked, clearly freezing her arse off.

'No. I prefer autumn.'

The coffees went down a treat, followed by a few sausage rolls that were not to be sniffed at. Tempted to go back for a third, Leigh had to practically pull him away to get back canvassing. Ever since he was a young teenager, Hudson's appetite had been enormous, lending itself to his eventual height and stature. This comparatively meant nothing when stood next to the bigger guys on the team, DS Hunt and DCI Hiraoka. Something about guys and wanting to stand bigger. Something primitive.

His mind wandered then to when humans were once more basic creatures. Neanderthals that hunted in groups and slept in caves. He pictured the crime scene and the one at Hyde Park. The viciousness of it. How barbaric and almost ritualistic it had been.

An image of a huge man built like a brick shit house sprang before his eyes. He stood across the street from them, by a pub opening for lunch. His eyes were cold and piercing. Hands as big as dinner plates.

It took Leigh swearing at him to snap him from his little nightmare escapade.

'Fuck! What?'

An impatient, highly decorated constable wasn't in the mood for complacency or larks. Instead of enquiring, she gave Hudson a kick up the arse. No time for reveries. 'No daydreaming, for fuck sake.'

'I was just thinking,' he started, taking out his notes and considering everything he had. 'What's the whole point of these lobotomies? Or whatever that word is for plucking out someone's brain. I mean, why remove them and not leave a message explaining? It's almost as if removing the brains and destroying their faces makes complete sense to the killer. As if we're meant to understand what it means.'

'Fascinating, Hudson.'

'What do you think it means?'

Leigh huffed, stopping in her tracks. Partly because she was exhausted and needed a break. Partly because he was giving her a headache. 'I think you've got your head in the wrong game here, Hudders. What does the evidence tell you so far?'

'Well, fuck all, so far.'

She gave him a finger gun. 'Exactly. So, as I said, stop daydreaming and help me with the rest of this canvass.'

Hudson nodded. 'Sorry. Yeah, sure.'

The detective felt admonished. Embarrassed. A dressing down now from two detectives. Perhaps policing in Gotham had left him with more time for creative thinking? All he knew now, more than ever, was that hard, air-tight evidence would be the only way to follow this case under Hiraoka.

Monday, 11th February

12:30

Hiraoka stood looking at the notice board, arms folded. Hudson approached, munching a leftover pasty. Leigh had finished her lunch, head down, glued to the computer, shifting through the admin. The pair both knackered from hours of canvassing and talking to the dead ends.

'Sir?'

The inspector grumbled. 'Grab me some pins from the stationary cupboard. And some tape. And some string.'

'We making a map?'

Hiraoka turned around, walked past him, and started shuffling through the case files on a spare table, picking out photos of the murders. Fresh shots of the girl in Soho had already been processed and sent straight up to them. The ink was dry only by an hour.

'OK, then.' Hudson marched off to the cupboard.

Then chaos descended, and before he knew what was happening, the pair were sharing a beautiful yet not-so-tender moment constructing what they finally dubbed as the murder board. The rest of the team looked on. Leigh, in particular, fascinated. It felt new and exciting for Hudson, having seen this sort of thing in fiction all the time, but there was never a need for a murder board in Notts. At least for his brief induction time in CID before moving. It was all just bits of paper and interview tapes. A few faces pinned up maybe, but nothing fancy.

Before Hudson's time, Gotham had a tiny police station. Long since closed and consolidated, amongst others, with Nottingham or surrounding stations such as the one that still operated out of Clifton.

'Right, where are we?' The chief inspector boomed out across the room. 'OK, we have murder number one. Some big, divorced City banker, Robert Short from Dagenham. Killed in Hyde Park, seven days ago, sometime between ten and twelve in the evening.'

He shoved a blue pin into a map of London, right over Hyde Park.

'Next is Soho,' prompted Hudson.

'Yes. Murder number two. A young woman, identity unknown, likely a university student. Killed in Soho. Yesterday. Practically around the corner.'

Hiraoka pushed a red pin into Soho, where an alley branched off the road running west.

Hudson passed him the string, which the chief inspector connected between the two pins. Satisfied, he labelled a post-it with *twenty minutes* and stuck it on.

'They're awfully close to each other. Could the area bare some significance?'

Hiraoka shrugged. 'Possibly, but that's not the take I'm having on this. The fact these people were here isn't important. Something doesn't ring true. How can a murder look both planned and spontaneous? We need to collect evidence that can link these two people together. See if any of our witnesses know Miss Russell or the two victims. Find a common denominator.'

Nguyen, who looked like he'd just gotten off the phone, piped up. 'Well, we don't even know who the victim is yet. No ID. I'm ringing through to universities and colleges in the area to see if there's any missing students from classes. Nothing yet. It's bloody murder getting through to the faculties and anyone who will give you a straight answer. I'm requesting student lists, but GDPR is a minefield.'

'Good start, keep the team in the loop. But we have a middle-aged man, divorced, and a student. If there's a link, it's a faint one. We need to know their lives. Their friends. Who they worked for and who they hung out with. Their cousin's cousins if we have to. The murders, though... frenzied, speak of something more. A plan. Take Nguyen's initiative. Start making calls. Let's light up this room. I want noise until Friends stops airing on TV.' He waved a hand, then slapped the board, causing an officer sitting near to jump. 'But right now, there is nothing here!'

Hudson chewed the inside of his cheek, picking up some of the notes from the questioned kids. He'd managed, not for some short miracle, to get most of it typed and processed when he and Leigh had gotten back from their gruelling sub-zero canvass.

'I'm sorry, sir, are we looking at two killers or one?'

Hudson was having a hard time keeping track. Were these the ramblings of insanity or genius? It didn't seem to be too coherent. It felt more subjective than objective, but the spontaneity of the murders made sense. A larger plan did not.

Unless they were short of time.

'A single killer. Look at the scene. In fact,' he started shouting. 'Everyone take a good look.'

The attention of any detectives starting to lose focus suddenly snapped to and followed his every move.

DC Leigh, who was sat on the edge of her desk, some of the oak panelling hanging off, folded her arms tight inside a navy blazer. Eyes narrowed. Keen as everyone else. Hunt and the others also with their arms folded. Attentive.

And Hudson awkward in the empty space. Hands in pockets. Aware of his shirt coming untucked. How fucking Baltic it was in the office with no proper heating, frost still building upon the windows. Half-eaten takeaways littering the desks. A fake plant in the corner somehow drooping. But very quickly, Hiraoka had arranged a series of map shots and other various clues with notes onto the board. More pins stuck on a broader secondary map of London.

DS Hunt, technically Leigh and Hudson's immediate senior, inclined his head and shouted across. 'Quite the collage there, sir.'

Hiraoka ignored it.

Finally done, adjusting the last pieces of string and bits of blutac, the inspector stepped back to admire his work. Hands-on hips. The deafening silence of minds whirring descended. Hudson could hear his own heart beating. The blood pounding. Car horns in the wind outside. Haskell's keyboard click-clacking behind a door. The noisy flush inside the toilets.

All heads turned as a particularly young detective appeared around the corner, wiping her hands on her jeans. Anderson paused, staring at the room.

'What? Hand dryer broke.' She cast eyes over to the board and the colour seemed to drain from her face. Hands dropping to his sides. 'Sir?'

Hiraoka closed his eyes and nodded. Hudson felt it too. It seemed to cling to everyone. A viscous tension stuck to everything. Had this team been here before? Of course, they had. This was one of the Met's top CIDs. But it felt like something they had all been in denial about and anxious about avoiding. That time was up. And Hiraoka addressed the room.

'I think we have another serial killer on our hands.'

A half-hour of chaos ensued, with Chief Superintendent Haskell making an appearance to hustle up everyone, before pulling Hiraoka into his small, segregated little office at the back. After their snooping was caught and the blinds were drawn, Hudson and Leigh busied themselves about compiling the next courses of action. Leads, statements, and seeing what they had in the way of clues, besides the shitty CCTV that was still being analysed.

Then it came, late into the afternoon. Word of an ID of the second vic. The Met pathologists were heroically fast, and it sounded like Haskell might have put in a nudge because even Hiraoka had expected the ID to take another day or two at the very least.

When the chief inspector reappeared, looking exhausted, Hudson straightened up and approached him.

'Nita rang when you were gone. We got an ID on the girl, which confirms what our witnesses and her friends say. She's a student at Royal Holloway. Nguyen got off the phone and found her next of kin live up in Abingdon, Oxfordshire.'

'Right, well, we head there tomorrow then.'

'Not tonight?' he said, eager to get a head start. Get back into Hiraoka's good books.

'No, I'm going to stay back. You go. I want to run through some old case files again, just got an itch I need to scratch. It's time you and Leigh went out and started picking up the leg work. Did she say anything else?' It seemed Haskell had talked about more than just the case. Hiraoka's operational style, too.

'Actually,' Hudson added. 'She did. Apparently, they found something interesting in her nose. Cocaine, sir. Must have taken some that night she was killed.'

Now that was interesting. Hiraoka looked round from the board and stared at Hudson. 'Let's pay Nita a visit. The cold case files can wait. Let's see if we can nudge along the toxicology report to back that up.'

It was the look in his eye when he mentioned the drugs, that really made him wonder what Haskell had been drilling into him for the past fifteen minutes. His features looked worn as if the exchange had lasted a lifetime. Beaten him into the ground.

During his short week with the team, Hudson hadn't given much thought to Hiraoka and Haskell's relationship. Wondered if it dated back years in the force, or perhaps even old friends? Whatever past the two shared, it seemed to sour. Had Hiraoka misstepped in a way that made Hudson's clumsiness look minor? His impression of the chief superintendent back at the station had been positive. Seemed like a kind man who knew how and when to be tough. Old school, but not the sort that landed you in litigation or bad press.

'Sir,' Hudson decided to ask. 'Everything alright?'

The inspector raised an eyebrow, studied the constable, and fixed his coat and scarf. 'Let's make a move before that snow freezes your car in again.'

Hudson hung back, taking out his phone and noticing a miss call from Krystina. He closed his eyes, pressing his thumb and index into them. *Shit.*

Monday, 11th February

18:40

Hiraoka was a genius. They arrived at the mortuary with gifts. A bottle of blueberry gin, and within seconds, Nita was her usual, bubbly self. As usual, the dead bodies were the main attraction and not old friends. But even this time, it wasn't for Nita. Today, it was another pathologist they wanted to speak with.

'Sorry gorgeous. It's your new assistant Charlie we want to speak to.'

'Oh, Charlie? Want to go prodding around yourself, now do we?'

Hudson watched the two flirt. No detective's course was required to know that these two had fucked on the odd occasion. Though realising the chief inspector was married by the ring on his finger, the idea soured quickly. 'Well, we don't want to get in your hair, and it's good to work the new guy.'

She laughed. 'Hiraoka, he's been here three years.'

'Exactly. New. Now may we pass?'

'You may.'

The three of them moved through to the autopsy room, where an alarmingly tall, slim man, with messy hair and a goatee, stood hunched over some vials, with a pipette in one hand and a scalpel in the other. When Hiraoka coughed, he spun around at lightning speed, dropping both.

'Greetings! What can I do you all for?'

'They're here for lady cadaver.'

'Ah, number four zero seven, Catherine Evans?' He shot a finger upwards toward the ceiling as if making a point. He tapped his chin, spun about again, and rushed to one of the tables. He pulled back the sheet with a quick jerk. 'Tada!'

Hudson tried to catch Hiraoka's eyes.

'Oh!' Charlie suddenly burst, shooting toward Hudson, thrusting a hand forward. 'We haven't met. Allow me to introduce myself.'

'Charlie mate,' Hiraoka said. 'We don't need—'

'Oh, but we do, chief inspector. We do. Always. The best of manners, of course. Well, where were we? Ah yes. My name is Charles Rupert Bouchard. I am here, largely at work in the autopsy room, but I work under Nita here by stature. My colleagues call me Charlie, so do feel free to also do so.' He positively beamed.

'Right well, I'm Detective Constable Daniel Hudson. What do we er... have here then?'

Charlie stared down at him, puzzled for a moment. 'Ah, yes! OK!'

He clapped his hands violently. The sheet went back further, revealing the naked, pale body of Catherine Evans. Her face had, like the man previous, been pieced together. It looked strange, made Hudson feel queasy. Skin like turkey ham. And the head, skull pieces on a tray across the room, the brain missing.

'Well, let's begin with stating the basic facts. We've looked at the congealing of blood toward the lower part of the body. The bruising. The body's temperature via rectal examination, and of course, general deterioration such as the eyes. Typically, it's acceptable to assume a TOD of approximately midnight to two in the morning. I assume this is good news, inspector?'

'Yup. Fits with what we have so far. Continue.'

'Excellent to hear. Right, well, I was invited over by Nita to look at the first body. Though not quite at Nita's level of expertise, I did indeed draw to the same conclusions as she. Broken neck, multiple lacerations, puncture wounds to the torso and face, and an encephalectomy to boot. Though, upon examination of this body, something did begin to dawn on me.'

Hiraoka leaned onto the autopsy table.

'Yeah?'

'But!' he blurted, causing him to jump back. 'Let me step back. You said you found her in an alley in Soho?'

Hiraoka was still collecting himself. 'Yes, what of it, Charlie? Is the location important?'

'Well, she most certainly hid away to take the drug. The cocaine I mentioned on the phone to Detective Hudson here.' He gestured. 'Simply put, she made a possible spur of the moment decision to duck away from the crowd to take this. Otherwise, she would have been caught. Suggests her friends either didn't approve, she was travelling with one other, or she was alone and ambushed. Soho has plenty of hiding spots and is notorious for drug abuse. That or it was taken mere moments ago in a club toilet. Toxicology has already been requested, samples sent, of course.'

'Good. Well, what if someone had been there with her?' Hudson said.

Hiraoka shrugged. 'Perhaps. Doesn't add up, though. Seems more likely she broke off and went to do it alone. Otherwise, either a very large and strong friend chose the moment to commit the murder or the same monster from Hyde Park. Both knowing she would be alone and out of sight long enough to do what they had to do. We can cover that with questioning throughout the week.'

Hudson jumped in. 'Right. But wouldn't that interfere, perhaps, with forensics? Charlie?'

'That's a fair question, detective. Though, as Hiraoka suggests, perhaps we come back to that subsequent to suspect questioning. Some of Catherine's friends in particular. I have found no foreign DNA on the subject. I doubt I shall either.'

'OK, then.'

Hiraoka nudged Hudson. 'Call that Lucy back in. Maybe she knows our vic? Or had mutuals?'

'Will do, sir.'

They watched silently as Charlie wandered around the body, drew down a light, and then beckoned everyone to come close.

'Look at these and tell me what you think. Nita, I'll fetch the other body.'

'Alright,' she said. 'Making a comparison of these penetrations now?'

'Indeed.'

Hiraoka and Hudson both leaned in, staring at what they thought were the same cuts. The same frenzied, deep knife wounds. What were they supposed to be seeing? They looked unremarkable, except for their frequency.

'Erm, sorry Charlie, not quite seeing the big show here. Is the neck break on the second significant?'

'Just. A. Moment,' he wheezed from across the autopsy room, wheeling the first body over next to them. 'Have a look at these ones as well.'

The group circled the young cadaver.

'Nope,' repeated Hiraoka. 'I still see nothing particularly remarkable. Other than the coroner's office has been so generous with this.'

'Initially, so did Nita and I. Until I went rooting into the flesh, looking for fragments. Of which I found, of course. We'll get to that later. For now, look at the tearing here and here.' Charlie pointed down with a small knife, detailing the skin's torn edge around the entry wounds. 'Now, look at the jagged ripping inside as well.'

'Not as straight in as we thought?' Hudson guessed.

Charlie popped his bottom lip and bobbed his palms upwards like a set of scales. 'Hmm, well, sort of but not quite so, I'm afraid.'

'Come on,' Nita commanded. 'Spit it out. You've been brewing on this theory all afternoon.'

Charlie reddened. 'OK. Well, I'm not entirely sure about the killer here. You have him down as a large, powerful, assertively confident person who knows what he is doing.'

'And?'

'These stab wounds suggest otherwise, especially on the first body. The second looks a little cleaner, almost like this is practice. Like he's getting better at it. But the neck break explains that. No need for an

85

inquest here. The victim would have been dead during the onslaught, with no resistance. It's why the puncture wounds are not as jagged as the first. '

Charlie stepped away from the tables, crossed the room to a selection of x-rays pinned up on an illuminated board. Picking up several, he returned and pointed to the images of Catherine's neck.

'See the shape of those lines here and here? This is commonly seen in victims who have suffered a violent twist of the neck sideways. Someone who breaks a neck via, for example, a fall or hanging would see more linear marks along here. A fall would show far more evidence of fragmentation and a shattering of the bone as well. This is all backed up by the following.'

The tall mortician placed the x-ray images into Hudson's hands and pointed to the bruising on Catherine's chin and left side. 'See here?'

The two detectives peered over carefully, noticing the dark purple markings.

'This shows the victim, if you may imagine,' he said, beginning to mime snapping an invisible person's neck. 'Was grabbed from behind, the killer's right hand grasping at the chin whilst placing their left on the back of the head. The force to snap the neck would lead to bruising marks like that, which, detectives, also proves the killer was right-handed. It also, very disturbingly, tells us that Catherine was stabbed post-mortem, unlike our first victim, Robert Short, thus raising questions about the consistency of MO, method, and the killer's motivations. Though if we are to look for a pattern here, it's in removing the brain. Very, very morbid. The killer isn't concerned with how they die, simply that once dead, their faces are cut post-mortem and their brains removed. It's the act of someone extremely mentally deranged. If my theory is right, they won't care how they kill their next victim, only that it's quick, effective, and allows them to do the one thing that ultimately identifies their signature. Their message.'

'Remove the brain,' Hiraoka said, digesting it all.

'Yes. Remove the brain. Not quite as a trophy, but more for our own attention,' Charlie replied, nodding.

Nita smirked at the pair. 'He's not too bad, is he?'

The chief inspector laughed whilst Hudson took a closer look. Attempting to digest the enormous amount of information they had been able to glean from the autopsy in such a short space of time. It was impressive but also incredibly overwhelming.

'Sir,' he asked. 'If that's the case, is it worth our time re-examining those old files for cases where the brain has been removed? If they even exist.'

Hiraoka mused. 'Charlie? Is this your professional opinion? Can I bet on this?'

Charlie stood up tall, nose out as if in indignation. 'Inspector, it is with my highest esteem that I present to you this evidence. And I am willing to wager a considerable sum that these are the wounds of an amateur, despite their image of intent and planning. If indeed they had previously murdered, I would not be at all surprised, but perhaps like many, they started on animals.'

Hiraoka clapped his hands together. 'Superb. That triples the workload. Nice work, Charlie, just what we needed after this media blow out. Fucking hate the Mail.'

Before the detectives made it out the door, the pathologist shouted back.

'Another thing! Chief inspector!'

The two detectives turned around, looking over toward the body, eyebrows raised. 'More?'

'Have you profiled this killer yet?'

Hudson squinted, trying to recall something. 'Not yet. Why?'

'I see,' Charlie mused, crossing his arms and looking between the bodies. 'Because the choice to perform an incredibly sloppy encephalectomy on these people and display them in the way that I've seen, really concerns me.'

Nita nodded. 'We've not seen anything like this, John, you know we haven't. This isn't some stabbing or shooting. It's bloody psychopathic.'

Hiraoka was pulling out a packet of cigarettes, Hudson actually hanging on their every word.

'Aren't they all?'

'Not just run-of-the-mill. This is on a whole other level. People are going to study this for decades. Other agencies abroad will want to have a look at this. It's the stuff of nightmares.'

This time, Nita stared him straight in the eyes, concern visible in her features. 'Don't get your cocky old Kyoto arse too mixed up in this. This is a bad one.'

Hiraoka winked. 'We'll be fine.'

Out in the cold, crunching their way back slowly to the car, Hudson decided to quiz his guv on what had just been revealed. His mind all fired up, suddenly full of energy and eager to work.

'Think the killer is more of a wimp than first thought? Nervous? Holding back?'

Hiraoka leaned against the side of the car, peering down the street, blowing out smoke. His sharp eyes pierced the walls and through windows. Hands already freezing at the tips. A man who had seen a lot, whatever that fucking meant. But he did look broken in. 'Not sure, Hudson. We'll need to learn more about Robert Short and Catherine Evans before we can piece that together. Shit. I suppose we can't rule it out, though.'

'Sir,' he persisted.

'Hudson…'

'I've seen that look before. My chief back in East Mids used to have the same one. Like looking into a storm.'

Hiraoka looked baffled, then chucked his cigarette away. 'You're an odd one, Hudson, but I've had worse. Let's get the fuck back to the station. Nice and early tomorrow. How long is this drive up?'

They plonked themselves down inside the warmth of Hudson's Renault. 'Er, not that long. A few hours tops.'

'Good.'

Hudson was about to slot the keys in when he paused. Sat and looked ahead through the windscreen.

'Sir. Humour me for a bit.'

Silence suggested permission.

'I've worked one accidental death. Manslaughter in the end. A few risky hostage situations and a missing persons. This is my first double killing. I've trained to link evidence, but this doesn't seem at all right to me. I know my CID experience isn't long, but it just doesn't really add up in my head.'

'You're not alone. It's Charlie. He's gone and fucking ruined our good news. Drive.' Hiraoka popped Hudson's bubble anticlimactically.

'Sorry?'

'Drive. We can discuss the rest at Fitz. Start by putting the cold case boxes away. Not priority. Then we can focus on the family. The friends. The sooner we can establish these victims' characters, the quicker we can start shaping the killer. See where these two connect. So don't forget to give that Lucy a call as well. Could be a lead.'

Hudson shook his head. He shoved the car into gear and took off, wondering what the hell he was even doing. A decorated investigative officer got into the Met after years of hard work. Yet now, in the company of Hiraok, he felt like a school kid, learning it all over again. The two years training in Notts CID almost worthless. And the nagging thought that if this killer was young, practicing, and holding back, what was it all leading to?

Monday, 11th February

20:03

When Hudson and the inspector arrived back at the office, the day shifts had left, leaving a few detectives milling around on computers or printing out paperwork. Other than that, it was absent of most, including Haskell himself.

In the corner furthest from the windows, where dusty amber lighting cast the desks in an eerie glow, Nguyen and Leigh remained. Both yawning just as much as Hudson had all the way back. His sleep pattern well and truly in tatters.

Their heads rose when the detectives approached, peeling off their coats and eyeing up the coffee machine. Leigh laced her fingers and stepped up with some news.

'Evening, sir.'

Hiraoka stifled his own yawn, chucking his scarf onto the coat stand and crossing his arms. 'Go on, what've you got?'

'We've been running searches based on Class A possessions in and around the area over the last twelve months to get a gist of supply and names. We've dropped narcotics a line but, since we're here, thought we'd get a little proactive.'

'And what have you produced?'

'A decent list of names, guv.' Nguyen spoke this time, joining the group. His large shoulders hung low. Tired. Hudson could see the fatigue in his eyes. The thirst for a drink eating away at him. He wondered then if he was aching to leave so he could sink his night behind a bar. 'Names that are common for the area. It's quite a list. I've pulled in a favour with the boys to see if they have anything juicy on file we can use but, that could be a while. Reckon we're best starting with that.'

Hudson nodded his approval. 'Nice. Chance of a lead?'

Hiraoka laughed. 'We need more than that. We can't play our pot all on the one hand. Risky. What else do we have? Any ideas?' He wandered over to get himself a coffee, still listening to his team for something tangible to get their teeth into.

Leigh, Nguyen, and Hudson exchanged looks. Hudson's face seemed to betray an idea because the other two urged him to spit it out.

'Hookers, sir.'

Hiraoka choked back the coffee. As he marched past them towards his desk, he clapped Hudson on the back. 'They're sex workers constable, let's not demean them further? Prostitutes, if you have to, not hookers. The idea is solid, though. Eyes in the street after hours and chances they could have seen something. Let's make a start tonight. Leigh, Hudson, you can take place just off Berwick Street. Nguyen and I will check an old classic in China town. If the night plays out well, I'll treat you all to some food.' He paused. 'Just kidding, I'm not fucking made of money.'

Hudson laughed more than the others at this, always a fan of dry humour. It was one of the few qualities of Hiraoka he enjoyed. The least of which was his penchant for acting like an overbearing arse and disappearing on his own little crusades. Whatever they were. Maybe that was what Haskell had pulled him up on the other day?

Eager to get going, small talk was abandoned in favour of haste. Coats and gloves on, the four were out of the office within the minute, splitting up when Hudson and Leigh had to head further east to Berwick Street. 'I'll keep an eye on him, guv,' Leigh jibbed.

Hands deep in his pockets, the unassuming facade of a Soho brothel looked down at him. Frowning a little and not at all keen to go inside despite the cold, Hudson turned to Leigh with a nagging question.

'How the fuck are these places still operating?'

Her eyes rolled. 'How do you think, dick head? They're not hanging out signs, selling two-for-one blow jobs. Their fronting everything is the issue, and we only bust them down when drugs get involved. They're usually very clever. But, we've gotten to know a few of the staff, so they should cooperate so long as they're still taking money.'

Hudson's eyes bulged. 'Taking money?'

'Calm down, Inspector Morse, I didn't mean that. Now stop being such a little white boy and get inside. They don't bite unless you pay them to.'

She was right. The insides were that of modern office space. Nothing about it spoke of paid sex or sleazy pimps. Buzzed in, they met a respectable receptionist adorned with very striking tattoos and earplugs. Out of the loop, her broad grin was sincere. Greeting them, she led the two shivering detectives up a steep staircase to a waiting room, on the table, candles, and copies of the economist.

'Not too shabby,' he muttered, grabbing a magazine and flicking through aimlessly as they waited. 'Been here before?'

'I have actually, Danny boy. Want to save your line of questions for the manager?'

He shrugged. 'Just curious. Work or pleasure?' He laughed, not taking his own digs seriously. But Leigh never answered, only giving him a teasing wink. Clearly fucking with him, which worked.

Before the banter could escalate, a tall white man in a baggy office shirt came through the door with a look that contrasted with their receptionist. This one was full of concern and anticipation. His eyes hovered over Leigh, only glancing at Hudson. Clearly, Leigh had been here before. Definitely not a social call.

'Hello again, Bob. How're things?' She stood, reaching for a hand to shake. Bob declined, instead of nodding to Hudson.

'Can I help you?'

'He's fine Bob, we're just here to ask you which girls were on shift a few nights ago. We've...'

Bob looked immediately distressed and snarled his response. 'He said you'd be here poking your nose around after what happened. Can't you enquire elsewhere? We have no information for you.'

Leigh wasn't in the mood for arsing about. She stepped up to Bob, face up in his, and spoke plainly for him.

'I'm not here to speak to his pet dog. Go get Emmanuel, or I'll have this place vacant within the fucking week.'

Hudson tensed. Anticipating an arrest to get physical, so he fingered for the cuffs on his waist behind him. It hadn't been discreet because Bob immediately calmed down and waved a hand at him.

'Calm down, detective, I'll go get him. Jesus fucking Christ.'

When he left, Hudson gawked at Leigh, opening his hands as if to say, *what the fuck was that?*

'Criminals only seem to respond to their own dialect. Don't worry about it. Manny will help us.'

'Sorry what?' he quizzed, eager to leave. 'Dialect? And who the fuck is Manny?'

A deep voice entered the room, and Hudson's stomach dropped. A finely dressed man had replaced Bob, suit clearly tailored around sinewy muscles, matched with a perfectly trimmed beard and loose head of hair. His eyes were grey as steel and pierced him immediately. A smile tugging at his hidden mouth, clearly enjoying the atmosphere the intrusion had caused. Manny seemed like the kind of person who revelled in conflict and commanded limitless control. Hudson had a word for him but right then and there, nervous as hell, it escaped him.

'I am, in fact, Manny. I apologise heavily for my executive, we are suffering a little from the weather. As you may imagine,' he finished euphemistically.

Hudson and Manny kept eye contact. The tension still palpable until Leigh stepped in to change the tune.

'Look. I just need the names of a few who were on shift. Ask a few questions. They don't have to tell us anything else. We just need some extra witnesses. A fucking teenage girl has been murdered.'

Without hesitation, Manny pulled out a small notebook, wrote down three names and numbers, and gave it to Hudson. 'There we are. Not a problem. Anything else, let me know, but I would appreciate a heads up before dropping in like this. It's not very professional.'

Hudson went to speak, but Leigh cut him off.

'Sure. Sorry, it won't happen again. Really appreciate it.' She turned to leave, but Hudson could see one more question on her lips. 'Know anyone who might be in the habit of snapping the necks of customers who don't pay? Perhaps even get a bit creative with their methods?'

Leigh remained vague, not wanting to aid the media by spreading the killer's MO.

Manny's mouth smiled in a way that left his eye's looking cold and harsh. 'I'm offended you would suggest I would be in business with such individuals or even know them by reputation. My answer is that of course, I am unaware of any such individuals.'

'Sure about that?'

'Detective, don't test what we have here. I'm doing you a kindness by letting you in.'

Hudson's heart doubled in beats per minute. He felt the air grow tense. Leigh staring this man down. After what felt like an eternity, she let it go. She apologised, shook his hand reluctantly, and turned to leave.

As she did, Manny made no attempts to hide his gaze. His eyes following their way up Leigh's legs to her bum, where they remained. 'Take care, detective.' And then winked at Hudson.

It was then, with crystal clear knowledge he knew exactly what this monster was. A textbook narcissist. He mustn't forget that. What worried him the most was the look shared with Leigh. It held history. Unspoken understanding, and all Hudson could think of was, how many mysteries and secrets lay hidden in this CID team?

Hudson rested his weight against the bar, staring into the swirling nectar of his beer. Looking up, he smiled at the bartender and took a long sip. It tasted strange. Bitter but not that kind he was expecting. A twang of iron and copper.

Turning away from the bar, he scanned the room.

It was empty. Not a soul to be found.

Outside the windows, he couldn't see any street lights. No cars. No people.

Unsure what was happening, Hudson turned back to mention it to the bartender but found himself alone.

'Hello?'

His voice echoed back.

Hudson took a double-take of the entire pub, before walking to the front door. Grabbing the brass handle, he pushed it with all his strength. Eventually, as if caught by the wind, it flew open, and Hudson was met with velvet darkness.

Shocked. His mind confused by what he was seeing. Or rather what he wasn't, he tried to scream and found himself tumbling over, falling into the black. Tumbling over and over.

When Hudson opened his eyes. He found himself back in his bed, at his flat in Brixton. Breathing heavily, sweating, shaking, he looked around his room.

The light from outdoor the door bled in. At the window, a small draft fluttered the curtain. Sound of traffic and voices.

Everything was fine.

Feeling restless, Hudson made to sit up but found himself stuck. His arms invisibly bound to the bed. His legs too.

Panicking, thinking at first it must be sleep paralysis, he gritted his teeth, working as hard as he could to move.

But it was fruitless.

Long, cold fingers touched his head. Hudson wanted to flinch and cry out but found even his tongue frozen in place. Trapped in his own body. Barely alive.

Out of sight, Hudson couldn't make out who those fingers belonged to, only noticed something large and metallic at the corner of his eye.

A hammer.

Before Hudson could scream, he felt its enormous weight meet the top of his head at the hairline. Blinding hot pain ripped through him like getting struck by lightning. It came again, and again, and again. Something warm and wet oozed down from his head as if his hair were drenched.

But Hudson knew it was blood.

The long, pale fingers went to work, and Hudson begged and prayed to pass out, but he wouldn't. Then, he heard a voice. Deep. And it told him they would start to ply it out. And that's when Hudson thrashed free of his prison, breaking free.

Then he bolted up. Awake. Sweating profusely. Coughing and coughing. Eisa came dashing into his bedroom, flicking on the light, her face pale with fright.

'Jesus bloody Christ alive, what is wrong? Are you OK? Daniel? Daniel?'

Hudson could still see their faces. Both of them. His friends and family shooting him. He threw the duvet off, stood up, and went to the window, gasping for air. Panicking.

'Daniel?' she asked again.

'Wha— what?' he said, turning to notice her there. 'Nightmare. Sorry. Fuck, it was a bad one. Did I wake you? My bad, mate, it was just... Jesus.'

'I'll overlook the blasphemy. What happened? Want me to go make a cuppa?'

'Nah, Nah it's OK, Eisa, no need to go and do that. It's just one of those things.'

She snorted. 'Not bloody likely. That was not usual. You're not getting overworked, are you?'

Hudson shook his head. 'Go back to sleep. I'll… I'm sorry. Won't happen again.' A small pause, collecting himself. 'Actually, I'll make tea.'

Tuesday, 12th February

08:12

Krystina was the first person he called the next morning before his shift. The nightmare was still very much fresh in his mind. He couldn't find the courage to ring home, especially to speak to his grandad, but instead, he managed to try his sister.

It was a shame she didn't answer.

Put out, staring at the screen, flicking aimlessly through news apps, Twitter, and Facebook, he downed his drink and finished off his breakfast at a nearby café, and made his way into work. Eager to start building up witness statements for the second murder.

Before heading to their office in serious crimes office in Fitz, Hudson had a catch up with Lucy, the history student who had been wandering Hyde Park the night of the first murder. He caught her on the way to lectures, showing her pictures of Catherine and a few of the other witnesses from the Soho murder. Much to his disappointment, Lucy recognised none of them.

He thanked her for her time and set off through the thick snow, drawing his coat in under his chin.

When Hudson arrived, eyes droopy, thick coat feeling heavier, he almost completely missed the office's new face. A black woman about the same height as Leigh. A thick pair of glasses and long glossy hair. Her small chin under the glasses made her look mid-twenties at most, so he was very surprised when Hiraoka introduced him that Kassandra Moreau had been working for the Met for a decade, specialising in online crime, and a few years his senior. Hudson couldn't help but recall just how white Notts' policing had been.

'Afternoon,' he said, trying to gather the energy to be polite. 'What brings you here?'

She rubbed her hands. 'Very excited to get started! I've worked mostly within narcotics, but a little resource shifting means I can work on my first serial homicide case!'

'Great. So, what sort of things will you be doing?' Instantly regretting asking, she barrelled into an in-depth explanation of social media, forums, and data-mining equipment. How she can track IP addresses, locate phones being used, and compile patterns of Internet browsing to match candidates for analysis. When she started to delve into even more detail, Hudson had to duck away. Feeling a little guilty.

'I'd love to sit back and go through more, but Leigh and I... have you met Leigh?'

'I have indeed. Charming lady. Yeah, she said she's driving up to Oxford today. Is that for the family?'

Hudson rubbed thumbs into his eyes, trying to get movement and life back into them. 'Yeah. Catherine Evan's family. I'm dreading it. How do you approach next-of-kin after what just happened? It's a fucking nightmare.'

Nguyen was passing them by with a file under his arm. 'Managed to vault over GDPR to get the information. University was being a little OTT but got the address of the family in the end. Just what I do.'

Nguyen seemed, if very briefly, to be trying to get Moreau's attention. Was he trying to flirt?

Moreau giggled, enjoying his flaunting show, but Hudson just wasn't in the mood. Spying Leigh chucking on a coat and grabbing a set of car keys, he tied the conversation off, apologised, and promised they would sit down later. What he was actually hoping for was that Hiraoka would be working closely for the meantime, eager to steer this case towards a resolution quickly before the Daily Mail's exposé on their case caused panic. Worst of all, if the Evans parents found out about how their daughter died by media, rather then the police themselves. Hudson couldn't bear the thought.

A slow thrum. Sound of the road peeling away beneath them. Motorway traffic light, easy to navigate. Hudson, once again the appointed driver, kept his tired eyes on the van in front of him, staring dead into space and matching speed. Feeling himself drift off, bit by bit. Thinking about the murders. Thinking about how quickly the case had changed.

How everything had changed.

His mother's words echoed inside his head, bouncing around amongst all the nasty shit. The bodies. Mangled skin and blown out skulls. Pale cadavers naked on metal beds. Distraught onlookers. Traumatised expressions. It was all beginning to feel like too much. Doubting his abilities as a rookie DC to help the team solve this case

An image of the journalist materialised in his mind. Long legs and hard eyes. She seemed so convinced and sure of herself. Her words. That there had been another murder. Ever since that morning, after canvassing the shops and flats, checking the meagre amount of CCTV footage, he'd been thinking about who might have leaked the information. Someone close to them? Someone in the force? The mere thought was nauseating, and he felt somehow responsible.

Not a day later, the Daily Mail published the details on a possible serial killer at large in London. It wasn't on any of the other papers, and it wasn't front-page yet, but it had caused an absolute shit storm. Today, the news channels had gotten a whiff and were discussing some of the details vaguely. Haskell had been the worst in that he was surprisingly calm about the whole thing. Which unnerved Hiraoka. Which unnerved Hudson. His explanation was that no one gave the story much weight, and there were still no details of the Hyde Park murder in the news. Just hearsay. Nothing in the major broadsheets or international networks. They themselves had little to go on as it is.

That didn't stop the bollocking. As was expected.

Immediately they were ushered from the station to go talk to the family before things got progressively worse. Hudson still couldn't shake the doubts and had begun to look at people in the office. Anyone near their desk, or anyone who had stopped long enough to view the case files or glance at the murder board. What would their motivation be for putting it into the public domain?

DC Leigh's nudge jerked him back, almost sending them left into the hard shoulder.

'Jesus!'

'Wake up,' she grumbled. 'The turning was back there.'

Half an hour later, they pulled into an idealistic street in the small town of Abingdon. The houses bordering pristine tarmac pavements were quintessentially English, trimmed with flower beds, well-cut lawns, and driveways packed with the best cars money could buy.

Hudson scanned the door numbers with Leigh until they found number forty-two. They parked, got out, and stood, staring at the house like it was going to say something.

Leigh waved a gloved hand over to the front door.

'Best I go with this one, Hudson, just to break it in. No hard feelings.'

'Yeah, fair enough.' He weakly surrendered. Feeling a headache surfacing from the long drive up.

Hiraoka had decided to take him off the bench. He didn't have much of a choice, but had a feeling Haskell caught wind of it. They really didn't have that sort of luxury now with two murders to work.

She approached the door, knocked only twice, and was greeted by a red, tearful faced Mr Evans with his wife behind him, petite, pale, and with a permanently frozen look of shock.

'Afternoon Mr and Mrs Evans, I'm Detective Constable Kukua Leigh. This is my partner, DC Hudson. May we come in and have a chat?'

Without a word, Mr Evans simply turned and walked back into the house, the door still open. They'd already found out. It was funny like that, how the police were sometimes the last to the punch. Hudson felt a lump in his throat rise. Kept his face down. He couldn't bear this. Not this one. It was somehow a hundred times worse. A kid barely eighteen years old.

The pair saw themselves in gingerly, closing the door and locating the living room on their immediate right. Hudson hung back in the doorway whilst Leigh stepped in, bravely, and asked for a seat. He noticed she'd taken a lot of cues from the inspector. Which lead him to believe she'd worked under him for several years at least. She seemed extremely confident.

Nothing was said. Only Mrs Evans whispered yes, and Leigh took the armchair adjacent to them.

Hudson found a stack of photo albums on the coffee table. A box of tissues next to it. Also, tucked almost out of sight, a large bottle of Glenfiddich fifteen year. Grief seemed to be hitting them hard.

'Mr and Mrs Evans. Let me begin first by saying how sorry I am for your loss. That we are completely at your disposal, and we will not rest until your daughter's killer is brought to justice.'

Mr Evans started to cry quietly, staring at the mantelpiece. Mrs Evans put a hand on his leg and looked at Leigh. 'Why?'

The constable was caught off guard. Stumbled on her first words. 'We er… we're trying to determine the motive. Building a profile, and we know the kind of man doing this. We are getting closer to the answers we all want. I promise you that.'

'What do you want?' she said.

'Anything. Anything about your daughter. No matter how infinitesimally small or insignificant, it may help us toward catching her killer. The one who has been terrorising London with his evil. We've caught murderers on the tiniest puzzles of evidence in the past, so we ensure not to overlook anything.'

Mrs Evans paused, digesting this. 'I won't let you in her room. Not a bloody chance.'

Leigh clicked her tongue, chewed it, and laced his fingers together. Composing herself.

'Mrs Evans, may I call you Anne?'

She nodded.

'Anne,' she said. 'We need absolute cooperation and help if we are to catch him. The smallest thing, even a note or an object, could link us to solving this.'

The parents looked at each other, the father coming out of his state, wiping away the tears. He turned to look at the detective then, shaking his head.

'No,' his voice squeaked. 'I won't have it. I can't.'

An uncomfortably long pause descended into the room. A faint hum from the boiler upstairs the only source of the sound. Leigh looked slowly over to Hudson and gave him the impression she was about to say something perilous. Something that could either save them or ruin it all.

Leigh clasped her hands together once more, leaned forward, and delivered the blow.

'Your daughter was a coke addict.'

Anne mouthed, eyes wide, like a fish gasping in the open air. 'What did you say?'

'Coke. Cocaine. Your daughter was abusing drugs, as far as we can tell, for quite some time. Her system was full of it when we found her. There w—'

'Get out of my house!'

The husband suddenly bellowed, causing Hudson to jump. Anne flinched, but Leigh maintained stern eye contact. Holy shit.

'No.'

'Get! G-g-get out! The bloody— get out of my bloody house!'

She stared at him, taking it all. Not blinking once. Completely unrelenting. 'I can't do that, Mr Evans.'

'Why!?'

'Because your daughter's killer is still out there. We need to stop them. Or they're going to do this again.'

This time, Mrs Evans began to quietly sob, and the father regarded her with naked earnest vulnerability. His face pale. The word *stop* playing around his head, over and over. You could see it in his eyes. The sense of finality the case required to get justice. That they were needed.

'Stop?'

This time, Leigh's face broke character. Hudson saw something different in her then. Something old. Something painful.

'If we sit back and do nothing, the memory of your daughter will be forever poisoned and stained by the knowledge that her vile, evil killer was never brought to justice. The man who hunted your little girl down will go unpunished. Other daughters and sons loved by their families could meet the same end. He will be allowed to tear apart lives if we don't do our best.' She took a beat then, pointing her finger with each word. 'We can't give up on each other. We need each other. It. Must. Stop. Here.'

Hudson drew breath, cheeks tingling. Watched the room as if he were floating. An outside observer. Mr and Mrs Evans seemed to absorb every word of this and look between each other, trying to read their expressions. After what seemed like an age, Mrs Evans took the reigns and nodded slowly.

'Not in my name, detective…?'

'Kukua Leigh, Mrs Evans. DC Kukua Leigh.'

'Kukua,' she said. 'Lovely first name, where's it from?'

'It's Ghanaian.' Leigh smiled, sensing success at gaining the family's trust. A giant leap forward and Hudson couldn't believe it.

The mother nodded. 'It's the second on the left. Please take care.'

She made to stand, but the parents hadn't finished. It was her husband's turn to speak. The tears had begun to dry.

'Don't make this front page bloody news. Do what you're paid to do,' he said. 'Protect us.'

Leigh caught Hudson's eye. He felt his stomach immediately knot, and a bubble of guilt rise up in his throat.

They had already failed them.

Wednesday, 13th February

13:02

Staring into his coffee, thanking DC Leigh for the favour, Hudson mulled over the events of yesterday. The interview with the family of the murdered student, how impressive and controlled Leigh had been. Her tact to further encourage them to support the investigation on a promise was even more encouraging, given the way things could have turned. Already Hudson's opinion of her was extremely high, but with far more years as a DC than Hudson, it made complete sense. That and her obvious talent for people. Their encounter with Manny only reaffirming his thoughts.

Catherine's room had been a gold mine. Books and paperwork detailing her studies at Royal Holloway University. A PC holding all her saved passwords links straight to her social media and emails. Everything open and accessible. However, they shut it all down, requesting permissions from the parents for access, or face the legal headache if they didn't. Additionally, special liaison officers were assigned to the family to get through the trauma.

Keen to keep making moves, both he and Leigh worked in tandem, going through the long archived history of her life online, trying to put together a list of suspects. But most importantly, they now had Moreau in the fold, who had quickly pulled out meta-data and various other files to work through. Hiraoka now taking a more back seat stance. More oversight. More meetings. But after only a few hours in, Hiraoka leapt up, grabbing his coat, and told Hudson he was making a one-man-only trip to the student union and Catherine Evans' faculty campus to do a bit more digging. Establish a wider pool of suspects. Speak to someone in charge who can move the investigation along.

Hudson, meanwhile, kept on shifting through until lunch. The work fatigue starting to weigh heavier and heavier. Mind drifting off into a land where he slept eight hours and had healthy gaps between shifts. The sort you got with normal civilian work.

A kink in his neck warned him to take a break, his dried eyes another warning to the fact. Admitting defeat, he walked over to the murder board with a cup of green tea Moreau had made everyone and pondered.

Tapping a Biro on his chin, he surveyed the picture of Hyde Park, the aerial shot, the picture of the murder, and the notes on the kill method. The murder board remained unchanged, except for fresh radius circles of a mile drawn around both murder scenes. Where they intersected, Hiraoka had stuck another post-it note. This one read *canvass.*

Before Hudson could finish digesting the new notes, Hiraoka was back, fresh snow on the shoulders of his coat and in his hair. Without taking a second beat, midway through taking off his scarf, he rounded up the entire office with a loud shout.

'Right,' Hiraoka began, waving a pen at the board and herding the officers in. 'This is our next area of interest.'

DC Anderson raised a hand. Barely visible from the back due to her small stature. Her mousy hair made her look young and timid, betraying her persistent convictions. Most of her success came from destroying the mental strength of her criminals. She often got the nickname Colombo for this reason alone.

'No questions, Anderson. Let's dish this out, then we can all get each other off over Q & A, deal?'

There was a resounding laugh before Hiraoka kicked it off again.

'Canvass. Let's get uniforms marching this area. Let's get constables in business, getting records of footage. Perhaps we can find a link. Perhaps we can see a connection between the two locations.'

A few of the officers made a few notes. Hiraoka didn't wait for them to finish.

'Next, we draw up a list of known traffickers of coke. We got a hit that the latest vic was a bit of a lover of the chalk, so let's see who her dealer was, who supplied that dealer, and so on. Perhaps we can get a grasp on what sort of person she was really.'

'Going for a drug angle here, Hiraoka. Not sit with narcotics?' DS Hunt had chirped in again. Hiraoka took the bait. 'No. Still a homicide. But by all means, Hunt, I will put you in for liaising with that department. In fact, I insist, that's a good idea. They'll have plenty of information we may be able to utilise in our case, even if it means closing the enquiry altogether. It also keeps you out of harm's way whilst others question the sex workers.'

Hudson tried hard not to laugh. Kept his head down.

'That's good enough for now. Let's get to it. I want an update this afternoon, so I can run this all by Haskell by this evening. Otherwise, you know, job losses and such. Let's get crackin' come on now!' He clapped loudly, getting everyone to jolt awake and rush away from their desks.

DC Leigh hung around to fuss them. 'Think we'll get anywhere with the drug angle?'

Hiraoka nodded, walking over to his own desk, turning on his screen, and falling down into his chair. Hudson watched on, fascinated. 'I do. Whoever followed the girl into that alleyway had to have been aware of her drug use. Otherwise, the odds of someone waiting for the opportunity to get her alone is too low. Why? Got something to share? Not going to pull one, are you?'

Leigh tried to backtrack, not meaning to question his decisions.

'No! I think it's a good one. Drug dealers can be questionable at the best of times, so I wouldn't put it past someone in drugs to pull this off. We might want to look further into the first vic. Robert Short. See if he had a history of drug abuse at all. I've still not spoken with local running clubs to see if he had any buddies.'

'We checked,' Hudson butted in. 'There was nothing, except a bit of weed when he was a kid, but that's just the PNC, so by all means.'

'It is possible. Maybe narcotics have something?' Leigh offered.

Hudson plopped himself down into his own chair, fingered a set of paper clips. 'That's... actually a really good shout. Sir?'

'Leave this with Hunt,' said Hiraoka. 'He'll coordinate Anderson and Nguyen if required. I want you focusing on the circle of friends. For both of them. We need to find a link between Short and Evans. Cross-check for anyone in the system with a history of violence, animal cruelty. The usual.'

Leigh and Hudson nodded. 'Sir.'

Back at the flat, shoving some semi skimmed milk in the fridge, Hudson pretended not to hear the anxious screams of his flatmate Eisa. But, after what seemed like hours, he couldn't ignore them anymore, so he decided to humour her. God, he would regret it.

And regret it he did.

'Have you seen the new episode of Ozark? It's fucking ridiculous. You know Darlene? Right? We—'

'I'll stop you right there mate, I don't really watch it.'

'What? I knew you were uncultured and boring but, really?'

'Yeah.'

'Gracious, Daniel. What do you watch?'

He hummed a little, resting a hand on the door frame. 'Vikings. Not really watched much in a while anyway. Been busy, you know?'

'Ah yes, Sherlock, of course. I've seen the news, but you'll be pleased to know I give literally not a single fuck. Not one! Look!' She opened her hand at him and emptied something invisible onto the floor. Symbolising all the fucks she did, indeed, not give. 'Not one!'

Hudson laughed despite himself.

'Right, right.'

On his way back to make himself something to eat, he checked his phone for Whatsapp and saw a notification. On Eisa's advice the other day, he'd given Jessica a message. To actually meet up. Holding his breath, he thumbed his way through the conversations and selected her name, the text in bold, waiting to be read.

Yeah, I'd be up for a few drinks, that'd be nice. Where did you have in mind?

Heart jumping, feeling like a right bloody kid, he waited about half an hour, then replied.

Nice, well, how about we meet at the Kingfishers for a few and take it from there?

Her next reply came a little more urgent than his, as he sat relaxing out on the sofa, halfway through a documentary on penguins.

Brilliant! I'd best dress to impress. See you tonight then. Xx

Hudson grinned, responded with something witty, something clever about how she didn't need to make much effort to look good and sat back. She didn't reply, but there wasn't a need. It had risen his spirits. Then cringed heavily at his message, which was more creep than romantic.

Almost on cue, Eisa swaggered into the living room, tablet in hand and a scowl on her face.

'Have you paid your internet bill?'

'Yeah, why?' he asked.

'The signal's gone, and I can't get it back up.'

'What?'

Eisa shoved the tablet under his nose. 'Look!'

She was right. No signal.

'That is odd. Well, I've got everything on direct debit, and nothing has bounced as of yet, so I shall keep you informed if something changes. Tried unplugging it? On and off routine?'

Eisa didn't seem to enjoy this answer, so she sulked off back to her bedroom.

Shirt tucked into a dark pair of chinos. Stylish boots and a deep navy jacket, Hudson felt slightly over-dressed yet still bitterly cold. He'd made the rookie mistake of trading sensibility for fashion. Though, to save himself, he'd brought a lovely thick woollen scarf, which he'd wrapped up around his mouth as he dashed between traffic toward the pub.

He was really looking forward to tonight. A real break. Monday had been a crazy one. Absolutely non-stop since the second murder. Tuesday following had been an emotional trial with visiting the second victim's family, and today had been even crazier. Tracking down the women who had worked the night of Catherine's murder had proved fruitless. But he had managed to drop by a few running clubs. As such, no luck. No one recognised Robert Short's face or his name, and Moreau had failed to pull up his name on social media against any local clubs in the area at all. Yet another dead end for a case quickly escalating out of control. He really needed this night off.

Hudson checked his phone. He was a few minutes early. Relieved by this, he decided against waiting outside and went straight into the pub, grabbing a pint and a glass of Chardonnay he knew she'd be after. Once he'd found some decent seating, eventually, he was only halfway through removing his scarf when the woman herself turned up.

Hudson swallowed hard, his eyes burning a hole into the wall behind her.

'Hiya, thought I'd get us some drinks in, white wine OK? You're looking lovely, too. Can see nothing's changed.'

'Aw, thank you, Daniel. You're looking quite nice in this jacket of yours. Good shout. Oh, and thank you! Chardonnay, I hope?'

'Of course,' he laughed. He showed them both to their seats and pulled her chair back. Being an old-fashioned gentleman and everything.

'So, how're things?' He began, sipping his lager gingerly. It tasted like watery piss. Better go for a Guinness next, he thought. Still hadn't quite grown accustomed to the London prices. Six quid for piss?

'Really?' she said. 'We're going to lead with that?'

Hudson looked a bit taken by her retort. Decided to force a laugh and change tact. 'I'm just having a laugh, of course, it's as good a place as any to start. Well, I'm doing just fine, thank you. How about yourself?'

'Not bad. Not bad.' He must have had it plastered over his face because Jessica jumped right in on it.

'Daniel?'

'Yeah?'

'Are you… are you working that case? Those…' She lowered her voice a little. 'Those killings they're talking about in the papers?'

'What are you on about?'

She looked around, waving to someone she knew, then put her attention back on Daniel. 'Hyde Park. Soho. It's all in the news. Some of us have been talking and think that you might be working on it. James says there's a picture of you in Soho actually, got caught by a photographer.'

'Really? Fuck sake.' He took a generous gulp of beer. Didn't expect to be talking shop so quickly into the first official date.

'Tough?'

'Vaguely, yes. Mind if we change the subject?'

The atmosphere immediately plummeted, and Hudson was wondering what he could do to salvage the moment.

'Sure,' she said. 'How's the flat?'

'Hilarious, actually. The lady I'm renting with, Eisa, she's a bit strange—'

'Eisa? That's her name?'

'Yeah, why?'

Jessica giggled, sipped her drink, and moved a strand of long blonde hair behind her left ear. 'Nothing. I knew an Eisa a while back. Do continue.'

'Well, she's a bit of an eccentric. Runs a book shop, so she barely covers the bills. Needed someone to lodge with her to just make it past the breakeven level. I was the lucky bugger who got the room.'

'Is she that bad?'

Hudson made a noise, stared off toward the bar, thinking. 'She isn't, actually. It's probably just the new move, new city, new job, and I've put the woman under an unfair assessment of what should be a good flatmate.'

She smiled. 'That's very logical of you.'

'I know! First for everything. So, how's this procurement lark you're up to? You mentioned I.T. last time. Had a lot of money in it, or something but you never really delved into the details.'

'Ah, right. Well, I don't want to bore you.'

'You won't. Crack on.'

'Fine,' she dramatised, taking another sip. 'So, after I got my masters, I fast-tracked a qualification known as CIPS. Chartered Institute of Procurement Specialists. Essentially it specialises in the field, so I went through that whilst you landed your work on the police up in Nottingham.'

'Oh, right, that was when you came down here?'

'No. That was my masters. I moved to just outside London to do the CIPS with a company. Forget their name, but I moved back into the capital to do my mCIPS.'

'mCIPS? That the masters equivalent?'

She nodded. 'Something like that.'

And the pair went into it. Completely absorbed by each other and Jessica jumped into the details of procurement and what she did. What clients she worked with and the critical tenders she'd overseen. It all seemed quite interesting, to be perfectly honest and Hudson was thankful for the fact. His mind was finally distracted from the mental images of butchered bodies. The haunting fragments of his nightmares.

What he didn't imagine was how bloody brilliant she would look this evening. She'd chosen to dress for the weather, of course, not like constable dip shit here, but underneath wore an elegant pair of trousers, hugging at the waist and flaring at the bottom with some heels, complemented by a long sleeve blouse, hinting at a little cleavage. It was classy and smart. She had definitely allowed the city to transform her, but really, Jessica had always been a cut above the rest. Always wanting to venture forth.

Maybe she and James would have been a good match. His goofy childhood friend still living in Gotham. They'd shared quite the ordeal a few years back, whilst Hudson waded knee-deep in detective exams. A missing girl in the village had sent the pair, with no backup, deep into the woods at night. He'd never forget the help and promised James he owed him one.

The bollocking he'd eventually received from the superintendent wasn't nearly as bad as it could have been. Hudson had managed to find the girl, unharmed, kidnapped by her deranged father, fresh out of prison. It had gotten him some fame around Notts.

'So,' Hudson sighed, a little fuzzy after his second pint. 'Still speak to James then? Mentioned to me on chat he'd moved south to Stevenage for work.'

She waved a manicured hand at him. 'Pfft, a bit. What do you expect, though? I know he's your best mate, but I always found him odd. He's always curious, hence why he's been following the case.'

'He's not that weird. But who wouldn't be curious, not that it's popping up in the news? He's always been a good friend.'

'Sorry, that was a bit harsh. He's doing quite fucking well for himself, or so I hear? Excuse me.' She finished off the last of the bottle and grinned at him. 'So, what spurred this on? Missed me that much?'

He'd been caught guilty of swirling the contents of his pint and confessed to slipping his concentration. 'What? Oh, sorry, just a bit tired. Erm, well, I thought, what with work, sorry to bring it up again, I wouldn't have much spare time for the foreseeable. So I thought, what the hell, let's make some time. It's been too long, hasn't it?'

Hudson knew that wasn't the answer she was after, a twinkle in her eye and a nip at the corner of her mouth. Those gorgeous rose lips. Thin at the top, plump at the bottom. It seemed unfair for him to objectify her like that, but bloody hell, she cleaned up good. It was just not his night to put on the brave face, admit his feelings. But it was just the first date, and all would come in good time. At least he hoped.

It was just nice to know he had another person to turn to here, what with everything going on. Not including any dangerous attempts at conversation with Eisa or trying to see his sister.

A knot of guilt twisted inside him. Hudson had to fix that. Make an effort to call her again. He knew he could be trying harder. Somehow, though, he felt he was stepping on her toes. Intruding. Knew from James' work as a solicitor just how busy life could be. Knew plenty well from Krystina already.

Noticing Hudson's attention skip again, Jessica took the reigns.

'OK. Well, yes, it's been nice. So where do you fancy heading off to next?'

'Oh, erm, we could go to—' His phone rang. 'We could er...'

It kept ringing, and, shaking his head, he checked it and saw it was Chief Inspector Hiraoka's name on the screen.

What the fuck now?

'One second, sorry.'

She smiled in understanding. Gave him the nod. Hudson dashed away from the table, threading his way through the growing crowds, and stood outside in the bitter February chill, planting the phone to his ear, expecting something awful.

Another murder.

'Good evening Hudson.'

'Evening, sir. How are you? Is something the matter?'

'Not exactly.'

Hudson stared at his phone. Checked to see if he had heard correctly. A gaggle of laughing teenagers bustled past, so Hudson waited for them to go.

'Sorry, sir, say that again?'

'I need you to do me a favour and meet me just north of East India Dock road? Know it? It's in Poplar. I'll text you the exact address. Need you to meet me here as soon as you can. Can you do that for me?'

'Erm, is this case related? It's a bit of, well, it's bad timing, sir. I'm sort of busy.'

'Sort of?' he said. 'Take opportunities where you can, Hudson, to garner respect, and now would be a good time to show some loyalty. Do

I need to find another constable?'

Hudson closed his eyes and felt his stomach drop. 'Shit.'

'It's case related. I've got a lead I've been tracing and need some backup. Did you put forward for more proactive tasks on the case?'

'Well, yes, but isn't this a little… unorthodox?'

'No, no, no, it's all fine. All signed off by Haskell. Just get here, and I can explain everything.' There was a pause. 'Tell her sorry.'

'How did you kn—'

'Just get here.' And he hung up.

The hardest bit after the call was looking into Jessica's face and telling her that he had to go. That tonight, he had to return to work at the beck and call of his chief inspector. The ass hole that had it in for him.

'Look,' he pleaded. 'This has really come out of the blue. Can you… I mean… are you free some other time so we can pick up where we left off?'

Jessica didn't attempt to hide her disappointment at all, gathering her coat. Picking up her purse reluctantly. 'Well, I can't deny this is shit timing, Daniel. But, if needs must. Are you sure this is work? I haven't scared you have I?'

'Oh no, not at all! I was having a great time.'

'It's just after I mention th—'

'Listen,' he said, putting a hand on her arm. 'It's been lovely. I just get called in like this every now and then. Nothing I can do. I'll give you a call though, yeah? Send you a message on Whatsapp.'

She nodded, smiling. 'Go on then. Dinner's on you next time.'

Hudson sighed with relief. 'Brilliant. OK, well, I'll see you later then. Thanks again!'

He left Jessica alone in the pub, stood there staring after him. Hands hanging by her side.

Wednesday, 13th February

21:16

Twenty minutes later, swinging his recently rescued car into a gravel driveway, Hudson's mood had evolved from vaguely pissed off to absolutely livid. He'd been taken advantage of and manipulated when he needed some time off the most. He couldn't deal with it. Not tonight.

Getting out of his car, he slammed the door shut and took out his phone to give him a ring. See where he was.

Just before he hit dial, Hiraoka came skulking out the dark toward Hudson.

'Put that away, I'm here.' A pause. 'You good?'

Hudson frowned at him. His eyes seemed to be different somehow.

Urgent. Alert.

But something more sinister lay further in that shadowed dark. It unnerved him. He hadn't seen it before.

'What do you mean? What am I getting myself into?'

'It's fine. Just follow my lead. I've been doing a few errands. Few calls. Traced back the coke to this location, so I'm about to make myself aware.'

Hudson rubbed his face in dismay. 'You've brought me here, on my evening off, to do a drugs raid off the book? I thought DS Hunt was liaising with narcotics, not us? Sir?'

He waved a hand. 'This is what proactive investigative work looks like. Haskell has given the clear on the team using what resource we have. I'm not asking for favours. I'm delegating work. This is an order constable.'

'Right. Well, what is this bloody place then?' Hudson replied, not that convinced.

Hiraoka pointed to a detached house opposite, a light on in the top room. 'There.'

'Any idea how many are in there? Weapons?'

'One or two. A knife at best. Low-level scum. Halfwits the lot, so it won't be too difficult. Know how to handle yourself, Hudson?'

A cold rush hit Hudson, and it wasn't from the blizzard rolling in. Small flakes beginning to settle on the cars and brick walls around them. An acrid taste in his mouth signalled danger. Something was very wrong with this picture.

'Sir? Really? Shouldn't we have a warrant? Back up?'

'Just do as you're fucking told.'

'Yes, sir, sorry.'

Neither of them bought his charade, and with the frustrations of no substantial leads or physical evidence of their killer, questioning a real person on a potential break was admittedly tempting. Hudson also felt intimidated, though he wouldn't want to admit it. Hiraoka stood a few inches taller than him, had a stern face, and a single word would have him off the force in a heartbeat. He'd have to just do as he's fucking told.

His terms.

They both walked up nonchalantly to the front door, and Hudson stood to the side. Still pondering how long this sort of behaviour had gone unnoticed by the others. Or worse, that it was simply swept under the rug.

Jolting him too, Hiraoka tapped him on the arm and nodded to the door.

'Kick it in, I'll go first. Follow a second behind and take the other rooms.' He pulled out two standard-issue police batons, handed one over to Hudson. 'Just in case.'

117

He took a few strides back and got ready to take his aim at the door.

'Give it a properly good one, Hudson. I don't want you tickling the door and giving them the heads up.'

So he did. Baring his teeth and breathing out, he slammed the bottom of his booted foot into the lock, causing it to splinter at the frame and shoot open.

Hiraoka charged in straight after, shouldering the door as it bounced back off the wall.

No call out of police presence. Ignoring the rulebook. He dashed into the first room and started going to work. Hudson followed.

The kitchen and living room were empty, so Hiraoka took the stairs, Hudson at his heels. They could hear a door upstairs slam. The noise of panicked footsteps. Someone trying to escape.

All around, the walls were marked and dirtied. But the blur of adrenaline had made Hudson tunnel-visioned. Focused only on Hiraoka. On finding the drug dealers. Whoever they were.

Kicking in the door of the last bedroom, they found a man, alone, failing to wedge open the window. Hiraoka crossed the room in three strides and grabbed the man by the collar.

'Don't you fucking move.'

In plain clothes, they weren't to be recognised as police officers, so, keeping their mouths shut, they could get away with what they wanted. And these coke dealers always kept quiet. Hiraoka had it all planned, it dawned on Hudson. The perfect mission. No accountability with or without reward.

He felt sick.

'Sir?'

'What?'

'The fuck is this?'

'Never you mind.'

Hudson kept his distance. Watching horrified at Hiraoka's unique investigative method. What would it take, he wondered then, to turn him in. Report him for misuse of authority and breaking policing protocol?

'You and your boys,' he started, growling heavily. 'Will keep your product off my streets. If I catch even a whiff of your presence that you've been dealing to young kids again, I will personally come find you and bring about an end that would make the devil himself shake. I will fucking destroy you all.'

The dealer wheezed in his grasp. 'B-b-bruv, fuck. C-calm down, yeah? Chill.'

'No. No one is chilling tonight, son. Now fuck off, and let your big boss know I came knocking.'

He dropped the man, who gasped momentarily for air, before legging it out the room. His hurried steps and swearing echoing outside for a few minutes until he had obtained significant distance from them.

An hour later, Hudson and Hiraoka found themselves in Hyde Park, staring into a curtain of fresh snowfall. Not too far away from the first crime scene. What had happened still rushed through Hudson's mind in a blur. The stench of the place. The graffiti. The mess. The frightened dealer. Hiraoka completely losing it. He didn't know what to think. What to do or what to say to him. His senior line of authority, who he had begun to elevate up beyond measure, had now come crashing down to be nothing more than a thug. But what power did he have over all this? What else was this DCI capable of?

'Why did you bring me in on that, sir?' His voice shook, part from the cold, part in fear.

Hiraoka didn't answer. Instead, just as he always did, he pulled out a pack of cigarettes and lit one slowly. After letting out a slow breath and a roll of blue smoke, he bowed his head against a sudden gust of wind and started to talk. His voice was uncharacteristically different.

'I had to. I needed to send a message of my own, and I needed to motivate you.'

'Expect me to buy that, sir? Given you have Hunt, Nguyen, and the rest at your disposal. You just needed me to safeguard yourself. How can I be good with this? This isn't policing. This is criminal.'

'I don't need you to be good with it, but your interests are in my interests. Vice versa. You won't report it, but it'll stop them dealing for a few weeks at least. Save a few lives, perhaps. Let us have a bit of breathing room on this case, and hell, perhaps even a lead. It's funny how these things can happen.'

Hudson frowned. 'A few weeks. I thought you said back there th—'

'You think my threats alone would get those twats to stop for good? Don't you think, by now, I know most of the big players in this shit hole? Indulge in some perspective, Hudson. Even for a kyu, you're really fucking naive. Sure you transferred to the correct job?' He blew out some more smoke. Waved a hand.

There was that word again. *Kyu*.

Hudson was pissed. This did nothing for the case. 'How does roughing him up get us closer to the killer? It doesn't even bring us closer to the student. All it does is betray Haskell, the team, and jeopardises the case.'

'No. It teaches you a valuable lesson. Rules are frameworks built by those with their own wobbly sense of morality. In this, not only does his seniors acknowledge the Met are willing to reach further to close this case by disrupting their business, but it also frightens them to potentially make mistakes. They were squatting in that building, and we weren't looking for information, so a warrant would have been useless. The visit also has no relevance to the case and isn't on clocked overtime. Sometimes, Hudson, you need to have extracurricular activities. That's the lesson.'

'But why?'

Hiraoka smiled, taking another long smoke of his Marlboros, and turned to him. 'As I've said, it's sent a message. Heat gets turned up. People start making mistakes.'

Hudson looked down at his purpling hands, trying to digest Hiraoka's morally bankrupt reasoning. The musings of a man who had either lost faith in the system or simply didn't care either way. The cliché of it all unnerved him. Sunk enough doubt into his mind on whether to file a complaint or not.

'Why are we here?'

'Don't you know by now?' Hiraoka smirked, tossing his smoke and tightening his bright red scarf. 'This is where the killer started it all. And it's where we have to keep coming back to. If we can't write the beginning of this story, we can't write the end. Sometimes you just have to start shaking trees.'

And with a condescending pat on the shoulder, he took a left out of Hyde Park and disappeared into the snow, leaving the young constable cold, confused, and terrified at what he'd helplessly let himself in for. His bright, promising transfer and move to the London Met, now evolving into a nightmare he couldn't climb out of.

Thursday, 14th February

03:27

The pair of them sat, half three in the morning, in their pyjamas, drinking their tea.

Silence. And then...

'Not going to tell me what happened in that nightmare of yours? You've had several now.'

Hudson stared into the carpet. Watching the beige yarn swirl and twist in his broken look.

'It's nothing. It was just sudden and shocking. I've forgotten most of it anyway,' he lied. 'Thanks for the tea, though. Soft side after all?'

Eisa scoffed at that. A harsh comment given the circumstances. 'Easy now. I'm quite the co-habitant. You are merely too quick with the bigotry. I'll put this aside as unease, fatigue and general nonsense. Consider your apology accepted.'

They both looked up at each other and laughed.

'Fine,' he said. 'Whatever.'

Hudson didn't get back to sleep that night. Instead, he sat up awake, re-playing the events of his nightmare over and over again. Each part in more vivid detail than ever. The empty pub. Tumbling into darkness. The fingers clawing at his scalp. The hammer pounding away at his skull...

But most of all, the talk he had with the chief inspector after roughing up some low-level coke pusher. He still felt that awful taste of betrayal to policing. His tainted morality and a wave of anger toward the man who had tried to bring him down his dark and corrupt rabbit hole.

At half five in the morning, Hudson chucked on his coat, grabbed his things and left earlier than he ever had for work. By half six he was at their Fitzrovia *base camp*, surprising the cleaner again.

'Oh, here we are. At it again are we?'

Hudson forced a smile. 'Yup. Things, OK?'

'Not bad love, not bad. Who am I to complain? And you?'

But Hudson was already closing the door behind him. She frowned, hands-on-hips and muttered something under her breath. Then went back to her cleaning.

At his desk, Hudson rifled through his paperwork. Looking for a place to start. Re-familiarising himself with the details of each murder. After an hour, faith and self-doubt rehoused themselves in his mind, and he threw it all down, put his face in his hands and choked back the tears. He didn't know how much time has passed until DC Leigh appeared, walking in with two cups of something hot and steamy.

'Good morning, ready to get cracking? How was your evening?'

Hudson checked his face was dry, sat up and smiled wearily. 'Tiring. Came in to get a little head start. Re-read the interview notes from the two victim's relatives. Nothing useful. Nothing at all. I suppose we won't start getting much done until today. How was yours?'

Leigh stood in a bright yellow puffer jacket, contrasting his own grey coat, long black jeans and winter boots. She pulled off a beanie dusted in snow to reveal her new afro had small braided bobs. It looked good. 'Not too bad! Went to watch a production with a friend. Had dinner with Dad. Got the nails did. Here, this is for you. I saw fresh footprints outside so doubled back and grabbed you one.'

'Cheers,' he said, taking a hungry sip. Immediately burning his lips and tongue. 'Shit.'

She laughed. 'Easy. You'll have plenty more reading material by the end of the day, fingers crossed.'

'You look taller today.'

'It's just my boots,' she replied. 'I'm going to add some extra notes to the board, want to help me out?'

Hudson stood. 'Why the fuck not?'

Leigh travelled the length of the office to the murder board with an arm full of papers. 'We've already ascertained where we want to question. Thanks to yours truly.'

'Nice.'

'But, there's something else. The time.'

DC Hudson tapped a finger on his chin, thinking. 'What about it? Both happened late at night?'

'No. Hiraoka ran this past me the other day. Only a small thing but I think it's quite important now I've been dwelling on it. Look.'

She jabbed a list of notes on the side of the map. 'First murder, beginning of the first week of February. Next murder, a week later.'

'And today is the fourteenth? So you're saying we're due another killing in a day or two?'

'No. I'm saying it could happen any time now. Or one has already happened, and we've not found it yet. Especially if they're escalating.'

Hudson paced, taking another gulp of his coffee. 'Ramping it up? Speeding up the frequency?'

'That's exactly what I'm saying. The urgency of the kills. The theatrics of it. The acts of someone unhinged. Strong and powerful as well. Knowing what kind of damage they can do, they will want to keep doing it. I think they're planning it right now. This could all be part of something larger?'

Hudson nodded. 'Not bad. I think Hiraoka might even go with that. How can we sell that in forensics though?'

'That's the damn thing,' Leigh said. 'All we've had so far are boot prints, some blurry CCTV which shows bugger all, and a foreign fibre the forensics team are yet to trace to a correct brand. We're waiting on multiple toxicology reports which, again, could take a month plus. Then there's Robert Short's phone records, which could also take a month to access. On top of that, Moreau is coming up dry on the girl's laptop. There is literally nil. Nothing.'

'I'm not entirely sure what else we can do until those reports come back. Question as many people connected as possible, I suppose? Run the CCTV over and over?'

Leigh rubbed her neck, trying to ease out a pulled muscle. She stood staring at the board, trying to consider an angle they hadn't looked at yet.

'At this rate, I'm never fucking making sergeant.'

Hiraoka, walking in with Chief Superintendent Haskell, spotted the two constables from across the room and gave Hudson a nod. His unblinking eyes trying to tell him something. Probably to make sure he kept his mouth shut about the other night.

'I sense an unease,' he grumbled ominously as he walked over. DC Leigh making herself busy again.

'Good Morning, DC Hudson,' Haskell boomed. 'You've made a habit of these early starts. You'll show your DCI up if you keep going. I highly recommend it.'

Hiraoka laughed.

Sensing the mood between Leigh and Hudson, Haskell pursued this aggressively.

'Feeling OK constable? Any errors in the recruitment process? How have you been settling in, I hear you've moved to Brixton? Bit bold but it could be Hackney I suppose,' he laughed at his own joke, winking at Leigh to show no harm meant.

'No, sir. Leigh and I were just discussing the case. Ideas of what—'

'You've read my mind,' Haskell interrupted. 'I was just discussing the case with Hiraoka as well. Follow me to my office, I have a bit of an announcement to make.'

Caught off guard, Hudson threw up an eyebrow, trying to get a clue from Hiraoka or Leigh as to what was going on. Leigh gave him nothing but a shrug. Hiraoka stared straight ahead.

Cramped inside the chief superintendent's office, they all budged up around his desk and waited for the news, as Haskell shuffled into his chair. Pausing momentarily to suck in his beer gut.

125

'Right. Well, I'll come straight out with it as I did with Hiraoka. The deputy commissioner has caught wind from the commander that things haven't been running as quickly and efficiently as they'd like following the second killing in Soho. They'd have appreciated this further forward by now, considering our reputation. It's been over a week. There is a dangerous lack of witness questioning and statements in general. Very little has been found in evidence with no results in sight.'

'Two killings in eight days, sir. With all due respect—'

'No, Hudson, with all due respect the commander is right. Now, Hiraoka has put together the murder board, with the help of Leigh, which I see is being actively updated,' he added as she began to gesticulate wildly. 'But that's not enough. The CCTV is consuming man-hours with no results, the reports from the labs and tech will take weeks, with no valuable eye witness accounts having been obtained. That's bugger all really, and it's an embarrassment to this team. Why haven't we made second or third visits to the relatives? Why haven't there been interviews lining up out the bloody door? We should have better witnesses by now. It's not as if we're tracking down a phantom.'

He shook his head, grabbed a bottled water from a small cooler next to his desk. Hiraoka was motionless. Didn't say a word.

Hudson worded himself carefully. 'What's our plan going forward, sir?'

'Glad you asked. As of this afternoon, the entire operation is to be re-structured. As it is, the specials team will absorb some uniformed officers from current cold cases and assist with the canvassing and be the feet on the street. Next, we will be momentarily, and I emphasise, temporarily, moving all detectives and other officers in this task force to be working full time on this. We're thin on the ground thanks to a few annual leaves and a departure.'

Leigh's mouth dropped.

'Gone this high up, has it, sir?'

Haskell pointed a finger. 'The commander is concerned with public appearance. We need to get a grip on this case before it continues to spiral out of control. Liaison officers are already up against it, and if bodies continue to pile up, our jobs will be the least of our worries.'

Hudson was trying to take it all in, his mind tired and drifting back to the nightmare he'd had this morning. All of them, at the bar, ready to kill. Blood in the snow, seeping everywhere...

'Hudson?'

He jerked awake, gawped pathetically at Haskell.

'Sorry son, am I boring you?'

'No sir, sorry I wa—'

'This is no time for me to regret recommending your application. We need all hands on deck. Can I rely on you, constable, to at least come to work awake and ready?'

'Sorry, sir.'

Haskell let out an exaggerated breath, his shoulders slumping, resting his large fists on the desk.

'Put your heads together, gather yourself and come back by the end of today with something. When the rest are in, Hiraoka, I want a full handover to the team. All other casework to be put on hold. Count our lucky fucking stars only DI Patel got lumped with court duty up north.'

'Sir,' Hiraoka intoned.

The three detectives left his office, feeling the mounting pressure more than ever. Hiraoka's hand came slamming down on his shoulder, gripped it firmly. A thing he'd started to get used to. A blatant but habitual case of personal space invasion. Old school power move.

'When I first took a homicide case in Kyoto,' he said. 'I got to the scene, mid-afternoon. Wore uniform back then, ironed fresh, hair done, wanted to be the big hit. The big fucking balls. The Sensei. Only when I got there, I threw up on the crime scene, tainted most of the evidence and got demoted to a desk job for twelve months.'

Hudson threw him a look, Leigh grinning as she eavesdropped from her desk. 'Twelve months? Do I have a demotion hanging over me if I can't take enough Gaviscon before the next job? Or enough pro-plus?'

Hiraoka frowned. 'No. Your problem isn't your stomach but your head, you need to... oh, one second. Oi, Nguyen! Is that pickle and cheese?'

Nguyen had just entered the office with an armful of food. A protein shake hanging from his belt clip.

But, try as he did, the smile faded from his face as he left the station, phone in his hand. Hudson thought about calling home, or calling Krystina, giving someone a message, but he just couldn't muster it. Felt like Haskell had deflated his ambition and any positive energy left.

Out on the road, soaking in the big city, monolithic buildings towering around him, the great Thames raging on, cutting through the concrete and metal of civilisation, it dawned on him then how much he'd gambled on. How big of a thing this all was. Bigger than him. This wasn't all just a career change. A lifestyle change. This was a change of world.

Hudson took out his phone and dialled. His sister answered. Waited for him to speak first.

'Let's do pizza.'

Thursday, 14th February

14:28

The main room filled quickly with officers, ranking from constable to chief inspector. Most of the headcount now filled with uniformed constables from Charing Cross and other nearby stations. An excited mutter buzzed in the air, a few nervous laughs breaking the tune. A sense that the stalemate, in this case, was going to be lifted. Hudson stood arms folded, up by the front with DC Leigh. Noticing a few uniformed faces from his training days. Felt like wanting to conduct himself a bit more conservatively. Set an example. Keep his mouth shut and listen hard to what was about to be said.

A few PCs in the back laughed loudly, just as Haskell made himself aware and walked to the front.

'Settle down now, I've got enough meetings today.'

Lifting a cup of coffee, he sipped it, watching the room fall quiet. Satisfied, he put the cup back down and continued.

'Right, as you are all aware, the Daily Mail, in all its fucking glory, along with a few other outlets, have begun spreading the wildfire. Headlines include Jack The Ripper Returns, London Bathed in Blood and The Surgeon. All in all, I had a very informative conversation with the commissioner himself on this, given our delightful serious crime unit was first on the scene,' he paused, eyeing them all. 'When I enlightened the commissioner that we had no physical evidence or proactive leads to a suspect, he wasn't all too happy. In this unit's interest, I pulled the resource card, which isn't far from the truth. We are lacking in ground presence from uniforms, we are lacking in technology and intelligence, and we need a better strategy. We have two murders, both linked by MO and yet not even a vague picture of who the murderer may be.'

Haskell's eyes fell on Hudson momentarily. A deep grey, hardening slightly. He knew.

'Today marks the tenth day of the investigation, headed thus by DCI Hiraoka and supported by DCs Leigh and Hudson. Now, so far, I have read the paperwork and the write-ups and the interviews have been conducted to a high standard, and all processes followed. It is just unfortunate that we have a killer who can disappear and leave no evidence. It now then falls to strategy to gain further intel. We will be doing that by an increase in technology and uniformed officers.'

Moreau, tucked away in the middle of the room, grinned at Haskell and waved. 'Spending my days on Facebook, you mean?'

Haskell laughed. 'Not at all. Right, a quick introduction. Right there we have Detective Kassandra Moreau, did I say that right? Yes? Detective Moreau from the MPCC Unit dealing in Cyber Crime.'

Moreau waved energetically, which was met with a little concern but some warmth as well.

'Moreau will be using her technical expertise to try and track the killer's movements online. Moreau has... do you mind?' Haskell asked.

'Go on, sir.'

'Excellent. Moreau has extensive experience in information technologies, both offline and online, including tracking movements and decoding decrypted data. She'll be our Q for the investigation, essentially, and will allow us to expand our strategy online, to ensure we're not missing any pieces. This includes scrubbing phones, laptops for further data that may be invaluable to the investigation. This will now be full time until further notice.'

'Got a for instance?' Hiraoka asked, resting his arse on his desk.

'That's your job, I'm afraid but to entertain the question, suppose our killer is doing a great deal of research on his projects? Making plans?

Running under a pseudonym, perhaps? We will want to track this behaviour and link it to the MO.'

Hiraoka nodded. 'Right.'

'Moreau's technical experience will also be used to establish patterns in kill methods. I understand, Hiraoka, Leigh and Hudson have already made quite the start on this but, as the commissioner has reminded me, we are falling drastically behind. And now, with the media soaking this up like sponges, we can't afford to slow down or put a foot wrong.'

He cleared his throat, opting for a bottle of water this time.

'Uniform constables and sergeants will support all investigative officers with extra canvassing. I want feet on the ground between Hyde Park and Soho. I want to know everything, any gossip. I want to know if anyone suspicious at all, regardless of build, has been seen hanging around these locations prior to the murders and then after.' He checked his watch. 'Right, duty calls. I'm to submit our operational review, so Hiraoka, if you could wrap up here.' And dashed off.

Hudson watched him go, his hulking frame vanishing under a large parka and out the door.

The DCI took the floor, a little more casually and concluded the talk.

'Our profile thus far is a male, between six foot and six foot four. No age or race yet. Uniforms, I'll be spending the rest of the day, regrettably, instructing you all on our canvassing strategy. It'll be split into several groups for the areas. Moreau, I'll be with you on the tapes, and then we can crack on. Detectives, I want all relatives, etcetera, re-interviewed to help us with a bullet poof time-line. You'll all receive emails of our plan. Good? Let's go.'

With a loud clap of his hands, Hiraoka smoothed back his scruffy black hair and went to his desk. The room began to disperse, the noise filling the space again. Hudson stayed where he was, watched the shuffling commence. Saw the uniforms head for the tiny meeting room. Watched his boss pull together some paperwork to brief them on their canvassing. The place was buzzing with energy.

DC Nguyen approached Hiraoka and looked to be deep in conversation. Hudson couldn't make anything out from his desk but cocked his head all the same. After a minute, Nguyen nodded. Hiraoka left, entering the meeting room with the uniforms. Nguyen turned, spotted the constable and made a beeline for him.

Back stiffening, Hudson straightened himself to full height, ready.

'Alright, Hudson? How's life?'

'On hold,' he said. 'I didn't expect such a high profile case in my third month.'

'Course not.'

Nguyen was well-liked and well respected by the unit. He wasn't a man of words, nor a man of comedy. So Hudson would soon learn to expect a certain bluntness from the man that, ultimately, wasn't born from any rudeness or a lack of empathy.

'Hudson, just a word with the guv. He wants me to work with you on a few things, whilst Hiraoka helps Haskell on our new strategy.'

Hudson frowned. It sounded like he was talking a load of shit. 'OK?'

'We'll go through the tapes again together, re-document them so he can run it by our new tech Moreau. That much I can do, I'm a bit caught up in my own stuff here. Two sexual assaults but I've had the nod. We're all hands on deck.'

'Alright, couldn't hurt. Fresh eyes and all that. I'll take it all, to be honest, there's been absolutely nothing.'

'We know. We all know. You've been dealt a shit one, the problem isn't the killer; it's how it got public so quickly. In an ideal situation, this would have remained internal for a few more weeks. It is what it is.'

Hudson rubbed his face, imagining that Hiraoka wanted someone else to take a hold of his leash. He glanced over at Leigh's dark eyes deep in concentration, typing furiously, picking up her phone to make a call. Perhaps he'd been more of a burden than he'd anticipated?

'It is what it is. Can I run you through my perspective on this, Newham? Newman... sorry?'

'Nguyen.'

'Nguyen, right.'

He nodded. 'Go on.'

'I've come from a village. Worked in a small city by comparison.

132

Minimal level of resource in comparison, very little in serious crime. We'd get maybe ten murders a year in the entire county, if that. But it all had patterns. Something tangible. Links usually to family or close friends. You know as well as I that statistically, it's close to home.'

'Don't tease me, Hudson.'

'We're in London. It's one of the most heavily CCTV'd places on earth. There have been hundreds of people, not a few dozen metres away. Yet, despite it all, we have barely a single bit of physical evidence, an eye witness account or a link between the victims, which may suggest a motive behind the killing. So far,' he said. He walked around his desk, across the room and slapped the murder board a little too enthusiastically, making one of the stray uniforms making the coffee, jump. 'So far, we have less than fuck all. We are so backward on this. I think the killer is deliberately leaking details to the media, blowing this all up like a theatre show. They want to ensure this is seen by as many people as possible, what do you think?'

Nguyen cracked a grin.

'What?' Hudson asked, a bit annoyed.

'You ever do theatre in school?'

'No, why?'

Nguyen shrugged, pulling out his phone. 'You seem a bit dramatic is all. Bit over-the-top. You're still in probation, so just follow your process and produce. You're not alone on the leak theory. Haskell's said as much, but I don't buy it. Journalists make a living off this stuff, so it's not hard for a few hungry writers to add two and two together. It's not like the crime scene tents were inconspicuous now.'

Nguyen strolled to the exit, thumbing through a few apps.

'How many murder cases have you done? Has the team done?' Hudson launched at his back.

'We spend more time with the devil than our own family. I couldn't tell you. Over a hundred for me, perhaps even more for some of the others. I don't dare think what Hiraoka has seen. Anyway, have the tapes and pen drives ready, will ya? I've got to make a call.'

The rest of the afternoon, Hudson begrudgingly went through the CCTV they had compiled down at Charing Cross Station. Again. And again. It made for a nice getaway from the overbearing, drab and dark colours of their Fitzrovia base. Charing Cross was far more lively and bustling. Their work pile consisted of numerous VHS tapes, CDs and pen drives, which meant for a real pain in the arse. Not to forget the additional online files sent over in dribs and drabs stored on the cloud. Otherwise, why make a job easier?

It got late pretty quick. The scene out through the windows still showing a steady fall of snow. Covering the rooftops around them. Hudson and Nguyen were yawning on and off, both not muttering a single word for hours at a time, scribbling away, re-organising tapes in order of any that displayed a man of gigantic stature. Labelling the discs and slotting them into separate cases. Compiling them into files where possible for duplication. Doing the same for the pen drives and cloud files. Finally, at around half seven in the evening, they stacked the last of them high and set aside their notes. Hudson let out a chuckle of relief and rubbed his eyes.

'Twice as fast as last time. Jesus. Genuinely, helped a great deal. I think we have, what...five? Five files and a tape we could use? Suspicious figures in the vicinity.'

'Four,' Nguyen confirmed, checking the notes he'd jotted down. 'Four that have any sign of a large male going passed. This is where my help ends. Count it as a volunteer because I know I will. It'll be going toward my development, but you'll want to let Hiraoka know.'

'What, that we have some positive start on a lead now?' Hudson laughed.

'Fuck no. That you might want to check your stats, go back to the morgue if you have to. Who's dealing with this one?'

'What?'

Nguyen stretched by the office door, swiping a hand through the air. 'Ya bloody body collector.'

'Examiner? Oh right yeah, Nita, we're using her mortuary currently.

Already near capacity.'

Nguyen smiled. A rarity. 'Ah yeah, she's a good egg.'

'Yeah?'

The two detectives re-piled the physical CCTV evidence into boxes and made their way back to the evidence room, a cold piece of crap right at the back of the station with a load of cheap metal cages. They signed for a key, and after Hudson had done snooping a quick look at all the various items, including a weird shaped lamp and a gun inside a plastic bag, they signed it up and left, giving the sergeant at the desk the nod.

'Remember,' Nguyen said, wagging a finger. 'Let him know. He'll be keeping tabs on uniforms for Haskell. They may want to alter their approach. But what do I know?'

That filled Hudson with heaps of confidence.

'Right, well, thanks again. Felt therapeutic. I suppose you're going to leave me with all the paperwork?' He brandished the large file in his hand. A collection of notes from their efforts.

'Therapeutic? No. And of course. Favours don't come in pairs, Hudson. That's your job.'

The detectives rolled their eyes, mocking the circumstance of their enslavement to police admin and said their goodbyes. Zipping up his coat at the entrance, waving to the desk sergeants as a set of uniforms came barrelling in from the snow holding a drunk, Hudson braved the dark and the wind on his return to Fitzrovia. His shoes thoroughly soaked through by the time he got there.

Finally, back in out of the weather, the constable slumped down at his desk, flicked the monitor on and saw he had a few emails. Closing his eyes, he pushed the heels of his palms into his eyes, rubbing them until he saw blotches. Silently praying this fiasco would sort itself out. He was never a religious man, but he was beginning to get desperate. He wondered how Hiraoka was getting on with the meat of the investigation. The timelines. Liaising with a much larger team to somehow deliver Haskell's increasingly challenging deadlines.

A pang of guilt.

Not sympathy for the man. Quite the opposite. Guilt for having felt any at all, for a man who seemed to cut corners to get an end result. Or, as he had worded it, to *shake some trees*. Whatever that meant. And guilt, moreover, for not having raised any of this with Haskell or his senior staff. Why was he holding back at all? Curiosity? Fear? He'd not long been in the job, so perhaps it just boiled down to selfish levels of survival?

Exhausted from his own thoughts, he threw down the large file of notes and began the long slog of typing everything up. Their horde of surveillance findings. A chance, just maybe, of finding their killing.

'Finally managed to pull your own head out of your arse then, Danny?'

Krystina saluted her small glass of whiskey, Hudson his pint of lager.

His sister stood only a few inches shorter than him. All legs and long blonde hair. Small nose and pointed chin. All reminders of her original Slavic routes before being adopted by Hudson's mother two decades ago. 'Really am sorry. Things have been a little crazy with the new case I'm working on. How have you been?'

Having managed a good hour of write-ups, he'd sacked it in. He couldn't put things off any longer. Picking up a call to Krystina, he named a time and a place to meet. Apologised profusely. She'd been quite scathing and then rounded off the call with a sincerity of kindness that almost gave him whiplash. Such was her way. But he was glad he answered. Satisfied he'd made the right choice for a change. If there was to be one area of his life that wouldn't end up in a shit heap, it had to be family. After the dust settles, or in this case, snow, a family is what held everything together. No matter how weird, estranged or already fractured.

'Busy? You forget what I do for a living, haven't you?'

'I haven't, but I'm just struggling with what I have on is all,' Hudson pressed, taking a quick and generous sip. They had bravely chosen to sit outside a Greene King, some very light snowfall adding to the persistent powder around them. The large heaters were working wonders, however, and coaxed a few more drinkers out as well.

Krystina laughed. 'Fine. But you need to schedule your time more efficiently. I'm a solicitor for several big firms and bill sixty hours a week. You made this big promise of coming down to reconnect, and it's not felt like that at all.'

Hudson nodded. 'You're right.'

'You have no idea what—'

'Krystina. I get it. I'm sorry but if you knew half of what I've been looking at. My trips to the morgue. Telling families the news. This isn't like back home anymore. I hope you can realise that and appreciate I've been doing all I can to meet up.'

She raised an eyebrow, swirling her whiskey before taking a gulp. Putting it back down gently, deliberately, she gazed back at her brother shrewdly.

'I have Jessica on Facebook, Danny. Just be honest with me.'

'What?'

A waitress picked the perfect moment to take their orders. As prophesied earlier, they were getting pizza. Hudson went something spicy, whilst Krystina went for a Hawaiian. Almost daring her brother to bring up the pineapple-on-pizza debate.

'I see what she posts,' she said after the waitress had left. 'What she gets up to. Dates she goes on.'

Hudson closed his eyes. He had fucked up, and there was no hope of ducking out from someone who had studied law for half their life. A nosy looking couple near their table had already picked up on the mood, which only seemed to aggravate Krystina more. 'Listen, that was just a spur of th—'

'No, I get it. You've already set up your priorities.'

'That's not it,' he protested. 'It just sort of fell like that is all.'

'Lie to me, sure, but don't lie to yourself, Danny.'

'I'm not lying.' Even as he said it, he knew it was wrong. He'd been nervous about touching base again. The truth was, he was a little bit afraid of her. Always had been. With her bipolar disorder, he never knew what side he was going to get. 'Can we just start again? I'm here right now. I'm trying to make an effort.'

The couple at the adjacent table had paused, drinks untouched, listening intently. Hudson could see Krystina's jaw pop.

'Melissa put you up to this?'

'Mum's got nothing to do with it.'

'Wouldn't have been the old man. He would have seen through your bullshit. You know I never asked for any of this, and I'm doing fine.' She stood up then, putting on her coat and gloves. Green eyes severe now, her previously gentle features suddenly fierce. 'Time I left, I think.'

Hudson mouthed like a fish out of water, fumbling for words. He stood up too. 'Krystina! Come on, sit down! You're not thinking straight.'

This hit a nerve.

'No, brother, I'm thinking perfectly fine. Tell me, did you move to London to make amends or was it to escape and clear your own guilty conscience?'

'I…' he began but couldn't finish. The couple at the table now openly watching, mouths also open.

Before Krystina left, she bent down between the two who had eavesdropped and yelled for a solid three seconds. The entire pub went quiet, heads turning to Krystina and Hudson. The bouncer at the door about to make a move. But before he could, his sister had already satisfied her need to cause a bit of chaos and left.

I reached for a Burr puzzle; the intricate wooden craft, one of the hardest to solve in the world. The object moved between my long fingers. The smooth sides glancing across for but a moment. Then, with a pause, I placed it back down and squeezed my bottom lip between a thumb and forefinger.

'No need for self-imposed limitations now?' I said. 'No. Not yet.'

I stepped closer to the window, my nose almost touching and traced the cold pane slowly, whispering my next words. 'I see you from afar. You seem happy. You seem challenged. I sense these movements may slow a little but do not worry detectives, it won't be for long.'

Thursday, 14th February

23:10

Without consequence, though with minor frostbite, Hudson never went home after his lonely pizza. Krystina never came back after she stormed out. Instead, he found that his feet and oyster card had put him outside their small Fitzrovia headquarters. The tumbled down conversion that housed the proactive Central West MIT. What was once a bustling hive with two dozen detective constables and various supporting staff, stood a ghost of its former glory. Stretched thin thanks to cuts and in the process of controversial mergers of units, it wasn't just Hudson feeling the strain.

Despite the place being of serious historical significance, and having been provided by a very generous donation, he hadn't arrived there for sightseeing but the old itch to work. Something coppers tended to get during the middle of a case. A bit like; Hudson thought, as he climbed the few steps toward the doors scrubbing away at a bit of ice on his boot, getting crap off your feet.

'What the fuck am I on about?' He muttered to his consciousness, nodding to a few late-nighters, the place almost empty. He took the stairs two at a time, waltzed through into the buildings main open plan room, wheeled his desk chair to the murder board, picked up his case files and slumped down.

A big fat sigh left his lungs. Eyes dry from sleep deprivation.

'Right.'

He placed down the folders onto the floor, arranged each folder by date, and eyed the board. On it, were pictures of the scenes tacked onto the locations. They'd already done that business, but there was still no link. Nothing discernible that made sense.

Scratching at the nape of his neck, he blinked a few times, then regarded the map again, tracing his eyes along the streets and roads of London City.

'Why Hyde Park? Why Soho? Why the brains?' he said out loud. 'Do you know these people? Have they crossed your path? Are you trying to tell us something?'

Hudson stopped, chewing his lip. Why was he here? Had he really needed to scratch that itch so bad? There had been no discoveries in the timelines. Hiraoka had been thorough, leading them inexorably to another dead end with their lack of evidence. No tangible link between the students or from anyone in Robert Short's life. At least so far.

Yet review it again he would.

Hudson fumbled over the files and looked at both Robert Short and Catherine Evans. Firstly, they never attended the same school. They never lived in the same area except for London and didn't even follow the same music tastes. No family ties, no mutual friends, nothing. Completely separate in every way, except where they both lived and died.

Hiraoka and Moreau had done a bit of mucky work on social media, and the case files were full of startling detailed information on the girl, but a lot less on the man. Was he shy? Or simply kept himself to himself? Why meet in the park late at night? Perhaps this eluded to a secretive lifestyle or relationship to the student? It made sense if his ex-wife resented him, but nothing evidenced it. Maybe that could be a theory to follow? A jealous ex-lover or admirer with a twisted sense of justice coming back?

No. It didn't add up. The removal of the brains spoke of something else. Something more evil.

A slip of paper fell from that file. He picked it up. On it was written, *Gang meet? Gang drug deal?*.

Gang meet was scribbled out, but gang drug deal was not. Hudson pondered on that for a second and thought about the way the attacker had killed him. The heavy, downward force with a knife. Measured, powerful and brutal, leaving the body largely undamaged but the face wholly destroyed. Then the scalping and the hurried amateurish job of surgically retrieving the brain without professional equipment.

Feeling like he was pulling on something, pulling at another thread, he checked the girl's file and noticed the same brutal attack. Perhaps this was the drug gang's method of kill? A gang member took a man out from orders or other means, and the girl was in the way? Maybe even a cult? They had toyed with the idea of a ritual because of how the brain was being removed post-mortem.

'But why there? Why make it theatrical? What's it in aid of?'

A deep, accented voice came from the shadowy edge of Hiraoka's desk.

'I've looked over the gang theory, Hudson, it doesn't seem right.'

The young detective shit himself.

'Jesus fu—, Christ. Sir. How long ha—'

'Long enough. I too enjoy unauthorised overtime.' He stood up from his desk. 'Pack that nonsense away, you can research ritualistic killings another time. I'm taking you for a drink, coke dealers withheld.'

The chief inspector thought his last comment was quite funny.

'Sir?'

'I've had a long, shit day or two. So I want to drink. Do as you're told, *Kabu.*'

And he did.

Overhead, in neon signage, glowing faintly behind the snow settling on top, read *Ronnie Scott's*. At the door, a few people still filing through behind the ropes, the bouncer handed Hiraoka a warm smile and let the pair through. Once they paid and sorted themselves out, Hudson followed his inspector through a warm, finely decorated corridor, before opening up into a tiny theatre. With perhaps the capacity of a hundred people max, including the band on the sunken stage centre back, red fabric seats with table lamps ran in lines along to left and right sides, with chairs dotted down in the middle, lower, and closer the stage. At the back, behind a cooper rail and some pillars, a luxurious bar built-in glass and gold served a few smartly dressed individuals expensive mixes and wine.

The walls dripped with history, and the place suggested a certain intimacy, with the moody red lighting in the back, the low ceiling and the warm, rich colours. The railings and holds looked gold in the light. It was an emporium of dreams, and he felt suddenly very welcome.

Hudson's mouthed his amazement. Was Hiraoka looking to soften him up after what had happened?

'Bloody hell sir, this is a bit... nice, isn't it?'

'They haven't started playing yet.'

The chief inspector led them both to the left, found a seat somewhere in the middle and plopped down next to a small group who smiled at them.

'Friendly in here too.'

'Shhh.'

Hudson regarded his boss for a moment, still soaking it all in.

'Run up and grab us something, will ya? Old Fashioned for me.'

After a violent assault on his debit card, Hudson returned a good bit poorer and settled a bottle of beer and a small glass of whiskey, crushed ice and some other stuff in it, onto their table. Though the bloke behind the bar seemed to eye him and Hiraoka a few more times than was comfortable, deducting a small percentage from the price. Police discounts always a bonus and evidence Hiraoka was a long time regular.

'Heard about those,' he said. 'Any good?'

Hiraoka took a sip and smacked his lips. 'Hmm. It's a favourite of mine. My first drink in the UK after I travelled over from Kyoto years ago. Quiet now, music's about to start.'

What followed next; the cacophony of musical pleasure, had been headlined as *Lemon Dame and the Rascals*, as Hiraoka would later tell him. A reasonably old black man took stage right, adjacent to the grand piano and started blowing out tunes Hudson had never heard. A young guy on the drums grinned the whole time, whilst a lady, with lightning-quick fingers, dazzled the keys, hitting a beat Hudson nor indeed many others in Ronnie Scott's, could keep up with.

Everyone's eyes were hypnotised. Rows of clicking fingers, smiling white teeth and claps. The atmosphere became electric, and for a good while, both detectives forgot all about the murder case, and the dead bodies rotting in Nita's mortuary. The empty case files. The no leads. The media hounds and the deadlines from the superintendent. All of that melted away, oozing under the seats.

When the last melodic firework fizzled and popped above the crowd, and they clapped hard and whistled their thanks, Hudson realised he hadn't touched a drop of his beer.

'Bloody hell,' he shouted over the noise. 'That was brilliant.'

Hiraoka looked at him then, his glass empty. 'Well look at that. They didn't replace my last with such an incompetent tosser after all?'

'What?'

'Nothing,' he said. 'Time to go.'

Still reeling from the experience, Hudson walked in silence, in tow with Hiraoka. The pair made a sight, both very tall heads cast forward, eyes blank but searching. Long parka coats, thick scarves, hands gloved. The night was slightly cooler than before, dry and not a falling flake to be seen. Made a change. Hudson was beginning to grow tired of the postcard weather. Too much disruption had come of it.

The snow wasn't melting either, making it feel like the world had stopped. At one in the morning on a Friday, it might as well have.

'Claim that on expenses then, sir?'

Hiraoka inclined his head. 'Does villains like me a justice, for a little time off.'

'Eh?'

'All work, you know. Suicide rates in Japan are alarmingly high because of our unprecedented work ethic.'

Hudson grinned. 'Bit of a brag there?'

'Don't be so stupid.'

'Sorry.'

Bit bloody odd this whole thing, Hudson pondered as he took a left onto Shaftesbury Avenue. His working relationship with Hiraoka had been strange at best. Patronising, distant and unsupportive. Not to mention signs of corruption and a very relaxed approach to process and transparency. How had he made rank?

'Watch yourself, son.'

Hiraoka tugged him back from a reverie in time to avoid a near-miss with a cabbie. 'Whoops.'

'Yeah let's not make it a third shall we?'

The pair crossed, hands in pockets, shoes slapping against the wet pavement.

'About that, sir, if you don't mind me talking shop? No? OK, well, forgive me for being a bit blunt, but is this some sort of way to make right what happened the other night? I've not worked anything this high level before, I'm grateful for the opportunity of course, but, I'm concerned is all. I want to know I'm not going to trip anyone up or cross any lines myself.'

'You think too much.' Was all he said.

'Sir?'

'I'm the senior investigating officer. I shouldn't have to have the chat. The one where I tell you how fucking old I am. What I've seen. You're not thick, Hudson. You've seen through my little play, but it's an honest one. It's not all about work.'

Hudson cocked his head. 'Old cop takes young cop to old watering hole. They develop a crucial understanding at a critical plot point? I knew that bartender seemed a bit too friendly. Still a bloody rip off for the one round. I'd buy the whole office for that price back in Notts.'

He ignored him. 'You're at it too much. You're trying to do my job. I don't trust you yet, constable. Focus on the case file management, going over statements, talking to people. Filling in the gaps. Revisit the crime scenes if you have to.'

'I'm still hitting the brick wall.'

'We.'

'We,' Hudson corrected. 'We aren't coming up with anything. But, I've got theories. Ideas.'

'Any you can tell me right now that you can back up with evidence?'

'No.'

A small smile, before taking out a cigarette and lighting it. 'Didn't think so. Keep at it. Be thorough. Triple check your files. Get the others to review. When we catch the fucker, we want our date with CPS to go easy.'

The two stopped by a taxi rank, and Hiraoka found an empty one for Hudson.

'How much to Brixton?'

'Forty-five,' called the cabbie in a thick eastern European accent.

Hiraoka swore quite a bit and fished out some money. Then he stood and met Hudson with his own two eyes.

'Get some proper sleep, rise and shine for tomorrow. We still have blanks in our timeline, and a better picture needs to be made of our killer.'

'Right, sir.'

'Good, now get in, and I'll see you tomorrow. Cabbie, get rid of him.'

The eastern European grinned and waved two fingers up to him. 'Righ' you are, Bozz.'

Nursing a surprise hangover that had come with entering his thirties, Hudson managed to figure out how to work Eisa's coffee machine and was just pouring himself a cup when she stumbled into the kitchen.

'Wow, taking liberties now are we? Is that how it is?'

Hudson kept pouring the jug into his cup.

'Erm, hello? Good morning sir, are you quite together? Detective Hudson?'

Hudson nudged another empty cup toward her and began filling it up.

'Good morning to you too.'

'Damn you to Hades.' She snatched at the cup, took a drink, wandered around the flat and then called back from the living room. 'Not bad, we'll have use for you yet.'

Hudson took his own cup, followed her into the living room, plonked himself down between two cushions and started drinking his sludge.

'Get enough sleep last night? Have those dreams been assaulting your peace at all?' Eisa asked her tone now sincere for a moment.

'No,' Hudson replied. 'Though just a short one. I got back late, so I was properly tired. Maybe that helped.'

'How would it?'

He shrugged. 'Mind's too knackered to conjure up terrible images? No idea.'

'Have you informed work? You said you'd be pursuing counselling. You should let your er, partner know, right? You have a partner and such, so you should probably inform him of these matters. They'll impair your investigative abilities no doubt.'

'No, not yet.'

He took a cautious gulp, winced, put the cup down and ran his fingers through his hair. 'Mum has a point. Something she said a while ago before I moved.'

'Oh?'

'I wanted to go into teaching, can you imagine? Mum fancied it for me too, but nothing was going there, and a vacancy in the police force popped up sooner. Maybe I'm just making excuses?'

Eisa went misty-eyed. 'And took the road less travelled.' Then laughed.

'Poem, right?'

'Fucking bravo, Shitspeare. Jesus. Yes, a poem. So, are you having second musings on your current occupation then? I should hope any future endeavours you might have included a substantial working notice, followed swiftly by fresh employment, which would supplement the rental payments without a hitch. Yes?'

Hudson grunted.

'You'd better.'

'It's fine,' he said. 'I don't have any plans to go into teaching. I'm too ingrained into the force. It's what I love doing. Or thought I did. This move to the Met, it's a big step. It hasn't been the smoothest.'

Eisa choked incredulously, batting a strand of hair from her face. 'Contrary to your relative stiff disposition, no pun intended Mr Morning Happiness, but you're not a piece of wood. Just because you've spent a good decade in one career doesn't mean you can't change. Why the hell not?'

For that, Hudson didn't have an answer and knew his jovial and rather annoying flatmate had made several good points. Instead, Hudson meekly surrendered, finished his coffee and put himself together for work.

On the walk to the station, he thumbed through a news app and checked the weather. The next day or two were due to be cold and dry, giving the snow chance to disappear but a fresh storm would be sweeping in to take one last dump on the capital. Not believing much of this, he checked a few other messages and saw something from Jessica.

I had a great time the other day, looking forward to another date sometime x

Hudson couldn't help but grin, feeling foolish to assume the world was so against him, and with his stride lengthening and his shoulders pulling back, he replied confidently.

Me too. Let's do tomorrow night. Free? X

He shoved the phone away, hid his hands in his pockets and marched on, gazing up at the steel skyline, melting into the cold, metal sky behind it.

Friday, 15th February

08:56

'Right,' Hiraoka said, leaning down on Hudson's desk casually, playing with a cigarette. 'We got a call this morning, prompted by some grace and miracle from our premature media explosion, who thought they saw something dodgy.'

'Really?'

Hudson was listening intently, this time without Leigh. She was out chasing the toxicology reports in person, following up on some leads Hiraoka had made at the university. Frustratingly, all of Catherine Evans' friends had air-tight alibis thanks to student accommodation CCTV. Yet to be verified, of course. Which meant they were back to listening out for gossip and rumour. So far, no link. But today, luck would finally change.

The chief inspector nodded. 'Yup. Something good from the shitstorm. The boys care for their mum, so we'll be nipping down in person. Have another look at the scene, see if it adds up. Then we'll go from there.'

Almost on cue, a very busy and exhausted looking Haskell whizzed passed them, an apple in his mouth and papers under his arm.

'Morning guv, another meeting is it?' Hiraoka shouted over.

Haskell glared at him, took a chunk out of his apple and disappeared into his office.

'Jesus,' Hudson muttered. 'The f—'

'Deputy commissioner I 'eard. Probably gnawing his ear off about all our shenanigans. Anyway, finish that brew, close your computer and let's get going.'

'What's the address?'

'Block of flats, eight, no, nine floor ups. Hopkins Street.'

Hudson grabbed his jacket, walked passed the murder board. 'Hopkins Street, Hopkins Street, Hopkins. Sir. That's right where—'

'I know. Shut up and get your keys.'

A little under an hour later, the detectives were climbing the stairs to a tower of flats, not spitting distance for where Catherine Evans had been murdered. Squinting over the wall, Hudson looked up and down the alleyway. At the bins, the rubbish and the slush. At how normal it all looked now and yet, a week ago, it had been the stage to a most brutal killing. Not forgetting, the second encephalectomy in the case. A medical term Hudson had no idea he'd be learning to spell, let alone repeating.

Shivering, he turned back and took the last flight of steps to floor nine.

'Same as before, I'll run production, you take notes.

'Sir,' Hudson intoned.

Hiraoka pulled out a sizeable knuckled hand and rapped the door. No answer. He banged again, and the pair heard shuffling from inside.

'Met Police from the Serious Crimes Unit. You called us an hour ago?' he boomed.

'Just a minute mate!' Came a young voice inside.

Keys jingled in the lock, and the occupier opened the door. A short, medium built guy in a Nigerian football t-shirt.

'Mum said she'd rang you boys, is it about tha' thing last week?'

Hiraoka scowled. 'You mean murder? Yes. Can we come in?'

'Whatever, mum's in the living room, straight through yeah.'

Hudson bit his cheek to stop from laughing and crossed the threshold. Out of the cold, they entered a minimal living area, with plain cream walls right the way through with a more warm, exotic theme in the living room. Lots of reds and browns. A large rug. A glass table. In the corner, opposite the TV, a woman with crutches on either side of the chair, smoking a cigarette.

He spotted a pair of tights wrapped up around the smoke alarm, and a window cracked open. Aside from the demeanour of the woman, the place looked nice. Respectable.

The young boy's mum was large, ankles swollen by water, but her face was kind. Hudson immediately felt a gentle instinct about her, something genuine and caring. A very motherly vibe, so, sitting down with Hiraoka and pulling out his notepad, he gave her an encouraging smile. This shit can't be easy, especially when it's happening right on your front door.

'Good Morning Mrs Hansen.'

'Miss Hansen.' She waved a thick finger at Hiraoka and grinned all her brilliant white teeth. 'And you're welcome. How can I help you fine men today? Can I get my boys to rustle up something sweet?'

'No, thank you. We're here to talk to you about what happened a few nights ago.'

'Well I knew you weren't the Avon catalogue collectors,' she laughed. 'Gimme a second.'

Miss Hansen checked out her boys, who were gaming in their bedrooms. Satisfied they were busy, she returned and offered them tea.

Hiraoka had found himself comfortable on the sofa. 'No, no, that's fine. Shall we start from the beginning? With what you saw?'

Hudson kept his gob shut. He'd fancied a tea.

'That sounds just fine,' she replied.

'Good. First I need to check with you that you have other spouse, family or friends who also swing by to look after you?'

'I don't, it's just me and the boys. Why do you ask?'

'We need to ensure you're not vulnerable, Mrs… Miss Hansen, before we take a statement and interview you.'

'Oh okay well, don't let these legs fool you, I can whoop ass if I need too!'

She laughed a ferociously infectious laugh. Hudson chuckled.

'Around-the-clock care? Are you able to make trips out yourself?'

'The boys are my angels. But there's a shop just around the corner, and I'm not that crippled. Been getting much better. This place has a lift too, y'know?'

The detectives both exchanged wounded looks. They hadn't.

'That's good to hear Miss Hansen. So, this is a temporary injury?'

'Yes and no, detective. My weight gives me problems, but it's healing. I can get around if that's what you mean?'

'How have you felt since the murder? Is there any cause for concern regarding anxiety? Nightmares? Security?'

Again, she laughed, perhaps even louder. But Hudson was more worried about how head-on Hiraoka was questioning her. Straight away calling it a murder. Why not describe how the killer mushed her face up like a stew, whilst you're at it? How the brain was plucked out like tuna. Just fucking drop it all on the table, Jesus.

The use of the word *nightmare* also caused him to jolt a little. Triggered unwanted images in his mind. His scalp peeling back like a swimming cap.

'Oh heavens no, don't you boys be spilling what little resource you got left on a hag like me. No, no, I am fine. I just feel, God's truth, so awful for that baby. What was her name?'

'Catherine. Catherine Evans,' Hiraoka said. 'We all do. The more info you give us, the more we have to work with and the quicker we can get this monster off the streets. Don't want him out there with your boys going back and forth to school, do you?'

She almost seemed to ignore them, her stumpy arm leaning over to grab a phone. Once she'd retrieved it, she thumbed through it and sighed. Then tutted. Then sighed again.

'Hmm, yup. That's what Bethany Shaw is saying in the DM! Said it's the return of the ripper!'

Hudson slipped. 'I wouldn't bet your piss on the stuff Bethany Shaw writes, Miss Hansen.'

The inspector coughed.

'Is it the ripper? I've heard they're also calling him *The Surgeon*.'

'I'll word it a little nicer than my constable informed,' Hiraoka said. 'Don't take your sources from the papers. Any factual information regarding the case will be revealed to the public by proper channels. Press conferences, that sort of thing.'

'Fair enough.'

'Right, so, let's start from the beginning.'

And Miss Hansen run them through, speaking a bit more candidly than was comfortable for Hudson. He took notes, walked back and forth, listening intently. She described how dark it was, how, in actual fact, she hadn't seen a thing, only heard some movements and looked out in time to see someone tall skulking around the corner. Only her description was...

'Very tall. All covered in a thick coat, scarf, hat. Just all bulky. Couldn't make out much.'

Hudson shot Hiraoka a look, but he didn't see it. Instead, he continued with his questions. Taking a moment, he walked over to the door, opened them and looked out toward the scene, the cold air biting at his face. He wiped a bit of slush from the side, watched it rain down onto the concrete below. Then, peering over, he imagined the little yellow triangles, the things SOCO had left dotted around the bins, where the body had been. Imagined how it had all happened. Ghost-like figures sprang from the ether. A tall man creeping up on the young student, wrestling her to the ground and then brutally stabbing her already dead body...

His bare hands gripped the sides.

Now, the area was empty, clean of blood. Leaning down onto the wall, he rested a hand on his chin and closed his eyes, trying to imagine how the killer would have startled the woman. That in fact, it had been the victim, concealing herself away to take cocaine, that had lead to the killer having opportunity. The killer in that respect had been a panther, prowling between streets and alleyways, on the hunt for someone vulnerable. Or maybe it had been somehow planned? It seemed too risky to pick at random if they wanted to murder in such a specific manner. It felt important. It had to be by design.

Hudson frowned. That didn't quite add up. With the drama of Hyde Park, both murders had happened close to the public. Out in the open, at the risk of being seen. All around him, dozens and dozens of windows looked low at the maze of sprawling grey. Plenty of potential witnesses.

But only one viable call in. Had the killer organised this down to a tee, or just naturally gifted at the art? Hudson didn't have a clue either way and hoped his wise old Japanese chief inspector did. The whole thing was giving him a migraine.

'So, no actual visual confirmation?' Came Hiraoka's voice from inside, muffled. Hudson walked back in, sat down and smiled at Miss Hansen. 'Nothing at all?'

'Well, I damn did! Tall thing too.'

Hiraoka shook his head. 'No, I mean of his face. Distinguishing features. We'd need something of his face to go by.'

'No, I didn't, it was dark! How can I see the damn face from up here? Think I'm Superman?' she accused tutting and shaking her head. 'I didn't even see the damn girl. Thought he was just, I don't know… Oh, Lord forgive me. I should have known something was wrong.'

'Didn't see the girl?'

'No,' she said. 'It was dark, and those large bins are in the way. All I could see was this man, this person just standing for a few moments, before walking away.'

Hudson considered it. Had just looked down over the edge just moments before. Knew that, at night, it would have been difficult to see her body. Though, her reluctance to come to the police saddened him. A behaviour all too common, unfortunately.

'Well, thank you for your time, Miss Hansen. I'll have a word with one of our boys to come visit and take the official statement, considering your current circumstances. I hope that's…'

'Oh no! I'd be happy too! Tell me when and where!'

'Whenever you can. As soon as possible, Charing Cross Police Station.'

There was a pause in which she beamed at him, and the two men rose up, towering in the tiny living room and began to shuffle out.

'Well, Miss Hansen, we'll be in touch.'

Twenty minutes later, Hudson came out the café juggling two hot chocolates and a small bag of pastries. He handed one off to Hiraoka and took a sip from his own. Narrowly avoiding a bit of black ice beside the car and wondering why, after all his sugar and caffeine intake, he hadn't gotten a case of the shits.

'She, er, seemed a bit eager, didn't she sir?'

'Mmm,' he noised. 'Classic looky-loo. Best it'll give us is a confirmed time stamp.'

'Looky loo?'

Hiraoka frowned at him. 'Love to nose around. Love to gossip. Drink that choccie, Hudson. Why the change-up again?'

'Machine broken, could only do tea or hot chocolate.'

'And you didn't go for tea?'

'Nah,' Hudson said. 'Didn't fancy it.'

'Right when I think I've decided to make do with your presence on the team and you pull a blinder. Hot chocolate before tea? Are you sure you don't swing the other way?'

'Sorry, sir. Come on, it's twenty-nineteen.'

Hiraoka shook his head. 'You are uptight, aren't you?'

And he was. There was something about the chief inspector that just made him shy away. His old fashioned stubbornness, offensive humour and frequency to break that personal barrier and thump you on the back. Despite the efforts of the other night, he hadn't forgiven his past activities. The guilt of what happened still gnawing at his conscience. That was something he wanted to forget. And quickly. Hudson didn't fancy contending with another potential criminal closer to home or to be sacked for gross misconduct at the very least.

But as he watched DCI Hiraoka tear at the croissant, minding his own business, his eyes glancing coldly up and down the road as if paranoid of someone watching, Hudson realised that it was a very real option for him to report Hiraoka. To let internal investigations know he was working with a dirty copper. That the severity of the case, the complexity, was being undermined by the SIO, ultimately jeopardising the entire MIT and Haskell with it. He started to feel a little ballsy.

And yet he was afraid. Would they believe a rookie?

The walk back to the car allowed him to stew on those thoughts. How caught up in the chaos he'd been with the nightmares and the case. Though who could he tell? His mother or grandfather? Jessica? Krystina maybe? Definitely not. But perhaps he should think about giving his family a call?

'You there, son?' Hiraoka shouted, waving at Hudson from the passenger side.

Hudson snapped to it. Looked at him dumbly. 'Wha? Oh right yeah sorry. Station?'

The inspector nodded.

Friday, 15th February

11:50

Back at their Fitzrovia headquarters, Hiraoka had Hudson type up the notes he'd taken and informed Haskell of the findings. It was almost lunch by then, so Haskell walked Hiraoka off toward a vending machine, leaving Hudson to sit with an open file in front of the murder board. It was beginning to dawn on him, glancing at the time, that a third murder, if this was a serial killing, could be happening any moment now.

A soft voice from behind him made him jump.

'Greetings, squire, what troubles thee? Oh, watch yourself there,' Moreau laughed, bending down to help him with the files.

'Alright?' he said.

'Yeah not bad. Getting anywhere? Haskell is giving some of us the nod to help here and there when we're not super busy on our own shit. That OK with you?'

'What? Oh God, yes, please, feel free to shit physical evidence.'

Moreau wrinkled her nose. Hudson backtracked.

'Erm, just kidding.'

She laughed again, walking passed him to regard the wall. The map, the notes, the whole collage.

'I get what you mean. How're the interviews going?'

'Slowly. I know Leigh has been down at Charing Cross helping. The uniforms are rounding up people they can, but from what I've heard, it's not good. We're having problems getting hold of the sex workers who would have been working on the same night. So far, we have Miss Hansen whom we've just spoken to.'

'Oh?'

'Yeah,' he said, tapping a pen against his knee. 'It's not looking great. Nothing solid at all.'

DC Leigh appeared then, ears burning, taking off her coat and showering snow all over the floor. She looked like she'd been busy and rushed on over, giving Moreau the nod.

'Afternoon both.'

Moreau smiled. 'What's cookin'?'

'Not much, just got back from Hilton Hotel in Croydon,' she said, chucking her scarf onto Hudson's desk. 'Catherine's family have popped down to London. Wanted to get closer to the investigation.'

Hudson's eyes bulged. 'Fuck, really? Does Hiraoka or Haskell know?'

DC Leigh paused, sucking in her bottom lip. 'Not yet. Speaking of which, her father gave me an idea. Has Hiraoka looked in to see if the killer has a military past?'

Moreau pointed to the murder board. 'Nguyen and Hunt have started working a satanic cult theory, doesn't that seem likely with the brain removals and the randomness of it?'

Leigh ignored her, instead hustling Hudson for a response. He flipped open one of the folders and tapped the paper. 'Yeah, thought he had. We ran what few stats we have of our killer with the Army, Marines, Navy, you name it. That was a particularly fun bit of admin, though to be honest, I owe a favour to Anderson. Useless with systems. Some of the desk officers at Charing Cross were not that helpful with PNC either, but, they don't have any records for soldiers AWOL of that particular build. Nor any previous criminal history. Odd isn't it?'

'What do you mean?' Moreau and Leigh said at precisely the same time.

'No one his size. His stature. The bastard's big, so you'd think he'd stand out?'

'Or maybe they aren't looking hard enough? Why would they? They have their own internal investigators. That and what do we have? Shoe size? Height? Projected weight? I'm sure they have hundreds that match that and not in the mood to run errands for us. We'd likely need someone far senior to warrant the records, with a far better profile of the killer. That's going to be dead-end until we get better leads. An actual profiler.'

Hudson sighed, chucked his pen onto his desk and rubbed his eyes. 'Maybe. Probably. Ugh, I dunno. I just want to start working witnesses, something I can do.'

'Tell you what, I'll go through CRD with you again, do another round, we'll go through the case notes again, check out gangs, see if there's anything missed. I've got stuff to do right now, but I'll pitch in end of day.'

'I'd give the big boys an update before you go full steam ahead.'

She nodded, smiling and slapped the murder board. 'Of course.'

Sure enough, by the time the sun had set and left the office illuminated only by the faint and headache-inducing neon lights of the city, most of the serious crimes unit had disappeared home. This left Hudson and Leigh at their desks, clicking through databases and disturbing websites in their hundreds.

DCI Hiraoka arrived a time before they got started, mentioned something about an errand he had to run, his face a little pale and washed out. It stuck with Hudson all evening, ideas of him off to do something else unsavoury. Punch up a few more dealers for leads. What sort of family life did a man like that run, he thought?

But did he want to know that? Did he want to accept that right now?

For a second, glancing over his monitor at Leigh, her dark brown eyes scanning the screen, nose wrinkled, thick bottom lip sucked in as usual whenever she was thinking, he thought about telling her. Letting her know his thoughts about the chief inspector. Maybe she was the key?

Hudson quickly thought otherwise. Easy way to stir the pot before it had brewed. Knew he would have to go about things more delicately.

Perhaps not just for his own sake but for the health of the team, too. Which only made the whole thing that much more complicated.

He hadn't buried himself back in work for long when DC Leigh shouted over.

'Oi, Hudders, get over here and give this a look.'

The man grunted, went over to her desk and leaned toward her screen, dry eyes squinting. 'What you got? Military records?'

She pointed. 'No, but I have this. A cult, small, disbanded years ago by the looks of it, carried out amateur investigations on the various killings in and around London during the eighteenth, nineteenth and twentieth centuries. Specifically to do with religiously motivated and satanic murders. Now, this website here, this blog, has been archived but, I traced it back to an old FB page they used to reach out. That is still up but again,' she added, throwing him a look. 'Hasn't been updated for quite some time.'

'Right so we're thinking they're not disbanded? That they're still hard for this devil worship shit and one of them has gone so far as to re-enact them?'

'Hmm, not so much. We don't find any carvings or bones at the crime scenes. Nothing weird and spooky, just the brains opened out, so it could just be an homage? A tribute?'

Hudson chewed the inside of his cheek, peered at the FB page. 'I dunno. Why bother? If you're into this type of thing, you'd want to kill on stage, wouldn't you? Get all the pieces together and follow through on authenticity? If you were a proper fan, the details would matter.'

'Why?'

'The theatrics of it? It's all about the theatrics isn't it, making a big drama so that everyone can see what you've done. It's essentially narcissism, that satanic stuff. I don't buy this fetish with Satan, it's just mental health issues.'

DC Leigh swung back in her chair and slapped her legs. 'There it is then. Theatrics! We have a brutal murder in Hyde Park, London's biggest and most famous park. Next, we have Soho, which is a huge city burb for entertainment. It's always full of arty types. Sex workers, drug users, it's a perfect setting, but an alleyway doesn't really tally up with a huge open park, does it?'

'Yeah,' he said. 'That one was out the way. See, nothing seems consistent. This must be pissing Hiraoka off if it's bugging us.'

'I don't doubt that, Hudson. I'll email this over, could be something to look into?'

He shrugged, walking over slowly to his desk to grab his jacket. 'Maybe. I'm still not convinced, no offence but Hiraoka will want to make that call. I appreciate this help.'

'No problem. Anything off the CRD for military history?'

'Nah.'

'No hits?'

'Fuck all. Literally nothing. Even cross-referenced it with PNC and HOLMES 2. Nothing. I have this sick feeling we've made an assumption somewhere in this case, and it's set us off on a completely wrong course, you know?'

They both shut their computers down, dressed themselves up for the cold and made their way out.

'What do you mean?' she asked, sliding a beanie over her head. 'Maybe you just need to review with the guv?'

'Yeah,' he said. 'I'll see him tomorrow morning. Get him before we start on any callbacks.'

They made their way outside, out into the wide street and noticed the sky looked eerily thick and dark, almost viscous instead of the jet black you'd expect, hazed by the amber glow of London light pollution. Perhaps more snow?

'Well, safe walk home an all that. You up to much?' she laughed.

'Yeah, cheers. Er, just meeting someone for a drink. Just a date, nothing major yet. But don't worry, I'll be plenty sober for tomorrow.'

Leigh kissed her teeth, shook her head. 'Whatever mate, see you tomorrow.'

Exhausted, cold through to his bones, Eisa's homebrew hot chocolate mocha, coffee thing or whatever the hell it was called, was a blissful treat to walk into when he plonked himself down on the sofa. The TV was on, streaming Netflix, and Eisa was in the kitchen, cooking up a treat.

Hudson had his feet up, his head pounding as the clock ticked past ten. Thinking still about those mutilated skulls. Brains planted down like trophies in the snow. His main objective tonight was to rid his head of anything morbid and just dive straight in with whatever his live-in-landlord was up to. No matter the cost.

Netflix was showing some anime, probably something Eisa had been watching previously. Attack on Titan.

'What's Attack of the Titans?' he asked cautiously.

Eisa made a choking noise from the kitchen. 'I pray I didn't hear you spill those words under this roof, Mr Daniel Hudson!'

He chuckled.

She came in a few minutes later carrying plates laden with a beautiful white sauce and beef risotto, garnished with mozzarella and parsley. Hudson was pleasantly surprised. 'What have I done to deserve this?'

'Must we trade deeds for this relationship to work?'

'Relationship?'

'Oh, Hudson, I'm not the villain. Eat your grub, and shut up. I'm going to educate you in good quality Japanese Anime.'

Hudson did as he was told and tucked into some of the best food he'd eaten in the last few months. Since Christmas, probably. On the TV, though, he was met with a barrage of fast-moving cartoons and a bizarre plot he couldn't quite grasp immediately.

Attack on Titan was definitely not something he expected himself to get into. The odd characters, strange music. Maybe it was just the craziness of it all that felt like just the right kind of medicine he needed?

'Given any notions toward the teacher thing?' Eisa called to the kitchen, Hudson choosing to clean up as a thank you.

He couldn't quite hear her over the running water but knew what she was asking about. 'Bit busy with the case. It's... it's not really something I have time to think about right now.'

Eisa scoffed. 'That's bullshit.'

'No, it isn't.'

'Yes, it is.'

'No it isn't,' he passed back, skimming the net.

Eisa appeared in the kitchen, her arms crossed matter-of-factly.

'I lied. I have heard you shouting in your sleep. Your nightmares have been getting worse. I have earplugs to soften the blow but, you need to get this all seen to.'

Hudson stared down into the sink water bubbles, saw a bit of risotto spinning toward the drain. Watched it go round and round before finally disappearing down the black hole. Knowing he would eventually have to open up the U-bend to fish it back out before it blocked.

'I will,' he whispered.

Friday, 15th February

19:45

I felt so excited. So ready for the next one. My technique more polished and practiced, allowing me to focus on the actual task at hand. The message I was trying to convey. They all had to know.

Truth is, I had been pondering a lot on the location of my next. It had to remain reasonably public but of course, something new. Somewhere safe, where I wouldn't be caught. The police investigations were beginning to ramp up. I had to be smarter now. But I already had everything planned, thanks to a little inspiration.

A small medium-enterprise cinema in Stratford had been run by the same guy for almost two decades now. Once old and dilapidated, now stood beautifully refurbished and kept close to its original classic fixtures from the nineteen-sixties. It meant that not only would it be cosy, discrete and contained, but the number of people visiting would also be minimal. It wouldn't be central and it just sort of felt right. Easy to pluck someone away from the crowd, do what I have to do in the darkness. And of course, public enough for it to be recognised for what it truly is. My message to you all.

Sometimes when I'm looking down from my flat window, into the street, I feel you crawling all over me like ants. Biting and scurrying along my skin. I hate it, and for the longest time, people, in general, have been like a pestilence to me. I've had to act, to fake and manipulate my way through life. It's exhausting. It went against everything I believed in. It went against who I really am. But the worst part is how other people perceive the world. An endless facade of mirrors and lies.

There needed to be ways of showing that to people. Media and education had failed miserably, and now hope was all but lost. There needed to be a way of unshackling people's minds from their own bodies—making them see. What I relished most about this whole mission of mine was the challenge it would offer. The intellectual, psychological triumph to pull all of this off. It sent shivers up my spine. Made me smile.

I looked over at the cinema in question, pulling myself away from such intoxicating thoughts and re-focused.

I was here now. This was it.

I crossed the road, avoiding piles slush where I could. I then pushed my way inside through turning doors, where I was greeted by the smell of polish, stale popcorn and some lingering deodorant from some fat, zero-hours idiot at the front desk. I reluctantly engaged with the specimen, bought a ticket and went to screen three down the hall for some drama/action title. The only film now showing at this time.

When I found my seat, I ignored it and carried on up, taking a spot towards the top, near a balding male in bright colours and a baseball cap with a *Pikachu* on the front. Satisfied this was the one, I took a seat and waited.

And waited some more.

Truth be told, I didn't remember a second of the film. I only recall the blur of colour and the drone of dialogue, interspersed with the crackle and pop of gunfire and explosions. Once the credits began to roll, and the crowd exited bottom right, I timed myself perfectly to walk just behind the guy in the *Pikachu* hat.

I was tall, so I caught his eye and just gave the nod. He didn't think anything of it. He grinned stupidly and made his way down the steps. Noticing some young teens at the bottom taking their time, I tapped him and pretended to make out he'd dropped something on the floor. And by the time he was upright, laughing at my bullshit mistake, the screen was empty, and my knife was already lunging upwards.

Unlike the other two, this one was juicy. In that, when the blade hit his upper abdomen, a jet of blood fired out from his mouth like punching hand soap quickly, dribbling thick and dark down his chin. It caught me full-on, hitting the top of my coat. The man's eyes were bulging like the other two messengers had, no chance to scream as I tore his life away.

In went my knife, a few more blows for good measure and he was down.

Conscious of time, I wiped the blade of excess blood and began cutting at his face. My stomach heaved momentarily as I realised after cutting his first eye in half, the man was still alive. He passed out quickly though, his breathing collapsing so I pressed the blade into his armpit and kept pushing until his pulse vanished.

A little shook, something I didn't anticipate, I tried to focus on what I was doing. Clearing that silly lapse in control out of my head.

Finished with the face, I pulled out the hammer, this time with a better hook and went to work on his skull, following a very very quick scalping. Like before, I was faster. I knew where to hit hardest, and soon the parts I wanted were dislodged and discarded. Next, I used the extra hook to wedge it beneath the brain and push against what felt like the stem, just like before. Only now, I had something to cut it. I felt the thick, gristle texture of it. Like bone and it felt impossible to cut. Here, kneeling in the darkness, bag slung over one shoulder ready to bolt, I very nearly lost my nerve until I finally heard a satisfying click when it snapped.

Done. *At last!* Smiling, relieved, I ensured my gloves were intact and reached down to remove the brain.

A noise from the hallway. I'd run out of time.

Heart pounding now, I fumbled the brain, dropping it unceremoniously onto his chest and darting out through the fire exit on the left. I smeared blood on the handle before attempting to rid myself of the gloves once I dashed through some corridor filled with boxes and spare fixtures.

The rest of the run was a blur. Wild and dark. A tangy iron taste in my mouth. Watery.

Outside in the snow, after vaulting a fence and sprinting across a street or two, I carried on jogging, my mind slowly coming back to me. It had lagged behind. Lost in the cinema. Amongst the seats. Staring down at the body.

'Fuck,' I panted, slowing to a quick walk to swap out my bloodied coat for a clean one. I scanned the terrace windows for lights and faces. No one was around. No one I could see and chose to leave it as it is.

I felt angry despite my efforts. Frustrated at such an amateur attempt. Ultimately, I would have to return home and consider where I went wrong, and what I could have done better until a small, yet warm thought comforted me.

The brain was removed. The face mutilated in their favourite place of all.

Because I knew people. You see it immediately. In their eyes and it was just a facade, really. But I had achieved it. I had torn away their mask, that shielded them from reality and exposed their true essence for all to see and judge.

For that was my message. And once my bag was tightened to my back and I headed toward the nearest underground, I realised then who my next and penultimate target would be. Something truly spectacular.

Saturday, 16th February

00:05

Huddled in a cosy Covent Garden tuck-away, Jessica's choice for a quick meet up was on point. He'd not fancied Eisa's judgemental interrogation and so offered that she may pick a spot out instead. It was late, cold, a fresh blizzard had reared its ugly head, yet Hudson was in good spirits despite everything else. For now, the grim details of his case at the middle of his mind.

Hudson's entrance into the café-bar brought in with it a flurry of unwanted guests. He apologised to a few shivering customers, shutting the door against the wind. And as he turned, he spotted her. Blonde bombshell hidden away in a nook halfway across the room.

'How's it going?' he said, throwing his scarf over the chair.

'Not bad, want me to get you a drink?'

Hudson was already pulling out his wallet. 'No no, I'll get a round in. What're we having? Shots?' he joked.

Her eyebrow danced upwards. 'It's not that kind of night. I'll have another gin though. What're you having?'

The answer was no idea. But he fancied something that would warm him up and also numb his mind a little bit. The autopsy pictures and pained cries of the victim's family interviews were locked away tonight, but never completely. If he stopped for too long, he replayed it all. And it wasn't going to do him any good.

So he ordered a double rum and coke, no ice.

'Cheers then,' he said, raising his glass.

'Cheers.'

'Tough night?'

Jessica crossed her legs under the table, swirled her gin a little. Thinking. 'No, actually. I think I've just been caught up in the monotony of my work projects. Needed a cheeky late one. And who better to do it with eh?'

Hudson laughed. Considered how she might be lying but left it. Any excuse for a drink together was good news for him. He loved being in her company. Listening to her talk, laugh and drink. Jessica's attitude seemed to lift his spirits. Perhaps that's what drew him to her more these days.

He took a generous sip of his rum. 'Christ, this is good.'

'It's my favourite hideout. Allows me to recharge after a tough day.'

'Amen to that. Could go for a second one of these. Drinks are lovely.'

'They are,' she said. 'But not what sells it. I could buy a gin or a rum anywhere. It's the location that matters. It has a way about it, makes the gin taste better. Something resonates here. Almost like it sees you.'

'Wow. Bit deep?'

It was Jessica's turn to laugh.

'Maybe the gin's gotten to me already. This is nice. Here. Us.'

'Agreed. We should make a habit of it.'

'Slow down there, John Wayne.'

'Can't fool me. But seriously,' he added. 'We're both pretty busy so anytime for a quick drink is valuable. One of the bigger perks of having moved down.'

She smiled at that. 'That's very sweet of you, Danny. I know what you're thinking. The other night. Don't worry about it. I know that sort of thing might be happening in your line of work.'

Hudson flushed. He had wondered when she would say something. The two had been unnervingly absent in approaching the event on Wednesday. Where their date had been cut short by a late-night escapade with his DCI. Something he wasn't going to be divulging to her any time soon, no matter how cosy they got.

'You really OK about it? I am really very sorry.'

She patted his hand on the table and shot him a wink. 'Of course I am, wouldn't be here otherwise would I?'

The hours melted away until closing, their witty banter not letting up for a single minute. Only on the quick trip to the toilet, did his mind saunter back to the case. The bodies. The details. The madness of it all, before consuming his thoughts with Jessica's beautiful face and lulling voice.

Was it morbid of him to be mixing the two?

Twisted, even?

Downing their last drinks, still relatively sober to both their surprise, they jostled out into a quieter evening, the wind having died down a little. Amber and white lights from nearby windows illuminating the alleys, creating a surreal haze that hung above the snow.

Hudson couldn't help but feel drawn to Jess. But didn't want to push things. For now, it was nice to have this, and it would be OK to just see how it all played out.

Before he could dwell too deep in any impending awkward silences, his phone rang, and he took the call without thinking, back in work-mode. Running on default settings.

'Hello? Leigh? Yeah, what's up?'

Jessica crossed her arms, clearly not too happy to have the moment interrupted.

Hudson closed his eyes when he heard what Leigh had to say. 'Fuck. Fuck fuck fuck. Want me over… I mean, are you on your way? No… only a few. I'm fine, I'll get a taxi.'

'What's happened?' Jessica asked. But it fell on deaf ears.

When the call ended, Hudson looked sick and was hurrying for cash for a taxi, ready to ring another number. 'I'm sorry, I've gotta go. It's… it's happened again. Work. I'm so sorry, I'll give you a call.'

And he was off. Jessica stood watching him through the dim light. Perhaps feeling like she was losing what small chance she might have with him. Perhaps feeling like, given his occupation, it may not be worth it at all.

Saturday, 16th February

00:50

The taxi got stuck midway there, skidding at some lights just outside Stratford. Hudson had to jump out with the driver, using the floor mats to wedge under the wheels. After a few panicked minutes, they dislodged the taxi from the snow pile, and they were back on their way. That's how a lot of this case was starting to feel like. Getting stuck. Getting moving again, and, as with most cases, getting stuck again. But there was something about this one. A detail or two completely missing. They had four flat tyres in a foot of snow.

A wild idea materialised when he climbed out onto the pavement, just a few hundred metres down from the crime scene. Leigh was standing there, wrapped up, miserable and with a cigarette hanging from her mouth. *He really fancied one, all of a sudden.*

'Cheers drive,' he shouted, passing him over what must have been money to cover all his utility bills.

Leigh got walking without pausing to wait. Hudson jogged to catch up, skidding slightly towards the curb.

'How long's this been up then?' he asked her, pointing a gloved hand toward the series of cars and forensic teams. A CS tent also erected. It looked chaotic. Even busier than the Soho killing. Hudson couldn't help but peer around for any looky-loos. Any journalists.

So far, nothing. But the word was out now. Only a matter of time for someone like Shaw to come sniffing. The street windows were already filled with curious faces, some stood at their doorways in dressing gowns and coats. Hushed whispers and kids on their phones trying to snap long-distance shots for social media.

Brilliant.

'I've only been here about ten minutes myself. Hiraoka and the others are inside. The body is in one of the screens apparently.'

'Not been inside yet?'

Leigh shook her head, stubbing her smoke out on a bin. 'Nope, too busy. No idea what the hell is going on. But I should imagine some of the same. A fucking cinema though, that's a step back. More private.'

Hudson considered that for a moment. 'Hyde Park was out in the open, public park and all. Soho killing was an alley so, a bit more tucked away. Maybe this is the next natural progression? Maybe this is the step forward?'

'You think so?'

'No idea, the whole thing is fucking nuts. If I can avoid looking at another body that'd be swell.'

Her eyes rolled. 'Obviously.'

The two constables showed their badges at the tape, stepped under and found Nguyen a few yards outside the processing tent, talking to one of the SOCO guys. They caught up, got their bearings and found out the murder had happened some two or three hours previous.

According to the showings board, the last film aired around eight pm. Hudson double-checked the run time and mentally estimated closing times. Maybe ten pm? Half ten? The time crept to almost an hour past midnight, so it left the killer a tight window.

'Where's the manager?' Hudson asked.

Nguyen shot a thumb over his shoulder toward a police van. There, still visibly shaken, a middle-aged black man stood talking to a PC. Someone Hudson didn't recognise.

Leigh and Hudson thanked Nguyen, walked over and gave a few easy smiles, nods of acknowledgement to the PC.

'Mind if we have a quick chat with the manager?' Leigh asked the PC, already stepping in to the free space.

'All yours.'

The uniformed constable stepped aside and went off somewhere else to be of use. Hudson and Leigh turned to the Cinema manager, a portly looking guy with a shaved head. Wearing two hoodies over each other and fingerless gloves. Looked more like a student than a business runner.

Hudson considered the man before they spoke. What might have caused him to completely miss the killer? Incompetence? Or plain unlucky? And he'd hoped the guy had the decency to load up new tapes for CCTV. That feeling quickly shifted to guilt. Why had he leapt straight to the attack, instead of considering how close this man had come to such a dangerous killer? He made a mental note to keep a check on himself. The safety of people came before anything else.

They reeled through the basics first. Name, age, place of residence, how long he'd worked there. Bradley lived nearby, just a few streets over. Probably how he'd managed to come back so quick and get questioned. Hudson took all this down.

'So, just over twenty-four years?'

'About that, yeah.'

'That's a hell of a long time.'

A smile spread across his face slowly. Dark brown eyes positively beamed. 'Yeah, it is,' he said. 'And I've loved every second. Been in love with film since only a kid. Since my Dad took me to see The Lost Boys. What a classic.'

Hudson scribbled away in his notes, wanted to have an accurate character build of him. He had a feeling they would be dropping in to say hello quite a bit during this investigation.

A third murder.

What the hell was happening?

'Thanks again,' Leigh said, nodding to the man. 'We have all your details. It's best you remain here with our uniformed officers. It's going to be a long night I'm afraid, but if you pester Nguyen over there, he'll get you food and drink.'

'That's fine. I understand. Just want to make amends where I can,

173

detective.'

Leigh shook her head. 'You didn't kill that man, Bradley. You're a victim in this in your own right. Take care now.'

By the time the two detectives had broken their way through all the tape and security, half an hour had passed, and Hudson was anxious as hell. He knew how Catherine had looked down in that slushy alley and only dreaded now how things had progressed in a warm building. First a shattered skull, a butchered face and an exposed brain. Then the same, only for a horrible attempt being made to remove the brain.

It didn't take a genius to guess what was next.

Hudson, followed by Leigh, entered screen three at the back of the establishment. Dark grey walls, old red and blue carpets. The faint, sweet smell of popcorn and cleaning products. Inside, the lights were on, showing in stark clarity all the mess that gets left behind after a show. It seemed to Hudson that the body was found before cleaning could begin. So how long had this screen been left unattended?

On the other side by the fire exit, opposite the entrance, lay a body surrounded by men in white SOCO suits already packing up. Petridis was among them, having a frank chat with DCI Hiraoka. Stood huge as ever, though his shoulders looked slumped in his large jacket.

As Hudson approached, it was Leigh who swore first when they saw the head of the victim.

He'd guessed right.

The brain sat displayed on the victim's chest. The pink, meandering surface blotted in congealing blood. The stem severed and the face below the folded scalp entirely destroyed. Hudson spun around quickly and gulped down a mouth full of sick. Took a few deep breaths. A ringing in his ears sounded for a moment, and he felt like he had to get out of there.

And then Leigh was in front of him, hand on his elbow.

'Lookin' a bit extra white there Hudson. Want to calm down with that privilege, yeah?'

It was enough to make Hudson smirk, and he stood up straight again, clearing his mind. Leigh looked more composed. A rock. Something for him to hold on to. He felt an idiot despite everything.

'Cheers.'

'Don't worry about it,' she said. 'Let's get it over and done with.'

Composing himself, he turned back and entered the inner circle. DCI Hiraoka towered over the rest. He seemed drained but vaguely alert, still on the clock with no sign of letting up. Yet another absolute unit who refused to remain glued to the desk.

'Morning sir,' Hudson said, arms folded across his front.

'Hudson. Leigh. Has Nguyen briefed you at all? Petridis has likened this one to *Some Kind Of Monster*.'

They both shook their heads.

'Monster is putting it a little lightly, sir,' Hudson said.

Hiraoka's face was deadly still. 'The album, Hudson. Do you not listen to Metallica?'

Leigh decided to interrupt. 'But we get the gist, sir. What's new? Any ID found on the victim? Anything at all?' Leigh stepped through, taking a closer look at the body.

'Not that we'd been able to see, no. We have an evening screening, last on the reel and a brief period between customers leaving and the manager coming in to clean. No cleaner. Did you speak with the manager? OK, good. Well, we got the call shortly afterwards at approximately quarter to eleven, which means, with the final showing ending at twenty past ten, we have an extremely small window.'

Hiraoka adjusted himself, scanned the room. 'No cameras, no witnesses. So, the theory here is an audience member. Someone who bought a ticket came in, waited until everyone was gone and then got to work.' He pointed to the brain, stepping around Leigh. Hudson tried to focus more on Hiraoka's hand gestures than the gore itself.

'This is new. Same MO, same cuts but the brain is now being exhibited on the victim's chest, rather than above the head. No doubt this is the same killer, but they've brought new tools, or done some training. And as before, the face has been mutilated. With the brain on

175

the chest, either this is a new decision, or they spent so long trying to remove the brain, they ran out of time. You can tell it was rushed, given the further blood splatter across the chairs there, the floor. We're getting an expert to come look at the blood splatters tomorrow.'

'Or they planned it poorly? Didn't give themselves enough time?' Leigh chimed in.

Hiraoka nodded. 'Which will be further explained by the sloppy smudge of blood on the fire exit over there.' Hiraoka jabbed a finger to the far back of the screen, the detectives following it and watching another small band of SOCO guys busy taking pictures. Another group, which must have been the North East BCU murder investigation team, first on the scene. DS Hunt looked busy speaking with them all.

No one said anything at first. They all stood in unison, allowing all that information to sink in. Imagining the killer planning the method. Executing the kill. And the rushed, sloppy getaway.

'Fuck,' Hudson whispered, grabbing his chin.

'What?' Leigh asked, standing back up after kneeling down to check the body for any further details initial forensics may have missed.

'Well, what's next? Last two murders were, by the looks of it, trying to remove the brain cleanly. They've succeeded. They've achieved what they wanted. So is this about perfecting a method, or sending a single message?'

'Or,' Leigh proposed. 'They've been training and, with the method nailed down, will ramp things up to more serious targets? These people seem like nobodies and no connections yet?'

Hiraoka grabbed some cigarettes from his coat, stepped through them and grumbled. He pulled one out and had almost lit it when he realised where they were. This seemed to piss him off.

'No,' he said. 'Fresh eyes. I want you two and the rest of the team on interviews. Haskell's already got PCs on local businesses and properties for tomorrow morning, some extra civilian staff called in, already, to run the databases. We need every customer in this place over the last week, starting with this screening. Any patterns. Any familiar faces. If they were planning, they would have come back at least a few times to judge the space. The time. They had to have known the manager's schedule.' He paused for a moment, cigarette hanging dangerously from his bottom lip. 'Hudson, Leigh, get on employment records. See if anyone missed shifts. I want this ransacked and documented until we have to purchase extra hard drives just to hold the fucking stuff.'

Leigh was already taking out her phone, messaging Nguyen and Anderson. 'Got it. What about the er… body?'

Hiraoka waved a hand, turning to leave. The two detectives followed, eyes following them. Uniformed officers, forensic experts, medical workers. Their expressions screaming one thing.

Catch this sick fuck. This is on you.

And Hudson was all too aware of that weight. That expectation to perform in the face of so much authority.

'The body,' Hiraoka continued. 'Shouldn't be a problem. I doubt the coroner is going to slow the train now after murder three. I'll keep you informed.'

He lit the cigarette, watched its end burning out in the crisp winter air. A single flake fell from the empty, black sky, threatening to out it. Hudson rubbed his temples, setting out a plan in his head. Sobered now from his drinks earlier with Jessica.

'Right. So, customers, manager, previous workers. Interviews, cross-check with PCs. I think the whole of us will be on that. Rest to do businesses and neighbouring premises. What about an ID?'

'That'll have to wait, as I said. I doubt it'll cause issues, but at this point, I'm doubtful there's a link between victims, rather a plan. This arse hole has picked locations, not people.'

Leigh seemed to dwell on that the most. Hudson watched her eyes glaze over as she fell into thought. Absently biting her bottom lip. Before he could nudge her, almost five minutes after they'd walked around to the other side of the cinema, into the back alley where their killer would have made an escape.

'I think John has a good theory there. Location not person.' She nudged a bit of snow off a chain-linked fence. The alley was wide enough to hold parked cars and room to walk either side.

Hudson seemed transfixed by the forensic team placing yellow triangles along the snow, away from the fire exit door. It stood open, wedged by a doorstop, with other SOCO guys inside the concrete hallway that no doubt lead in toward their crime scene. 'Yeah, you think?'

'Well, we've been looking for a pattern in the wrong place this whole time. What do you think?'

'What do I think?' he repeated. 'Well, I'd like it to stop fucking snowing for a start. Could this killer at least share some consideration for convenience and the bloody cold? But on a serious note, I think Hiraoka is right, too. Cashless payment methods. No CCTV. It means, if we are to assume we won't find ID lurking on our victim, we are stuck with another John Doe that'll lag this investigation further. What with each of these happening within a week of each other, it only gives us seven days to obtain his identity, find a link between the other victims, locate the killer and stop this.'

Leigh turned away from the cinema, instead looking past Hudson to gauge where their killer might have run to. Something like morbid humour in her eyes.

'No pressure then?'

Saturday, 16th February

04:26

When most of the team had gotten back to Fitzrovia, the room was chaos. Phones were ringing, and detectives dashed back and forth, compiling notes and revisiting the murder board. Everyone was on shift. The space filled with extra staff from Charing Cross.

Haskell had rallied the troops.

Hudson had files of his on the desk and about his fifth cup of coffee. Lukewarm by now. He checked the time on his monitor and managed to make out something like half four in the morning. Had time really slowed down that much? Was he trapped in this? He picked himself up out of the chair and crossed the dingy, dark red carpet that filled the entire place. Approached the single pane windows that rose up to the high ceilings. Looked out into the snow. Down over the cobbles and dust bins.

A black figure moved. Not suddenly but slowly. A gradual motion that caught his attention. He looked round to the mouth of the road and swore he had seen something watching. Someone. Convinced he was going mad, he rubbed his eyes and stepped away.

'Watch it dick head!'

DS Hunt, who looked alert and on the warpath, glared at him with contempt. Hudson wasn't in the mood for more of Hunt's shithousery. Not tonight. He supposed he should have left it, but he didn't want to.

If he was going to make it through his first serial murder case in one piece, he wanted to smooth out the kinks. And Hunt was one big fucking hump in the path.

'Sorry, what was that DS Hunt?'

Hunt couldn't believe what he'd heard at first and wheeled around, files mid-shuffle.

'Hudson, grow up and get back to work. We don't have time for this.'

But he was already boiling inside. Whether from lack of sleep or because of the nightmares, or maybe because they couldn't catch a killer who made a habit of removing people's brains with a bloody hammer.

'DS Hunt. I'm doing what I can. Speak to me like that and I'll drop it in my review with Haskell. I haven't stepped on your toes once since I've started, so drop this façade of alpha cop and get off my back.'

'Did you just fucking threaten me, constable?' Hunt rounded on him, face within inches of his.

'I'm extending a courtesy, sir,' Hudson replied, his head buzzing with adrenaline. Never the best in confrontation. 'Please step back.'

'You're on thin fu—'

A loud boom came from the entrance, and a heavy silence fell across the room. DCI Hiraoka was back.

'Have I just arrived at the circus? What the hell is going on here?' His voice boomed, rattling the place to the cobwebs.

Faces looked on meekly. Guilty. Some fearful. This was the first time Hudson had seen Hiraoka explode like this. But also the first time he'd seen such respect, mingled with fear in so many of his colleagues' faces. This wasn't a man to cross.

And then he looked at him.

'DC Hudson. With me, now!'

Without the luxury of spare private offices or interview rooms, Hiraoka wheeled him back outside into the cold. He guessed it was all part of the punishment. Have him writhe and squirm, slightly off comfort. Stew in his actions and accept a good beating.

Hiraoka pulled out a cigarette. Lit it with a match, this time, and threw the stick down into a drain clogged with slush.

'DC Hudson. Explain to me why I have to parent you, three murders deep into a case this big? I'm quite lost. Even I can't solve this one. So please, I'm all ears.' And the chief inspector crossed his arms, cigarette balanced, smoking aimlessly.

Hudson could really smell the tobacco this time around. That dark, sour, roasted blend he loved to burn. It churned his stomach. It also made him sick how Hunt had managed to side-step and put him in the cross-hairs.

'Sir, DS Hunt got aggressive, I was simply backing myself up. And frankly, since I've started this case, he's been a constant bone of contention. A constant rub. I should have said something sooner but had no idea he'd kick off like that.'

'That's not what I saw,' he said. 'It looked a lot like you were going at him. Maybe I didn't see the full picture, eh?'

'With all due respect, guv, you weren't th—'

The cigarette was gone, and Hiraoka was suddenly right up in his face.

'Three. Fucking. Murders. Apologise, get your shit together and don't you ever answer back to me in such a disrespectful tone.'

Hudson couldn't believe it. Mouth wide open, he didn't know whether to shut it, or go back at him, to take the moral high ground. Which was somewhat ironic, because Hiraoka slapped him on the shoulder and said. 'Because DS Hunt isn't worth it. Don't rise to him. I don't fancy being hung out to dry by Haskell after my new rookie kicks off against our second-highest rank on the team. Suck it up, apologise and focus. I need everyone's mind on this. I can't afford dismissals when our MIT is already running on fumes. Got it, *Kabu*?'

'Kabu?'

'Means cub,' he said. 'Get used to it.'

Still thoroughly rattled from the telling off, and with the adrenaline from last night beginning to wain, he collapsed into his desk, groaning at the time on the computer. Eyes burning, barely able to read a word on HOLMES 2 or any of the other million databases. Without much of a fight, Hiraoka gave him the nod to catch a few winks. As it happened, there were a few old, moth-eaten sofas round the back of the room, where the shape of the building portioned off the make-shift kitchen. It meant that the only people who would be interrupting him would be those coming to get a brew. Hudson would be long gone.

His sleep was restless. Not quite warm enough, he drifted off cold and was plagued with nightmares. Stirring and groaning in his sleep. After about four or five hours, he jolted awake, sweating and found Nguyen sat on the end, looking concerned.

Hudson swore. 'Fuck sake.'

'You look like shit, mate.'

'Thanks,' he said, getting up and immediately going for the kettle. He noticed the headquarters sounded a little quieter. No murmur of voices or keyboards click-clacking. 'Where is everyone?'

'Had sense to go home to their beds you nutter. I'm about to clock off now. Anderson and a few others are coming in to take over. Coming?'

He shook his head, stirring the milk into his coffee slow as hell. 'Nah. I'm going to stay on, probably clock off end of day.'

Nguyen clicked his fingers. 'Well, don't invite me to the funeral. See you later mate.'

And not once did he mention the nightmare. How fucking idiotic he must have looked jumping up like that. Sweating, looking terrified and mentally strained. Hudson felt a wave of respect for the man. His sense of timing and knowing what to say and when to say it. Maybe there was a good friend in Nguyen?

Hudson made his way back to his desk, fresh cup in hand. He looked over the latest witness notes and squinted up to the murder board. Reciting things out loud.

'Hyde Park. Sloppy encephalectomy. Three dozen cuts to the face. Seven puncture wounds to the body and abdomen. No trace DNA found in the environment or on the victim's body and clothes. A few partial boot prints.'

A quick sip. And onto the second.

'Soho, Hopkins Street alley. One week later. Cleaner removal of the brain. More cuts to the face. Neck snapped clean in a twisting motion. Two puncture wounds to the chest, downward. Better eye witness than Hyde Park. No DNA in the environment the or on clothing. No CCTV evidence yet.'

And the latest. Just twelve hours ago.

'Stratford, local cinema. A rushed encephalectomy. Messy. This time placed on the chest. New. Face has been completely disfigured beyond reconstruction. Two puncture wounds to the chest and underarm. Whole cinema of leads and potential witnesses. No CCTV. Running scene for DNA.'

He pressed the palms of his hands into his eyes and groaned. Trying to understand why on earth someone would be sneaking around London, removing the brains of people completely unconnected? So far, nothing connected them. It was just one endless nightmare he found himself caught in.

Draining his paper cup and throwing it into the bin, he looked over to new techy Moreau's desk. Her chair sat empty. She wouldn't be on shift for a while. Perhaps Moreau could look into social media patterns. Fan groups. Go deeper with the satanic cult theory. Connections between the victims via those pages or something else? So far, they had no forensics physically linking the killings and it was putting a strain on them all.

Why? What's significant? Nothing in his research proved it was gang-related, or cult-related. It seemed out-of-place. No symbols used or written messages. No positioning of the bodies. It didn't add up. Could someone be ballsy enough to pick people at random on the fly? Have the capacity and intelligence to pull it off without leaving evidence? Or were they all underestimating the intelligence of their killer? That, in fact, this was all carefully and meticulously planned, and the purpose of these killings aligned more to their sick and twisted view on reality?

Feeling he needed to contribute something before leaving, Hudson approached the murder board with a permanent marker and wrote, *Did all victims have mental health issues?* And set the pen down.

Perhaps that was it. The removal of the brain. Destroying the face.

Picking at random. Maybe it was to do with the killer's mind? Perhaps somehow, somewhere, the victims had left a bread crumb trail online of their mental suffering.

A divorcee struggling in a high-stress job. A young woman studying at a high-stress university. A middle-aged man, forgotten by all and lost in his films. Maybe his stab in the dark would find something?

Maybe not. It was a long shot theory at best.

Sunday, 17th February

11:00

'Are they usually this difficult to budge?'

Hudson queried Hiraoka about the latest call to the coroner's office, juggling two green teas Moreau had made them both for their trip. They'd parked around the corner on yellows next to a pub, with the mortuary located opposite. He'd overheard jokes about cutting off the road, merging the two buildings into a B&B. *Beer and bodies.*

'No,' he said. 'Famous for not giving a toss about police process, only their own to follow. This is a different game now, detective. Eyes up.'

The pair crossed the road, stepping carefully over black ice, cutting tall silhouettes against a low, winter sun that bled deep orange between the buildings. Their shadows stretching long across mounds of slush.

Hudson was beginning to tire of the weather. The gridlock traffic and constant snow. It had been almost an entire weekend since the third murder, and the investigation had come to a complete standstill. Media attention was through the roof, with newspapers throwing about wild ideas of copycat killers, Satanists and liberals taking revenge for Brexit. Hudson couldn't remember the last time he'd had a full day off. Everything was merging into one, hideously long ordeal.

As he reached for the front door to the building, a squat, red-bricked build with neat hedges out front, a single flake landed on his hand. Mocking him.

Well, that's what it fucking felt like.

When the detectives rounded the corner, following the underground pipes to Nita's cosy cavern of cadavers, they saw her hunched over a laptop, lab coat on, typing away furiously. Her head tilted at the sound of their footsteps echoing off the walls.

'You know I'm supposed to enjoy these visits, boys. Frankly, I'm not so bloody joyous.'

Hudson was a little surprised to see Hiraoka grimace. He obviously cared a great deal for what Nita thought.

'It's a bad one,' he said, moving straight to the autopsy table and looking into the empty skull of their third victim. A middle-aged John Doe still not identified.

Nita finished typing and walked on over. 'I've never seen anything like this, John. Nothing. And it's unnerving me somewhat. Look here,'

Taking a pair of fresh gloves, she motioned the two detectives round toward the head and pointed towards the brain stem and edges of the shattered cranium. 'Looking at the damage there, what is your first impression?'

'Better standard of work,' Hudson blurted before Hiraoka could chime in. 'Not much, it's still brutal. But it looks better than the last.'

'Exactly, Hudson. Exactly. They're learning quickly. The damage to the brain, too, was minimal. Only minor damage to the medulla. But I don't have it here it's being screened for further forensics. Very little bruising to the top tissues. That said, all the usual impressions across the gyrus, the surface of the brain, from being held. The brain is incredibly soft. Resting a fresh brain on the ground or the chest of a victim for mere seconds will completely contort the ventral surface.'

Hudson and Hiraoka exchanged a look.

'Still no foreign tissue? No DNA at all?' Hiraoka enquired, shoving his hands in his coat and walking around the table. 'Nothing?'

Nita shook her head. 'Sorry John. It's clean. They're very meticulous and careful. You've got a real smart monster on your hands. I don't envy you. But, we may have hit the jackpot.'

'Oh?'

She walked over to her desk and picked up a plastic packet next to the victim's clothes, which were all laid out neatly. As she came back, the detectives could make out an ID card of sorts. Hiraoka took it from her and grinned. 'Excellent. Where the bloody hell was it? SOCO never found anything on their person.'

'In his shoe, if you'll believe it? Clifford Biggins.'

Hiraoka and Hudson exchanged another look, this time a bit more comical.

'His shoe?' Hudson frowned. 'Why the hell would anyone keep a driving licence in their shoe?'

'Not a driving licence, constable, take a closer look.'

They did. Hiraoka passing it over to Hudson who realised, they had several quite pressing problems. One, that they would never be able to match the face with the card, and that they would be spending a lot on phones, calling around to find out who this person's carer was, and how they'd been out on their own without supervision.

'Fuck.' Was all he managed, passing it back over to Nita.

Hiraoka did a lap of the body. Thinking. 'So, any ideas? We're running on fumes here.'

'Well,' she mused, bottom lip popping out as she shrugged. 'It's all a bit theatrical. Very definitely mentally disturbed. You've probably gotten that far. They seem to be on a bit of timer or just very eager to carry out their plan. Perhaps even stuck to a weekend schedule. A regular nine-to-fiver. Whatever it is, they have one and are gearing up. I'd say they have someone in mind, rather than a series of killings. They want to hone their craft and advertise their progress. Very egocentric and all the other classifications. Warped sense of reality.'

Hiraoka nodded. Hudson was quietly shocked to hear how similar her notions resonated with his own theories. It seemed to sit quite well with what the team had put together so far as well. But the idea of an ultimate target seemed interesting. Hudson wasn't so sure, though.

'Report today?'

'Tomorrow you cheeky bastard. You know I'm not a miracle worker, John. The toxicology for Robert Short is still in progress, from what I've heard. Did you the favour of asking because, despite not trading in miracles, stock prices in sheer fucking charity are high as ever.'

The big man raised his hands up above his heads, then bowed dramatically, motioning for Hudson to leave with him. 'I see Charlie's energetic personality is rubbing off on you. I'll leave you to it. We'll await it patiently and see you again soon.'

The last thing they saw before closing the door was Nita flipping the bird.

Listening to quiet radio chatter on a quick lunch break, pasty in hand, Leigh stood at the windows of their Fitzrovia office, looking down into the mews, seemingly waiting for the snow to melt. Or perhaps, hoping that if she stared long enough, it would all melt on command.

Hudson approached with a leftover sandwich, picking bacon out from his two front teeth. 'Alright?'

'Yeah, yeah just thinking,' she murmured. 'You?'

'Yeah, knackered all the same.'

A faint smile appeared, and then she chuckled. 'This what you were after?'

'You know, I would say no, because it'd only make me a sadist to say otherwise. But, it is what I wanted, I think. I just didn't expect how, well, messy it is. And traumatic.'

He surveyed the last nodule of bread, just to do something with his hands. The pair barely had longer to contemplate the wisdom of policing when Anderson came over, clutching some paper. Looking as miserable as the rest of them. She was quite tall. About the same as Jessica, Hudson thought. Instead, Anderson was a lot slimmer, wore glasses and looked like significantly less capable of coping with anyone's bullshit.

'Well, I've been making a whole bunch of calls. Few more running clubs in and around London. No hits except two I think we should follow up on when we can. But as you arrived, I had just got off the phone with a local London charity for mentally disabled and vulnerable. This is awful.'

Leigh turned, grabbing the paper on reflex to decipher his scribbles. Anderson hurriedly continued.

'He was in a support network. He would have had carers check in on him. Completely on benefits. He gets to do little social trips and events, thanks to the aid, and this cinema trip was one of them. Judging by the lack of carers at the cinema, I would hazard a guess he's completed a programme and can go out and about on his own.'

Hudson furrowed his brow. 'Our latest vic?'

Anderson nodded. Her long face pulling in a grimace. It pained him to learn the news.

'And?' Leigh probed impatiently.

'I rang the number on the back in the event it gets lost. No answer. I'll keep calling until we get through. The killer hadn't known to look for it, so only his wallet, phone and other items were gone. It's a stroke of luck but, god damn, the poor bloke.'

The lump rising in his throat came out of nowhere. He imagined this man, living a trialling, difficult life under meagre benefits and disability support. Only to meet some senseless fucked up end, at the hands of a deranged serial killer, watching a film in what was meant to be his safe place.

He made an excuse to go for a piss, ending up in the cubicle bawling his eyes out, trying to keep the noise quiet.

Grabbing a bit of tissue to sort his face out, his phone buzzed then and checked it at the sink.

It was his sister. Timing as always.

'Ello?'

'We still good for tomorrow evening? Is everything OK? I haven't said anything have I? Are you all OK Danny?'

He didn't need this right now and pushed his thumb into his left eye. 'Er, yeah. Yeah, we're still on. Sorry, it's quite manic at work.'

'Danny, leave work at work. Family is more important.'

'I know.'

'But do you though? Why haven't I seen you more? Look, I've got to go, but we'll have a great time, I promise! I have loads of ideas! Things we can do! See you soon!'

And she hung up. True to form, just like almost every other call. Hudson was too tired and upset to react and simply pocketed the phone, turning on the taps to splash his face. When he resurfaced, he caught sight of himself in the mirror. A long, drained face with shadows beneath the eyes and a week's worth of stubble. His brown eyes looked empty. His cropped hair untidy.

What he'd give for a solid eight hours.

Hudson promised himself to only work a few more minutes, but the subsequent interviews conducted at the station had made it feel like an eternity. A variety of characters had arrived. Those who had been at the cinema on the night of the murder. Bradley, the cinema owner, was being extremely cooperative and helpful. But that didn't stop the moviegoers themselves from being painfully inconsistent and unreliable.

The door to interview room 2b swung open, and a distressed looking DCI Hiraoka appeared, lighter in hand.

'Any joy, sir?' he asked, falling into step.

Just like before, the Charing Cross station was packed busy. With the weather being as bad as it was, you'd have expected crime to take a bit of a dip. That wasn't the case, as it turned out. They jostled past a drunk at reception who was arguing with two desk sergeants.

'Nita's theory now resonates more than ever,' he conferred, lighting up his hundredth of the week. 'The chaos feels masterminded, detective. Have you any updates for me?'

Hudson shrugged. 'We're still eliminating names. It's a cash-only register, so the hope of tracing transactions is zero. Part of the *charm* of a small cinema.'

'Fuck sake.'

'Exactly,' Hudson agreed. 'It feels masterminded. The only thing Bradley has are receipt copies. But we've added up numbers so we can at least get a picture of blanks. Go from there. We're also looking at public transport. See if we can nab CCTV of people travelling in and leaving around the time-frame. It's… It's….' A yawn broke his sentence. A long one, he couldn't stifle and felt water stream from his eyes. 'Long work.'

The chief inspector nodded, wrapping his scarf around his neck. Pushing his hair out from his face. 'You've overstayed yourself. Get home and sleep. You're useless to me like this.'

Hudson got the impression he'd stumbled into his good books, but he was right. He yearned for his bed. Looking out into the neighbouring street. Taxis and buses making their way through the slush. Shoppers coming to and fro. A monster somewhere out there, amongst them, planning their fourth.

'Best bet is CCTV at this point. Matching faces between the three locations via public transport. It's just going to be really time-consuming, and we've not got the biggest team. Reckon Haskell will pull more resource in?'

Hiraoka laughed. 'Doubtful. We're stretched already with other ongoing cases. But, the media are up-in-arms, so it would seem prudent. We'll see, constable, we will see. For now, we await formalities from this shit storm and an ID, pending DNA corroboration. Then, it's more of the same. Families, friends, anyone. We'll find a pattern. A link. We just need to keep going.'

He housed his unlit cigarette, shoved the packet into his coat pocket and went back inside. Hudson watched a little in disbelief he'd passed up the opportunity to smoke. But it dawned on him as he stared at his back, that his slumping shoulders betrayed to him just how tough this case was proving. It had all started off as one, horrific event. None of them really knew just what sort of grim nightmare it would grow to become.

They were all feeling it now.

Monday, 18th February

09:30

The extension of Eisa's charitable side seemed to know no bounds. After the gruelling double shift and murder over the weekend, he'd collapsed on the sofa and slept right the way through for fourteen hours. Upon waking, she had a fresh coffee brew on the go. Strewn across the kitchen counter, various papers and her laptop. The bookshop downstairs, which he'd been meaning to visit, was suffering a dip in trade. She was struggling, he knew it, but never once did she project. Instead of gratitude, he felt guilt. As if he was imposing on her.

It dawned on him, as he drained the coffee and wrapped up warm for his snowy trek into the city, that he could have done far worse in terms of living arrangements. He'd gotten luckier, perhaps, than he gave it credit.

The chill was high that morning, his phone telling him the temperature sat at minus three but *felt* like minus thirty. A cloudless, pale blue sky betrayed Londoners of warmth with a blinding, low hanging sun glinting off the icy cold Thames. London looked picturesque under blankets of snow. But he'd quickly learnt over the last few weeks that was just a facade. Hiding the rivers of blood now flowing freely in out-of-sight dark corners and spaces in the city.

With the inquest into the third murder back quickly, ID to boot, it didn't take long to trace kin. It also meant they had a place of residence for Clifford to check out to proceed with their next enquiries. The confirmation of murder was expected, with further details supported by Nita's impeccable documentation. It meant they now had three, clear-cut files which they hoped would start piling up.

At this rate, they'd need a truck to deliver the files to the CPS. Just open the doors and pour it out onto the pavement. Get cracking.

Hudson got off the phone with the victim's family, Leigh pausing to listen and started turning off his computer.

'That was Martha Andrews. Closest next of kin we can find for him.'

'Oh?'

'Yeah, which is pretty depressing actually. Clifford Biggins' parents died when he was young. No other immediate relatives except his father's side has a brother who had a daughter... I think. Cousin? Anyway, I've written it down, and it's their last proper relative.'

Leigh raised eyebrows. 'Small family?'

'Seems like it,' he shrugged. 'Maybe Martha had the bright idea kids weren't worth it? And it sounds like this poor guy wasn't in any position to have kids of his own.'

'Fuck that is depressing. I've spoken with Hiraoka so we can get going when you're ready?'

Hudson nipped away for a quick piss before their drive south to Croydon, in the complete opposite direction of Stratford. The traffic was predictably busy, crossing the Thames into Battersea, with countless cars and buses sitting at red lights. As they moved further south, snow on pavements turned from the usual icy slush to fluffy white. The parks around them looking almost untouched except for a few shitty snowmen.

Taking a right passed Clapham Junction, they pulled into a small estate of flats. Leigh got out before Hudson could turn the engine off and scowled when he closed the door.

'You're a terrifying driver!'

Hudson scoffed. 'No, I'm not, I'm perfectly safe in the corners.'

Leigh navigated her way up the pavement, careful not to slip as they looked for the right flat block. 'No. More like Tokyo fucking drift. I'm almost certain I clenched hard enough to drop a dress size.'

'You can drive next time then, Miss Daisy,' he laughed, catching up to her. Bringing in the coat a little tighter. Winds picking up around the taller buildings. The sweeter smell of trees surrounding them on the walk up.

'Bingo. Next time, may just do that, Hudders.'

After the verbal sparring, they rang up to the fifth floor and met Martha outside in the hallway, not before Hudson triple checked there was a lift. He hoped all of their enquiries wouldn't land them in tower blocks. He didn't have quite the fitness for all the steps. His first few escapades in the London underground used to absolutely knacker him.

Martha motioned them into a modest one-bedroom flat, neutral tones, tidy with a few magazines about. A half-drunk cup of tea on the table. Very average. It showed that she cared about her home, but knew not be so reckless as to overspend on niceties like a Ming vase or a five hundred inch TV.

'So,' Leigh said, thanking her for a cup of tea she handed over. 'Thanks again for the short notice, we really appreciate it. I understand you were close with Clifford?'

She nodded. Her eyes looked pained, crows feet pinching at the corners. Wispy thin hair barely reaching her shoulders. Her features and posture betrayed what her flat hid well. Something seemed to be fighting her. Perhaps on a regular basis and keeping things tidy were a way to focus on something else. 'I was. Well, as much as I could be. I'd visit when I could.'

'What stopped you?'

'Nothing stopped me,' she replied, slightly taken aback. 'Life just takes over sometimes. You do what you can with the best of interests. It doesn't mean you love people any else. I'm sure you might understand?'

Hudson nodded his agreement. He understood very well. As Leigh continued to question her, he checked his phone absent-mindedly. He was to meet his sister later today. It'd been difficult to organise, but that's how life often played out. Work had other ideas. So did their killer.

'Sorry, Miss Andrews. We don't mean to offend.'

She laughed. 'That's OK. Well, fire away with your questions. I know you both have a job to do.'

He was quite impressed with how well she took everything. How composed she was in general. She helped with providing them with more information about Clifford. Confirming his last two addresses. Checking the ID they brought with them, verifying that it was indeed Clifford's from what she knew. Also mentioned about his disabilities, his habits. Where he went to school. Where he lived. Everything to get their teeth into. But concluded the man could never have produced an enemy mad enough to do something so evil. Hudson and Leigh just couldn't wrap their heads around why their killer would choose someone like Clifford?

As they left, their suspicions about her cheerful demeanour were immediately quashed, hearing her suddenly sob quite loudly from inside the flat. The detectives shared a solemn look, sighed and made their way out.

When they got back to the office in Fitzrovia, stuck behind some cyclists one part brave, one part stupid, it seemed to resonate well with Hiraoka who felt now the victims were random, but that the method was very much planned. The leading theory. Haskell remained constantly informed and, whilst repeatedly pulling the DCI into meetings and conferences down at the station to berate him on results, he was quietly positive and trusting in the team. After all, it was his.

Hudson's phone buzzed with two messages, so he took a seat at his desk to take some weight off his feet, pulling up some emails with digital CCTV images to review.

The first was from Jessica. They hadn't picked up from where they left off the other night. And he hadn't text back either. It was a short text. Just asking how he was. Hudson couldn't help but smile. Letting something like warmth fill his chest when he typed back a response. He could do something end of the week. Maybe another drink Friday.

The second was from Krystina. He would run late for their catch up if he didn't leave soon. She'd found just the right gaming café in Towerhill, not far from where she worked.

After some glamorous cataloguing of more CCTV and paperwork, Hudson was out just as the sun had gone down, wrapping his long coat around him and shoving his hands as deep as he could into his pockets.

He bumped into Anderson at the door, Hunt passing them by and choosing not to make a quip.

'Hey, get those addresses for Clifford? Any joy?'

'Sorry,' she said, looking like she meant it too. 'Hunt's had Nguyen and myself visiting witnesses from the Stratford cinema. We're going to go check it all out tomorrow if we can. Might be worth checking his belongings, help with the ID. He lived alone, right?'

Hudson nodded. 'Yup. As far as Martha Andrews knows.'

'Martha?'

'Closest next of kin. It's all he has in terms of family.'

Anderson hung her head. 'I really am sorry, Hunt is on my arse. I think he's set this one back but we'll be visiting as soon as we can. Everything OK with you?'

Hudson lied to her about his optimism for the case and his own health. Not just because he was running late to Krystina, but Hunt's peering gaze shifted them apart quicker than they'd wanted.

The tubes provided a brief escape from the cold, some of the lines now reopening thanks to a great effort of clearing London's innermost centre from ice. The gritters had done a cracking job, Hudson had to admit. But then again, you couldn't afford a city like London to grind to a halt for too long.

Reaching the café almost an hour later, he spotted her at the window, arms crossed and green eyes searching the streets.

Hudson jogged the last few feet across the road, gave her a quick hug which was returned in kind and quickly went inside to get their table.

Krystina ordered a couple of lemon milkshakes and pulled out a card game. Something to do with combustible unicorns with swords and guns. Without a word about how long it'd been since they last saw each other or their previous calls, his sister started dealing cards.

He waited until they had their hands, scrutinised the rule book and thanked God it was simple. His mind a complete mush.

'I go first,' he said, placing a unicorn down holding an AK47 with a purple background. 'Glad we're finally here. I've been wanting to do this, but work has been absolutely mental.'

Krystina seemed to ignore him. Staring at her own hand, long fingers tracing over the edges of each card, placing two next to Hudson's and announcing the effects.

'One of your cards to discard please, Danny.'

'You alright?'

She looked up at him, and it gave him goosebumps. 'Of course I am, I'm already winning! You never were good at games.'

Hudson rolled his eyes. Fell for it again for the millionth time. Her personality change was often hard to track, but he was getting better. Expected the weird conversations without context. The mood swings. The anger and obsessive behaviour. She used to hurt herself as a teenager. A way to express herself during some of the more challenging years in school.

His mum had been crushed. Feeling as if she had failed as a foster mother. He knew how hard they must have felt. Failing to live up to expectations.

'What have you been up to, anyway? Busy?'

'Busy, busy, busy, Danny. Always busy. Never a dull day as a property lawyer.'

Hudson smiled and said ironically, 'I don't know how you manage the case loads. Ever thought about going into criminal law at all?'

No response, just concentration on playing. Hudson wanted to keep up the conversation. It was wrong to give in to silence and let her win. 'You look a little tired. Getting much sleep? I know all about that right now.'

Krystina looked up at him after making her play and crossed her arms.

'I look tired?'

The tension rose substantially, and he immediately regretted it. 'Sorry, I just wa—'

'I'm not wearing my best makeup today. Been too busy to get the stuff I usually use in Boots. That and I've not been resting that well. As you say, case loads are hard to manage. But I'm doing fine. Thanks for asking.' And smiled serenely, as if nothing had happened.

Letting out a steady breath, thankful for the blessing, he noticed that an hour later, he was alone on a bus home and Krystina was long gone. Her voice still bouncing around in his head. And he felt a staggering wave of frustration hit him. Gripped the handrail until his knuckles turned white.

Was he completely inept? Why couldn't he bond with her? Before, he had considered that after everything she had been through in the past, for her mental health, she may have put up walls. But for Hudson, he prided himself with how he approached people. It was imperative to his job.

So why couldn't he get through to his own sister?

A familiar, dreaded thought crept in. That dark smoke seeping in through the ear. The truth.

She's not your sister. Just an adoption.

You share nothing but a fondness for citrus beverages and board games. There the similarities ended.

Growing up had been volatile. Full of drama but also full of love. They shared plenty of happy memories, but as they reached their late teens and Krystina graduated in law, several years ahead of her brother, they grew apart.

Maybe that was it? Perhaps he was fighting a battle that didn't need to be fought? But there, nagging in the back of his mind, his mother's voice. Asking him to look out for her. To promise to make sure no harm comes to her. And he had promised. Not because of any obligation to his mum or even to his own conscience. But because despite all the shit they had been through, as young kids, sat in the long grass, staring out across the fields, they had been best friends and promised under that large oak tree, to always protect each other. No matter what.

Tuesday, 19th February

08:02

Very quickly into his career, Hudson realised coffee wasn't going to cut it. He felt he needed something with a little more kick. Not for the first time, he saw some coppers drinking a little on the job. Often discreet and toward the end of a shift, but drinking all the same. Hudson had spied Nguyen, one of the team's bubbliest, tipping something into his cup before he climbed out of his car one morning. Once, too, in the office. It really shook him for some reason.

He had this picture of the man. Indestructible. Never too vocal, but always there when it mattered. Hard worker. Well respected in the team. So it was a bit of a blow when he saw him do it.

With the day bitter, gloomy and still icy as shit, Hudson decided to do the grim jobs he had been postponing. Calling the families of the victims.

The phone rang twice before the widow picked up. Clearly not that impressed.

'Hello, it's DC Daniel Hudson here. I wanted to speak with you again regarding the passing of…'

An audible sigh. 'Yes yes, you've had your poxy grief officers or whatever you call them out here. I've said it a million times. I mean, how often do I have to spell it out for you idiots? I'm not at all upset about this as bad as it sounds. Can you just leave me alone?'

'I'm sorry to hear that, but I actually wanted to ask you some questions. Perhaps we could get together for a chat if possible? There's a few things I wanted to tie off.'

Hudson wanted to know more about the woman. They didn't have enough. It wouldn't be out of the realm of possibility if she knew a few shady characters. It could be a lead they were completely overlooking. But thus far, the list of friends and family she'd provided were dead ends.

'I thought you had everything? I gave you a list, didn't I?'

'Yes of course, but—'

And she hung up. Hudson groaned, tapped the phone against his head in frustration and placed it back down. Leigh crossed the office in time to see this unfold. She grinned.

'That's not how you work a phone y'know. Not had your training then?'

'Ha ha,' he laughed, sitting back in his chair and crossing off another name on his list of calls. 'Trying to make follow-ups and Robert Short's ex-wife isn't playing ball. I'm tempted to book her for obstruction. Anything.'

Leigh leaned onto the edge of his desk, casting her eyes down onto some of his paperwork. 'What about the drug lead? Checked with the narcotics chaps on it? Isn't Hunt meant to be liaising with them?'

Hudson clicked his fingers. 'He is. Yeah, I don't know what the latest update is on that actually.' He wanted to avoid that topic of conversation, not eager to be reminded of last week. Nor to have any excuse to speak to such an overbearing bellend. 'Feel like I'm grasping here. No bloody leads. No DNA, no proper eyewitnesses we can trust. CCTV cross-analysis is still in the very early days. That could take weeks and weeks. Toxicology reports for Robert Short, Catherine Evans and Clifford Biggins are still in process, let alone the others. It'll take months. It's wank. Seen the news today? It's really blowing up like a treat. All sorts of names now. The Surgeon. London Lobotomiser. Return of the Ripper. It's getting ridiculous.'

'So get up off your arse then?' Leigh offered, shrugging as if to suggest that shit doesn't get done whilst you're sat around making calls. 'You've got to exhaust all enquiries to establish leads. No use going over old ground that's been analysed by at least all of us, twice over.'

It suddenly clicked in his head then. Lead. He remembered there would be a TV appeal done later today. Journalists would be there, maybe like the idiot who showed up in Soho at the second murder.

Bethany Shaw.

'It seemed off she would know about the pattern. How would she know that unless she was tipped off by someone?'

The deepest frown imaginable appeared on Leigh's face. 'Where do you keep your meds? You must have lost them. Mate. Pattern? Who was tipped off? Have you finally fucking cracked?'

Hudson waved a hand, started a quick Google search. 'Journalists. I need to track someone down. Blonde one that was at the crime scene few weeks ago. Bethany Shaw. She mentioned something about the case that seemed a bit off. Want to have a chat. Find her number or email for me.'

'Like what? Are you inferring a leak? Hiraoka has all their contact information uploaded from his last trip with Hunt, why not just try again with her Uni friends?' Leigh asked.

'Dunno. Maybe, but that's what I want to ask her. Just seems off, though, doesn't it? I get why she came to Soho on the second murder, but I'm still not convinced how she linked them. Nothing had been formally released. No press conferences.' He made a few extra clicks and slapped the desk. 'Bingo. LinkedIn you've done it again.'

Leigh leaned over to look at the screen. 'What's your play?'

Hudson laughed, already dialling her number. 'We don't need one. We're acting under the SIO, first on the case. She won't be able to pass this up. Not in a million years.'

Within the hour, both detectives were stood impatiently outside of a Caffè Nero in Piccadilly. Here where the traffic ran busiest, monstrous mounds of slush had built up against the curbs, some kicked about by the hurried commuters and brave bands of tourists.

Halfway through a terrible dad-joke Hudson had heard the other day when shopping, a very tall blonde woman in heels, long coat and glasses came sauntering down the street towards them, grinning from ear to ear.

She extended a gloved hand immediately, eager to get things rolling.

'Hello, detectives. Kukua Leigh. Daniel Hudson. Thank you ever so much for meeting me. I must say it's a little uncharacteristic, but I understand stories can often shed light on investigations. Journalists have always played a vital role in criminal cases. Shall we nip inside?'

'Ye—'

'No, thank you, we won't be too long.' Leigh interrupted Hudson, taking the wheel.

'OK,' she said, a little taken aback. 'Not to worry. Well just for the record, I'm Bethany Shaw, I work for the Daily Mail. I'm currently helping to cover this awful case of the London Lobotomiser, wanting justice for all involved and to locate this evil, deranged psychopath as soon as possible. Where would you like to begin?'

'Not here. I think it's best we speak a bit more privately.' Leigh said, aware of how public they were.

'I picked this spot deliberately, detective. I don't trust what you might do to me behind closed doors.'

'I beg your pardon?'

Shaw smirked. Hudson could only imagine she was enjoying this. Antagonising Leigh. But he had a feeling there was something he wasn't reading. Something personal between the two.

'You've never been a fan of me, have you Kukua?'

'Can't expect me to list the litany of racially charged bullshit you call journalism?'

'Ouch. I thought we were here to trade information, not insults?'

Leigh's hands started fidgeting.

'Hudson, this is a waste of time.'

The journalist looked at Hudson. 'Do you have something for me, detective? Perhaps we could have a chat, just you and I? Don't think I'm going to get anywhere with this one.'

Leigh wasted no time in getting straight to the point. 'Who leaked you the case information? Who tipped you off?'

Shaw frowned. 'I beg your pardon? I'm not sure what you're implying here bu—'

Leigh was already in her space, nose to nose. 'Give. Me. The. Fucking. Name. Before I shove your head so far up your own arse, you'll taste what you ate for breakfast. Are we crystal-fucking-clear, Bethany?'

Hudson was stunned. Didn't know whether to say something or ask her to repeat it so he could record it for later viewing. Either way, it wasn't as effective as Leigh had maybe hoped. Disgusted by the outburst, Shaw wrestled herself away from the detectives.

'How dare you,' she spat. She turned tail and stormed off up the high street, pulling her phone out.

'Shit,' Leigh said. Then decided to shout it a few more times, making a few young kids walking passed scream in fright.

'Fuck, what was that about?' Hudson asked.

'I'm sorry.'

'Don't be sorry, she's obviously a piece of work. Is there a situation between you two we should be aware of?'

Leigh closed her eyes, frustrated. 'You know what Hudders, I think I best keep out of this. And I may have fucking blown it. There goes our lead.'

The two paused for a second to think and gather themselves. Leigh swore again when she realised the worst and Hudson clocked onto it too. They would have to act fast if Shaw was planning to put this into an article. Or post it on social media. She had both their names and this would potentially be career-ending smears. At the very least, they'd be off for the foreseeable future.

Hudson's stomach dropped afoot. He motioned to Leigh, and the pair walked off in the opposite direction, looking for somewhere a little more discrete and off the beaten path to talk. Stepping into a tuck-away beside some construction, Hudson dove straight into it.

'We need to speak with her. Convince her of the importance of this lead. If she publishes anything, with our names in, we're fucked. Haskell will flip. Hiraoka will butcher us alive.'

'Don't you think I know that! Jesus, fuck,' she swore, pacing back and forth. She clearly looked distressed. Annoyed with her outburst. It was the first time Hudson had seen her like this, so unprofessional and out of control. It made him uneasy, just like when he'd seen Nguyen swig some whiskey on shift.

He was watching his team literally fall apart. Tearing at the seams.

'Let me reach out to her, alone,' Hudson said finally, clutching at his chin, trying to think. 'She will close herself off to you now after that. Let me talk to her, see what I can do. At the very least, get the lead from her before she publishes it.'

Leigh swore again, kicking something down the alley. 'Fuck it, alright, but nothing risky. And do it tomorrow after she's cooled off. No way she'd publish this too early. She'll want it done right if she's going to do it.'

Wednesday, 20th February

05:49

Hudson sat bolt right up, sweating, clutching his bedsheets. Looking around his room, frantically, trying to get his eyes to adjust to the darkness. He hadn't yelled this time, not to his knowledge. No footsteps from the other bedroom. No sign of Eisa rousing at all.

Cracking open the window for a bit of sub-zero fresh air, he flopped back down onto the wet duvet and stared up at the ceiling. Trying to pinpoint the exact moment his mental health started to collapse like a deck of cards.

What the fuck is going on?

When had Hudson lost resilience like this? He'd never been one for nightmares and now, what, it had been several weeks?

Sensing he wasn't going back to sleep, he chucked on some clothes, brushed his teeth and was out the door at the crack of dawn.

It was something of a ritual and a habit now. Few days of work. Everyone in a flap because there had been another murder. Friends and friends of friends giving weaker and weaker statements. Then going home stressed, over-worked and tired. Having a few nightmares. Getting up and heading to work early. Throw in some awkward conversations with the chief inspector and there you have it.

The life and times of Daniel Hudson.

He hadn't realised just how long he'd drifted off into his own head when he almost spilt hot coffee on his hand at the office. Snapping out of it, he glanced behind him to see no-one was there. Over on Nguyen's desk, he spied some of the CCTV analysis that was being done. Linking up timelines with supposed entries of travel for the killer.

Nothing yet. At least he hoped they would stumble on something. Right now it seemed like their best avenue.

Knowing the stuff was all sitting at the station and not here, he reluctantly wrapped up, taking his coffee and braved the weather.

Snowfall had avoided London now for a good few days since the weekend storms. The only thing that really remained now was a smattering of ice and residual amounts of snow where it had been piled up high. Instead, Hudson now had to watch out for wet snow, puddles and rogue bits of black ice.

On the way down to Charing Cross, he decided to take a moment to sit. In his backpack, he'd carried a thermos of hot soup. Not your usual breakfast item, but Hudson was in the mood for comfort good.

He spied a bench halfway down the high street to plonk his arse down, not before attempting to sweep up a dry patch. It felt nice to pause. Sit still and watch traffic zip past, people going about their business. It was still dark, barely eight o'clock so he managed his soup via a shitty street light and the glow from the Greggs behind him.

A small portion of soup spilt. He licked his finger. Checking the time on his phone, it was closer to half-past and figured he could be here all day if he wanted. Better to make a move whilst he still had the energy and review the CCTV. So, reluctantly, he tightened the thermos lid and placed it back into his bag for later.

I have to confess, seeing him across the road from me shit me up a little. Right there, over on the bench, tucking into something. For an instance, I considered the idea he may recognise me. I don't cut a small figure, so I hastened to move away, but the idiocy of this soon removed doubt and fear.

Look at you. Alone, feeding yourself lies. Feeding yourself small, morsels of nourishment to keep going. I regarded how pathetic it looked. Like some small rodent lapping up scraps before its inevitable demise at the hand of fate. That's precisely what awaited this detective. Fate. And at my own hands.

I splayed them then. My fingers. Spread out my large hands and pretended to move my burr puzzle. Imagining each segment were a slice or component of this man's life. I watched him go for another gulp of his soup.

I moved another piece.

I sensed then how far he was to discovering me. That they were, no doubt, trying to find a link between the murders.

Of which there were none.

I moved another piece and smiled.

And that smile widened as opportunity occurred to me like brilliant light. I saw it there across the street. Innocent and waiting. If I only followed, I would learn so much more to my advantage. Got closer. But it would apply a certain amount of risk. Risk which I would ultimately savour. For it was a challenge. A new sub-plot to my narrative. This meaning of mine. The reason I did any of this.

This opportunity was a necessity to further my plan. I saw that now, plainly.

I tucked my hands back into my pockets to keep them warm. The morning sky grew lighter as the sun crept out behind the clouds. A smell caught my nose, and I relished the moment. Logged the sounds and the taste on the air.

And then Hudson rose from his perch. So I followed him.

Wednesday, 20th February

13:15

By lunch, Hudson had already given up after obliterating his eyes going through endless station CCTV. It would take years to sift through. On top of that, a call from Leigh reminded him of a planned date he had with a particular journalist. His visit to the station short-lived. An attempt was made at casework, but right now, if he didn't get on top of this mess with Bethany Shaw, they were all fucked.

He gave her number a call on his way out, wrestling with his coat and almost choking himself somehow.

No answer.

Outside on the steps, zipping up his parka and tightening his scarf, Hudson gave her number another ring and swore. Still nothing.

The city was bustling now, office drone's hunger for a Tesco meal deal overshadowing the evident danger of traversing the snowy pavements, so he fell into step. Allowed the crowds to carry him like a poo stick downstream. All the way into the centre. Hudson was bending his neck back to get a look at Nelson's Column at Trafalgar Square. It looked impressive under the ominous overcast. More so for the bits of snow and ice clinging to it and on top of the lion statues.

He tried calling Shaw again.

'Hello?'

'I've seen your missed calls. What do you want, detective?'

Hudson paused to consider his reply. It had to be tactful. 'I want to apologise for yesterday. For myself and on behalf of my colleague. The case has placed a bit of a burden on us, and that stress came out in an unhealthy way. I'm sorry for it.'

'I'm not in the habit of accepting such quick apologies, detective, but I'm happy to meet, as I presume is the purpose of this call?'

'It is.'

'Fine then,' she said. 'We'll meet at Caffè Nero again, by Piccadilly Circus. Alone this time, I'm not the biggest fan of that hot head partner of yours.'

Hudson bit his tongue for the sake of the bigger picture. 'Yep, that's fine, see you in half an hour?'

'I'm busy, let's make it an hour.' And she hung up.

He didn't mess around, immediately pocketing his phone and making a bee-line almost back the way he came for Piccadilly Circus, jumping straight on the nearest tube. When he arrived, a little sweaty despite the cold, he reached the coffee shop with no one waiting outside. It was only when he peered in through the windows that he spotted her at a table toward the back.

After a deep breath, he stepped in, deciding against a drink and going straight for her table.

'Hi, thanks for coming,' he said, pulling out a chair opposite.

She seemed engaged with her phone. Typing away furiously. When she was finally done, she placed it onto the table and laced her fingers. Hudson hoped those last strokes weren't the final edits to her next article.

'What do you have for me?'

He frowned. 'Sorry?'

'What do you have for me? We can't trade without you having something to offer. This isn't how things work.'

'Excuse me, can I just remind you who you're speaking wi— sorry, sorry no, please.' He tried to calm her down as she made to leave. He sensed there would be no bullshit. She'd been tested enough, and no amount of strong-arming would work. Hudson was fucked.

'Shall we start again? I'm running out of patience here, detective. Last chance.'

He gritted his teeth, fished around for ideas. 'Well, it's clear I want the lead. The person you spoke with at the murder scene some week and a half ago. So what is it you want from me?'

'Isn't it obvious to you yet? You do know I write for a paper, don't you? I'm not a gossip columnist either so let's stop jerking each other about, please.'

'That's case sensitive information, you know we can't divulge anything publicly, especially without my superintendent's consent. Besides, we have fuck all anyway.' Hudson closed his eyes slowly. Immediately regretting what he'd just said and the journalist simply beamed at him.

'Go on, you've started digging. Might as well finish.'

Her face taunted him more than ever. He wished he'd ordered a drink now, or something to eat at least. So he had something to fiddle with. Instead, his hands were balled into fists beneath the table. Flexing. Clenching around his legs.

'We have yet to determine a suspect. We are currently out dry.'

'Nothing at all? Isn't that a bit concerning now you're three murders in? Why the incompetence?'

Once more, he had to clench and just bare it. 'No. It's a unique case. Look, I've said plenty enough, can you just tell me who spoke to you that day, please? It's only fair.'

She grinned at him, spent another few minutes on her phone then decided to stop toying with him.

'She was tall. Blonde. Didn't catch her name but she had a look about her. Bit creepy to be honest but she seemed to know a bit about the murder. I assumed she was either a fellow journalist or someone who loved following this sort of thing as a hobby. Maybe a PI with something to gain. Why, do you think it's a potential lead?'

Hudson's eyes flew open. 'Did you get a name?'

'No, she wanted it to be anonymous.'

'Wanted what to be anonymous? The tip-off she gave you?'

The journalist nodded, flicking some hair behind her ear and making a move to go. But Hudson wasn't done. He had a thousand questions and wanted at least half of them answered.

'Wait a second. You have nothing else? Come on!'

She shrugged. 'That's your problem. But I have a better story to write, thanks for the business.'

A wink and a wave and she was gone, leaving Hudson seething. He swung his fist into the table, causing a few customers to jump and yell. Taking cue, he got up and left a few minutes after she had and pulled out his phone, dialling quick.

'Leigh, you at Fitzrovia or the station?'

'Fitz, why?'

'Hiraoka there?'

A pause. 'Yeah, what's up? You found something?'

'Like you wouldn't fucking believe.'

This one was for Chief Superintendent Haskell, who sat waiting in his office, Hiraoka in one seat opposite but with no sign of Leigh. Hudson closed the door behind him gently.

'Where's Leigh?'

'She's at the station, you must have passed her. She's confirming an ID problem with our third victim. Turns out it may not, in fact, be correct.'

His heart dropped.

'Fuck sake. Sorry sir,' he quickly added, looking at Haskell with fear of retribution. The old man waved a hand as if his apology annoyed him more than the swearing.

'I'm told you have quite the update for us. Leigh updated us after some persuasion, so we know you've met with a Daily Mail journalist. I hope you have a damn good reason, boy, why you decided that was a sensible idea in the middle of a serious murder investigation.'

The weight of their eyes felt heavy. Hudson swallowed, scratched his neck and stepped forward, collecting his thoughts to speak his case.

'Back when we investigated the second murder of Catherine Evans in Soho, I noticed a journalist at the crime scene.'

'There are many journalists hanging around at crime scenes, constable, please try and be more specific.'

'Yes, sir,' he apologised. 'A journalist, in particular, managed to get my attention and mentioned something about the case which would not have been made privy to the public.'

Before Hudson could continue, Haskell jumped in again. Clearly agitated by the whole ordeal. Hiraoka looked livid. Glaring at Hudson as if he had done him a personal betrayal. And in many ways, he had. Behind his back.

'What sort of case information?'

'She mentioned the pattern and the link to the Hyde Park murder before any formal announcements had been made.'

Haskell moved his weight onto his elbows, resting his chin on his fists. 'Go on.'

'Well, it struck me as odd. Not that she couldn't have deduced it herself, but with the way she said it. It was a hunch and we've had no leads, so I wanted to follow it up. We tried to convince her to provide the lead and, following a reschedule, I've been able to speak with her and—'

'Constable,' Haskell barked. 'Have I upset you in any way?'

Shocked by the suggestion, Hudson didn't know what to say at first. 'N-no, sir? Sorry, I don't follow?'

'Because one would assume I have, if you felt you had the balls to come into this office and lie in front of your SIO and chief superintendent. Why is it, constable, you feel the need to lie? I'm providing you with a chance here, to provide me with a clear explanation of the events that occurred. Otherwise, I'll make it my business to treat this transfer as a poorly judged secondment. Back to Gotham you go.'

Hudson's stomach plummeted. He couldn't believe it. The sack? His lips went numb as he fumbled his words and tried to explain.

'We, er… we met first, and it didn't go according to plan, sir. Sorry. We were worried about the lead and… Leigh got agitated. It really pissed her off and she threatened to publish a story of police abuse of power. Worried about the repercussions and the clear misunderstanding, I rushed to meet with her again, knowing she would more than likely do so with me than with Leigh in the picture. So, today, I managed to speak with her again, and she was finally, after some persuasion, able to give me the lead.'

Haskell stared deep into Hudson's self. His very soul and Hudson knew full well a small detail was missing. Hudson collapsed under his intense gaze, his dark, piercing eyes beneath a sweep of grey and black hair.

'Sir, I have to inform you that in exchange for the lead, I did confirm that we had no ongoing suspects.'

Hiraoka was the first to react. 'Oh for fuck sake.'

Haskell simply shook his head. 'What the hell do you think you're playing at constable?'

'I… I didn't consider it too compromising at the time, and I really needed that lead, sir. We really needed something on this case.'

'Then do tell me what the fuck you traded with her?' he suddenly roared, standing up and slamming his fists into the desk, causing even Hiraoka to flinch.

'Someone knows more about the case. Someone tipped her off before she arrived at the crime scene. Someone out there knows about the pattern, about Hyde Park. Bethany Shaw described her as being a tall, blonde female, quite stern-looking and gave off a creepy vibe. It's my bet, sir, that this person knows something that we don't and we need to track them down. Could be a private investigator or perhaps even an accomplice to the killings.'

Haskell was fuming, but Hiraoka jumped in to save him. 'CCTV, guv. If Hudson is right, CCTV will show the person of interest at the scene. We just need to go back over evidence. Nguyen has it all catalogued.'

The chief superintendent pointed a finger. 'Thin, fucking ice. Very thin. Had this been nothing, I would have put you on leave effective immediately. As such, you have gotten very, very lucky. You owe your chief inspector. Go work this lead now, whilst I deal with the inevitable shit storm of tomorrow's papers. Hiraoka, I want clear supervision on Hudson from now on. Get Hunt on it if you're busy. No unauthorised overtime, or meetings at all. They're all to go directly through me. Clear? Now get out of my fucking sight.'

Wednesday, 20th February

15:28

'I'm really sorry, but it's the wrong person. ID was planted. Our victim's not Clifford Biggins.'

Moreau delivered the blow when Hudson popped down to the station to meet up with Leigh. Apparently, Martha Andrews had just received a call from her Clifford just a few hours ago. That he was very much alive and well and that they had found the wrong guy. Asked why he hadn't been home, it was discovered no officers had been round yet to visit the property. He had been home and was simply getting over a nasty cold.

'Fuck,' Hudson said, slapping a hand to his forehead. 'Anderson's drop the ball there. But his… ID…'

'Identity theft,' Moreau declared almost dramatically. 'Can you believe it? Stumbled on an entirely new crime.'

Leigh shook her head, downing her drink and lobbing the empty cup into the bin. The three side-stepped as a rush of officers came jogging down the hallway. 'So that entire witness work we did was a fucking waste. Do we even know who this bloke is then?'

'Not yet. We postponed some of the DNA work because we had the ID so we will find out in a day or two. Until then, we're in the dark, and it's being treated as a John Doe situation. But, in the meantime and probably why you're wondering what Moreau has to do with this, I am working here to see if I can trace anything online. Clifford's handing over his phone so I'll file requests with his provider to track his movements. Leigh will pop down to see the chaps in Stratford, and grab those statements from Clifford. See if we can figure out how he had his ID pinched.'

'Nice,' Hudson said.

She wobbled her hand. 'Sort of mate. He's apparently a bit withdrawn and difficult to question, so it'll be some work. Can only try.'

'Hiraoka and Haskell know?'

'Oh, of course, I let them know all my habits,' she winked, slapping him on the arm before he could react. 'I'm just taking the piss. Leigh told me what you were in for.'

This time, he rounded on Leigh. 'You knew my neck was on the chop?'

'Out of my hands, Hudson and you know that, don't you turn on me now.'

'I might add as well, Hiraoka did drop me a line with a full update, so I already knew mate. Don't go flipping out. Chill your beans here and gather yourself up, alright?' Moreau had a special sort of approach to conflict, but no matter how unorthodox it was, it did seem to work.

Hudson couldn't help but like her. He couldn't stay angry for long and grinned.

'Sure. OK, so, what now then? We go review CCTV, and you go make some calls?'

She made gun signs with her hands. 'Bingo. See you guys later?'

'Yeah, cheers Moreau you're a fucking legend. See you later.' Leigh hugged her and turned back to Hudson, not entirely done. 'We need to get on this bitch hard, Hudders. No playing now. Ready for a sprint? I know you've got to clock off on the usual for being misbehaved.'

Hudson opened his palms to her.

'So this is what a rock and hard place feels like?'

Sometime around four, Nguyen had joined them to look through the CCTV files. Word had gotten around that Nguyen was neck deep. Hunt and Anderson showed up later and got stuck in, using up all the computers. It was a real show of effort that only motivated Hudson to work harder.

They all took a couple of days each and went through it frame by frame. It was arduous, hungry work. So much so by half five, they had ordered in an enormous round of pizzas and chicken wings. All of it promptly demolished.

Finishing off the crusts using leftover dip, Hudson started to nudge through his frames, looking for anyone that might match the provided description. Tall, blonde, female. He'd also lost track of time, which was fortunate for him, as DS Hunt was the only senior officer in the building. For a moment, Hudson caught his eye, wondering what he would say. Maybe he'd send him home? Maybe report it straight to the guv? Instead, he nodded and went back to his own work.

'Hudson, what exactly did she tell you? I feel like I'm wasting my fucking time here. Pizza or no pizza,' Leigh blurted, picking up another slice.

'What I've already told you. A tall woman with blonde hair hanging around the crime scene. It might be that she was well off-camera, we need to keep checking.'

'Right, but why are we checking hours before or days after? Why Hyde Park and this shit hole in Stratford?'

He grunted, throwing down his crust. 'Because, if they are hanging around that scene, they may have hung around the others. Just keep looking, seriously. Oh! She was right!'

Hudson's own footage caught up to the early morning after the night of Catherine Evans' death. From a long angle, he could barely make out the end of the street. As he whizzed by the time stamp of the murder, reviewed numerous times to show no sighting of their killer, police presence began to materialise, tape hung from end to end, blocking out people who started to crowd for a peek at what was happening. But when the time stamp hit early hours, and Hudson and Hiraoka had arrived at the scene, he'd almost choked on his pizza in his hurried fumble to hit the pause button.

'Here she is! Talking to Bethany Shaw!'

The other detectives got up, even Hunt, and walked around to his computer.

Nguyen clapped him on the back. 'Isn't this the footage we ran over a hundred times last week? We didn't find anything. It barely shows the end of the street.'

'I know. But it catches the end of the street where the journalists were huddled and look. It's her. The blonde that Shaw was on about.'

Sure enough, they watched a very tall, heavily dressed woman with long blonde hair poking out from a thick woollen hat, approach Shaw, speak for perhaps thirty seconds, before turning away and walking off.

'Hey,' Leigh said. 'Zoom in, see if we can see her face.'

Hudson froze the frame, tried to zoom in, but her face was partially blocked by her hat and coat. 'No joy.'

Hunt returned to his desk, smoothing down his shirt and pointed over at the constable. 'Well, Hudson, time for you to go before Haskell buries his foot up your arse to the knee, so I'd leave this here, and we'll take over. Write it up, we'll see you Friday, bright and early.'

'Day off?'

'Those are the orders, don't bother questioning them.'

Deflated, he nodded and made quick records of his work before getting up and making for the door. Coat zipped up and his new woollen gloves on tight, he made to say goodnight to everyone. But as he turned to survey the office, they were already engrossed, gesticulating and fussing over trying to capture clear face shots of their mysterious blonde. Smiling sheepishly, he caught only Anderson's eye, nodded and left, feeling like they'd had a very small win.

Apparently, exhaustion was an excellent remedy for night terrors. Hudson went unscathed through the morning and finally woke, to his alarm going off incessantly. He busied himself with his phone, rubbed his eyes and staggered out to the kitchen, realising he had a day off today and wouldn't be due in until tomorrow at six am. A glorious sense of relief hit him, but it came with the familiar taste of anxiety. His work being picked apart in his absence, ready for a fresh grilling on his return.

But also, the feeling of dread. An ominous sensation that the killer may be heavily resourced with actual human support. Maybe that blonde wasn't a PI? Perhaps they were linked to the killer in a fair more nefarious way?

Knowing it'd gnaw away at his mind, Hudson made some breakfast and fired up the Nintendo Switch, chucking in some game about a prince saving a princess, and escaped reality. He must have been gone for hours. Blissfully free. Mind unoccupied by work. Hudson galloped through the kingdom, fighting beasts and saving village folk through quests. Only, when Eisa emerged and announced the shop was shut for the day, did it dawn on him how he had lost grip of time, stomach gurgling.

'Oh shit, sorry I was meant to pop down, everything alright?' he yawned, stretching across the back of the sofa.

Eisa grinned. 'Of all things to kill time with, Breath of the Wild is a superb choice, and I hold no ill will against you for it. The shop is fine, though I am exhausted, as my demeanour may denote. Though I am somewhat disheartened by your lack of visits. It really is quite lovely, you know, being surrounded by books.'

She practically collapsed into the seat next to him and rested her head on his shoulder.

'Keep playing,' she said.

And so he did, until the room was pitch black and the only light came from the humming glow of their TV, and the distant mountains of Hyrule.

Thursday, 21st February

19:15

For most normal people, days off were a time to see family. Fall in love with your hobby all over again. Go exploring or catch up on lost errands. But for detectives such as Hudson, it meant escaping life and doing sweet fuck all. And he had loved it. The evening had flown by, and it would have done so until much later, had he not received a text from Jess.

Fancy dinner? I'm actually free tonight if you can make it through the whole date? Xx

Hudson eased himself out from a sleeping Eisa and propped her up with a few cushions, wrapping her in a throw from the armchair. Tiptoeing to his room, he sat down and considered his reply. A bit wounded from her wording

Sure, where do you have in mind? Xx

Keep with the two kisses, Hudson. Play it cool. You've had a few dates with this one now, don't blow your chances. This might actually be a semblance of normality creeping in.

A flash in his mind's eye, and he pictured a butchered head on his bedroom floor. Hudson flinched and jumped back momentarily, then realised, of course, nothing was there. He breathed in quickly, then slowly and knew he needed to get out and drink. Do something. Anything.

There's this nice tapas place in Tower hill I like the look of. Say, meet there in an hour? Xx

No need to think about that one.

Sounds spot on. See you then, Jess xxx

He stared down in horror. Three kisses. He panicked a little, considered amending it but thought he'd just make things worse. Suddenly feeling like a teenager all over again, he savoured the butterflies, smiled despite himself and pocketed his phone.

Time to smarten up, Hudson.

He decided to make an extra effort. Pulled out a dark blue blazer and a white shirt. Then, daring himself, he pulled out some chinos to go for the preppy look. It was a bit young of him, but what the hell? He finished everything off with a pair of brown Chelsea boots, an overcoat and scarf.

When he arrived at the tapas restaurant, he was again blown back by how well Jessica always managed to dress up. It looked like she had also made the extra effort too, opting for a medium-length green dress and dark black tights, with black heels. She giggled after noticing how he was looking at her. They made a few jokes and went in out of the cold, eager to get some preliminary drinks in.

After a brief deliberation on what to eat, they settled on having a bit of everything, with regular servings of wine in between. Just what was needed.

'Finally pulled me away from work, thank you! And couldn't pick better company if I tried.'

'Cheesy, but obviously true,' she laughed. 'You have been a hard man to get hold of. I'm guessing this work is something of a lifestyle, am I right?'

'Very bloody right.' He neglected to tell her he'd been on leave, for no particular reason.

Jessica took a sip from some red wine the waiter had brought over to their table. 'Mmmm, very nice. Try some. Here.'

She passed over her glass. 'Oh, that's fine, I'll pour my own—'

'Try it,' she insisted.

So Hudson did. Shaking his head incredulously and having a quick sip, not wanting to thieve from her round. 'You're right. Very nice, not too sharp either.'

'Lovely.'

Hudson watched her suck in her lip as she took the glass back. 'Perfect for tapas. Now, where is this bloody food?'

After fifteen minutes or more of work chatter, the food finally arrived by two waitresses, who filled the space on their table with an assortment of tapas foods, salads and sweet potato fries. Hudson's eyes bulged at so many options, whilst his wallet quietly whimpered. It was a week until payday yet.

They fished about, grabbing bits here and pieces there. Being adventurous and cracking a few jokes about just how adventurous they were. Jess started to bring up University and some of the old memories. It was nice to take a trip down memory lane. Those late-night drinking games. Stumbling into lectures, half awake. Surviving for days on tinned ravioli because student loans had cocked up and your part-time wage was primarily for booze.

It took an hour and a half, but there he was, drunk. Still feeling exhausted from the endless shifts he'd been pulling. It seemed to show a little on his face, as he tried in vain to listen to Jessica's story about capitalism and socialism. His eye's drooped once or twice enough for it to be a problem. She stopped talking. Crossed her arms.

'Am I really boring you?'

Hudson jolted. 'No, no. Sorry, I've had a long run of hours, and it's only just hitting me is all.'

Expecting the full force of retribution, he was pleasantly met with an offer. 'Well, to be honest, me too. I'm surprised we got this far. I'm shattered. I couldn't tempt you in crashing over at mine? Strictly behaved, you know. Just because I'm feeling kind. It's a bit of a trek back to yours.'

Somewhere by the back of his neck, he flushed red. Felt how warm he'd gotten and couldn't stop dropping his gaze from her eyes down to her lips. Her neck.

'Er… Are you sure? I'm quite fine getting back.'

Jessica laughed quite loudly, swirling her wine. 'It's fine, I'm not threatening you. Shall we get the bill? I insist on dutch, none of this chivalry bollocks, thank you.'

Hudson grinned. 'Sure.'

They paid after a short interval for the waitress. It came to something in the three figures, so Hudson felt at bit relieved he was so tipsy. They walked outside slowly for a few minutes, silent, towards what they knew to be the nearest taxi rank and stopped, coats wrapped up tight as a cool wind started whipping through the tall buildings around them.

'So, here we are,' she said, visibly a little put out by the end to the night. Hudson sensed it too, didn't know if he had the courage to just say something. Anything.

'Yeah, I'm glad we finally went out on something like a proper date. We both deserve it, don't you think?'

Her eye's widened, and she scoffed a little. 'Brash of you! But I agree. We do deserve it. Would you consider this a date then, Danny?'

'Of course, what would you call it?'

A twinkle in her eye. 'It's getting late, then. Fine if I leave you here?'

'Well,' he said, heart suddenly pounding as he took the dive. 'How far do you live? Could share?'

'No it's fine,' she replied, stuffing her gloved hands into her coat pockets and looking up and down the street. Not as if waiting for someone, but deciding which route to walk home. 'I'm fortunate to live within walking distance.'

'That is convenient,' Hudson said.

'Oh, it's very convenient. Close to all local amenities.' That twinkle in her eye again. 'Take that as a yes then?'

Hudson winked. 'Twisted my arm.'

The next time Hudson checked the time, it was close to midnight. He was out of breath, covered in sweat and lay spread-eagled across Jessica's queen-sized bed. Silk sheets and feathered pillows. Crisp lines and fine art on the walls. Modern interior decor. Started noticing the more subtle details after what must have been his second orgasm of the evening.

Feeling a bit tender, euphoric yet still sensitive, he got himself up and hobbled to the bathroom, where she was still tidying herself up. He knocked, stumbled through, and met with her bare figure, wrapped tight in a robe as silky as her bedding. Hudson's eyes fell straight to his favourite parts and reached over to stroke her back.

'The best thing about that place was definitely the order-to-go dessert they had on offer.'

She chuckled, pressing her hands onto his chest and resting her forehead onto his nose. 'Always this cute after sex?'

'Maybe?'

Another laugh. She finished cleaning her makeup off, brushed her teeth and gave Hudson free reign of the toilet. After a quick piss, he too washed up, brushed his teeth and waddled back to the bedroom. When he stepped in through the door, Jessica tossed his mobile phone across the bed towards him.

'That was flashing, by the way.'

Fuck, he thought. Not another one, not now.

Not keen on finding out, he gingerly held it as if it might infect him and opened up his messages.

It was DC Leigh. They were on a late shift and had found another shot of the woman they were looking for. This time, at the first crime scene outside of Hyde Park. Further away than anticipated. He sat on the bed and fumbled a reply quickly, not wanting to be taken away from Jessica for too long.

Before he could lean over and kiss Jessica, the phone flashed again.

'Oh for fucks sake, give me a break.' He checked the message and saw it was from DCI Hiraoka.

Get your arse in, now.

'Jessica, I'm really sorry I've got to go. The guv himself has...'

'Seriously, Danny? It's middle of the bloody night!'

'I know, I'm sorry,' he apologised. 'But I have to go. I don't have a choice in the matter.'

Jessica fell back into bed, turning away and wrapping herself in the covers. 'Don't let the door hit you on the way out, Danny.'

'Jess… please…'

No answer. He wanted to stay. Talk it through longer, but the case called. He had to be there. Especially if he wanted to avoid Hiraoka's inevitable wrath. He dressed quickly, tripping over her shoes and a stray Rubix cube, grabbed his coat and dashed out the door, sending a few things off her side table flying.

Friday, 22nd February

01:50

Hudson could still smell her on his clothes. That sweet Miyake perfume she always wore. Recalled the soft touch of her skin. Her eyes in the dark. Smiling back at him.

When he eventually arrived at the office in Fitz, the office was buzzing despite the late hour. Space he still found unorthodox. To him, it seemed so odd not to work out of the station. Something he had been used to back in Notts. Having a separate space for the MIT meant for an almost 24/7 incident room on the very worst crimes.

Crimes like this one.

Some of the desks had been moved, and Hudson could see Leigh and Hiraoka had been hard at work, Anderson as well, who was still flat out.

'So, we've got another hit?'

Leigh nodded, picking up her notepad and flicking through everything she'd jotted down. 'Yup, and it gets better. So far, we've tracked a bit of her movement. Here.' She tapped a circled note on her paper. 'She was seen leaving the east entrance of Hyde Park further down the road sometime during the TOD.' A pause. 'Are you wearing perfume?'

'Yes, that's how I spend my evenings. Moonlighting as a salesperson at a Debenhams kiosk.'

A few of the detectives laughed.

Hiraoka stood up, a freshly rolled cigarette in his hand. 'Kukua herself put it together. This is fantastic policing, and only wish I could take the credit. My news, however, is a little tamer.'

He couldn't deny feeling wounded. All of his and Nguyen's methodical efforts with the CCTV had truly procured nothing. Yet Leigh had done so with ease. Hudson was surprised by the tang of jealousy, but it was only because he wanted to prove himself.

'Remember the fibre found on the body of Miss Evans? You may not have. Charlie came across it on a second look after the autopsy just a week ago. I've been running back and forth on this since.'

Hudson hadn't. Didn't recall reading it anywhere in the reports. As Hiraoka handed the case files to him, he ran through and realised that he had utterly failed to follow up the inquiry on a foreign fibre, thanks to his obsession with the CCTV work. Not even SOCO had mentioned it initially. But it explained to some extent why Hiraoka has seemed equally as tired, dashing about. But to omit it entirely?

'Analysis back?'

The large man nodded.

'And the toxicology reports? No?'

'We played too many bonus cards with Nita and the blood analysis. So, I'm not too surprised this took a while. Be lucky to have it next week. Needless to say, here it is.'

He slid over a second file to Hudson, which he opened and rifled through, taking a look at the summary analysis page underneath a few paper clip pictures of the fibre. Skimming through some of the chemistry jargon, he flicked to page two, then three and finally got some sense of it all.

'So, they've managed to label the fibre then to something a bit expensive? So, whoever was with Miss Evans on the night of the murder, was wearing a pricey coat? I mean, that could be quite a few people...'

The chief inspector held up a finger. 'Nope. It had a smudge of the victim's DNA on it, proving the fibre was displaced during the murder. It's also a fibre of a very particularly pricey material currently being traced to the manufacturer and then retailers. Essentially, we highly doubt this is from someone on a low income or student grants. This is the killer's fibre, without a doubt.'

Hudson read further, chin resting in his hand. 'I'll let you have a read through of that, Anderson and Leigh can update you on the findings, but I wanted you for another reason.'

'What's that, sir?'

'After the little chat, two days ago. I think a little good deed may go a long way.' And winked on his way out for a quick puff.

Anderson frowned, made a motion as if to suggest Hiraoka was on his crazy ways again. But Leigh peered sternly at Hudson. She knew exactly what he was getting at.

'Yep, and if I were you, I'd get some coffee down your Gregory, pisshead and make some final work on these tapes. We don't have long.'

'You know, I was going to ask, where do you want me to time line?'

She squinted at her computer, clicked a few times with her mouse and motioned to Hudson's own desk. 'I've sent it over to you now. We're building up a map of this woman's movements. Distinguishing features will be the blonde hair, height and gait. We all know how she walks so, if you need any notes, holla at your girl.'

Hudson knocked his knuckles against the wood. 'Coffee then? Who's in?'

Every hand in the office shot up, including a few officers drafted over to assist the admin.

'Great.'

A loud bang woke him, and realised he'd passed out at his desk. The culprit, naturally, had been Hiraoka. Which meant the three or so hours he'd stolen out of overtime would be all he'd be getting today.

Moreau was in on the early shift, overlapping with theirs. Much to her delight, Hudson begged for some of her extra-strong brew, because coffee was not going to cut it today. Not a fucking chance. Anyone worth their salt knew the same poundage of tea to coffee, yielded far more caffeine.

Two bags a cup it was.

Practically shaking by midday, Hudson felt satisfied, in part, with the cataloguing and paperwork he'd gotten through. Miraculously, should any of this lead to a conviction and trial, it would all need to be in perfect order. Should the miracle happen and catch the bad guy and the prosecutor needs to bring it home, a single piece of evidence, or lack of, could bring the whole thing tumbling down. And Hudson wasn't about to let fatigue be the architect of some sloppy admin.

After lunch, and a few more of Moreau's teas, a very enigmatic Hiraoka barged into the room carrying a folder of photos and a phone to his ear. Speaking in hushed tones, flipping from Japanese as he mumbled and back to English on the phone.

Hudson and Leigh, still knackered, exchanged a twitchy glance and got up to follow him outside. Once he ended the call, they pounced and begged for an update. Something. Anything that wasn't admin or CCTV trawling.

'Sir, give me a flea comb. I'll go over to Hyde Park right now and find piss, shit and spit for the report. Come on, give it to us,' begged Leigh, practically putting her hands together.

Hudson chipped in. 'Anything, sir. Is the toxicology report back in? Does Hunt need help with narcotics? Perhaps we could follow up in the fibre brand, find buyers and locate customers?'

Hiraoka regarded them suspiciously, as if they were his two young children, brewing a prank unbeknown to him. 'What is this? Shouldn't you be chasing for the report?'

'Nothing, sir. We're just going a bit stir crazy.'

'You need some work to do, is that it?' he asked, taking out his phone and weighing something up in his head. He looked at Hudson, then at Leigh and really seemed to be wrestling with his conscience.

'Here,' he said. 'Hold this. I need a smoke.'

The chief inspector gave Hudson the folder whilst the man himself lit up a Marlboro. He took a long, deep drag and slowly exhaled, not giving two shits how much went back into the constable's face.

'Sir? Can I take a look?'

'That depends. Are you in the mood for a bit of interviewing down in Croydon? Remember Miss Russell? Robert Short's ex-wife, who was ever so lovely?'

Leigh wasn't put off. Despite the fact Miss Russell had been very uncooperative, it still meant getting out into the air. Even if said air was frigid cold. 'I do, sir. What's the nature of the call? Any reason we're going through re-interviews now? What's changed?'

Hiraoka chuckled, flicking ash to one side and shaking his head. 'What's changed? Really, Kukua? You're the smartest one amongst us, and you're asking what's changed? DC Hudson, open that fucking folder, would ya?'

So he did. And inside, were screenshots from all the CCTV footage they had of that tall, blonde woman. Same style of coat. Same build. Same stance. Hudson laughed and felt the biggest smile spread over his face. 'Bit of a grasp, isn't it?'

Leigh didn't respond. She touched her afro absent-mindedly, then her face. Trying to find a comfortable place to rest her hand. Eventually, she just had to hold the photos and think in physical terms. She rifled through them and looked at the Hiraoka. 'We show her these. What's it going to do?'

'Not much. But maybe she can help identify her. See how she reacts. You never know. Either way, it'll be a ticket to speak with her. I know her character, and if you walk in there with nothing, she'll hold her cards close to her chest.' He took another long drag and stared up at the cloudless, winter sky. 'If you go in with that folder, however, it's a trade. An offering almost. She'll feel that we're not possibly going after her and she'll soften. Hopefully, she's connected to the first victim. That link is absolutely key. Best case scenario, she wears a wig and has helped orchestrate this with someone else's help. Worst case, we close that line of enquiry.'

'Worst case?' Leigh scoffed, handing the pictures back to Hudson. 'I agree. Bit of a grasp.'

'Don't we need to mirandise her if we're questioning?'

'We'll tight rope it. Nothing direct. If she gives herself away, then we'll go official.'

'Can't hurt,' Hudson admitted.

'No, but it's a waste of time.'

'Not necessarily. Nguyen and Anderson have exhausted a long list of Catherine Evan's friends, and it'll take longer to run through people she's worked with, or studied with or more. But we'll need to tie them to Robert Short anyway. On top of that, we don't even have a true ID for the third victim, so we come back to the first.'

Hiraoka had stepped back a little to finish his cigarette, letting the two have the floor.

The constables listened but did not yet seem convinced.

'Why back to the first victim?'

'The first one matters somehow. Maybe it's how it all started, and she knows a tiny detail that'll help unravel the end. It'll unspool like a massive bog roll, but we have to pull at the stuck end.'

'Really?' she grimaced. 'That's your analogy?'

Hiraoka stubbed his cigarette out on the cobbles and clapped his hands. 'On that shitty note, I think I'm leaving this in capable hands. I shall work on the fibre and ID with forensics. Cross-reference and put Anderson on a re-visit with Clifford, our fake victim. I want you two to interview Miss Russell. Leigh, keep an eye on him. Orders from above, sure you can understand, constable?'

Hudson gave the nod. Time to see what their ticket might buy them.

The tension was palpable in the living room. Hudson felt that in all honesty, they'd used their ticket just to get through the front door. Now, with both detectives sat opposite Miss Russell, they didn't feel a chance in hell in getting anything new. Even with the photos in the folder on the table.

Hudson reached for the coffee she had made them. Wondered for a crazy moment if it was laced with poison.

'Miss Russell. Thank you for letting us come see you today on such short notice. We both really appreciate it. The police appreciates it, and as you can imagine, this case has achieved some, er... significant coverage. So we're keen to sort of cover all bases if you will.'

'Fine, just... can you get to the point please?'

'Absolutely,' Hudson concurred. 'Straight to the point. Are you aware of Robert Short ever having an affair at all?'

She sighed, sitting back. 'Is this about those photos? I've had your uniforms drill this into me as well. In fact, I'm getting pretty sick and tired of this police harassment.'

'Please answer the question, Miss Russell.' Leigh wasn't in the mood to fuck about. Not today.

'No, not that I am aware.' She rolled her eyes. 'But, what does that matter? We'd been split for some time. Loser lived on his own anyway. Ransacked his place?'

Hudson nodded. 'Our detectives and officers have been through his things, and nothing has come up suspicious. Nothing on his computer, no paperwork incriminating him. Nothing. There's no context to it. What context there might have been are on his phone. Which has long since been destroyed by the killer.'

'Are you certain he didn't have any enemies? Women he pissed off? Was he part of any groups or cults?'

'Groups? Cults? Course he fucking wasn't. Guy was dull as dishwater. You would know that if you had done your work properly. Are you done here?'

Friday, 22nd February

12:45

By the end of the week, the chill was that much colder, the air drier and the sky looming heavy, threatening to empty one last payload. In a steady, mechanical motion, my arms and legs pumped back and forth. Back and forth. Guiding me along the edge of the Thames, toward the Houses of Parliament. The centuries-old facade rose tall and majestic out of the icy heart of London, the spire of Big Ben disappearing into the descending gloom. Reaching the road, I checked my watch.

A new record. My stone-faced expression. As expected.

I made a left up the steps and across the bridge, taxis and buses trundling by. Uniform and in order. Crowds of people filed their way across, many in suits and coats, dozens of tourists wrapped in heavy scarves. Some homeless, holding up cards. Wanting something for nothing.

Tucking my nose up, avoiding the whiff, I gave these dregs a wide berth, tip-toeing closer to the road. Picking up the pace, I ran on past Big Ben and on toward Millbank.

On this side of the Thames and in the shadow of Westminster, the ice on the pavements stuck hard, leading me to tread a little more cautiously. Slowing the pace, I turned left off Millbank and into the gardens. There, I jogged up to a sculpture upon a large stone square. Sculptures of bronze men.

The Burghers of Calais. I knew it to be, hands on my hips, breath rolling out in small clouds of steam in the cool air. Setting my feet wide apart, directly in front of the monument, I stretched my sides, working out the thighs as well.

The monument was a strong and powerful one, I thought. Representing the English's consistent efforts, over a period of one hundred years to capture the port of Calais. To think of such strength, such persistence, was immeasurable by today's standards. In that, the history intrigued me.

Finishing my stretches and scanning the beautiful memorial park around me, I remembered that in fact, Phillip had been so determined not to let the English in, it had resulted in starvation and the eventual surrendering of Calais. Where the stereotype stems from typically. The truth, of course, being so much more impressive and heroic. And yet futile.

The French rarely surrended. Another falsehood. Another lie.

A smile played on my lips. Thinking about the detectives, trying to hold siege against the attacks around the capital. That no matter what, they would starve in the face of impossible force, leaving them no choice other than to surrender.

But the battle had only just begun, and my most significant message was yet to be executed. Assessing my surroundings, I smiled broadly, inhaling the bitter air and the smell of ice. Now I felt truly alive, just as the soldiers had before me.

'You into that sort of thing, Hudson?' Hiraoka quipped, gesturing at the elaborate graffiti wrapped halfway around the shop next door.

Hudson nudged a small pile of undisturbed snow from a fence, looked over then at a large green octopus, a skull for a head smoking a huge joint.

'Well, it's colourful, you have to admit that.'

Hiraoka grumbled.

'What? Not a fan of art?'

'That ain't art.'

'Why not?' he laughed, followed him up the path to the door. 'It's just expression through visual aid. Anyway, is this it?'

'Yup, crackpots the lot.'

Hudson watched him knock the door. Hands like rocks.

'You don't look impressed.'

'It ain't the paint, son, it's this. It's this *lead*.' And exaggerated the last word for added effect.

Since Hiraoka had sent him and Leigh on a dead-end errand to interview Miss Russell, Hiraoka had followed up on the fibre work and CCTV analysis. In the process, Moreau had been doing a little background work into Satanists. They had found that not only did a website blogged by a local resident mention rituals of human-brain removals, but that part of his traffic originated from Catherine Evans' laptop seized for evidence when visiting her student flat. A small link, but one nevertheless. If they could only follow it now to see where it went, maybe it could link the other victims? Hudson would no doubt have to work the other two, one still nameless, into the picture.

The door opened and a young man, perhaps no older than Hudson, peered inquisitively through a pair of circle rimmed glasses.

'Afternoon, are you police officers?'

The detectives exchanged a look.

'Yes. What gave us away?' Hiraoka joked, voice completely flat.

'Sorry, I just, I guessed. What can I do for you?' The pale, mousy haired man grinned nervously, gripping the door frame.

'Well,' Hiraoka said, going for his badge. 'We'd like to talk to you abo—'

The man flew at them, charging barefoot between the pair, up the path and into the road. Hudson lost his balance, slipped on the slush and into a bush. Hiraoka stumbled and shouted after him.

'Oi! Get back here!'

No joy. The mousy haired man in glasses pumped his arms wildly, flailing as he sprinted furiously up the road, avoiding the ice.

Hiraoka jogged after him, his longer stride coming to an advantage.

That and his huge boots. A few people on the street looked on, a few teenagers in hoods laughing and clapping. Getting out their phones to take a video.

The detective pursued and, as Hudson pulled himself up and charged out into the road himself, he saw the large figure of John Hiraoka rugby tackling the poor man straight into the ground.

He cried out. Game over.

Hudson stirred a sugar into Hiraoka's cup but left his alone. The small man sat opposite, name of David Green, took two sugars. Hiraoka's eyes were firmly on him at this point, but something of a grin lingered behind them. A twinkle, perhaps. What did he have planned?

A knackered living room light bulb hummed overhead, giving him a headache.

He rubbed his eyes, took hold of his cup and then focused on the weasel-faced man opposite.

'Right, David,' he started, sipping his tea. 'I think we got off on the wrong foot. You happy to start afresh?'

'Yes yes, of course, yes a fresh start, do go on. I… I was just—'

'OK, calm down,' he said. 'What's your full name?'

'David. David Green.'

'And you live alone? No family? Girlfriend? Boyfriend? Pets or anything?'

The detective hadn't noticed any food bowls or extra cups on the table.

'Nope. Just me.'

'And what do you do for work, David?'

'I work at a café in Camden. Suits me well.'

Hiraoka raised an eyebrow. 'How does that pay for your rent?'

'It doesn't. I also freelance as a writer and SEO consultant.'

'SE-what now?'

'It's website tech stuff, guv.' Hudson interjected. He rooted around for a spare pen and dated the notepad before they got going any further.

Scratching away what they had so far.

'We found your name on a website. We found a few, actually, but your one was the most… promising shall we say? Very extensive, updated regularly and quite frankly disturbing.'

'There is nothing wrong with it. Nothing wrong, detective.'

The man's voice was nasal but oddly deep for his stature. Something about his presence made Hudson nauseous. He continued to scribble.

'We'll be the judge of that. How long have you run the website?'

'Er, a little over four years.'

'Four years? And what's the purpose of the website?'

'It's a fansite. I populate the pages with interesting facts and details pertaining to satanic rituals. We have a forum—'

Hiraoka frowned. 'We?'

'I. Sorry.'

'Sure?'

'Yes. Well, I run it, but we get lots of enthusiastic contributions.'

'What, like theories on the killings? Fanfiction?'

Hudson and Green looked at Hiraoka in a new way. 'Sir?'

The chief inspector waved a hand impatiently, taking another sip of his tea. 'It's what they do on these nutter sites. They speculate nonsense, create conspiracies and write up erotic short stories about it all. It's fucked up.'

'No no, detective, we don't do any fan fiction. It's entirely professional. We're almost like yourselves, really. Detectives. Solving the mysteries of this world. Worshipping our true Lord.'

'Really?' Hudson blurted.

'Well, yes,' David said, all fear seemingly ebbing away. 'We spend a great deal of our time and money digging into old public records, reading old historical literature. Interviewing fellow Satanists, you name it.'

'Private Investigators, eh?' He glanced over at Hudson. 'Interesting. Well, you may guess then why we're here?'

Green's eyes lit up. 'Are you fellow Satanists? Surely not?'

Hudson and Hiraoka looked at each other. 'He's not half the size of our profile.'

238

'Well,' Hudson shrugged. 'Might be an accomplice?'

'Yeah, could have. Knows the tall lady in the video. Maybe they're good friends? Might even be on speaking terms with our killer? Could be a fan of that serial killer in L.A. from the eighties.'

'Ramirez?'

'Yeah, that's the one. Like Richard Ramirez.'

Green squirmed as the detectives toyed with him. The realisation burst his fantasy bubble quickly, and the stuttering returned.

'No! I had nothing to do with them! I investigate only!'

'We're not entirely convinced though,' Hiraoka pressed. 'You'll need to come down the station and let us know the details; otherwise you'll be down as a major suspect.'

'But why?'

Hiraoka leaned back, swirling the contents of his cup before putting it down on the table.

'Look. It's quite common to have copy cat killers and frankly the nature of these killings is very reminiscent of previous satanic work. Satanic worship. Brutal, sporadic and unrelenting. It stands to reason a man who runs a website, glorifying satanic murders, would want to replicate them to further their interests. Start off by learning the basics before getting a little wild with design. Am I making sense so far, mate?'

The small man had turned white. Head still shaking back and forth. 'No. Sir, no, I wouldn't. You see I don't need to replicate, why would I? The Lord has not asked it of me!'

'OK, OK. Shut up.'

Both detectives stood, leaving the man utterly perplexed. It took him a moment to splutter some semblance of language out his trap.

'Wait. You're not... you're not taking me?'

'Oh, yes, we are. You're coming down to Charing Cross station. We want an extensive list of all your contacts. People who have used the website, people interested in this sort of... stuff. And I mean, fucking everyone.' He warned, pointing a finger.

Hudson led the way out the door a few minutes later, Hiraoka leaving him to handle their suspect, bundling him unceremoniously into the back of his Renault Clio. As he placed the keys in the ignition, he glanced back into his rearview mirror. At David Green. He sat with his hands clenched in his lap. Terrified.

Maybe he did know their accomplice? Or perhaps even the killer himself?

Pulling out into the road, making a right in the direction of the city centre out of Shepherd's Bush, he couldn't help but think this all felt too convenient.

Late that night in Fitzrovia, the silent office snapped awake when Hiraoka slammed down his phone and grunted. Fatigue wore on them once more as the week drew to a close and outside, despite the new falling snow, revellers congregated outside bars and clubs to get well and truly pissed.

'Everything alright, sir?' Hudson asked, leaning back on his chair to stretch.

'No, it bloody isn't. Green's alibi checks out. Additionally, Moreau has just emailed me more details on this satanic business. Says key elements are missing from our murder scenes, meaning this has all just been a wild goose chase. Just fodder for the file. No links whatsoever with Robert Short or any mutual parties.'

Leigh gawked. 'What?'

Hiraoka just rubbed his face in his hands. 'Yup.'

'Fuck.'

Hudson echoed her sentiments exactly. 'So where does this leave us now? We still don't have an ID on victim three? We haven't traced the fibre yet to the source, and we can't locate the woman from the CCTV footage to ID her as well?'

He stood up, needing to move and went over to the Murder Board they'd started to neglect. He wrote down everything he said and stuck it down onto the map of central London. Saw pen marks along roads outside Hyde Park, around Hopkins street in Soho, and a few roads in Stratford. The mapping they had done for sightings of their mysterious blonde.

'If any of this is something to go by, the next kill is going to happen any time now. The week is up.'

Hiraoka was up too, but had reached for his coat.

'Get some sleep, team. Hudson, Haskell would have a heart attack if he knew you were still on the clock. We come back, fresh-faced, Monday morning. Should they murder tonight, or tomorrow, there is still nothing we can damn do about it. But get rest and tackle this again another day. In fact,' he boomed, looking around at the other detectives. 'That's an order. Off home, the lot of you. Go on. Get. Arigato!'

With not too much reluctance, everyone cleared out their things. Except Hudson. The guilt from his presumptive actions behind the chief inspector's back were still raw. His fears of another nightmare in bed loomed like a creeping shadow, but the hunger to work was more vital than ever. Just one more bit of CCTV. Just one clue in their notes and interview scribbles. Something would come to light. He'd missed something and knew it.

Leigh stood at the door, hand on the frame. 'Sure now, Hudders? Nguyen's got word we're all going for pints.'

'You're alright,' he said, ignoring his phone buzzing, a text from Krystina. He grabbed his mouse and logged back into his computer. 'I'll see you Monday. Have one on me.'

Friday, 22nd February

20:01

Finally, after the agonising wait of preparation and planning, it was time to action the rest of my plan. The next big message. And I'd never felt so much excitement.

Stood at the edge of Wandsworth, in thick winter gear and even thicker boots. I strolled up the road, running a gloved hand through the snow on top stone walls bordering tiny gardens. Hedgerows of holly, frosted trees and frozen ornaments in the cold. It all looked festive and beautiful despite the time of year. I had no care for it, personally, but it did look rather quaint.

Halfway down the street, hands in pockets, I peered around for anyone that might end up passing me by. There were none. Not a soul to be seen.

I was utterly alone.

Choosing my spot carefully, I found the house I wanted, squatted down between two BMWs across from the place and hid in the shadow. Should anyone walk passed, they may look down and see someone tying a lace. In a neighbourhood like this, no one would stick around. No one would take a closer look or ask questions. Not in a posh bit of South London like Wandsworth. No one was observant here. I was virtually invisible.

A half-hour passed.

I waited patiently. Keenly. Checking a watch tucked neatly beneath my gloves. Then looked back up at the door. Still, nothing. So I waited longer. Letting the snow slowly gather on top, camouflaging me that much more to the surroundings.

A low, deep rumble and the soft crunch of tyres under snow alerted me at last. I watched and waited for the car lights to dance by. It parallel parked into a nearby spot. Out climbed a man. A large, stocky man in a long, expensive-looking coat. Once out, he rummaged in the boot for what must have been a shopping bag, then trudged over to the house I'd kept tabs on. The man went in, closed the door behind him.

Time I made my move.

Slowly, on my haunches, I darted across the road, making sure I wasn't being watched. I slotted myself between the next pair of cars and then, even slower, tucked my way partially beneath the vehicle. I would not be seen. I would not be noticed.

This time, the wait was longer. The door opened again and a light, feminine voice called back into the house, telling her husband she was off out. The soft click of heels came down the steps and passed me. Then, a few moments later, another rumble and crunch of snow as a taxi pulled up to whisk her away. A taxi or an Uber, I didn't know or care.

As the car disappeared around the corner, I slowly removed my boots, beanie and gloves, pulled out from the bag my next outfit. Once changed, I shoved everything else in the bag, hid it under the car and stood up, straightening myself. Taking a deep breath, I timed it a good few minutes before slowly making my way up to the front door. Each step slow and exciting. My tongue tasted the bitter air. The cold was sweet. I was eager to do it. To see it happen again. How had I lived so long and deprived myself of these pleasures?

Taking in a deep breath, filling my lungs and rapping the door, I prepared herself for the next stage.

The man answered the door.

'Hello? Can I help you miss?'

'Oh, yes, sorry! I'm told to meet Miranda here?'

'Miranda? She's just… I'm sorry, you are?'

'Oh, forgive me,' I laughed childishly. 'I'm a friend of Miranda's from work. She just let me know she's getting a taxi in. Is she here?'

The man shook his head. 'No, sorry, you've just missed her.'

'Shit! Ah bugger,' I sighed, looking up the street. 'Listen erm, I know this is a bit ridiculous of me, but could I just stand inside out of this bleedin' blizzard until I ring a taxi or something?'

'Yeah come on in. Take your time. I'll let Miranda kn—'

'No! That's fine. I'll give her a message now.'

I smiled at him. Almost entirely bald. Large nose. Strange sort of good looking but not that good. Weird really. I stepped in out of the cold and into his hallway. A large open corridor of panelled oak and cream walls. It was very nice, yet somehow modest. I kind of liked this man's taste.

'Right,' I said, continuing my lies. 'I've sent her a message. Dear, I'm so sorry to put you out like this. I've only gone and walked half an hour here thinking I'd catch her just in time.'

'Half hour? Where have you walked here from? In this weather?'

'Oh, you know. I needed to pick up a few things from Sainsbury's. Then thought I might as well walk the rest of the way here.'

The man frowned, looking around. 'Where's your shopping?'

'Oh, what?'

'Your shopping. Where is it?'

I drew a sudden blank, realising I'd lied myself into a corner. This target would be one of the toughest to trick. I couldn't get complacent tonight of all nights.

'Didn't have what I needed. One of the things I've asked her to get. You know Sainsbury's don't do strawberry Prosecco?'

'No, sorry, I er... I don't. Didn't take Miranda for a Prosecco fan.'

'Oh, she isn't usually, but she's just got into it with us. '

'Right.' His face furrowed deep, seemed to decide all was fine, so left me in the hallway and disappeared further into the house.

Beginning to fear that he wouldn't take the bait, I swore and turned my phone off. 'Fuck!'

No answer.

'Shit. Erm, excuse me!?'

The large, bulbous faced man came sauntering back. 'What's wrong?'

'It's my phone. It's just died. Can I use yours? I am so, so sorry about this.'

He laughed at that, closing his eyes and shaking his head. 'Don't be. You're obviously having a bit of a nightmare. Friend of Miranda's is a friend of mine, I suppose. Here, come on in, excuse my poor manners. Work has me completely exhausted these days.' He showed me in, looking a bit guilty, leading the way to the living room. 'Take a seat. Want a cup of something whilst you wait for the taxi?'

'Oh yes,' I said. 'That'd be lovely actually, yes please.'

I watched him leave, turn left, further into the house. A few moments later, I heard the kettle click and start to boil.

Ah. The kitchen.

Eyes narrowing, a smile on my lips, I stood up and scanned the room. Noting the objects in place. Noting the layout and size. Just in case.

Cocking my head, I called out to him. 'Do you have a bathroom I could use?'

'Yes, second on the right before the stairs.'

I left quickly, going into the bathroom and checking my reflection. Inside my coat, a longer, sharper knife. More sinister and cruel than the ones I had previously used. This one had been long delayed and was worthy of more attention. Time to go to work.

Leaving the bathroom, knife in hand, chucking my coat on the sofa, I entered the kitchen with it hidden behind my back.

'Oh, you're making tea?'

'Yea, want coffee instead?'

I feigned a laugh. Noticed the coffee tin over the other way and made my move. 'Yes, please. Coffee.'

The large man turned, reached for the coffee and never saw it coming.

Racing forward, crashing into him, I plunged the large blade into the base of his left shoulder blade, then out and again into the base of his neck as he fell face-first into the cupboards. Crying out, he slumped down onto the kitchen floor, scrambling about with his arms.

This one was putting up a fight!

As he turned to face me, I went to work on his chest, plunging it in, hard and fast. It took a lot more effort than the first man I'd killed, to penetrate the chest. It was firmer, more solid, and I had to duck and weave to escape his swipes or have my DNA find a home under his fingernails.

His face was a picture. Eyes bulging in surprise.

Fear. Despair.

He clawed at me but failed. Not quite reaching. Soon, the blood seeped out, his life force flowing with it and he slumped dead against the cabinets, hands palm up in a steadily growing pool of his own blood.

I finally let out a gasp of air. 'Fuck, that was too close.'

I stood, steady, stepping away to take it all in. His heavy body slumped and lifeless. Wasting no time, concerned about the noise that might have been heard from neighbours, I turned on the TV, wiped the remote and came back to the kitchen with my hammer.

My hand hovered in the air for a moment. As if second-guessing my entire plan. Amused more than anything, I instead took the seconds to savour the opportunity I'd carved out for myself. A chance to do real work. Something that mattered. Then swung the hammer down hard enough to shatter the man's skull.

After twenty or so minutes of carefully scalping, opening the skull and completing my best encephalectomy yet, I gingerly held it up and placed it onto the kitchen counter above the body. There, it stood fleshy pink, its surface glistening and wrinkled. Satisfied with my latest work, I felt I could start to pack things away, make my stage exit.

So, meticulously, I looked myself over and began removing things that had gotten hit. I meandered my way through the living room and to the bathroom. There, I placed a thick layer of tissues down and laid my stuff down on that. Then, running the taps, I began a hasty clean, so I could depart without leaving any marks. After what seemed like hours, I finished up, put on my coat, washed my face and flushed all the tissue down the toilet.

'Double check,' I told myself. 'Don't be careless. You have plenty of time. Leave the kitchen; that can remain as it is.'

And I did. His wife wouldn't be back for hours. Perhaps not until the next day. So I squatted, pulled out some surgical gloves and looked for blood. For stray hairs. For anything. I noticed a few things and set them right, then left the bathroom. I went to the hallway, dropped my shoes on the carpet and returned to the living room.

'Hmm, it's missing something,' I mused, looking to the kitchen, still seeing the wide-eyed man staring blankly out ahead of him. 'Something special. This calls for a change.'

I raised a finger. 'I think a note would do well.'

I looked about the house, careful of what I touched and where I stepped. Along one of the hallways, I entered a little study. There, I took a pen and paper, returned to the living room and mused about what I would write. Drawing a blank, I walked back to the kitchen, admiring my handy work.

'I need inspiration! Give me something!' My eyes lit up almost immediately. 'I've got it!'

Almost half an hour passed, and the note was finished. I'd taken great care to ensure the letters were evenly sized, some of them a little awry and the lettering as masculine as possible. I was well aware of linguistics and the forensic department they had in the Met, and they were looking for a large man. Who knows, he may have girly handwriting? But this was perfect. In capitals with some very generic habits. I was good.

Sealing it off, I took the note and placed it on the man's lap.

Chief Superintendent Haskell of the Metropolitan Police. My face exploded with joy.

'Oh, Haskell, you really didn't see that coming, did you? Victim of your own case? The one bringing your department and shoddy police network to its knees. All helped along by the sheer incompetence of poor recruitment, a fucking half-wit and old fool. Pathetic. It's been a pleasure toying with you all. But this was definitely an itch I needed to scratch.'

And with that, I turned and left. Outside, I skulked low and dived toward the car, grabbed my boots, bag and beanie. Changed quickly and then zigzagged around the vehicles over the course of another half an hour. The timing deliberate, to throw off any possible onlookers who had caught sight of me from their windows. They'd assume me to be a neighbour, or just a local. Nothing of bother. Perhaps even, by glance, a stray fox.

Never a woman who had just brutally butchered a senior member of the police in his own home.

I couldn't stop smiling. Jumping for joy. I was back in the swing. Fourth kill under my belt, and what a kill it was. Perhaps the most poignant brain for display yet. Truly, my message could not go ignored now. The city, indeed, the entire country would now see.

And as I rode the tube back home, I already knew who my fifth would be.

Friday, 22nd February

23:12

Something stuck to his face. Hudson rose his head, groggy, grabbed at a piece of A4 lined paper and peeled it off.

'Ugh.'

Looking up, blurry-eyed, he realised he'd fallen asleep at his desk. The time a little past eleven in the evening. Rubbing his eyes, he looked around the office, oddly enchanting and a little spooking in the darkness. The only light, a strange half amber glow, seeping in through the windows.

Then something else. As he stirred, sitting back in his chair and rubbing out a knot that had built up at the bottom of his neck, Hudson thought he saw something blue flashing, then lights flickering on, and then the sound of rushing footsteps pounding up the stairs.

DS Hunt came charging in, looking relieved to see him there.

'Said you were here. Working late against orders.' He paused, face pale and struggling to get the words out. Angry almost. 'DC Hudson, we've got another murder. We'll be having people arrive shortly, more from the station. Neighbouring MIT's. Uniforms. We've also got Scotland Yard coming down and then someone from the other station in Wandsworth. Armed police too. Get your things.'

'Wait, what? What's going on? It's fucking two in the morning.'

'It's Haskell, Hudson. He's been killed by the surgeon.'

The blood rushed away from him. His skin cold, eyes wide. A pump of adrenaline shot through him then, and he found himself walking toward DS Hunt in a dream-like state. Grabbing his coat and keys.

'Lead the way.'

Hunt drove him there, the pair silent. It wasn't until they crossed the river that Hudson quizzed him on the location of the murder. Grabbing a coke from his glove box to get a quick boost. Hunt told him it was at his home in Wandsworth and that the whole place was on lockdown. It was utter chaos. They'd have to fight their way through to get to the scene.

'Jesus,' Hudson swore. 'Is this really happening?'

'I know,' he said. 'This will be national security now. The Mayor is to make an announcement tomorrow as well. Fuck knows how the media will take this, but it won't be good. We still don't have a fucking suspect, and that won't look good on Hiraoka. We'll have to make this a twenty-four-hour jobby. This is it. Ah, here we are.'

Hunt pulled up at the end of a street, waved at some uniforms in their high vis in the snow. They came over, checked their badges and then waved them in. Hunt parked up almost immediately, a massive convoy of police vehicles, ambulances and other vans congesting the entire road.

'Fucking. Hell,' Hudson whispered, climbing out of Hunt's BMW. 'It's a fucking circus.'

'Wait until you get inside. But before you do, wait for Hiraoka. He's fucking pissed.'

Hudson was dreading that. His reaction. How it would hit him, but as he slowly moved his way through the crowds of police and other law enforcement officials, he bumped into DC Leigh, who was in tears, leaned up against a squad car.

She was being comforted by DC Nguyen.

'Hi both, I've just been told. Jesus Christ. Leigh, how're you holding up?'

'How the fuck do you think, Hudson? How do you fucking think?'

250

She started crying, failing badly at holding it all back. 'I can't. I need a walk.'

She stormed off with Nguyen at her heels, his face also run with tears. He threw Hudson a filthy look, leaving him standing helpless and guilty.

Shit.

Carrying on, he soon found Hiraoka descending the steps to the front door of a large terrace house. It was quite a nice place. Big. The sort of house, he supposed, Haskell would have lived in, after a long career in the police force.

Hiraoka spotted Hudson, shook his head and then walked over to meet him.

Out of the corner of his left eye then, a shape darted from the crowd, hands clawing at the air, screaming loudly. Her soul in anguish.

Miranda Haskell, his wife.

Officers tried to restrain her, but Hiraoka intercepted her, fighting her attacks and attempts to break free and bolt into the house to find her dead husband. Eventually, the strength left her, and she sobbed into the chief inspector's shoulders. Hudson watched on in pain, a lump in his throat. Hiraoka slowly ushered her away from the front gate, back into the street with two liaison officers by a police ambulance car. There, she collected herself momentarily before breaking down again.

Face etched with grief, Hiraoka walked his way through the crowd to Hudson.

'Don't rush to head in there, Hudson. It isn't pretty.' He paused, staring around helplessly. 'Haskell. I can't fucking believe it.'

'I'm still in shock. His poor wife. What are they going to do now? Hunt thinks this case will be turned on its head. Matter of national security now with police officers getting killed. Could escalate.'

Hiraoka shook his head. 'Nah. National security, yeah, but we'll just get even more resource. We'll be overseen now. And Miranda, she'll be looked after. Make sure she's... she's... shit! Fuck fuck fuck!' He threw his cigarette packet at a tree and paced the pavement, face in his hands. Swearing quickly in Japanese.

Hudson winced. He hadn't heard him lose it or swear quite like that since the time they'd busted up the crack head down in Poplar almost two weeks ago.

'Sir?'

'Come on,' he said, after taking a moment to gather himself. Combing his hair out of his eyes. 'Let's both go in. I need to process this alongside you, really. I'll show you what we have.'

The pair made their way up the steps, passing SOCO members, other officers standing guard and a few other seniors making notes and wandering the halls. It really was a fucking circus. As they crossed the threshold, people were bagging up any item they could get their hand on. Dusting surfaces. Taking pictures. But the real action was in the kitchen, where a significant bit of tape stretched right across the doorway.

Hudson approached anxiously, navigating the strategically placed plastic stepping blocks to avoid damaging potential evidence.

'In there?'

Hiraoka moved his head just a little. 'Yup. Need a bag?'

'No.' And he didn't.

The face was butchered beyond recognition. Hudson noted the look in his face, the sheer shock. His mouth still gawking at whatever Chief Superintendent Haskell had last seen in his dying moments. Tongue lolling out down the side of his ruined mouth. Half of his nose peeling off and his left eye all but gone.

'Fucking hell,' he swore, holding it in.

No one said a word. It was silent. Everyone just quietly going on about their job. No one had the energy. Emotionally and physically exhausted. Everyone was in a state of shock. Their one and only; the big man himself, was gone. Taken down by what the news was calling a satanic monster lurking the streets of London. And now, after this, it would catch on like wildfire.

Hell had come to London.

He could picture the headline now. And the gaggle of Met officers trying to piece together a case on fuck all forensics, poor eyewitnesses and no leads whatsoever.

The killer was winning.

'Evening detectives.' Came a very well pronounced voice from the door.

The pair turned to see a man of medium height, a slight paunch hidden in a jacket and open shirt. Despite being clean shaved and wrinkle-free, the man looked ancient with a full head of hair. It was his eyes that gave it away.

'Sir,' Hiraoka said, reaching out and shaking his hand. 'Oh, sorry erm, sir, this is Detective Constable Daniel Hudson, my new detective constable on the case. Hudson this is Co—'

'Commander Michael Elms. I've heard a lot about you.'

'Elms will do fine, son. Good things, I hope.'

Hudson nodded.

'I'm told one of our finest is dead in his kitchen?' He asked.

'Yes sir, SOCO are still processing the scene.'

The commander beckoned them and lead the way out of the house, sidestepping passed numerous experts and Met officers. Out on the steps, a few neighbours up the street peering over from their own stoops, Elms spoke bluntly to the detectives.

'Things are going to change. A senior officer, one of our finest, is dead in there. Murdered. I plan to hold the entire special force accountable, beginning with you two. I want to know why this killer wasn't in custody after the second killing. I want every damn crumb and seed on this whole case. Is that perfectly, crystal clear?'

'Yes sir,' they both muttered.

'Good.' And he left, taking the steps slowly and walking away toward the tent and pulling out his phone.

Hudson let out a breath he didn't know he was holding. 'Shit.'

'Shit indeed, Hudson.'

'Who's he calling?'

'Everyone. Commissioner, deputy commissioner. They'll be calling the Prime Minister, the Mayor. Everyone, before the Daily fucking Mail slams a headline on this by breakfast.'

He groaned, picturing the titles. Picturing the fiasco a Bethany Shaw horror column would cause, and how bad it would make the Met look.

The killer would be lapping it all up, of course, being out in the limelight. All the glory and fame they were seeking. It was all theatrics.

From behind a group of uniforms, Petridis in white overalls walked out of the house and down the steps to the front garden, making for Hiraoka's attention.

'Sir, got something you might want to look at.' And produced a sealed bag with a piece of paper in it.

'What's this? The note?'

'Yup, we've done our bit. Thought you might want to get a head start on that until we finish processing.'

The chief inspector nodded, carefully taking the bag and peering intently at the contents.

'Odd.'

'What does it say?' Hudson asked.

'One sec.' Hiraoka walked back into the house and looked at it in some light. 'Capitals, handwritten, not very long. This is new.'

Hiraoka read it a few times, shook his head and thrust it at Hudson.

DEAR DETECTIVES

I EXPECTED MORE. A LOT MORE.

MY EFFORTS TONIGHT, I HOPE, HAVE NOT BEEN IN VAIN AND YOU CAN BASK NOW IN MY GLORIOUS AND RIGHTEOUS MESSAGE.

DO YOU SEE YOUR TRUE SELVES NOW? I HOPE I HAVE HELPED TO SHOW YOU WHY I DO WHAT I DO. PERHAPS THEN YOU CAN UNDERSTAND AND WORSHIP THIS AS YOU SHOULD.

WE ARE NOT WHAT WE ARE.

SEE YOU SOON.

Hudson re-read it a few times as well, letting the whole, narcissistic tone of it seep in.

'Fucking hell, the prick's a psychopath!'

'We already knew that. The man is clearly growing hungrier for fame. After that media blow out, he's gone and done this.' He pointed into the house, composed himself for a moment. 'High profile killing. A police officer. High media coverage. A note. He must be out there somewhere jerking himself off, waiting for the news to hit.'

'Jesus.'

'Door-to-doors already?' Hudson quizzed, seeing a few uniforms dotted up and down the street.

'Yeah, only a few. They'll do the night shift. We'll come back first thing and grab the witness accounts. We have to have some consistency and solid statements going forward. We want to nail this bastard.'

Hudson nodded, giving the bag back.

'No, you pass that on. We need that with forensic linguistics asap. Know where to go?'

'Yup.'

'Good. Get that over, go home, grab a wink and a shower, and I'll see you here again first thing.'

Hudson paused on the steps, still not taking it all in. Least of all, a free sending home by the guv.

'Sir? What about the suspect? Are these Satanist groups dead ends? Have we missed something?'

Hiraoka waved a hand. 'No use with SOCO here. I want you fully wired because tomorrow will be...' He checked his watch. 'Today will be a busy day. Nothing's a dead end yet.'

'Yeah, okay. And sir, are you alright?'

The chief inspector stood, silhouetted in the doorway, one hand gripping the frame for support. 'No, Daniel, I am not. Haskell and I were...' He paused. 'He was a good friend.'

Saturday, 23rd February

06:07

Strangled screams and the sticky wet of blood woke Hudson. Jolting upright, he noticed a carton of silt lemon tea juice. The source of the *blood*. Taking in deep breathes, he sat up on the edge of the bed, feeling the carpet between his toes. Chucking the empty drink into the bin.

The nightmare had been different this time. A new location. Someone else had been with him. He could feel it. But the way he died was the same. The horrid sensation of his scalp peeling back. The hammer coming down and waking up with a start.

The acrid taste tingled beside his tongue, his throat clenched and, with a sudden whoosh, Hudson felt hot bile jump out from his gut and splash right between his feet.

A voice at the door roused him. 'Oh, Jesus, Daniel,' Eisa cried.

In mere moments Eisa had the coffee on, cleaning up the mess whilst Hudson was left huddled on the sofa, nursing his head. Shaking.

'You going to add medical costs to the rent?' he asked, wrapping a blanket around himself. Hudson was a tall man, well built but his weakened disposition and huddling made him appear a child again.

'Spare me your wit, Daniel and drink this.'

Hudson took the cup, watched his thespian friend plop right next to him, hands fidgeting.

'Sorry mate.'

Eisa just shrugged. 'It's about that time, isn't it?'

'Yeah, work.'

'I've got a lot to do today, sorry I can't offer a more sympathetic and caring version of myself. Lots of cataloguing and orders to do. Not to mention money. It's all a bit chaotic, as it were. I'll have to leave you to it. Do try and take it easy on yourself today. Hydrate yourself thoroughly, is a good bit of advice too. Helps avoid those nasty headaches from the stress. See you tonight.' And she just got up and left the room. Closing the bedroom door behind her.

'Eisa?' He called, but no answer came. Instead, Hudson was left alone, nursing the morning filter, inhaling the drug. Was this all getting too much for him?

Before he left, he noticed a bag by her door. A black backpack. Wondered if, maybe, things weren't going so well with the shop. He really should go down and visit the place sometime soon, when this was all over.

Popping another bit of gum in and swirling some freshwater around, Hudson wiped a runny nose on the back of his coat jacket, waiting for Hiraoka. When the chief inspector appeared, black hair slicked back and a fresh cigarette already glowing in his hands, the man had a look about him. A man who'd get things done. But it was still dark at this time, so the faint, luminous glow from the street lights only made him appear more sinister.

'Morning guv.'

Hiraoka nodded, taking a drag.

'Nice walk?' Hudson jibbed, trying to lighten the mood.

'Cab,' he grunted. 'Waited like a good boy?'

'Sir, only been here a few minutes.'

Hiraoka put out the cigarette on a wrought iron gate beside him. Chucked it under a car to his right and shoved his hands into his coat pockets. Like every other day, he wore a long, dark grey overcoat, set up by the same bright red scarf. 'No time to waste, come on.'

He knocked the front door of a house at random. Tall, black with a brass knocker. Most of the houses here on Haskell's street were reasonably pleasant. His wife had been a doctor, and so both their incomes had afforded them a small luxury.

Haskell…

The man was gone. How could that be? His booming voice and presence filled the office. Gave Hudson that small vial of warmth and courage to go on. But no more. The air was empty. Instead, left with the constant threat of the chief inspector.

Fear now permeated everything and everyone. A horrible, itchy sort of anxiety that circulated the Met. Anyone could be next if the killer was now targeting coppers. Anyone.

They spent the next hour or two up and down the street, knocking on doors catching people before they left for work. Most were hurried, and so information obtained was loose at best. In short, not a single bloody witness and nothing suspicious except a missing cat.

The pair were growing steadily impatient and angry by the time they reached yet another door further down.

'Good Morning, I'm DCI Hiraoka, this is DC Hudson. We're here to ask a few questions regarding the murder last night.'

A blurry-eyed man, short, his dressing gown half undone, grunted at him. 'Wha?'

'Yesterday evening, your neighbour, our Chief Superintendent Haskell, was murdered in his home. This occurred between nine and eleven pm. We wanted to ask you a few questions about what you may have seen or heard.'

'Nuffink.'

Hudson shifted next to Hiraoka. 'Nothing suspicious over the last few days, perhaps? Anyone loitering?'

'I just fuckin' told you, didn't I?'

Before the pair could retort, a loud, shrill voice came from inside the house.

'Alfie, who is it?'

'No one,' he shouted back and closed the door.

Hudson's mouth fell open and gawked at the door. Then turned to Hiraoka. 'Sir, did he ju—'

'Yup.'

Hiraoka knocked on the door.

No answer.

He knocked again but a little harder. He waited patiently till the door swung open and the old short arse was there, growling.

'Wha? I'm busy!'

The chief inspector drew out his badge, showed it to the man then pointed a finger down the road toward the house Haskell once lived in. Once cooked eggs in. Made love to his wife in.

'A copper worth two of you was taken from us. Lived in that house over there. We have a few questions that need answering, so if you'd do me th—'

'Piss off. I tol' you before. We don't know nuffink, mate. Ask someone else.'

Hudson made to butt in, but Hiraoka was quicker. Calmer.

'Sir, these questions will only occupy a little of your time.'

The loud squeal from inside came again, except this time it was giving commands. 'Shut the door, ya letting in the cold! Come on!'

On cue, the old man started closing the door again, grumbling, when it thudded to a stop inches from the latch.

'The fuck?'

Hiraoka used his foot to push it open, grabbing it with a free hand.

'Invite us in, answer our questions, or I'll have you for possession.'

Hudson got more uncomfortable, started looking up and down the street to see if anyone was watching. He was doing it again. But in light of recent events, he couldn't care less today. Maybe more tomorrow, but right now, he was fuelled more by revenge and anger than any semblance of logic and control.

'Sir?' he asked. 'Should we?'

'Let us in.' Hiraoka asked one more time. A shocked look on the old man's face and a slump of his shoulders hinted they had won, thought the small man kept shooting the detective fearful looks as they crossed the threshold.

Large, open, full of light, the place was a complete shit hole. Betraying its gorgeous exterior facade. Old phone books and letters filled the corridor and, being led to a dining room on the right, this too was piled high.

Hiraoka kicked something in his way, heard a cat dart from the room.

'Don't clean much, do you?'

'Wha' d'ya want?!' he wheezed, slumping into a battered Chesterfield, lighting up a cigarette and shuffling some spoons into a drawer beside him. The chief inspector saw plain and clear. So did Hudson. What kind of dirty game was he about to play now?

'Think I'll stand, if you don't mind. But I want to ask you and your girlfriend what you saw last night.'

The man licked his bottom lip, looked up at the detective and coughed. 'She's not here. She's... at shops. She's at the shops. Sorry detective.'

Hiraoka hung his head.

'I. Just. Fucking. Heard her! She's upstairs, go fucking get her!' he roared, rearing up to full height and terrifying the neighbour.

A small squeal came from his throat as he cowered away, stumbling from the room to call upstairs. 'Babe, babe, come dan 'ere. Policemen got questions 'bout over the road. Nuffink else, honest.' The man turned to Hiraoka. 'Promise?'

'I promise.'

'Sir,' Hudson said, interrupting the scene. The old man startled. 'Can I er... just nip outside? Gotta make a call.'

Thunder stormed in his eyes. But nodded and waved at the door. 'Be quick.'

Out in the fresh air, Hudson fumbled for his phone and dialled home. When it answered, it wasn't his Mum who answered.

'Alright Grandad?'

'Phwuh! Hello there Daniel. Bit early, isn't it? How's the city treatin' ya eh? Been a good while now since you last called.'

'Not too bad,' he lied.

'The whole village still talks about that girl you saved.'

'Really? Old news by now, surely?'

'Yeah, but it's Gotham, innit?'

Hudson grinned. 'Yeah. How is she doing? Elsa?'

'Not 'eard much, but I know she's with her Mum now. They moved south. Kettering, I think.'

'Ah right. Er, is mum there?'

'Nah, she's popped out. Why?'

Hudson paused, peering down the street at the crime scene tape still strung across Haskell's home. 'Er, nothing. I actually don't know why I called. Well, I do, but I just wanted to just… you know...'

A deep laugh crackled a little from the other end. 'Stop wafflin' for cryin' out loud.'

'Sorry. Well, how's things up there? How's the memory?'

Hudson could almost hear him shrugging matter of fact. 'Well, still good. Only one or two things every other day. You sure you're alright?'

'Yeah,' he lied again. 'It's all good. Just… busy. Right well, tell mum I said hello.'

'Will do kid, ta ra.'

'Bye.'

Before he walked back in, he dried his eyes, sniffed the snot back up, and straightened his coat. No time for rest.

'Pull a chair over,' Chief Inspector Hiraoka asked of Hudson, just as he started looking at the murder board.

Hudson wheeled a spare one to the empty floor, sat down and produced his notes. 'Gunna go through that woman's statement then are we?'

'We are indeed.'

'Hunt doing the statement?'

He nodded. 'Yup, but we'll go over your notes. What was your first impression of her, what was your gut feeling?'

Hudson frowned, fiddling with the corner of the desk. 'Erm, I dunno.

Scared, I suppose, why?'

'No seriously, what was your genuine first impression of her. The vibe you got?'

'Scared. I'll stick with that, I think she was scared.'

'Does that marry up with your notes?'

'Erm,' he stalled, flipping through his notebook. 'Late evening, had been drinking, hallucinated a giant cat running beneath the cars. I'm going to say no.'

'No, of course not,' Hiraoka shouted, clutching his head and scaring a few of the uniforms behind him. 'She's mad. Our first possible witness to anything odd is a drug addict, who was drunk the night of the killing and saw a giant cat. You sure you haven't cursed me, Hudson, I had a good thing going.'

'He did you know,' laughed the all-too-familiar sound of DC Leigh. 'Alright both? Moreau's done another batch of tea if you want it?'

'Oh yes, please,' Hudson gasped, grabbing a cup from her hands. Hiraoka ignored this.

'Suit yourself. So, I just saw Hunt taking some properly rancid bitch down to the station. That our witness number one?'

Hudson took a slow look at the inspector, took a steady sip of his herbal blend and had an idea. 'What if the cat, which was the killer fleeing, snagged on any of the cars? DNA? Fibres? Something to match what's already being profiled? Maybe match it with the door at the cinema? Some way to link the crime scenes aside from MO?'

Hiraoka shook his head. Standing up, he stretched his arms wide. 'We'll have to wait for forensics on that. Again, we're looking at weeks or months on those reports, if we do find anything. Anything else?'

'No, sir.'

'Fucking amazing.'

DS Hunt dropped the papers onto Commander Elm's desk, stood back and gave Hudson a strange look. It hadn't taken long at all. Alarmingly quick, in fact, for Elms to fill in the space that Haskell had left. Of course, it was all interim measures, but the level of authority was enormously daunting for the detectives of Fitzrovia's central west murder investigation team. As a commander, Elms would oversee the staff and help develop and present how the case and operation would look going forward. Particularly to the public, a matter of grave importance.

Public perception.

They were also in mourning. Had lost not just their leader but a friend to many. Hudson only regretted not having the chance to get to know him more.

The sergeant tapped the files with a long finger.

'That's the statement, sir. Fits with Hudson's scribblings, but it looks bad.'

'Yes,' Hiraoka charged in, standing beside Hunt in a power play. 'It's a weak witness, but it confirms they were outside waiting. Confirms they may have been planning and…'

'Shhhh,' Elms sounded, putting a finger to his lips.

'Sir?'

'Shhhh,' he repeated.

Hudson stiffened then and clenched his fists inside his pockets in anxious attainment of the verdict. They'd fucked up.

Elms picked up the statement, slowly read through each bit meticulously and re-read it. Once done, he placed the papers back in order, set it down and crossed his arms.

'Again.'

No one said a thing. Not at first. Hudson kept his gob shut and Hunt had to show off how big his balls were.

'Sorry, commander, could you clarify what you are meaning?'

'Conduct the door-to-doors again. Properly, this time.'

Hiraoka chuckled. A laugh with no warmth in it. He pressed against Haskell's old desk and tucked his chin in, his voice almost muffled. 'With all due respect, sir—'

'With all due respect, Detective Chief Inspector John Katashi Hiraoka, I have heard quite enough of the failings of this investigation.

All your past achievements do not wash away the stain on this unit. The Mayor of London shall make a formal announcement tomorrow. A delay. Can you imagine why that might be?'

Hiraoka met his eyes. Waited. Hudson stood rooted to the spot. Shocked at hearing his full name being voiced, making the man he feared seem so vulnerable. Exposing the belly of a wolf.

'Your books were not up-to-scratch. The whole thing is a mess. And if someone doesn't straighten this circus out quickly, we'll have another box to put into the already overflowing cold case locker. Do I make myself perfectly, crystal, see-through, transparently clear, detective?' He roared the last but one word, causing everyone to piss themselves a little.

He bowed his head in the traditional Japanese mannerism. Something Hudson hadn't seen him do before. Hiraoka forgot himself a little, tapped the desk and left. Seemingly annoyed. Followed by Hunt and Hudson.

'Sir,' he called, following him to his desk, Leigh looking up from hers, Nguyen turning from the murder board and Hunt in step with Hudson. All wanting to immediately round on the chief inspector.

'Sir.'

Hiraoka ignored him, reaching for his phone and pausing. Looking conflicted, he tapped the phone against his palm, paced a little, the others watching nervously.

'Right, we have some details back from Nita and Charlie. The type of blade used in the murder. I want you, Hudson, to go with Hunt to nip off and do that, me and Leigh will take another stab at this door-to-door. Nguyen, round up any stragglers, look at the note, push those linguists on that. See if we can put together a bigger profile.'

Nguyen nodded, immediately dialling up the forensics team. Moreau in the background, busy.

Hunt, who stood quite a bit taller than Hudson, planted a hand on his shoulder. Hudson bit his tongue.

'Guv, sure you don't want me to come do those? I've been known to he—'

'I know. That's fine. Just work with Hudson whilst we do this. It's...'

Hiraoka checked his phone again and swore. 'Er… rotate. Yeah, it's good to rotate.'

Hudson frowned, noticing the look on his face. 'Alright sir?'

'What? Yeah, come on, chop-chop let's not make the man angrier than he is.'

Saturday, 23rd February

13:30

Hunt opted to drive. Sought an opportunity to flash his BMW. Hudson hadn't been that fond of the man, seemed a bit cocksure of himself, but couldn't argue how comfortable the ride was to Nita's mortuary. Since joining the team, Hunt gave him the impression he wasn't welcome. A missing piece that didn't fit.

At regular intervals, the sergeant had sought to belittle him, ridicule him in front of the other detectives and staff on the case. Not to forget the events just a week or so ago.

Stepping out, Hudson almost slipped. Black ice had frozen under the fresh layer of snow from the other night, making the roads and paths that much more dangerous. He remembered seeing something about that in the Evening Standard. Watch out for black ice.

'Steady on,' Hunt laughed, edging himself carefully across the pavement.

Hudson gave him the bird behind his back.

Inside out of the cold, rubbing hands, Hudson reluctantly followed Hunt's lead and met Nita downstairs amongst the raw concrete walls and exposed pipes.

'Hi both, where's John?' Nita fired, tucking a clipboard under her arm. She looked thoroughly miserable. The news had travelled fast.

'He's on other calls,' Hunt said. 'We're told you have something?'

'Straight to business then? Fine.'

Nita directed them into her work area, put the clipboard down on the desk and walked over to the storage units. Grasping the middle one and opening it, she pulled out their man from the first murder. Mr Short, the city banker divorcee. Then, she pulled out the one just next to it, the girl from Soho. Catherine Evans, the young student from Abingdon.

'Right, Charlie is busy. I'll show you these two first, shall I?' She looked up at Hunt, challenging him.

He smirked.

'Right then, did Haskell come this way?'

'No,' she said. 'He's with Wandsworth. Let's just get to business, shall we?'

Hudson gave her an encouraging smile and put his hands in his pockets. 'You said you had a clue on the brand of knife? How did you manage that?'

Nita lunged at this. 'Not easy, come take a look at these.'

Pulling on a fresh set of gloves, she opened the body bags and revealed the cool, white, pallid cadavers. Naked. Lost from the world. Except they were littered with frozen marks, their faces crudely reconstructed from the terrible damage. Wating to be returned to next-of-kin for appropriate burial. Though perhaps cremation, in Robert Short's case.

Hudson held himself together. Saw that Hunt had no problem at all and hated him just a bit more for it.

'Here, we have multiple entries, frenzied, almost passionate. A lot of strength was used to make such cuts but, after a lot of work, I've been able to compare knives. If you look at this one here, for example.' She tugged at the one on Short's stomach first, opening the dry wound. 'The entry is deep, precise, and the flesh around isn't jagged. Suggesting that the victim was caught off guard. Surprised. No movements to stop their attacker. But notice their width? I've measured them all, and they're all between one inch and one point two inches. That's very precise. And the depth, though they vary depending on the muscle and soft tissue it's plunging through, measure at only four inches.'

Hunt folded his arms, peering down at the wound. 'So, a knife measuring one inch by four inches. That's hardly narrowing it down, is it?'

'No,' she said. 'It isn't. That's just the first step. Next, I analysed how the flesh and muscle were torn. How the skin broke upon impact. It's very clean, suggesting a purpose-built knife, not a kitchen implement or the sort. So we've narrowed it down again. And, based on its size, it's likely to be a hunting knife or a small, handheld military-type instrument. Look here at the girl too.'

She walked around and opened the bag to Evans. Her face put together again, and the body a litter of lines and cuts. Nita pointed at a few chest wounds and compared them to Short.

'See the similarities? The girl's wounds are a bit deeper due to her incapacity and strength, but the stab wounds are very much alike. The same can be said for our John Doe, but he was sent off for further analysis at another Morgue with more capacity, in Hampstead.'

'That's not usual, is it?' Hudson asked.

'It's not. No. But a bloke there wanted to help.'

'Elms?'

She nodded. 'He probably had something to do with it. Out of my hands. Literally. Seems this is now beyond any of us.'

Nita put away the bodies, walked across to her laptop and brought up a few pages. 'We, naturally, have an extensive catalogue of blades and knives to compare. I took note of the sharpness and the size and filtered through. Presented with a few dozen knives, I picked out the lot.'

'Bloody hell, that is a lot,' Hudson said, shaking his head.

'Yes, it is. Had to buy some of them myself for testing because we didn't have copies. So, I went to the local abattoir and stuck a few piggies.'

Hudson cocked his head back. 'What?'

'She's taking the piss, Hudson,' Hunt grunted. 'Want to skip to the conclusion? I'm assuming you tested each of these blades and came up with a variety of matches?'

'Nope. Had to hire some help.'

'Help?'

Nita shook her head. 'I'm barely eight stone. The killer is profiled at a minimum of fifteen based on the weight of these attacks. Plus the height. I got a guy in to stab some test blocks. Measured the stabs and made comparisons.'

Hunt laughed. 'Is this why the case has lumbered on? Been playing about down here for over a fortnight?'

Nita didn't respond, keeping whatever she wanted to say to herself. They all knew damn well that the following experiments would take place at the lab, not down in the mortuary. Nita would have simply supervised.

'We established three matches from a collection of several hundred. Two large pen knives and a small handheld military grade knife. I have them here.'

She opened up a box to her right and showed them both the tools of death.

Hunt smirked, picked one up and lunged suddenly at the constable.

'Fucking hell!' he shouted, but Hunt was laughing, putting the knife back in the box.

'Er, I'd appreciate it if you behaved yourself whilst in my office, detective. Doubt Elms would look kindly on a sergeant playing pranks, especially insensitive given the time and circumstances.'

At the mention of his name, Hunt shook his head. 'It's a joke, calm down. So we have these three, is it? Nice. What about Haskell's? So how does this profile our killer?'

She shrugged. 'That's your job, isn't it, Detective Hunt?'

Hudson smiled.

'Humour me,' he spat.

'My notes are emailed to John. I'll be sure to CC you in next time.'

Hunt shook his head, nudged a scalpel around on her desk before choosing to depart, leaving Nita behind in her dungeon of death, amongst the cold and the soulless. For such a cheerful woman, it really suited her. Hudson couldn't bare it. Things didn't change much above ground, the air still bitter and dry, with big gusts whipping in to crack at their skin, bite at the exposed bits. But at least there wasn't the putrified smell of decay.

'Time we got back and delivered the news,' Hunt said, happy to be done, too.

Back at the station, Hiraoka still absent, Hudson walked straight over to the murder board, unbuttoning his coat. Hunt went to his computer, opened his emails and peered over at Hudson from across the office.

'Hudson, what're you doing?'

He peeled his eyes away from a photo of Catherine Evans and glared at him.

'I'm reviewing what we have, but I think it might be worth calling up a list of knife shops in London. Making a few rounds and checking sales and CCTV for the last few months.'

'No. Hudson. We need to be reviewing case files, making sure what we have is up to scratch. The portfolio of evidence is under your remit. Anyway, Moreau can work the online orders and see what sort of traffic and UK shipments have been made under those specs. Call around.'

Nguyen, somehow slipping in to the feud without being noticed, coughed. 'If the serial killer is relatively new to this, as is suggested by the forensic evidence we've already reviewed, then I think checking retailers for recently purchased equipment is a good shout.'

'Mate,' he implored, opening a hand toward Nguyen. 'We have to cover all bases. Elms isn't going to want any stones left unturned now, is he?'

'It's a waste of time not looking into it.'

Hunt laughed, shaking his head and waving a hand over at Hudson. 'Crack on with those calls by end of play then. Nguyen is old fashioned and forgets how to do proper police work. Getting a bit aged, our boy is.'

No laughs from around the office.

Nguyen ignored it all, walked straight to Hudson and pointed at the murder board. 'Focus on this. Follow John's lead and ignore this prick.

Take a look at what you have and review for gaps. Like the CCTV trawl we did, just go back over. We can't afford to fuck this up, even on a procedural level. So if you have to go over the files again, do so. But personally, your time would be much better spent on the phone and checking specialist knife sales. Worst case, it's another avenue we've blocked off. Because it wouldn't be entirely unlikely they purchased it off the books. Especially given their extra-curricular activities.'

Hudson nodded. A sense of self-respect and honour exuding from the stocky man. 'Planned to regardless.'

'Good.'

'How're things going here?'

'They're not,' he grunted, hands on his hips. 'What did Nita have to say?'

'Three matches to the blade used in the attack.'

'Well, let's have a look at the models, shall we?'

Hudson led Nguyen around to his desk. Within minutes they were whizzing over the models, checking prices and accessibility in the market. Pasting down the descriptions, Hudson suggested the killer had to know a lot about knives to buy one of these. Powerful, sharp, just short enough to conceal in a jacket, just long enough to cause maximum damage. Nguyen was inclined to agree. They had a professional or an extreme enthusiast on their hands.

Updating paperwork until the later afternoon, Hiraoka got back in with Leigh, with a few more statements from witnesses corroborating what the smackhead had said earlier. Statements would be made tomorrow, but crucially, it gave them a bit of breathing room. They delivered Elms the good news, which he took reluctantly.

'Anything on the note?'

Nguyen, hands behind his back, responded in his signature calm manner. 'Not quite yet, sir. Our best forensics team are analysing it. Anderson is on the case, chasing them for any preliminary findings. So far, they're trying to determine the gender of the text and the intelligence. They're basing this off the lexical density and some other lingo I'm not really up to speed with.'

Elms smirked. 'Nor am I, Nguyen. I want that solved tomorrow morning regardless of weekend plans. Cancel them. This is your priority.'

'Yes sir,' the room mumbled. Leigh went to leave when Elms caught them.

'Before you lot go, I have the courtesy to inform you that as of Monday, internal affairs shall be interviewing each of you regarding the leak within the Met.'

A moment of silence.

Hiraoka was blunt. As if he had been expecting it for a while. 'Right. Night sir.' And left.

Hudson's suspicions about him only seemed to grow. Was he covering something else?

The rest were left up in the air, not sure how to respond after that. They all nodded, acknowledging the responsibility of what was to come and left together. A leak in the Met? Hudson seemed to shift uncomfortably for a while. So did the others. They shut down their computers, grabbed their coats and left without muttering much of a word to each other. But it seemed to slowly dawn on Hudson. If the killer was able to do this so regularly, without detection, then kill a chief superintendent in their own home, what's to say it wasn't someone on the inside?

Hudson sat alone in the pub, staring down into his pint. Waiting. Making small talk with the landlord. A man who was certain his girlfriend would turn up in no time. He was a smart man, and he deserved it. Sure enough, ten minutes into their riveting conversation on Wenger, Brexit and roll-on deodorant, Jessica turned up, all smiles.

She took a seat next to Hudson, offering him an innocent grin. He returned it gladly.

'How's the case?'

He shrugged, taking another drink. 'Can't say. Classified. It'll all be in the fucking news by tomorrow anyway. We've just lost someone and… mind if we just talk about something else, yeah? How's work been?'

And Hudson fell back into the chair, melted away and let Jessica talk at him. He chimed in now and then, making a comment at the right time, before going back to his pint.

By ten to eleven, the last orders bell rang, and Hudson was on his fourth. He could tell that she knew he was upset. Jessica wanted to console him. Interrogate him about what had happened. There was a sort of hungry sadness in her eyes. Like she was desperate to tell him something. But Hudson just kept on shutting her down. Shutting her out.

He met Jessica outside a few minutes later as the crowds starting spilling out onto the frosted streets.

'Off home already?'

'Yeah, early day and all that. Sorry.'

She smirked, her thin lips producing a dimple on the left. Hudson loved that dimple. 'Daniel, don't apologise to me, I get what you're doing. Why do you think I never pestered you tonight? It doesn't matter you were off in your head, it really seems the job is getting to you. I don't care, I just want to know I can be here for you when you need it. Are you sure you don't want to stay out for a few more? Come back to mine?'

'Nah,' he repeated. 'I better get back.'

'It's Saturday, Daniel, come on. Takeaway at mine after?'

And then he shocked himself. 'Maybe some other time. I'll message you tomorrow.'

She looked genuinely hurt by his rejection.

Sat on a night bus, staring down the walkway, through the windscreen, he could see Jessica's face in the blotted swirls of neon and chaser-red brake lights. He felt an idiot. Felt stupid, but more than that, he felt sick and exhausted. More so his mind than his back. A lot less to do with the physical side of the job, more to do with trying to hold on mentally. Trying to feel like he was actually working for a living, not just tagging along.

The bus jolted to a stop, and he almost forgot to get off. Hudson muttered another apology that night, chewed down on his tongue and shuffled up the street toward his flat. When he finally got home, a faint drizzle of sleet and ice falling, hands frozen, he realised he couldn't face Eisa. Knew that if she consoled him or said just one word, he'd just break down and cry. It was just a shame he didn't have that with his own sister Krystina. But maybe that was his stupid fault, too?

Sunday, 24th February

10:40

Bakery goods always seemed to do the job once the temperature had plummeted. Hot pies. Cooked pasties and maybe even a cake or two. Hudson wasn't counting calories; instead, he was counting hours. Days. Until the inevitable. Another murder. More bother from the media.

Reading the Metro newspaper on the way into the city, Hudson scanned the front pages. They detailed the latest goings-on about a crazed monster terrorising the streets of London. The still incorrectly named London Lobotomiser. Adding new glamour and chaos to the spat of knife crime plaguing the capital.

It got to him, so he'd sent the paper flying over the seat into the lap of an unsuspecting OAP. An apology seemed to get him off the hook. As it happened, the man had actually been building up the courage to ask for it; a sudoku or two lurking on its back pages.

Close call.

Hudson stood outside a weapons dealer in Hammersmith, one of many he and Hunt would be visiting. A shop that sold a variety of goods, including fishing equipment, archery gear and even hunting knives. The signage out front convinced the public of one thing. The finest gear in London.

The snow seemed to be falling at a steady rate since last night, building up a new layer of fresh powder. Hudson ruffled out a few flakes from his hair and stepped into the shop. Knocking the snow off his shoes on the step. The door chime ringing out.

Hands in pockets, Hudson browsed the isles, noticing the counter at the back. A tall, bald man with a thick beard eyed him up suspiciously. His arms and neck adorned in a variety of tattoos.

From shelf to shelf, he checked different types of fishing and hunting bait. Hooks, nets, contraptions. Over on the wall, above hunting equipment, hung giant bows. Wooden limbs. Longbows. Carbon fibre setups. They all looked extremely expensive. A loud shout from the back of the shop confirmed it.

'That one on the far left will fetch ya about three grand, but you can grab that other carbon one for under two thousand five. You looking to get into shooting? Hunting maybe?'

Hudson slowly walked over toward the bows, still fixated on all the tools on show. 'What makes you think I don't shoot already?'

The cashier laughed. 'Come on, mate.'

'Fair enough.'

A short silence fell. Obviously getting the hint, Hudson wanted to be left alone. He continued to peruse and at long last found what he wanted. On the stand, held out for easy viewing, a stunning four-inch hunting blade in a glass case. Hudson raised a hand and bellowed loudly.

'This one. Can I have a look?'

Five minutes later, a key was produced, and the case was opened. Gingerly, the cashier handed Hudson the knife and smiled.

'Beautiful, isn't she?'

Hudson nodded. 'Very. How much?'

'Er, that one? Could use that for skinning small animals. Foxes. Even badgers. I reckon about four seventy-five.'

The knife expert judged that to be too expensive, seeing the look on Hudson's face. 'But I assure you it's worth every penny. We only had a few in stock, and that's the last one.'

Hudson was immediately interested. He rounded on the man, forgetting all about the knife in his hand. The cashier hadn't and eyed it cautiously.

'How long ago? How many have you sold?'

'Er… a couple, I think. Yeah. Two. Why do you ask? Mind if I er… take tha—'

'Two? When? When did the two buy it?'

'Hmm, well, I think the er… Mate. Could you put th—'

Hudson wasn't in the mood for playing and pulled his badge out. The cashier immediately relaxed as if getting the chance to finally let out a long fart.

'Listen. This is all part of an enquiry. I need to see any CCTV you have from the times those two people bought knives like this.'

After the atmosphere calmed somewhat, the knife was bought reluctantly by Hudson, his wallet wincing and copies of the CCTV were copied to a pen drive.

'Very nice. Very high tech considering most places I check in on.'

The shop owner laughed. 'Mate. I may look like a hick ass country animal hunter, but when it comes to tech, it *has* to be up to date. Not used a VHS in almost fifteen years. Not a fucking chance.'

He grinned. 'I really appreciate this. Do you have copies for yourself? I'll be making copies of this as well. I have all your details, so again, thank you for this. We'll be in touch should we find anything.'

'Not a problem.' And waved him out.

Pen drive deep in his jeans pocket, Hudson queued for a time at a café, ordered something to go whilst pulling out his phone. He gave Leigh a quick text about what he'd found but didn't receive an answer. Everyone busy. Everyone on overtime.

Haskell had just been killed. Their acting chief superintendent of the central west murder team. It had shaken the Met, including the detectives and surrounding stakeholders. All of which had to be reassured and spoken to at length by Hiraoka and Elms, not to mention the commissioner and deputies too. Time-consuming work. It meant an added gap as well. They were short on inspectors, constables and other levels of rank as it was, let alone a loss like that.

Before he could sip his coffee in the now pounding levels of snow coming out of the sky, Hudson saw a text back from Leigh

Already at Charing Cross. Guess who I'm with?

Hudson sent his reply back immediately.

Who? I'm on my way now. I've got something you'll be very interested to see.

A delay. Hudson got drinking and made his way to the nearest tube station. When he looked back down, the reply had come.

Third victim. I've just interviewed a witness who was at the cinema. One of the missing names. He's still here. What have you got?

Jumping onto the tube, his signal beginning to fail, he managed two words before it went.

The knife.

When Hudson charged in, bringing with him a storm of snow onto the floor, he made straight for Leigh's desk and dropped the pen drive and a parcel onto her desk. A grin spread right across his face.

'A present for you and a present for Nita. Fuck it. For the whole team.'

Leigh looked down at the items. Picked up the pen drive and studied it.

'What's this?'

'His porn stash, the little perv,' Nguyen laughed, coming into frame. It seemed a little off-tone for the big man, which is what made Hudson chuckle. Leigh wasn't in the mood for playground bullshit.

'It's footage for the days that purchases were made of these knives. Timestamped from receipts going back a good few months. I left quick, so I haven't actually had a look through yet. Thought we should all get the pleasure. Where's Hiraoka? Hunt?'

Leigh shrugged. 'Out. You know we have to sit on this now until they're back?'

His face fell. In his haste to jump on it, he'd forgotten standard procedure regarding the obtaining of new evidence moving forward. It was always run by the leading investigator first. Brought to the team. You couldn't have constables milling about giggling over new material behind the backs of senior officers. It was a recipe for disaster and dismissals.

'Fine,' he said. 'What about your witness? Heard there was a break with the moviegoers back at Stratford.'

'Got him down at the station with Anderson, had to come back and grab a few things here.'

'Brilliant. Does he have an ID?'

'That's what we're hoping to find out,' she said. 'Coming?'

Not five minutes back at Fitzrovia and the detectives were out the door and heading south to Charing Cross Station. Today, his feet ached. It was potentially the most walking he'd engaged in since his hiking adventures back up north. The balls of his feet twinged, heels throbbed with the dull agony that came from too much pavement pounding. That hard, stomping, dash when walking at pace. He wasn't hot though, the weather had seen to that.

Great big gusts of snow whipped the detectives as they bundled into DC Leigh's vehicle. She cranked up the heating and got them there in a flash. In truth, the car was still freezing cold by the time they parked up, the distance being that short. With the snow falling heavily and threats on the radio of a fresh dumping of powder from a second storm, a walk outside seemed less and less appealing now.

Hudson tried his phone in the car before getting out. Dialling for Krystina but no response. His text messages had been read, but no reply. He'd call again tomorrow, maybe. See if she was feeling better. He didn't blame her for the cold shoulder he'd received since last time. Pondered on ways to make amends and start anew.

'Reckon there'll be fresh disruptions tonight?' Hudson asked, zipping up his coat, navigating a pile of slush toward the station's back entrance.

Leigh fumbled her phone, not really concentrating. 'What? Oh, yeah, probably.'

'You alright?' he asked, holding the door open for her as they approached.

'Yeah.'

'Sure?' Hudson persisted, not satisfied. 'Look. After Haskell, I know you—'

She stopped in the hallway, letting two uniforms pass them before speaking. Her long finger pointed right in his face, her dark eyes narrowed. Full of anger and fatigue. 'Don't you fucking dare. You've not been around here long enough to remember the fucking door code, let alone what Haskell ever fucking meant to the team.'

Hudson held up his hands. 'Hey, sorry, I wasn't presuming anything.'

'Just fucking… just keep it to yourself, alright? Let's just get through this shit show. Then we can fucking talk.'

The detectives moved silently through the station, taking a flight of stairs to the room in which Anderson was holding. She seemed to be having a jovial chat with a portly old man. When they entered, Anderson looked a bit gutted. Like the good times were coming to an end.

She stood, Leigh walked in, said hello to the man whilst Anderson introduced him to Hudson.

'Hudson, this is Mr Sbiera. Am I saying that right sir? Sbiera? Brilliant. Could you explain to the detectives here what we've been chatting about? It's been lovely meeting you, but I have to go.'

The old man's face dropped. 'Oh, must you go, pretty lady? I have so many story. I watch all the movies.'

Anderson shook her long hair to and fro. 'Sorry, Mr Sbiera. All the best now. Buh bye.'

Hudson looked over at Leigh, for a cue. Then back at Mr Sbiera and smiled.

'Hello Mr Sberia, I'm Detective Constable Daniel Hudson, very pleased you've come in to speak with us today. I'm sure my colleague has briefed you on why you're here?' He adjusted his tone, feeling uncomfortable. Awkward under Leigh's quietness. 'Could you begin by describing the events of the day you visited the cinema, starting with breakfast? I understand you were there, Friday the fifteenth?'

Leigh sat back in her chair, arms folded. Listening. Mr Sbiera replied.

'Well, yes. I was watching movie. Good action film, though not too happy on director. Very average.'

'What was the film?' he asked, genuinely curious.

'Oh, I forget!' He chuckled. 'But yes, I was there, detective. I was there.'

Mr Sbiera licked his cracked lips and allowed his watery eyes to look around the room. They hovered on Leigh for a little while. He smiled but only got a faint grin back. She was definitely not in her best moods, and Hudson worried it would distress the witness.

'So, Mr Sbiera. Can you walk me through what happened that night? From leaving your home, to leaving the cinema?'

And the story began. Hudson leaned forward on the table, fingers laced, listening intently. It was five minutes in before he grabbed a pen and notepad by Leigh and started scribbling notes. It all seemed normal, no signs of odd characters, nothing out of the ordinary. Then, as the tale turned toward the end, where Mr Sbiera recounted leaving the cinema, he made a comment about the noise and smell of the screening.

'There was annoying rustling of snacks. I always hate this,' he said. 'Always in this screening at night. But I still go! Though not too unhappy. It's a nice time to go watch a movie. Though, I do remember it smelled nice, like expensive perfume. And the people seemed nice. The staff always nice. I love the owner. Though, I do not think this is relevant to you, detective. I am sorry. I do not remember anything of a strange man. Everyone seemed so normal.'

Hudson couldn't hold back a sigh of disappointment. 'It's fine,' he conceded. 'Memories are tough to recall and aren't always accurate. It's really not your fault at all. You've been a great help for coming in and providing a statement.'

DC Leigh was already up, thanking him and leaving out the door. Mr Sbiera looked a bit taken aback and suddenly placed a hand on Hudson's.

'Catch them, will you? I fear something ungodly happen here. It's not right.'

The young detective felt unnerved but nodded all the same. 'We will, Mr Sberia. We'll do our best.'

Monday, 25th February

09:00

Ben Thompson, Mayor of London, adjusted his tie at the podium and fidgeted with the mic. Casting his eyes to a crowd of journalists outside Scotland Yard, he paused, collected his thoughts and spoke.

'As of last night, the investigations into a serial killer, whose identity remains unknown, culminated with the murder of a highly ranked, highly esteemed chief officer in the London Met. His name, Richard Haskell, who leaves behind his beloved wife, Miranda Haskell and many friends and family who loved him very much. It is with great sadness that I announce this but know that I come here today not just to grieve but to announce our strength. This cities strength and our resolve and confidence to obtain justice.

Crime in London, under this government, has struggled. But what we will do now, going forward, from this incident, from this tragedy, is to work together. And not just as a police force but as a community. As a city. It takes not just the hard work of our police officers to make this great city safe, but its people too. Work with the Met, cooperate and help bring this heinous and despicable killer to justice.

A hard worker, father and friend was taken from us on February the second this month. Robert Short. A daughter, a young student with a bright future, was also taken just a week later. Catherine Evans. Then, the poor life of someone still unnamed just last week. Now, we say farewell to one of our finest police officers. Today, the commissioner and I will work tirelessly and communicate closely until this awful case comes to an end.

But let me first assure you—any who may be watching now that you are still quite safe. These streets of London are some of the safest in years. Under no circumstances be unwise; please go home in groups late at night, be vigilant but do not halt your daily lives for the sake of this mad man. Do not present him with such an easy victory.

It is my belief that the Met have all the capable resource and ability to bring this killer swiftly to justice. That with the constant work, effort and determination of our fine detectives and uniformed officers currently in the field, we will end this nightmare once and for all. No questions. I will now pass over to the commissioner…'

Hudson grabbed his chin, looking around the room at the reactions. In the background, Commissioner Peter Smith took the mic to make a further address. Commander Elms, alone in his office, listened intently on his own laptop.

'Jesus,' Nguyen gawked, a cup of cold coffee sat loosely in his hands. 'Can't believe how far this has escalated. Never in a hundred years would I imagine someone would have the fucking gall to do this sort of stunt. Can't fucking believe it. He's just gone…'

Hudson shook his head. 'I feel sorry for her. Mrs Haskell. Before I left the scene that night, she was stone-cold still. Face blank as anything. Never seen someone hit so hard before. She needs our support.'

'And she's getting it.'

Hunt jumped in. 'Counsellors are already on the case. She's part of the family, she'll be looked after very well. Getting access to the very best grief liaison officers the Met has to offer.'

'Yeah?'

'We're not known for being accommodating to the wellbeing and mental health of fellow officers, let alone the public and the victims, Hunt. I wouldn't hold your breath.'

Hudson was a little thrown off by his sudden warmness. Standing up and stretching, the room began milling about, returning to desks in a quick attempt to file emails away before the commander got their attention. They knew he'd want to say a word or two.

As if on cue, he'd barely sat down when the man himself took the floor. He spotted DC Leigh by the murder board, arms crossed and face critical.

'Ladies and gentlemen, Wandsworth is our breakthrough. This fourth murder has provided us with exactly what we need to close this. We've already conducted numerous door-to-doors, physical evidence in the form of a handwritten note is already being processed and analysed. This is it. We can NOT allow this one to fall through our fingers. If you have questions, come see me, don't let it get out first. Goodness knows this unit has had enough of it.

'Chief Superintendent Richard Haskell was a fine officer with an outstanding record. He was also a great friend. I had the honour of working with him a few times and knew him when he was just a sergeant. I; and neither should any of you, forgive the evil acts that have lead to him being robbed from us. Pool all your energy and brilliance into tracking down the killer. I know we can do this. This team was created for the purpose of solving the very worst crimes. Minds specifically selected for being the best tools for the job. I want to see that the hiring process didn't make any mistakes. I want every other MIT and unit in London to look up to us as inspiration. Of what to emulate.

'Hiraoka, you have something to add?'

'Yes, sir, thank you.'

The chief inspector took the floor, a little closer to the murder board and slapped a big hand across it.

'This is it. Right here. This is our method going forward. Shove a sticky note up on the right here, just off the map if you have a thought. Walk past when you have time and digest it. Get some ideas flowing.'

He peeled off a picture of David Green from the satanic website. 'We interviewed this man, cleared him. We checked the contacts he provided, but of course, that isn't enough. We need to close in on this. Look further. Leigh, I need you to look at some of the other sites we found. Nguyen, go with her and conduct some visits.'

'Sir,' they both replied.

'The hunt has begun, and we'll catch the bastard. We do it for

Haskell's sake. Do it for his wife. But also for the others who died meaninglessly. Any confusions about what your current work should be looking like, come either to myself or your sergeant.'

'Sir?' Hudson held a hand up, fumbling with his watch.

Hiraoka nodded.

Hudson found himself standing then, going numb.

'We have a potential suspect,' he said, taking a deep swallow. A murmur rippled through the office, and Leigh looked over, annoyed. Looking betrayed a little. Hunt positively seething at having the limelight snatched from his grasp. 'I've been able to track down a knife shop that sells the particular kind of blade that matches what our reports from Nita evidence. Same one I'm betting that was used to kill Haskell. The business owner only owns one shop, so has given me a pen drive for the CCTV on the days the receipts are stamped for the sales of those knives. My bet is, whoever is in the footage, is potentially our killer, or at least linked in some way. Suspects we can track down for questioning.'

Hiraoka and the commander remained quiet, wanting to see this play out. Then Hiraoka boomed.

'Why was I not informed of this yesterday, detective?'

A laugh interrupted any chance for a grilling. It was Hunt. Sat on the edge of his desk, grinning from ear to ear.

'Really? This is fuck all! I know a dozen places that could sell this type of knife. It's a non-story. Guv, seriously, it's another fucking dead end by Hudson.'

A few in the office seemed stunned to see Hunt kick-off at Hudson so openly. But it hadn't been the first time. Hiraoka wasn't in the mood for office politics. It was part of his character and ill-timed, given they were now considering any potential leaks in the force.

'That's enough, sergeant.'

'I had given Hudson strick instructions to review our current case files.'

'Are you confirming, sergeant, that you withdrew Hudson from investigating a potential lead?'

His jaw clenched. 'Hudson should be held responsible for deviating regardless, including responsibility for all administrative tasks for the lead.

Commander Elms considered it. 'Very well. I want the rest of you working on identifying the third victim, reviewing the forensic analysis. Hunt, you can head that and Nguyen, I want you and Anderson reviewing victim circles. DC Leigh, I expect an ID by tomorrow as well. This is not acceptable.' A pause. 'Moreau, please assist where you can. I want these deadlines met without excuse. Are we all understood? Excellent. Dismissed.'

Hunt winked at Hudson before getting out his phone, dialling and leaving the office. It could only mean that Hunt weighed up the odds in his favour. That the knife lead was a duff, meant getting him out of the game for the rest of the team to focus on the potential of a lead on the satanic route. When the sergeant had his back turned, he gave him the middle finger.

Moreau floated over some time after lunch, the office empty save for DC Leigh on the other side, spending her hours on the databases cross-referencing missing persons with their photo of the victim. He had spent plenty of the day slowly and meticulously going through hours of CCTV footage.

'Fucking brilliant, isn't it?' he barked, giving Moreau a little start, but she smiled anyway.

'What's up?'

'This. The fucking knife peddler doesn't have date stamps on purchases. You'd think with all his tech… Anyway. I'm having to go through the entire day, and so far, the one knife's been picked up by an old man, about five foot tall.'

She scoffed, looking over at the murder board. There, the silhouette image from earlier CCTV capture, showing some big figure, somewhere over six foot. Heavily clothed and disguised. 'Not them then?'

'No. So I'm now shitting myself wondering if this other buyer is even it? I've still got to follow it up, I suppose. Another bloody face for the board.' He hit pause and print screened the image where the old man's face became visible. 'I've put myself in it now.'

'I've started trawling online for knife enthusiasts. Not much of anything, to be quite honest, but it shows research. I'm sending it over to Moreau to see if she can run any tricks up her sleeve. Ascertain geography and so on. At least narrow down parametres. Could open up our suspect pool.'

Hudson looked up at her, noticed she had a short weave in today. It was Leigh who preferred it *natural,* as she'd mentioned once. Hudson liked both. But when it came to his own hair, it was always a simple number two on the sides, five on top.

'Hmm, well, I'll be jumping fo—' He stopped speaking. Moreau popping out from nowhere, feet as silent as a cat, frowning and then peering in to look at the screen.

There, clear as day, a tall figure in a woolly hat entered the shop. Looking closely at the gait, the legs and the long blonde hair coming from beneath, it was clearly a woman. Granted, she was tall. It wasn't a six-foot-three brick shit house of a man, either. The mystery shopper picked up the knife, seeming to study it for a while and then left.

All three of them jolted up. Hudson's mouth dropping.

'Rewind!'

They did, stopping frame-by-frame to check the blonde lady. It was too obscured to make out the face, but one thing was sure, they'd gotten their big break.'

Tuesday, 26th February

10:52

As instructed, Hudson ceased his unauthorised, self-imposed over-time stints. Which was a challenging feat given the threat level and urgency of the case. The prolific nature of their killer.

Adding to the already bursting catalogue, a fresh worry brewed slowly in his thoughts after their big find on Sunday. That the CCTV may not play out quite as he'd hoped. Optimistic or not.

Hudson swayed on the balls of his feet, staring at the murder board, a cheap coffee in his hand. Small drinks were taken as he mused, tapping the marker pen on his knuckles. Taking a sigh, he wrote down underneath *knife*. Purchased online? Black market? Blonde woman? Six foot?

Lobbing the pen onto the top of a cabinet, he turned to see Hiraoka meeting his gaze. Wrapping a scarf around his neck. Eyes narrowed. Assessing.

'Oi, Kabu. Remember Valentine's?'

Hudson nodded. 'Yeah, Ronnie Scott's, right? Whiskey, jazz, all that? Best friends with all the bar staff?'

'Yeah, well, how about tagging along for another ride?'

Hudson looked around, but Hiraoka was already waving his hand impatiently. 'Elms is with the deputy commissioner across town. Get your coat. This isn't a request.'

'Where're we going?'

'Bar in Mayfair, we have someone waiting for us there.'

He frowned, snatching his coat and gloves and walking out with him, making sure to slam the door on the latch. 'Who?'

'Mrs Haskell.'

Hudson always gawked openly when he walked the poshest, most exclusive areas of London. The primary location being Mayfair. Its long streets of red brick Georgian terrace town housing, with beautiful, black-framed windows, steep awnings and long glass windows lettered in fine gold. Luxurious restaurants, fine tailors and fashion boutiques. But Hiraoka had led them to a small, dainty looking bar just a few buildings down from an enormous Porsche dealership, nestled right on the corner of the street.

Both detectives cut cold, morbid figures, snowfall still relentless and unforgiving. Obscuring their view through the bar window. It had proven quite difficult to drive there in Hudson's beat-up Clio. He had no idea why Hiraoka insisted on using his car for every trip, either.

'I dread to think how much a pint of Carling costs in there.'

Hiraoka regarded him, pulling the scarf down from his mouth. 'They don't sell Carling.'

In they went, the atmosphere quiet and classy. A few very well-dressed individuals dotted about the place having quiet drinks. Hudson wasn't exactly council estate born and bred, but he still felt oddly out of place. Like he hadn't quite scrubbed up enough to be let in. The tones were neutral, clean and modern. Overtly expensive non-essentials gave the target customer away, from the chesterfield furniture to the staff's white-collar uniforms.

Up at the bar, with a short drink on the rocks, sat a woman with long black hair, bare legs crossed beneath a skirt, arms over the bar. She had her phone on, tapping it occasionally. Hudson followed in Hiraoka's shadow, not keen on introductions following his death so soon.

Mrs Haskell turned before the inspector could speak. 'Good Morning,

John, nice to see you. Who's the pup?'

Hudson chewed his cheek, eyes trying not to betray his shock. She had a look of severity on her. Though her lips were full, eyes stern yet soft within. Mrs Haskell didn't exude the callous nature her tone implied. She was much more complex than he had first thought. Hudson was immediately fascinated, despite the putdown.

'This is Detective Constable Daniel Hu—'

'I'm sure he can speak for himself.' She said. And she motioned to him. 'Go on.'

His voice cracked. 'DC Daniel Hudson ma'am.'

'You can drop that. Call me Miranda or Mrs Haskell.' Miranda turned then to Hiraoka, offering a seat. 'You know I never liked that ma'am bollocks you boys love to use.'

'Miranda, it still sits odd with me too. Back in Japan, we used different terms of address which were much more clear. But we're not here to talk about my past or manners of greeting, are we?'

'No,' she said. 'We're not. Daniel, take a seat now. Let's drink.'

Alarmed at how early it was to be knocking back the booze, Hiraoka shot him a glare as if to suggest, *it's the whiskey or your job*. So Hudson followed suit.

'So, what is it? I owe you one, John, but I'm grieving, so don't waste my time.'

The chief inspector nodded in that same formal Japanese manner he had done so before. Old habits died hard, it seemed. Hiraoka clearly held Miranda in high regard. The only other person he'd bowed to being Haskell and Elms.

'We need to know if you saw anything. Noticed anyone in the street before you left. Anything. It could be something you wouldn't consider out of the ordinary,' Hiraoka said. 'Anything that comes to mind.'

Miranda took a drink. Looked a bit like a bourbon. But then again, she had just lost her husband in the most gruesome way. He inwardly cringed, wondering how they'd revealed that to her. How she would have reacted. Miranda seemed extremely capable. Strong. Powerful.

'I recall no one. The street was empty when I left.'

'Empty? No one leaving their homes? Getting into cars?'

'No,' she repeated, staring over the bar. 'No one. I remember because it was snowing. Plenty on the ground, and I looked up and down the street. The idiot Uber had parked a few extra houses down, and I fancied the fucking walk, believe it or not. I saw not a soul.'

Hudson frowned, something clicking then in his head. A small pinion of thought moved into place. 'Mrs Haskell, if you don't mind, what time did you leave?'

'About eight o'clock.' Her reply came without pause. Burnt into memory.

'Was the night out planned at all? In advance, I mean?'

'Tickets to the Royal Albert, Rich had bought them for my friends and me. He wasn't going. Had work commitments, or so he said.' The last part came out strained. Bitter

All Hudson could say was thank you.

Hiraoka coughed and motioned for Hudson to wait outside. Suspicious but not keen on pushing his luck, he said his goodbyes and left. Wrapping his scarf up over his face, the wind began whipping its way through the street, biting at his exposed skin.

Ten minutes later, Hiraoka returned, pulling up his own woolly neckwear. 'One more trip,' he said. 'And care to explain what that was?'

Hudson shrugged. 'Street was empty. Unless they were hidden, they couldn't have been long behind her.'

Hiraoka fumbled a cigarette out in his gloved hands. 'Why?'

'Well, say you've found out where Haskell lives. You'd know his routines. The killer has been eluding us up until this point, so I'd wager now they're pretty fucking tight. If they knew his routines, they'd possibly be aware that Miranda was going out that night. So, it makes sense that they'd be waiting, or at least be in the house not long after.'

'Hmm,' the chief inspector intoned, taking a drag and directing them south where they'd parked the car. 'Food for thought. I'd save that for Elms. It's not me you need to impress anymore. I've got my measure on you. Time to bring out the guns for the commander.'

Police tape still hung outside the Haskell's front door, the two detectives stood quietly, finding no words to speak. A cool breeze whirled at their coats, telling them to get in out of the winter. Ducking under the tape, nodding to a pair of heavily equipped officers carrying Heckler & Koch G36C carbines, much bigger than the MP5s they more commonly wore. No fucking about now.

Hiraoka and Hudson gingerly stepped through into the living room and then round to the kitchen on the left.

Hudson held his breath.

'Nice and tidy,' Hiraoka breathed, shaking his head.

Before, the ruined remains of Haskell lay slumped low in a pool of his own congealing blood. Splatters covered the walls. His nightmares now including him, lumbering forward, arms outstretched begging for him to finish it. A hellish image burnt into his mind along with the others.

An absurd groan escaped him, and Hiraoka looked round.

'Alright? Want a minute outside?'

He raised his eyebrows, not expecting that sort of response. 'Nah, I'm alright. Why the guns outside? Tape and all?'

'Elms. He's ordered a watch on Haskell's house.'

'And his wife?'

'Watched. There were a few other plainclothes detectives in that bar we were just in. You wouldn't have spotted them. She's not being put into protective custody, the threat seems low given the MO, but we're taking steps.'

'Makes sense,' Hudson agreed. 'Though I doubt this type of killer would return to the scene.'

'I doubt it as well, Hudson. Let's have a look round, shall we?'

And the pair broke off, scanning every inch of the place. As the SOCO had dusted everything, taken pictures and the lot, the men didn't hesitate to rifle through magazines and upend furniture. They already done the works previously, but they wanted to be thorough.

Moving back into the dining room toward the back of the house, Hudson saw a picture up on a bookcase. Holding the frame in his hands, the young detective looked back at the eyes of his dead chief superintendent, smiling with his gorgeous wife on holiday. Peru? Bolivia? Somewhere like that. They looked happy as hell, young despite their true age.

'She's pretty, isn't she?' A deep voice came from the door.

Hiraoka, his expression unreadable, folded his arms and cocked his head up to the ceiling. 'I won't lie to you, Hudson. This is one of my toughest. With spending cuts, it was the units best move to bring you in. We didn't think the case would be like this.'

'I'm aware of the situation, sir,' he bit back, placing the picture back down. Angry now. 'Let's just keep looking.'

Twenty minutes later, Hiraoka rested a foot against the wrought iron fencing outside, taking another smoke. Hudson decided not to join him and took a piss in the downstairs toilet.

Finishing up, turning the taps on to wash his hands, he noticed a bit of dirt in the sink and clicked his teeth. Nothing close to OCD, Hudson still couldn't stand scum build-up on ceramic. Dirt of any kind. Scrubbing it off, he felt a bit better and admired the clean sink.

Then he spotted it. Beneath the basin, where the sink met the floor. A line like a crack running up against the white porcelain.

'The fuck is that?' He bent down, rubbing it with a thumb to see how deep.

The crack peeled off.

'It's a fucking…' His eyes bulged. 'Guv! Guv! I've got a fucking hair here!'

Hudson heard his chief inspector's footsteps pounding through the house, his figure looming suddenly in the doorway.

'Where?'

'Here. You got an evidence bag on you?'

Hiraoka shook his head, turned around.

'We could use a sandwich bag or—'

'No, Hudson,' he growled. 'I don't think the killer is dropping hairs in other rooms for our benefit. Come on.'

'What?'

'Get up before you make a fool of yourself.'

But Hudson wasn't having any of it. He went back to the car, found a packet of bags, went back in, and put the hair inside. Then returned to the car afterwards after checking he hadn't missed anything else.

'You know, hair is one of the worst ways to establish DNA?' Hiraoka attacked, starting the car and staring down into Hudson's lap. 'If, by chance, it has a follicle, to begin with.'

Hudson knew it was a gamble. 'We'll see.'

Good news rarely came with no cost. A call back from Vauxhall labs told them they were busy. Very busy. A long catalogue of entries to work on and, as such, the hair would be delayed for a week minimum. On top of that, it would prove very difficult to get DNA of a single hair. On cue, Hunt made a remark about a waste of resources, but Hiraoka shut him down in front of Elms, iterating that nothing was to be ruled out. That all foreign DNA had to be eliminated and traced to provide suspects. Another unexpected intervention from Hiraoka on Hudson's benefit.

He tried to get a read off of him, knew he didn't need to fight his corner. Knew he was quickly becoming the detective to avoid in the office. Fumbling his way through the case like Bambi on ice. Proving Hunt right. Felt his self-esteem take another battering.

Just as the sun was setting in one of the first clear evening skies in weeks, Hudson rested up against the station wall outside front, redialing his sister. This time he got through to her.

'Hey, long time no speak. How are you?'

'Hi, Danny.' Her voice betrayed no emotion. 'What do you want?'

'About the other week. Listen, I'm just…'

A huff from the other end. 'Just fuck off. Don't come down to London and play the brother. What sort of piece of shit does that?'

Hudson looked down at the phone. She'd hung up.

Wednesday, 27th February

04:17

Hudson dropped the TV remote onto the sofa and rubbed his face. Getting up, he noticed Eisa standing in the doorway. She looked more prominent than usual. Taller. More muscular.

He called to her, squinting into the darkness.

No reply.

Eisa lifted her hand, showed something in her grip. She walked forward then, brandishing the large knife. Hudson gawked, stumbling backwards, hands up. Eisa got closer, her long legs gaining ground quickly. Hudson tried to cry out as she raised the knife over her head to strike him, but he tumbled. Tumbled back and fell through the floor.

His stomach lurched, the sensation of falling punching the air from his lungs. Abruptly, his face kissed the hard cold of concrete. Disorientated, confused, he spat blood and looked up from the floor.

An alley? Not just one or two but hundreds. Branching out from each other. The bins and fences and graffiti blurred together, creating a seemingly endless network. A sharp pang lanced through his head, and Hudson cried out. What was this?

Hiraoka tapped him on the shoulder, and Hudson turned quickly. He smiled, a kind smile he didn't recognise and immediately he felt better. The inspector, peaceful and calm, nodded over toward one of the alleys. A bid to leave this place. To go.

Obliged, he smiled also and turned to leave.

Dark walls rose then around him; the light snuffed out spare a red light in the distance. Hudson realised he was stood in a cinema screen. Alone. Hiraoka nowhere to be seen. Instead, he saw Jessica looming towards him. She smiled, reached up to his head and started slicing at his scalp. The pain immeasurable.

The ooze of hot blood began to dribble and flow down his face. He began to scream. The cuts going deeper. He just wanted her to stop cutting him. To just stop!

'STOOOOP!' Hudson screamed, bolting up in bed, drenched in sweat.

Reality came, jerked him awake, like being pulled quickly out of something thick and viscous. Then the warmth of his bed. Solid. He was safe. At the foot of his bed, Eisa stared back, her eyes revealing shock. Panic.

Then she spoke to him quietly. Barely a whisper. 'Daniel, hand in your notice. Quit that place or leave here. I can't do this anymore, Daniel. I can't do this.'

Hudson burst into fragile tears. 'Neither can I.'

The man across from the desk laid out two bottles of water. Then a pen, some paper, a folder and finally sat back, hands in his lap. Aside from his crease-free shirt, the man looked incredibly untidy. A crumpled jacket, dishevelled hair and a five o'clock shadow deep grey and dirty.

'So we've managed to get this escalated, I'll be billing them, of course, for the service, but it is under my understanding, correct me if I'm wrong Mr Hudson, that the case requires your therapy as a top priority.'

Hudson nodded. He'd turned up casual. Light jeans and a shirt, a woolly jacket thrown on over it. He crossed his legs, knocking his boots together, and looked at the man closely. Wanted to know how serious he'd take him. After all, he felt stupid enough being here as it is.

'Sorry,' Hudson apologised. 'What's your name again?'

'Dr Podelcki.'

'States?'

'Sorry?'

Hudson laughed. 'Your accent, sorry. I'll go with east coast.'

Dr Podelcki smiled broadly. 'Good guess. Queens, New York, for your knowledge.'

'Absolutely, well great erm, yeah, where do we start?'

'First, Mr Hudson, I just want to roll into this very casually, get to know you, perhaps you'd like to get to know me and then we can do a few other questions. Nothing too formal. How does that sound for you?'

'Yeah, fine.'

'Excellent. Excellent. Okay, right, so where are you from?'

'Gotham, Nottinghamshire. Up north.'

'What's that like? I hear the Sherwood forest is stunning.'

They both smiled. Hudson described the trees, the mountains, the country walks. Being spoilt for nature and adventure growing up. Appreciating that side of life.

'What did you do at school?'

Hudson laughed. 'English. English Literature. Even history club. Don't tell my flatmate that, though.'

'Not a fan?'

'Oh, she is. She loves the stuff.'

'Was your degree also in Literature?'

'It was, yes. With some modules in sociology.'

Dr Podelcki nodded, writing a continuous stream of notes after that. Hudson watched him, watched the pen gliding backwards and forwards. Waited for him to stop. It sort of calmed him, oddly. Maybe he was just overthinking it?

'Any interesting stories? Memorable moments during your time at University? Which one did you go to?'

'Oh erm,' he pondered. 'I went to Warwick University. Got lucky. I wasn't predicted the best grades, but I scraped through. Had a word with admissions, and yeah, it was great. That was one memory, but I suppose, a second memory, I was part of the hiking club and the drinks society so, quite a mix… no pun intended. So, on the night, me and my friend James and Peter were all behind the bar at this big event. We'd been practising our drink mixes and juggling for weeks, and we just weren't getting it. But, we nailed it, the night was fantastic, and people were cheering us on. Honestly, it was just fantastic.'

Dr Podelcki smiled. 'Sounds like a great memory. Perhaps you could put something together for me one day?'

'If I still have it,' he laughed.

'So, after university, I presume that's when you joined the force?'

Hudson nodded. 'Yup. Well, sort of. I struggled to find work. It was 2009, spent the summer doing odd stuff and, of course, only been a few years since the 2007 London bombings. I suppose the heightened sense of terror made me think about other things. I loved my village. My family and I thought policing people's safety in the community would be better than joining the military. I'd be home, doing the work here.'

'That's a very noble reason.'

'My family thought so. I actually...' He paused then, licking his bottom lip, reading the room and thought, what the hell. 'I actually wanted to be a teacher. But, I applied to the local police force. They weren't recruiting at first so, not good, but I got in eventually, and by late 2010 I was on the beat. Felt great.'

'It sounds like you're very proud of your past. Lots of happy memories. So, let's go forward and see what's bothering you today. I understand you are currently helping lead the investigation into the serial killer at large, is that so?'

Hudson nodded. 'Yes, that is true. It's about that. I feel I'm pushed back a bit. Just supporting the others.

'Go on.'

'I've erm... I've been having these nightmares. They're bloody awful.'

Dr Podelcki scribbled down some more notes, not looking up. He prompted Hudson to ignore him and continue. 'What happened in these nightmares?'

'Well, it always starts off sort of the same. I'm somewhere familiar, like a pub or a street. Except it's always empty. There's no one around. Then, I hear something, or someone I recognise alerts me. I get dragged into somewhere dark, or someone grabs me and...'

'And?'

'I know what they're doing. They're copying what the killer is doing. My friends, my family. Some of them people I don't know, trying to remove my brain. Sometimes, the pain I can feel seems so real. Like it's really happening. That probably the worst part.'

He scribbled again.

'Do these nightmares repeat themselves?'

'No. Well, sort of.'

'They're unique every time?'

'Yes. Well, yeah unique as in the setting and who kills me but it's always them trying to scalp me, go for my head.'

The psychiatrist looked up from his notepad and raised an eyebrow. 'This could very well be some traumatic stress from the investigation bleeding in. You're feeling that stress and experiencing nightmares as a result. As you confirmed yourself, the events in your dreams, the attacks, are mirroring that of which you are investigating.'

And the conversation went on like that for almost another hour. By the end, Hudson felt exhausted, but a weight had most certainly been lifted. As he left, shaking Dr Podelcki's hand, walking out of the station building and in the direction of the Thames, a realisation hit him he never anticipated reaching.

If anything, the consultation had convinced him that he wasn't sure he could stomach another killing. Now, with barely any leads to go on, time marching on as it does, a fifth seemed even more certain. If the killer was continuing their weekly schedule, their next body was due in just three days.

Pulling out his phone, he swore, noticing a few missed calls and messages. The truth of it was he'd been ignoring people on and off. Part of the anxiety, according to Dr Podelcki. With his mind so occupied, he'd let other things in his life slide. Krystina had made sure to remind him of that. She'd taken the brunt of it.

Thumbing the screen as he walked, his numb hands clasping the phone awkwardly, he sent her a message and pocketed it again.

Perhaps it was time to hand in his notice? It'd be a short one considering his term there. Maybe the quickest resignation in history? The idea of ditching Hiraoka in the middle of the investigation made him angry. Made him ashamed, but the other side of the argument was equally as strong. His own sanity and health.

So what should he do? Maybe he was unfit to be working within the central west murder investigation team? Maybe Hunt and Hiraoka had clocked it day one that he wasn't capable? A danger to them all. Framing it like that, it made only more sense to Hudson what he needed to do for the good of everyone involved.

Wednesday, 27th February

10:46

When Hudson wandered over to his desk, back from a quick slash and some more shit coffee, the bloke from internal investigations had arrived. He caught him chatting with Elms and Hiraoka, clearly discussing the logistics of interviewing working detectives during the current case. When Hudson's presence became known, Hiraoka gave him a look. It conveyed a simple message.

Don't fuck it up.

A few moments later, some awkward handshakes and water refills, Hudson sat down at a desk in an empty office they used for storing extra paperwork, opposite Mr Michael Hutchings. A long, wiry man whose ghostly complexion made his very body look a bit haunted. Still, he couldn't have been more than fifty?

'Morning Detective Constable Hudson, how are we today?'

'Very well, sir, and you?'

'Not bad, not bad, shall we get straight to it then? Lots to do.'

He nodded. 'Absolutely.'

'Who is, for the record, your SIO?'

'Detective Chief Inspector John Hiraoka.'

'When were you first assigned to this case, and how were those procedures carried out?'

'Er.' He paused. 'Sixth. No, the fifth of February. I had been assigned with DCI Hiraoka the week before, beginning inductions before Christmas. I came back in January to settle in, finish my inductions and some minor work. On the second, I was first assigned to the case. My first homicide.'

Hutchings scribbled away, making strange humming noises as he did. 'Did you find it at all odd to be assigned so early to a case? Had, indeed, your induction not finished yet?'

'It had, sir.'

'And how long was the induction for? I presume you shadowed a DTO?'

Again, he paused. Trying to recall the acronym. *Divisional Training Officer.*

'Yes, sir. For a few days. Then I spent double that sorting out the IT systems. There was a bit of a technical faff, so it was finished after Christmas. You know, I was progressing quickly due to my advanced training before as an investigative officer in Gotham, Nottinghamshire. It's this, along with the quickness of my training that I....'

Hutchings held up his pen. Thin fingers and long nails. 'That's very good, very good. Let's stick to the questions. We'll be out on time, just please bear with me and follow along, yes?'

'Yes, sir. Sorry.' A small, acidic bubble of anger popped inside him. He thought, *what a twat.*

For almost two hours, the questions persisted. And repeated. And repeated again for several hours. Wanting to know every detail of the case. When each case had begun, how he and the chief inspector had carried out questionings bagged evidence. For the most part, all was well, but of course, for his DCI's interest, he left out the coke dealer's pseudo-interviewing down by the docks. That wouldn't look good, and the mere omission of fact left a bad taste in his mouth.

Folding over his papers, slapping his arms down, Michael Hutchings grinned ear to ear, held out a hand and shook Hudson's firmly.

'Thank you very much. If I were to be so bold, detective, I am much more concerned about the appropriate behaviour of senior officers in this team. You are quite new here, still in the probationary period.

Constables with barely two years working CID should not really be held accountable to such a full extent as, perhaps, others may be.'

Hudson frowned, pausing as he rose from his chair. 'Sorry?'

'It would be in your best interests, Detective Hudson, if, during these investigations, you keep a careful eye on your inspector. Any issues at all, you have a duty to immediately flag or risk complicit behaviour.'

Before Hudson could leave the room, the man's wispy mouth appeared next to his ear. A warm, damp sound tickled him and caused a shiver. 'Don't trust him.'

Eager to escape, he launched out of the room and headed straight for the smoking area. Outside, the cool, bitter air still frosty from the other night. The night of Haskell's murder. Hudson hunched over in nothing but a jumper, arms folded, staring out across the courtyard.

'Bollocks,' he said. 'Bollocks fucking bollocks!'

A few hours later, Hudson watched Hiraoka exit the meeting room. Catching the young detective's eye, he walked over and grabbed the other half of his BLT sandwich.

'Cheers, son. Bloody glad that's over.' He took a large bite. 'Lovely.'

'This is ridiculous.'

'I know it is, Hudson, but we've got ropes to walk. Can't be choosy right now, let's play their game. You learn that back home?'

He shrugged, snatching up his Mars bar before that disappeared too. 'Not to the same extent but you cover the theory in policing college. It's all there.'

'Good,' he replied, not sensing Hudson's sarcasm.

The chief inspector polished off the last nodule of bacon and bread inhumanely quick, then clapped his hands. 'Right, Moreau, tech geek.'

Someone shouted across from the other side of the office. 'Cyber Crimes Specialist and hired tech hero will suffice, John!'

'Good grief, she's got good hearing,' he jibed.

The pair walked on over, her desk surrounded by tech equipment. Several screens, two keyboards, a laptop, a few hard drives hooked up, and some pretty impressive looking stationery to boot.

'Wow,' Hudson intoned. 'Quite the setup. New additions just in? Even Eisa would be impressed.'

'Who?' she asked.

'Never mind.'

Hiraoka clapped. 'Shut up, Hudson. Moreau. I've had an idea. I'm assuming you've scanned social media?'

She nodded, re-combing her thick black fro and adjusting her belt. 'Yup.'

'Facebook, Twitter, everything?'

'Yes, detective. Even Bebo.'

They laughed. 'Bebo. Right, well, what about dating websites, cybersex forums, that sort of thing?'

'Nothing. However, I've finally made progress with what was recovered from Robert Short's flat. Remember the laptop?'

Hudson had not but recalled it mentioned in the case files for Short. He knew that when they questioned Miss Russell, his ex-wife, Anderson and others had visited the premises to recover anything that might be used as evidence. The laptop had, unfortunately, been more than just password protected. An encrypted security feature that Moreau had struggled with.

Ultimately, it left a hole in their investigation. They hadn't been able to exhaust all opportunities with the victim, ascertain leads, or even connect him to the other victims. Their only options were social media, which, perhaps by sheer coincidence, had shown that Catherine Evans liked fan pages of Satanists. Unfortunately, Short being their only identifiable victim with a very blank social media digital footprint, they'd come up dry.

Until now.

'I've finally been able to gain access. Good news and bad news. What do you want first?'

Hiraoka nodded. 'Let's leave dessert for last.'

She nodded. 'Bad news—the browser histories and login credentials for email accounts are not pre-populated. There is no evidence of communications or anything that link to either the murder or the killer's identity. The good news is there is a calendar on here that indicates he was set to meet people throughout the week. We have diary entries all over the place with initials. For the night of Robert Short's murder, we have MJ. Now, this could be anything, but my first guess is initials. I've gone through all the names we currently have. I've also looked at mutual friends and can't find a single MJ, but it's early days. Otherwise, the laptop is a bust.'

'Fantastic work. Any joy with Catherine's? I know you've already done a few runs.'

'No, sorry,' she replied. 'Nothing. I've been tossing around theories in my head. Perhaps the killer didn't know any of these people? Perhaps only knew Short? Started off with something familiar. Easy. Then worked up to strangers, but those more vulnerable just in case. Or maybe they did know them all, but from past lives and had planned this whole thing years in advance. I'm just not sure. Either way, our only lead thus far digitally is that initials in his diary for Monday the fourth. MJ.'

'Brilliant update, I'll let you crack on.'

She nodded, giving them both a huge smile and went back to her screens.

Commander Elms made a cameo, pausing at the desks, gripping a large handful of folders. 'Another meeting, I shall be back later this evening. I'll want our daily round-up. How're things progressing so far?'

'Sir,' Hiraoka addressed stiffly. 'Moreau has found a potential lead through the recovery of data from our first victim's laptop. Initials MJ, could be the killer, or at least a clue to our first real suspect.'

'Excellent. Hudson, I'll read the CCTV report later today. And our second vic? What about our third? The fourth?'

The group paused a millisecond at the commander's omitting of Haskell's name. Intentional?

'Evans, we have nothing thus far except eyewitnesses corroborating each other on a tall figure being in the area, all dressed up. Matches the attacker's profile. The third, more inconsistent accounts from cinema-goers and two people still missing from the audience. As for Haskell, sir, linguists are still analysing the note, and a hair is being processed by the lab now.'

'A hai—'

Hiraoka interrupted. 'Nothing solid. Just to rule out. We want to ensure a thorough wipe of the place.'

Elms nodded. 'Right, well, good good. I shall have us all reconvene later. As you were.'

Gone, Hudson and Moreau looked to Hiraoka.

'It's fine, let's just see where this MJ thing goes. Moreau, keep us in the loop if you get any viable hits with this.' He stepped away from her desk so he could shout out across the office without blasting her ears to pieces. 'Listen up! We have new intelligence. MJ. Initials found in Robert Shorts' laptop. It's down in his diary for the night he was killed. I want someone on PNC, HOLMES 2, everything. Check case files, witness lits, anything at all. Any name pulled within the last five years and start a list. I want the list run through Sergeant Hunt, who will coordinate our best approach to narrowing down the search parametres. Do not exclude gender. We have a blonde woman waiting to be identified at our crime scenes, so let's not miss an opportunity. Clear?'

A chorus of acknowledgements and even a positive nod from Hunt by the window.

'Great. Let's get the bastard.'

Before Hudson met up with Krystina, the sun already setting with shop lights and advertising screens glowing iridescent against the snow, he battled with a vicious headache on his hike to the Thames. His eyes aching, pulsing in his sockets. After passing the London eye, he stopped by a local chemist and picked up some co-codamol and a bottle of water.

Downing the whole thing, Hudson chucked the bottle, immediately feeling a little better. A gust of wind whipped at his coat, ruffled his hair and following a short walk, saw her there. Waiting quietly in the cold.

He thought about what Hiraoka had said about Hutchings. When his big speech about their new case directive was over, the chief inspector wasted little time in berating and interrogating him on his meeting with the IOPC *boogeyman*. Hudson was honest. Explained the dates and times he started the case. What he was involved with and how he felt. Kept to the facts. More importantly, he failed to mention the little trip down Poplar. Hiraoka seemed appeased, but for Hudson, his soul felt that little more tainted. Hutchings had warned him, and he'd ultimately sided with the chief inspector. Through fear? Probably.

Staring out over the Thames, the houses of parliament in full view, Big Ben and its tower fully encased in scaffolding, Hudson brushed off great lumps of snow so he could rest his arms on the wall and stare out into the icy waters. After a few minutes of day dreaming, the sun already set and the glowing Victorian street lamps casting his shadow in three or four ghostly directions, Krystina's click-clack of heels through the slush alerted him.

'Hey,' he said lamely.

'Let me guess? Apology?'

Hudson nodded, meeting her cold eyes as best he could. Saw her defensive body language, hands tucked up into her armpits. Mouth buried in a grey snood.

'I am. All I'm doing here is my best. I just want you to know that's all it is. Mum and Grandad aren't here. I am. I give a shit.'

'They don't,' she said, brushing off snow from the wall so she could lean also. Peering instead at her gloved hands. 'No matter what they did, I never felt like I was home. Especially Mum. I saw it in their eyes every day. They couldn't handle me. Moving to London has been the best thing I could have done.'

'They do care about you.'

'Liar.'

Hudson sighed. 'They do. But you know as well as I do, that supporting you with what you have isn't easy. They did their best.'

'I'm not a fucking charity case, Danny. I'm not disabled or high on the spectrum. It's fucking bipolar.'

'I know.'

'Do you, though? Do you?'

Truth is, he didn't. Despite the help from doctors and psychiatrists, even a little Googling on the side, he'd never know how she coped. What went through her volatile mind on a day-to-day basis. What made it more painful, as a brother, was the inability to shift the weight. To help.

'No,' he said finally. 'I don't. Haven't a fucking clue.'

She smiled then, turning to look at her younger brother. His brown hair flapping in phantom gusts of wind. A few snowflakes melting on the collar of his coat. 'Finally, something that isn't bullshit.'

They laughed. The tension immediately eased.

'Maybe you don't want support. Maybe I am clueless after all these years. But I can't sleep at night, knowing that, as a family, we could have done more. Whatever that is. There's a whole bunch of reasons I moved to London. Wasn't just on some crusade to clear my own guilt. Maybe a part of it, sure, but I happen to fucking love you as well. You're still my sister. If that means you ragging on me over the phone one day and playing board games the next, sign me up. I don't care what it looks like.' He bit his lip, feeling himself getting unexpectedly emotional. 'This case. Krystina. I wasn't lying. It's a real fucking horror show. I'm not coping how I thought I would. It's nasty. And if I'm being honest with you, I need my big sister.'

She'd listened to every word, eyes unblinking, before turning to face him and putting her long arms around him. 'Danny, why didn't you say that in the first place? You don't have to be the protector all the time.'

He laughed, a small weight falling away from him almost immediately. 'I tried.'

'Let me get you a coffee before we go back to it,' she offered, pulling back and dusting snow off Hudson's shoulders. 'No rest for the wicked, is there?'

'No,' said Hudson, images of brains flashing in his mind. 'There isn't.'

Wednesday, 27th February

21:50

I couldn't distinguish what separated it. What distinguished the difference between the four. Each a sweet message savoured in the moment. The first had been difficult. New and challenging, but it had lived up to how I'd imagined it. Had set the tone. And the rest were easy. Even Haskell. That was the best yet. But I couldn't quite put my finger on it. The note had been a leap but one that was necessary to get the ball rolling onto my fifth. To nudge the detectives on track. To understand what I was trying to tell them.

Then I realised what it was. Power. Control. The choice of doing something so meaningful. To take a life in the name of that cause. To expose them like that and reveal their trueness. It was intoxicating and liberating. I couldn't stop now. Why deny myself a calling I'd been searching all my life?

I stared down from my window, the street lights a smudge of pumpkin glows, illuminating the shadowy swarms of late-night commuters and early week drinkers. I watched them disturb the slush, disturb my moment of zen. Milling about, false lives hidden behind a facade. Mindless vermin.

Reaching for the burr puzzle cube, I toyed with it, pondering the difference between the bittersweet of winter and the bittersweet of killing.

But which was it?

Did I want control? No. Control was a fallacy for those with too small a mind to comprehend the chaos of reality.

Was it power? Absolutely not, I grinned, fumbling further with my puzzle. Power corrupted. Power fuelled greed and led to complacency and weakness.

Power was relative.

Killing was for the process. The motions of it. For my entire life, through whatever medium it was, studying for my degree, a sports competition, a contract at work or taking the life of my first-person, it all boiled down to the same thing.

The challenge. The art of it. The message it conveyed.

Knowing in the moment, the true extent of oneself. How far you are willing to pitch mind, body and soul to accomplish the goal. And with robbing the life of Chief Superintendent Haskell, it had been the ultimate experience. But more importantly, I was happier. More fulfilled, which meant my own life in the office; visiting friends, family, were taking its toll. Shackling me into a world where I no longer belonged.

Rummaging through the fridge, I fell into a reverie, gazing at a tube of tomato puree.

That's what it feels like, I thought. Stuck on a feeding tube. Like in hospital. I hated hospitals. Hated that sense of enclosure, being tied down, force-fed food and meds, controlled. It all reeked.

Suddenly, the idea of living in London forever, building a career, and getting a house made me feel violently sick. I rushed to the sink and poured myself a water, drinking it slowly. Once the nausea subsided, I tipped the rest away and wiped my mouth.

Focus on the blood. The letter. The chaos on the news. The perfect essence of each brain, beautifully displayed at each scene.

I pulled out my phone, flicked through a news app and brought up what I wanted to see. The vast spread on the murder of Chief Superintendent Haskell. A fresh smile spread across my lips as I skimmed it, taking in the positioning, the grammatical metaphors, the bullshit of it all. London was practically begging for more. They loved it.

They loved the excitement murder brought to everyone's dull and useless lives. I had not only revived myself but had revived everyone else. Everyone was a winner when I won.

Fuck, I was a new wave fucking renaissance. One day they'd immortalise me, write books, poems, documentaries and movies. I was already something great.

But it wasn't going to end there. That wasn't the point. No. Why would it be?

Leaving the phone on the counter, I went back to the window and gazed down into the street, a snowfall building now in great flustering sheets. My eyes took in the details. The Victorian render, the bricks, the glass, the trees.

I would leave this place soon. After the final one was done. Just one more, to finish things off. After following and watching them for the last week, leading to my Haskell victory, I knew now who would be the best way to end the show. To finalise my metamorphosis.

It would be him. No questions about it.

I picked up the wooden puzzle, began moving the pieces back and forth, my long digits flicking fast across the mechanism.

A friend. Someone close would need to go. Need to die. It'd have to be the worst yet, the most cunning. Otherwise, it wouldn't send the right message, and I wouldn't be able to sever the ties.

The wooden sections clicked into place as I finally solved it. My perfectly manicured hand placed it down, lightly, onto the bookcase. I folded my arms, smiled and made up my mind.

'Detective, detective. You've grown happy with her, with them, in this place. But I know you regret it.' I turned away from the window, crossed the room and grabbed my jacket from the sofa. 'And I think, Danny, I can help with that.'

Hudson was nowhere to be seen. Home, exhausted and coming under frequent scrutiny about the possibility of a leak. Hiraoka, on the other hand, had his suspicions. He knew the lad was young, not used to homicide, but not a complete fucking idiot either. There had been a leak, he was sure of it, but he didn't pin Hudson down for it. He could see it in his eyes. There was doubt there, but not disloyalty. Decades of experience taught him how to read people.

So what was it? Just a slip-up? A conscious choice to leak? A private investigator he'd gotten in bed with?

Tired, pushing away a cold cup of tea, Hiraoka put down the phone to Charlie. Nita was off work, but Charlie was still plugging away, looking to earn his stripes. The pathologists report on Haskell had been fast-tracked and was probably one of the quickest reports he'd ever received. Of course, the preliminaries had been discussed, but what lay within the file would hopefully shed light on what their case was missing.

Hiraoka opened it, spread out the documents, pictures and began reading.

DSI Haskell, sixty-eight, male, five foot eleven, sixteen stone.

Forty-nine years in the force, due for his fiftieth later that year.

The chief inspector, not too young himself, adjusted the chair and started skimming his old boss's details and went straight onto the examination notes.

Avoiding the images of Haskell, laid pale and naked on the table, the bruising around the puncture wounds, the Y shaped stitching down his torso hideous and dark, the notes on the autopsy were thorough yet depressing.

Lacerations to the torso, groin, arms and neck. Deeper wounds, he read, to the groin and torso. The face was mutilated, destroyed much like the other victims. And like the others, an increasingly cleaner encephalectomy.

He rubbed his eyes, pressing the thumbs into the lids and sat back. Pulling open his desk drawer, the inspector plucked out the reports on all the killings. Opening them all to the pathologist's reports, spreading them over his desk, he began comparing. Everything seemed similar, but the photos provided the differences.

Hiraoka got up from his desk, taking the photos with him and pinned them up on the Murder Board. Done, he stood alone, middle of the floor, the office completely empty, dark and quiet. The thrum of the city muffled outside. Someone moving something elsewhere in the building. And Hiraoka focused.

All four slashed to pieces. All four were attacked in surprise when they were most vulnerable. This suggested planning and someone who wasn't so physically imposing. How could someone so large creep up on these people? On Haskell? And why had they left a note? To invoke an emotive response? Send a more literal message? Hiraoka looked over at Haskell's lifeless visage. Bit the inside of his cheek.

The cuts and stab wounds told a different story. The first kill, compared with the work on the DSI, showed a progression of skill. It proved their theory that this was someone new at the gig. But nevertheless, intelligent and an excellent planner. But this just confused things more. Were they dealing with a genius who just lacked dexterity? Someone young honing their craft? Or perhaps someone who had help? All victims were white British. All lived in London. How was this significant?

Then there was the note. Hiraoka only had a photocopy right now, as the real deal was still being analysed by the linguistics team. Why had they deviated? What was the motivation? Perhaps building up to something?

A few keystrokes later, he stood puffing slowly on a cigarette. This time Mayfair's. He'd been so occupied with the case, keeping tabs on the young blood, that he hadn't run to stock up on his old favourites. The slightly more tangy taste hovered in his mouth, and he grimaced.

'Fuck.' Hiraoka gagged, casting a look at the white stick, the paper burning slowly, unfurling into black ash.

'Sir?'

Detective Nguyen's voice roused him from behind. No idea he'd been there, or really that he'd started smoking again.

'Just muttering to myself. Why aren't you home? I didn't sign you off.'

He didn't bother asking him about the smoke in his mouth. It was none of his business. As a point, especially over the long years of his varied career, he made a habit when he could, not to pry. Because of course in the working hours it's all he ever did. Pry. A prier and not the pariah, that much was certain.

'Quality checking some databases just to cover us, sir. Last thing we need is anything turning up behind us that could expose vital evidence. It's not glamorous but, well, you know. Now with the guv on us after… y'know… double-checking Hudson's paperwork.'

'I do,' he mused, taking another distasteful drag.

Nguyen approached the handrail leading down the disability ramp, leaned over it, halving his stature and craned a head up to the boss.

'How's Hudson doing? Off the record.'

Hiraoka grinned, raising one eyebrow and flicking a dot of ash. 'Off the record?'

Nguyen nodded.

'It was Haskell's call. The man was… a genius. A mountain. He had an idea and followed through with it. I can't shit on the man for it, especially now. So we work with it.'

'Sorry sir,' Nguyen rebutted. 'I shouldn't have brought it up. Just curious. The guy sticks out, and it's more than just coincidence our solid record is getting tarnished by this serial killing.'

The eyebrow danced again, but this time the chief inspector turned to look at Nguyen. Interested.

'Have you come to gossip, detective?'

'No no no, no guv. Nothing like that. I just think the man—'

'I'll stop you there before you embarrass yourself further, detective. Not his adoring fan, I take less kindly to shit-stirring. Most of all, during a case of this level. If I find you sniffing about trying to undermine this squad again, I'll hang you out myself.' He paused to look the man in the eye. See if he'd just been stupid or not. 'Crystal?'

Nguyen nodded, taking a quick smoke. 'Crystal, sir. I was just out of tact.'

'Totemo yoi.'

Very good.

The chief inspector replied in his native, not bothering to translate.

A tension hung thick and heavy between the pair, though Hiraoka couldn't give a shit. Nguyen tried to make amends and cooked up an attempt at small talk.

'So, why the Mayfair's then, sir?'

Hiraoka decided to entertain it just this once. Why not?

'Just something temporary. Not the real McCoy.'

'Masquerading as the real thing, I think. Can't beat roll-ups.'

And something suddenly occurred to him. A notion. A figment of an idea that blew his mind. The note. The slashed faces. The build of the killer. The figure in the CCTV. Seemingly disappearing.

Hiraoka lunged forward, grabbed Nguyen's smoke, took one long puff, gave it back to him and thanked him. 'Arigato, my pedigree chum. You have just given me the inch I needed.' And dashed off, leaving the still bruised and slightly breathless constable confused.

Wednesday, 27th February

21:50

Flirting for midnight, even the most dedicated of police officers and assistants would be found at home. Either sleeping soundly or nursing something a little strong over ice. For some of the most revered lab assistants and morgue physicians, especially on a high profile case, that rule didn't apply.

And chief inspector Hiraoka knew that all too well.

Rapping his knuckles on the door, Arnold, one of the lab technicians, eased it open, feigning a smile.

'Bit late, John?'

'Late yourself, but I know you vampires never sleep. Secretly gorging yourselves on the blood samples.'

Arnold laughed, patting down his white coat and closing the door behind Hiraoka.

'Erm, if you're here regarding the DNA and, indeed, the hair found at the crime scene, I insist that the report is being compiled and will be on your desk tomorrow.'

The two regarded each other. Hiraoka didn't budge a bit, opened his hands, palms up and grinned.

'That your best?'

Arnold shook his head. 'Come on, John, even through my obsessive work ethic and insomnia, I have not been able to finalise and complete the test. There's still other parts of the report I need to type up. Yada yada, you know. It'll be with you in the morning. Go to sleep.'

'Wow, better. Though you lost it at the end. Can't be giving your man orders.'

The dropping of his arms to his sides relayed defeat, and Arnold let out a deep sigh. 'For fuck sake. You'll have me out on the streets one day.'

Hiraoka shrugged. 'All for a good cause, though.'

'It's not bringing anyone back from the dead. What more can you do in the next eight hours?'

The chief inspector stared at him.

Arnold went wide-eyed. 'Sorry, forgot who I was talking to there.'

'I noticed. The report?'

'Well,' the technician started. 'That part is true, it isn't put together but, of course, you'll settle for the preliminary.'

Arnold turned and lead him down to his station, where a particularly expensive-looking microscope stood beside an array of laptops, several racks of test tubes and some other things Hiraoka dare not ask about.

'Off the record…'

'I've heard that twice tonight. This better be fucking good Arnie,' Hiraoka scowled, leaning close to him and staring at his laptop.

'Well, interesting. The hair found at the crime scene, marked AP4568a, was female. There was pulp at the root, nDNA, which allowed me to run a few tests. It was enough to ascertain sex.'

Hiraoka grumbled. 'His wife then? She had left an hour previous to the killer arriving. On a night out, perhaps getting ready in the bathroom?'

Arnold nodded.

'That information was used as context, in this case, just to be thorough. Unfortunately, no match. So the hair, as far as we can see, is completely foreign.'

'What?'

'Well, with no other residents at the address.'

'And they hadn't had visitors over in a few weeks,' Hiraoka added. 'It could have been the intruder. But hang on, you sure it was female?'

'That much we're positive on. I've hung back late to run this through our database, see if it gets a hit. So far, nothing and of course, you'll get the full version tomorrow on your desk. We're pulling serious overtime down here because of the killings.'

'Shit.' Was all Hiraoka could muster.

Had Haskell been cheating? Raising this with Miranda could be suicide, but he would have to see her sooner or later. 'I'll have to question Miranda to be sure. Oh, before I forget, any joy with that bloody toxicology report for Robert Short?'

Arnold simply shook his head. 'Still in process. Sorry. Same for the others. I'd give it another week.'

'Bollocks.'

A wave of the hand, a thank you, leaving Arnold a little baffled. Just like Nguyen. Because Hiraoka was on the rampage now, this was how he operated. He wouldn't rest until the hints, clues, and leads amounted to a delightful piece of evidence pointing to the killer. It's how he'd gotten the promotions, the respect.

The move from Japan over to the Met in the first place. Exemplary detective capabilities, the reference had said, apparently.

And it was something he'd be keen to impress upon Hudson if he somehow survived this case. Create respect through legacy. But more importantly, survive.

Something about this one didn't settle right in his mind. Like a disjointed piece of wooden framing, causing everything to creak and groan, books and things to slowly slide off. It wasn't a quick fix, and it would require everything being laid out to start repairs.

Which gave the chief inspector another idea.

Alone. The building empty; Hiraoka sat in the middle of the open floor, channelling his inner spirit. Slowly, and in the faint light from a nearby desk light, the chief inspector peeled open his eyes and looked out across all the files, pictures and notes spread out on the floor and pinned up on the murder board.

An image jumped into his mind's eye. Shadows from the CCTV footage. Of a woman seen at several of the locations on the day of the murder. Could this, with the hair, make her a suspect? Could a woman be capable of such attacks? The realisation had felt like a punch to the gut. It had winded him.

Then for the second time that night, he was wrong. Wrong about his solitude and peace as another crept up on him, though this time the voice was female. Gentle. Hiraoka didn't recognise it, his heart thudding. Slowly, he turned around, ready to jump quickly, go for the legs.

'Finally, on the ritual phase, sir?' Cracked DC Leigh, a backpack slung over her shoulder, a canister probably holding some delicious Japanese tea as a bribe. The best. And he knew it because his nose inhaled the fumes hungrily. And his heart slowed.

'Fucking hell, warning first?'

'Sorry, sir. Had a gut feeling you'd be here late. Couldn't sleep either, frankly part of it is sympathy for you. Mostly anxiety to find a suspect. ID the third victim. Close this absolute nightmare of a case.'

Hiraoka pointed at the canister in her hand. Slender, ebony fingers, clasping it with profession. Someone who had known Hiraoka for a while. Becoming comfortable and familiar with the process.

'First, two cups?'

'I'll pour.' She smiled.

The two were quickly at work, wordless on Hudson's very apparent absence in the case lately and lack of results. It was quite clear now he would be shelved if anything came of the evening's results. But it had been worth a try. DC Leigh had definitely tried.

After an hour or two, intermittently interrupted by bouts of yawning and slurps of Yokoshima blend, Leigh plucked a linguistics report on the note. It was dated today and on the pile of stuff left on Hunt's desk.

'Sir,' she called from across the office, opening the file. 'Didn't see this come in, did Hunt not send it over?'

'What's that?' he called, crossing the office and looming over. Leigh sat small in the shadows, a lamp light illuminating the pages. It was the oddest part of his ritual. That he wouldn't use the main light, conferring it messed up the flow of his thinking. That it was better in the dark. DC Leigh just thought he was getting old as shit.

'Bastard!' Hiraoka exclaimed, plucking it from her hand a little unceremoniously. 'But not much here anyway. I mean, the bastard's still a bastard but, fuck it's... hang on a second...'

He found a note regarding some of the consonants, particularly how the S's and the L's were written. Hiraoka read it in his head, which prompted Leigh to stand and peer up over his arms.

'Sir?'

'Sorry. Give it a read. I need to find those CCTV tapes again. I... what did you put in that tea?' He asked, his face pale, worried. Something Leigh hadn't seen in years. Not since the football fights.

'Nothing. Why?'

'A very controversial and potentially fucking worrying theory has crept into my mind tonight, and I need to confirm it. I need to ground myself before I go mad.'

He turned to rush off, but DC Leigh called after him, a little pissed at being shoved aside after so much work. It was nearly four in the morning.

'Sir! Sorry but, do you mind the cliff hangers? What is it?'

The chief inspector shook his head, looking back down at the report, thinking of the hair, the Soho eye witness. 'Our killer may very well have an accomplice or...' He paused. Composed his thoughts. 'Or our killer is, in fact, the mysterious blonde we've pegged as a private investigator, likely the one who spoke with our journalist friend has been playing us the entire fucking time. We need to speak to Bethany Shaw.'

Thursday, 28th February

07:20

Battered, exhausted and still feeling the punches from yesterday, Hudson nursed himself on the way in with a double shot of coffee. Light snow hinted at a storm receding. Respite from the month-long freeze. Maybe spring was just around the corner? News had mentioned that overground lines returning to use. Snow starting to melt quickly now as temperatures slowly rose above zero.

Through muted sips, he gazed out the bus window, not feeling the walk. Listened in on public transport chatter. Read through a few pages of the Metro. The usual. Just to occupy his mind. When his stop arrived, Hudson realised how nervous he was about going to work. Rocking up at Charlotte Mews to another meeting with IOPC. Hutchings himself. Or to Leigh's judging glare.

He hoped she was in better spirits.

Barely over the threshold, he was met with a strong wall of smells: coffee and takeaways. At the board sat Anderson, hair tied up, drumming a pen against her face. On the floor, surrounded by papers, were Leigh and Hiraoka, completely a mess.

As Hudson approached, they looked up, blurry-eyed, sleep-deprived but with a glint there. Something had happened.

Leigh spoke first. 'Shall I tell him, guv?'

Hiraoka waved a hand. 'Why not.'

'What's going on? Have you been able to ID the third vic?'

Leigh's smile spread further. 'Better. We're building a picture of the suspect. Been here all night, and Hiraoka managed to have a chat with the lab, get a report fast-tracked, which we hope to get today and…'

'The suspect looks to be a woman, blonde. We have forensics.'

'The hair? They ran tests this quick?'

Hiraoka nodded, Leigh still grinning. 'Indeed. As I said, only because of the nature of this case, of Haskell's passing, that we were able to do so. That and there was pulp on the hair.'

Hudson grabbed a chair, pulled it over to the floor of scattered case files. Wondering if they just couldn't be arsed with computers anymore? It screamed BBC crime drama. 'Hang on, so, pulp on the hair? I remember from an assault case back in Gotham, they said you can only get DNA from a hair if it's got that pulp at the end, which you only get if the hair is properly yanked out of the scalp.'

Hiraoka nodded. 'Precisely. Now, why would there be a hair yanked out in Haskell's house?'

This one hit him. 'No idea. I mean… there's no signs of struggle, is there?' He asked them both, glancing over the murder board for clues they noted down. 'Yeah. No signs.'

'But why else?' he persisted. 'Why else would you find a hair pulled out like that? Think about it. Where it was found. The CCTV footage.'

Hudson struggled. So he walked over to the board and scanned the pictures. The grainy print outs from CCTV footage showing a dark, tall figure in the vicinity of the Soho murder, then Stratford down the road from the cinema. No CCTV had been found by Hyde park or in Wandsworth yet, but it was just a matter of time. He pictured the clothes. The fibre found at the second crime scene. It started to slot in. Tall figures. Expensive fibres. Blonde hair.

'Leigh, do you remember the fibre found at the murder scene for Catherine Evans?'

She furrowed her brow, bouncing on her haunches. 'Er, I think it was a luxury item, tracing the manufacturer still. Probably a woolly item or something. I don't think it'll come back until next week.'

Hiraoka stood up, enormous and stretched. 'Come on, constable. Follow the reports we've had. What have witnesses seen?'

'A male. Big. A shape shi—' And it dawned on him. His eyes widened, and he considered the forensics. 'She's been changing. She's been disguising herself? Fucking hell, so she's just used her height or what, chucked on some doc martens, a baggy coat and a woolly hat and just carried that off?'

The chief inspector pointed down to the floor. 'No. There's more to it. We need to dig further as it doesn't explain the strength of it. It means our suspect is definitely strong enough to overpower quite well-built men of some height. Her own stature has been an advantage. So has the surprise of her attacks but…'

'Check martial arts studios?'

Anderson from across the room shouted back, a pen in her hand. 'On it already. Got a list to run through if you fancy a help?'

Hudson nodded. 'Sure. So, what's the full update?'

'That we're looking for a woman, anywhere between twenty-one and forty. Peak physical health, intelligent and with a strange psychosis. We've also been tracking down Bethany Shaw to bring in for questioning. The woman who tipped her off is definitely our main suspect.'

Hudson was already at his desk, firing up the computer to start his calls. 'Bethany Shaw? No answer on the phone?'

'None. We're hoping maybe she'd pick up for you unless we swing by the offices and pick her up?' Leigh suggested.

'Fair enough. That's a huge lead, I'll get on that right away. What about this er… Psychosis?'

Leigh nodded. 'It's the theory we built up last night. Remember the satanic angle we started exploring? Well, it could be just her. There's no satanic symbolism or evidence that removing brains from random people is the work of a Satanist. This could be the deranged workings and plans of someone who has severe dissociative disorder and schizophrenia.'

'Fuck.' Was all he could muster.

Before he set up to call the first number he'd found. A dingy shit hole near Lambeth, teaching MMA, Hudson looked over the monitor at Hiraoka and cleared his throat. He thought about the IOPC. The fuck ups and made to say something. But Hiraoka began mumbling to Leigh and the moment was lost.

Just get to work Hudson. That's how you clear all this up. Good police work. No substitute for it.

Several hours of calls into it, with no luck on Bethany Shaw, Nguyen showed his face. He looked tired himself. But his darkened eyes looked different, and noticed he kept spraying himself with deodorant. Was he still drinking? Hudson didn't have time to dwell on it. Hiraoka, fully into the swing now of lead investigator, throwing out orders, commanded Nguyen to pursue old cases of animal torture. Check for any female connections.

Moreau swung in a half-hour later on the same shift. She must have had a sixth sense because she came bearing a fuck load of tea. A large brew was made, drinks were passed around, and the tech genius got to work on making more headway with social media and online presence with the list of names officers had procured during their database searches. Nothing of interest yet.

Hudson sipped his tea, picking up the phone to a Ninjutsu dojo in Tower Hill. He eventually got through to someone on mobile. It sounded like someone young, but professional. A very well-spoken accent and seemingly happy to be of assistance.

'So, in essence, we need to check your memberships to see if we can match our suspects. Would there be a suitable time for me to come by?'

'As long as it complies with GDPR, of course, I'm happy to help.'

Hudson smirked. He'd taken the damn GDPR seminars last year before his transfer. Dull, but it was worthwhile. The new data protection laws in the EU governed any and all bodies, companies and individuals working with or within the European Union. It sought to further protect people's privacy regarding data. And it worked.

'Absolutely, I can bring documentation with me. Are you free today?'

A pause. 'I can meet you at the office in the hour?'

Hudson didn't expect a quick response. 'Great. I will be arriving just myself, DC Daniel Hudson. Once again, thank you very much for your help and I will see you soon.'

Leigh was looking up from the floor at him. 'Hit?'

He shrugged, standing up and grabbing his coat. 'No idea yet. Got a few to visit. Anderson's checking some too. All have had some pretty big blondes training with them, so now it's elimination time, I suppose?' Then he had an idea. A niggling thought and caught the chief inspector's attention by raising his hand.

'Sir, it might be a good idea to speak with Evan's parents. They're still in town for a few days. What do you think?'

Hiraoka considered it. 'I'll speak with Miranda. Hunt is in later, so I'll let you have the overtime and go for a chat.'

'Brilliant, thank you, sir, really appreciate that.'

He left with a bit of a sour taste in his mouth. Hunt. It was Hiraoka's way of letting him know he wasn't off the leash just yet. He wanted a tight rein on him, with Elms tip-toeing around in the background, IOPC still in close proximity. No doubt stacking up files at Charing Cross. It told Hudson that, despite reassuring him that the meeting with Hutchings had gone fine, he was still worried about what he still might say.

Hudson treated himself to a little music between trips. His back and forth investigations really dragging in the late afternoon. A little Black Keys and The Bellrays helped to break up the monotony. The rumbling groan of buses. The screeching sound of braking trains on the overground. After his first visit to the Ninjutsu dojo, he started to slowly rack up a list of names and addresses. Each fed directly to the team via a secure email system. This was all part of their way to comply with GDPR. Secure data, always in structured environments, password protected or encrypted.

As he sent them through, Moreau worked her magic. Tracing the individuals, breaking a few GDPR rules on the go. And by the time Hunt had come in to start an evening shift, no luck was to be found.

Fucking typical, he thought.

Hunt didn't seem as enthused about travelling with Hudson to visit Mr and Mrs Evans either, but he knew what the inspector was up to, felt all too willing in that sense to keep an eye on the young constable.

'That Hutchings fella giving you the shit then?' Hunt pestered, picking at his fingers as he swung the BMW round in the Hilton hotel car park.

'It's going fine. Just doing their job, aren't they?'

'As long as you've not got anything hidden in your closets, Daniel, you should be fine.' He shut the car off, got out and closed the door with great care. You could tell he loved his motor. 'You are squeaky clean, right?'

'Of course. Just like the rest of you.'

Hunt laughed out loud, cocking his head back. Flashing his stupid fucking teeth. 'Calm down, snowflake. Just say the right thing, and he'll be gone. He's not as scary as the other fuckers make out. Right, we meetin' them in the lobby café, yeah?'

Hudson nodded, checking his phone. 'Yeah, let's go.'

When they arrived, the parents immediately recognised Hudson and shook his hand in turn. With Hunt, they were a bit off-balance but returned the welcome all the same. After a little introduction, they all sat around the table, Hunt ordering in some drinks.

'Thanks for me—' Hunt began. Mr Evans interrupted.

'We've spoken a few times with DC Hudson before. And, Leigh, I believe? Is there any news? My wife and I assume so based upon such a meeting?'

Mrs Evans added, 'Spare the details. We… heard about how it was happening. The way she was…'

Mr Evans tapped her on her leg. 'Come on now. You said you wouldn't.'

'Oh, I know, I know.'

The detectives sat and waited as the pair seemed to wrestle with each other. Mr Evans composed himself again and sat forward, ignoring his drink. 'What do you have for us?'

Hudson wasn't in the mood for Hunt stepping all over him. He wanted a rapport with the Evans family. This was his first case. Hunt was just a bystander, trying to enforce rank. Really just a glorified desk bitch who liked being in the field. Any opportunity to antagonise the rookie.

'We can't divulge anything during an ongoing investigation and gathering by the media, you may already know quite a bit, correct?'

The parents nodded. They'd clearly seen the grizzly details of how the killer performed their signature encephalectomy on their victims. The sheer evil of it. How they have moved on to killing a high ranking police officer.

'We need to know more about any social issues Catherine may have had. Anything at school, university, or at home? With anyone in particular? Was she romantically involved with anyone you remember? We are trying to build clearer pictures of the victims. Any detail, anything at all, could prove invaluable.'

Mr Evans grunted. 'Aside from what we've already provided you, no. She wasn't disturbed or having a dodgy relationship if that's what you mean. She did date a chap. Mark, for a while, but we knew about him.' He shifted in his seat, looking for anyone nearby. 'Look. I know we aren't supposed to know but can you please just give us something.'

'I'm sorry,' Hudson replied. 'We genuinely can't. It could jeopardise the investigation. Are you able to provide Mark's contact de—'

'To hell with the investigation!' Mr Evans roared. Mrs Evans flinched, and Hunt stood up in reflex. 'Where the fuck is the killer? What have you idiots been doing? You, Hudson. You look barely old enough to wear a fucking suit.'

He was taken aback. Stunned by the outburst. Staff nearby looked over, and a receptionist looked to be reaching for the phone. Hunt flashed his badge and shook his head.

'Mr Evans. Look. I'm really so—'

'No you're not,' said Mrs Evans, in an almost hushed voice. Contrasting so much to her husband. 'None of you are. Despite the horrific way our daughter was robbed from us, you sit idly by, allowing even your own officers to perish. The state of the Met is a shambles. How can we trust you? You come here asking more questions about our Cathy, clearly evident you haven't a bloody clue where you're going.'

And before the detectives could reason further, they left for their room. It couldn't have been more than two minutes. But it had felt like a lifetime, caught in that high energy. The sheer tension following Mr Evan's outburst.

Hunt looked over at Hudson, nodding to the front door. Once outside, he pulled out his car keys. 'Well, that went about as exactly as I thought it would.'

Hudson frowned. 'Fuck off, did you.'

'I beg your pardon?'

'Sorry, *guv*, but you didn't help the matter. I re—'

Hunt stood over him, a finger in his face. Nose inches from his own. Hudson's stomach knotted as he prepared to fight.

'Watch. Your. Fucking. Mouth, Daniel.'

No other words were exchanged. Hudson just stood there, disgusted. Fed up. He threw up a hand, pocketed his phone and started walking off down the street.

'Where the fuck are you going?'

Hudson didn't reply. It was late. Just shoved his hands into his pockets and focused on getting as far away from the hateful prick as possible.

Thursday, 28th February

21:50

Later that night, Hudson's planned route home was cut short. Instead, he found himself tube hopping, battling through the crowds in Knightsbridge. The snow almost entirely slush at this point. Numbed to the marrow, Hudson clutched at his sides and breathed hot air into his hands.

He didn't get quite why he'd come to Hyde Park. Not only was the park under higher security, with the gates shut much earlier and it being much more difficult to sneak in, his curiosity was nevertheless piqued.

Hudson stood by the wrought-iron fencing, eyeing a police officer further down by the gate. The sheer paranoia created since the first killing was incredible. Such a vast and powerful city suddenly felt so fragile. People getting home earlier, avoiding alleys and parks. Sharing rumours and hysteria over social media. London felt delicate, and with just another killing, it could all fall apart.

Maybe that's what the killer was after? But why the brains? Was that a message all along? Revealing the brain of London's citizens for us to see? Maybe a message they just couldn't decipher? Plain to see only for the killer? It all felt like wild guesswork, and Hudson doubted that even with all of Hiraoka's experience, he could replace a professional profiler's work.

His hands gripped the fence, stared back into the trees and pictured that tall, dark figure. The shapeshifter. The surgeon, hammer in one hand. Knife in the other. A twisted, bloody scene. Hudson made to peer further, but his phone flashed.

It was Bethany.

Meet me tomorrow, at two o'clock, Tower Bridge.

'Do they know?' Hudson whispered to himself. 'Do they know we're on to her?'

That notion suddenly hit him, turning back to head home. That this masked, crazed serial killer had been female the entire time. The rookie behaviour; a prejudiced and biased view he'd held during the investigation. Such an obvious detail overlooked. But comforted himself on the witness reports they had received, all giving the gender as male. It could be worse, but with that Hutchings bloke circling, he was practically shitting himself.

The following morning, Hudson peered into Eisa's room.

'Hello?'

No answer.

He rummaged about the kitchen and went downstairs to check the store but saw no signs of a note. Nothing to indicate a reason for shutting up shop. Worried now, Hudson pulled out his phone and sent her a text.

'Where are you? I've not seen you. Not like you to go out on a bender...' He considered out loud. Heard his own voice back and dismissed it. 'Nah, definitely not like you.'

Showered, shaved and finally dressed by quarter to seven, Hudson dove out the door with the objective of the last working day of the week to keep his shit together.

Since things had escalated, Hiraoka, the lead investigator, had brought Leigh further under his wing and pushed him back toward more menial tasks. Lots of database admin. Calls, the lot. Since Haskell's death, the team's general confidence in him was at an all-time low. More so than when he first joined, fresh from the country without a clue on Met procedures. Not really.

And that's why you'll stay a constable, Hunt had mocked him the other day.

The morning was instantly occupied by another meeting with Hutchings at the station. More bland white walls, recording stations and cups of water. Endless droning to boot. But Hudson knew the gig now, focused on just recalling all the facts and cooperating. IOPC would be reviewing all officers working on the case, but Hudson was first up as fate would have it.

'Don't suppose you could shuffle a certain DCI up to the top of that list of yours, eh?' Hudson joked poorly, leaving the session just before lunch.

Hutchings wasn't impressed. 'Unless you have a serious allegation to make, constable, I would highly advise against jokes made at the expense of senior officers. Particularly so soon into the role.'

The sheer willpower not to fall apart, climb up inside his own arse and die, was powerful. The embarrassment from his stupidity. It set him on a trajectory back at Fitzrovia, where he spilt coffee on Nguyen.

Finalising a quick chat with Elms, who looked eager to get going, holding a large stack of folders, Hiraoka soon spied the commotion.

'DC Hudson,' he cracked. 'Send me over Bethany Shaw's statement when you can. It'll be a fascinating piece to cross-check with what we have thus far.'

'I er,' he started, but Hiraoka was already there.

'Of course not. Hudson, I want something by close of business. If we can link Bethany Shaw's statement of the suspect with what we have thus far, we could start tracking down our…'

A loud shout boomed from across the office. Leigh was jumping up, raising her hands. Her cockney really shining through. 'Fuckin' found 'im!'

'Third vic?' Hiraoka jogged across the office, everyone standing around Leigh's computer to check on who the man was.

'Indeed. Adam Smith, if you can believe it, Bristol. Born 1976, Adam has been missing for the last six months. Last reported in Swindon.' She sat back, running her fingers across her afro, a massive grin on her face. Despite how Hudson was feeling himself, he couldn't help but smile too.

'Fucking great find.' Hudson said.

Nguyen, packing his bits up to head home on a half shift, frowned at the screen. 'Swindon? What the fuck made him come all the way here? Film wasn't that good. Saw it myself.'

Hiraoka wagged a finger. 'Such wisdom Nguyen. I want you to trace this back, Leigh. We need to see what his movements have been over the last six to twelve months. Moreau,' he called. 'Social networks. Online presence. Credit cards. You name it. Let's get this rolling. See what he has in common with the other victims.'

Moreau pointed up a pair of finger guns and clicked her tongue. 'Gotcha. Adam Smith though, guv, a bit of a haystack, that.'

'But you'll do it. I know you can. Leigh, who called it in?'

'His brother, Joe. Apparently, Adam left home and dropped everything to be with his girlfriend here in London. Never kept in touch, and the family filed a missing person. That's why it's taken so long, guv, we've had to expand to other counties. I'll be taking the road trip as soon as I can.'

'Brilliant. Find the girlfriend. Hudson, with me.' He walked the distance between them, waiting for Hudson to throw on his coat and gloves. He nudged him out to the courtyard and lit a cigarette.

Hudson waited for what else he had to say.

'How was the meeting with Hutchings?'

A shrug. That's how best to summarise it. 'Fine. I've already told you, though, sir. Is everything alright?'

'I'm just making sure you're not doing anything stupid, kabu.'

'So,' he said. 'I know there's T's to cross and I's to dot. It looks bad, Haskell getting killed. It looks, like... it's really fucking terrible, and I've not slept a wink so, I can only imagine how you and the rest of the team are feeling.' He picked at a thread of cotton on his glove. Dared himself to see how much it'd fray. 'But I'm really trying. I am. And as for the leak, I had nothing to do with it. But I'm committed to working this through. I promise you that guv.'

The chief inspector seemed to soak every last word in. Savoured it. Looked at Hudson as if looking at something he'd seen before. Like he recognised it from somewhere. Maybe from his time on the force in Japan. Either way, his face unnerved him.

'I believe you,' he uttered finally, flicking ash down toward a drain which had now revealed itself, no snow left on the cobbles.

'Thanks, sir. Well, I'll call in once I've gotten Bethany.'

He nodded. 'Very good.'

Hudson kicked through the puddles and slush and made a right, feeling Hiraoka's eyes on the back of his neck the whole way. But now, he felt a little better. As if the number of people on his side had shifted in his favour. He picked up the pace, pulling out his phone to call Bethany.

'Come on, you fucker,' he grumbled, scaring an elderly person at a bus stop. 'Pick up!'

In just a month, Hudson had already grown sick-to-death of cafés and coffee in general. Back in Gotham, he had the occasional latte but was known for his lemon tea addiction. Here in London, his chance for a yellow carton of sweet goodness was sidelined quite often, by the same, bitter sludge knock off crap. Maybe he was just fed up? Stood outside Caffè Nero, waiting for Bethany Shaw to show up, freezing his tits off, he wasn't in the mood. And there was someone he had to speak to first.

Jessica passed him his coffee five minutes later on their walk toward Piccadilly.

'So, anything I should be worried about?' She joked, flashing him a grin.

Hudson melted immediately. 'No, no, not at all. I just thought I owed you a better apology is all.'

'Well, you are a bit shit with messaging back.'

'I know.'

'And calling in general.'

'I know,' he repeated. 'It's been a bit of a nightmare. I've been terrible with everyone. This is something really unusual, something I've not seen before so, I just want you to know that it won't be long. Things will be wrapped up, and I promise to spend more time with you. Make more time.'

She let out a little laugh, shaking her head.

'You still don't get it, do you?'

Hudson frowned.

'Get what? Have I put my foot in it again?'

'It's not about taking me out, I just want to be in the loop. I feel severed. Like I'm not involved. Like I'm just on the sidelines, a bottle of sauce to squeeze when it suits you.' She paused. 'Excuse the analogy.'

'Oh no,' Hudson winked. 'It's a good analogy.'

They both laughed, taking a seat on the steps in the centre. A band played nearby, and pigeons filled the air. The smell of cooking sausages wafted over from a nearby street. Hudson's stomach growled.

'Hungry?' she asked. 'I've got a flexy shift. We could take a long lunch?'

Hudson checked his phone and could kick himself.

'I wish I could, but I'm meeting someone.'

'Oh right,' she said, casting her face down, then looking off away from him. 'Yeah, no, I'm being silly, but I'm sure we'll have a lovely date in store this weekend? Right?'

He nodded. 'Of course.'

They both shared a quick kiss, nothing too awkward, and Hudson tried to dash across the road without looking too eager to get away. Pulling out his phone again, he made to call Bethany but immediately spotted her angry expression in the crowd just a dozen or so yards ahead.

Concerned, he walked up to her slowly, hands upturned.

'You okay? We can reschedule if you'd like, but this is quite important. Got the DCI breathing down my neck.'

The journalist gesticulated angrily. 'Have you been pulling my fucking leg? Or is this part of investigative work now at the Met? Probing people for data? Sweeping up whatever crumbs you need, God. You guys make me fucking sick. Forget it.'

She turned and left, leaving Hudson open-mouthed.

Once the stun had worn off, he gave chase and tried to reason with her.

'Hey, hey, what was that about?'

No response. She took her phone out to dial.

'Oi! Talk to me!'

Bethany stopped, clearly livid and hung up whoever she was calling. She looked back from where they came and then up at Hudson.

'How long have you had her on detail? If you knew she was the lead, why bother me in the first place?'

Hudson frowned, shaking his head. 'Sorry I'm not following? Had who on detail? What lead? Are you talking about the woman we've traced? The one who tipped you off?'

'Yeah,' Shaw spat. 'Your fucking girlfriend, by the looks of it.'

It didn't clock at first. He looked back up the street and remembered Jessica. Then turned back to Bethany and sort of bumbled his words like a toddler trying to push the square-cube into the square hole for the first time.

'Jessica? What, the er… the tall blonde I was just with?'

It was Bethany's time to frown, now equally confused. 'You don't know?'

'Are you sure? Are you sure it was the woman I was just with?'

'Very. I remember a face. Part of the job, or maybe just my perverse side swinging. But yeah, that was her. So you've been ignorant of the obvious this entire time?'

Hudson turned to her, neck flashing red. This couldn't be true. The theory now hitting him like a freight train. That Jessica was the lead, the suspect and the one who visited the second murder scene. The one they'd been hunting this entire time. Going out for coffee. Catching up.

Sex.

Without thinking, he pulled out his phone, scrolled through his contacts and went to dial her.

Bethany lunged, grabbing his phone. 'No. Not yet.'

'Hands off! I know what I—'

'Evidently not, Sherlock fucking Hudson. Call her now, and you'll spook her. Fuck, where did you graduate from? Are you sure you're meant to be working in CID?'

His hands went up into his hair, clutching tight. He couldn't believe the possibility. Wouldn't let it sink in. His world started to bend and twist at the seams. A sudden rush of nausea caught him off guard, and he buckled, grabbing the nearest wall for support.

'You OK? Detective?'

Standing up, gasping for air, he pressed at his temples, composing himself again. 'I'm sensing there's some sort of little binding deal you're going to weave out of this?'

Bethany Shaw grinned wide, handing back his phone. She pulled out a small planner and a pen. 'Oh, I'm old school. When this inevitably blows up, I want first dibs on coverage.'

'I can't autho—'

'First. Dibs. Or I start spinning a yarn of my own. This is a big story, Hudson. Your little girlfriend there knows the man bludgeoning heads around London. That or she's doing it herself.'

His head sunk, and he tried to focus. Biting his tongue on the potential theory that she was helping another woman. Refused to tell Shaw that, in actual fact, Jessica could be their killer.

A sudden rush of blood in his ears. The noise made him feel sick again, making it hard to concentrate and keep a poker face. What was he going to tell Hiraoka and the team? Dared to picture Elms' reaction.

Hudson glowered at her before leaving. 'I'll see what I can do.'

337

Friday, 1st March

15:20

Hudson gazed up at the long windows of their base of operations, watching the dripping of thawing ice on the gutters. The sound made a strange thud on the way down, ricocheting off the metal awning by the door. A memory echoed in his ear, like a whisper in a cave. It was Hiraoka, back four weeks ago when they stood in Hyde Park.

Hoshoku-sha, means predator, he'd said, referring to the ferocious, savage and almost precise manner in which the killer had torn the face apart and scalped them out in the open. Brutally smashing away at their skull to pull out their brain.

It was hard to swallow. That notion of a predator. A killer that ruthless. Someone Jessica could be tangled up with. Helping, even. The mere thought that she was solely responsible was even more absurd. She wasn't the type. To orchestrate, that was one thing. To carry out? No way... He flicked open his phone. Swiped through her profile pictures on Facebook. That unassuming, intelligent and beautiful smile. Nothing about that face said psychopath. Nothing about it told him she was bereft of empathy or lusted for power, dominance or the suffering of others. Nothing in her past pointed toward a break in mental health or revealed an underlying dark side.

It must be confusion. Perhaps a wire crossed somewhere. But it was a lead, and it meant she'd have to come in for questioning.

Taking the stairs up slower than usual, he plucked up the courage to approach Hiraoka.

Ten minutes later, things had escalated beyond his control. The whole team were on the floor with Hiraoka at the murder board. Elms was sat on the sidelines, his flop of grey hair atop a face filled with curiosity and patience.

'I met with Mail reporter Bethany Shaw earlier today, who has confirmed an unexpected detail that could start opening up this case for us. I wanted to get a lead on the informant she spoke with at the crime scene in Soho. She mentioned before about it, and when I approached her, she seemed pretty angry. That's when she noticed the woman I had just been speaking with and said I was full of shit. Turns out she was the informant and the one who tipped her off beforehand.'

Leigh's eyes flew open wide. 'You fucking knew 'em?'

'The fuck is this?!' Hunt shouted.

Hiraoka raised a hand and called for silence.

The atmosphere was suddenly electric, tensions high and all eyes now on Hudson. Angry. Distrustful. All except Elms, who continued to survey the scene with the same look of interest.

'Hudson,' the chief inspector said. 'Who is she? This lead? How is she connected to you? Was Shaw entirely confident about the ID she made in the street?'

'Yes, she was. She was pretty positive. And she's a close friend. I see her from time to time for a catch-up and...'

'Now would certainly not be an opportune moment to begin muddying the truth with lies, Detective Constable Daniel Hudson,' Elms intoned from the desk to the left. Heads turned, and Hudson felt himself shrink beneath his aura of authority. 'Care to rephrase?'

Hiraoka looked fit to burst.

'We've... we've been dating for a few weeks. Maybe a month.'

'So basically the entire time this case has been live then?' Leigh shot.

Hudson froze. 'No. No, it can't have been. We've been dating longer than that, I'm sure. I'm...'

He was drowned out again by sounds of disgust and incredulity in the team. The idea they had been thrown to the sharks by their own detective made them feel sick. Betrayed. Whether Hudson had meant it or not, it was all adding up now in his own head. But that still didn't explain her knowledge of the case, nor plenty of other holes in the theory.

Hiraoka clocked this and called, once again, for the team to quieten down.

'Accusations aside, this information only confirms that the informant that tipped the journos off after the second murder is known to a Met detective. While concerning, that does not itself prove they are directly involved with the murders, let alone committing them. Hudson, what is an honest account of your girlfriend's character? Her profile, from a professional perspective?'

Leigh laughed, but Hudson ignored it. 'Empathetic, caring. Intuitive and intelligent. I've known Jessica for ten years. I went to university with her, and she's never shown signs of being malicious or even a little odd. No mental health issues or family problems I was aware of. If anything, I wouldn't be at all surprised if she's been trying to reach out to me to confess and has not felt safe or brave enough to do so. I feel that it's far more likely, sir, that someone is coercing her somehow to help.'

'This is horse shit,' Leigh said, shaking her head. 'With everything we have so far? How the fuck does it not point to Hudson's girlfriend? Why not just bring her in now for questioning, get the alibis?'

Hudson's face had gone pale. He slumped back down in his chair, picking up a file and turning to the notes Moreau had made on Robert Short's laptop. The diary they found. MJ.

'MJ,' he said dumbly, standing up and handing the report to Leigh. 'Jessica's last name is Meyer. It's her initials back to front. It's her. I'm so fucking sorry.'

Hunt chirped up, fists visibly clenched. 'I knew taking you on since day one was a huge fucking mistake.'

'Sir,' Leigh gesticulated, looking a little exhausted, passing the file over to Hiraoka. 'Hunt has a good point. How can we trust anything Hudson is saying?'

It felt like a punch to the gut. Hudson doubled over in his mind, reeling from the blow and couldn't bring himself to look her in the eyes. That feeling of knowing he'd betrayed her and the team like this. It was absolutely a shared feeling at this point.

Hiraoka turned to face the murder board and rubbed at his growing beard.

'Because, DC Leigh, I have thought the accomplice, and or killer, could be female ever since Haskell was taken from us.'

The room fell silent. Elms turned his gaze to Hiraoka and tilted his head in surprise.

'John,' he said. 'Why am I hearing of this now?'

'You're hearing it now.'

The room tensed.

'I knew Haskell. We were close. He was old school, sir. If a strange man had rocked up at the door, he would have told him where to go. If it had been a woman, then he may have given her a second chance. Besides, a woman would have gone more unnoticed, given Haskell lives with his wife. Someone glancing out the window wouldn't have suspected much. It was dark..' Hiraoka jabbed the board with a long finger, and Hudson, along with the others, followed it intently. Hypnotised now.

'Haskell's wife left not thirty minutes before for drinks with friends and the show at Royal Albert Hall. If we look at TOD, we could even set a timeline down that the killer was at the front door as close to ten to fifteen minutes after Mrs Haskell. This means that had the killer been female, she may have very easily duped Haskell with a story about missing her to share a taxi. The killer knew where Haskell lived. It wasn't random. This was a deliberate move. Calculated. Which is why a note was left this time. The killer is aware of our inability to catch them and is revelling in the challenge. Which also leads me to believe that the reason to knock on that door when she did, was to use Haskell's wife's departure as a ploy to gain entry. To surprise him.'

'Fuck!' Leigh gasped, putting a hand to her mouth. 'The hair in the bathroom.'

Hiraoka nodded. 'Foreign hair found in the downstairs bathroom.'

She turned from Hiraoka to Hudson. 'What colour hair does Jessica have?'

'B-blonde. Dirty blonde, I think.'

Leigh turned back to Hiraoka. 'You think we could place her in that house?'

Before the excitement could start to whisk everyone away from grounded reality, Elms stood and walked into the floor to take centre stage.

'Let's not get ahead of ourselves just yet. But what you have, at the very least, are grounds to enquire.' He turned to Hiraoka, his eyes squinting up at the large man. 'What are your thoughts, John?'

His eyes were not on his chief in command, but instead of the young detective who now stood in judgement for his actions, plenty of the team still regarding him with disgust and hurt. Then it came to him. A way to confirm their suspicions, to clear Hudson's name. Prove or disprove his own theory that Jessica was an accomplice and to at least find out who she was working with.

'We need to question Jessica. Ask her where she was and see how it plays out. We have some very shaky circumstantial evidence. I'm conscious that Shaw is our only tangible link to Jessica being at the second crime scene. It's a bit of a leap. But if she knows we're cornering her, she may react. Make a mistake. And I have just the thing.'

Saturday, 2nd March

09:20

Leigh and Nguyen juggled cups of coffee after realising they'd started drinking the wrong ones, following a tragic error by the barista to not label them.

'How do you even stomach that shit?' he said, swirling a mouthful of his own cup of brew to get the taste out.

'There's fuck all wrong with mocha. Sort yourself out.'

'Bollocks. Chocolate and coffee? Are you mad?'

'Quite a common combination, not sure why you're crying.'

Nguyen took another swig of his latte and shook his head. Deciding against another retort. Instead, he craned his head up to inspect the top row of windows of a beautiful Edwardian building, converted into flats above Kensington's charming shops and boutiques.

'So, this is where Hudson's bit on the side lives then?'

'Apparently,' Leigh said, checking the time. 'And I'd classify her more as a suspect at this point.'

'So, you believe any of that shit then?'

'What shit?'

Nguyen turned in his passenger seat, one eyebrow raised. 'That he's completely clean of any wrongdoing. Passing over information. He could easily have been feeding her bits and pieces here and there just to look all big bollocks. Come down to London, make it big, impress some pus— Ow!'

Leigh had thumped him. 'Shut the fuck up.'

'You know I'm talking sense.'

'No, you're not. Why would he risk a job he's recently transferred to after years of applying just to get laid? No, doesn't sound right.' But even as she said it, Leigh wasn't entirely convinced. She hadn't been privy to his internal investigative meetings with the boogeyman, but it didn't mean there wasn't a whiff of distrust. They had all thought about it.

Nguyen sensed her uncertainty. 'I'm right about this. I'm not saying he's maybe doing it intentionally, but it doesn't add up any other way.'

'Unless she's somehow the mastermind behind it all?' Leigh offered, popping a lip and showing her hands. 'We have to entertain that possibility as well.'

The detective coughed on his coffee. 'You think a woman, no offence, could pull these murders off? Have you seen the reports? The weight behind the attacks was evident in the wounds.'

'Have you not read what I've sent you, then?'

Nguyen sighed, pulling out his phone to check. 'Sorry, what do we have?'

'For starters,' she said. 'She has a strong academic and athletic background. We're not dealing with just your average person here. Anderson and Hudson were on the right track with martial arts. She's trained in MMA for several years.'

'Fuck.'

'Exactly.' Leigh rapped his phone screen with a nail. 'Read what I bloody send you next time. Anyway, the others should be setting up now, and we've had no sign of Jessica. Let's hope she turns up.'

'Yeah,' he said, glancing up at the flat windows again. 'Let's God damn hope so.'

In a large Volvo estate, parked on double yellows around the corner from the Natural History Museum, DCI Hiraoka and DS Hunt sat patiently, checking wires they had hooked up to small microphones by their ears. Behind them, and stationed in various other streets, sat specially trained officers fully armed to the teeth in case of severe escalation.

Hunt rested an elbow on the window edge and aimlessly watched people walk by, his gaze occasionally stopping on a few attractive women and giving them a cheeky smile or nod. With no luck, he sat back and huffed, starting to fiddle with the car's central console.

'No joy, what's happening to this town,' he moaned.

Hiraoka tapped some ash out the window. 'It's because, sergeant, you look like you're on day-release. And keep your hands off the car, I didn't polish the interior to impress you.'

Hunt laughed. 'Brutal.'

Silence returned in the car, their eyes watching the roads, looking out for Jessica. Time rolled on slowly, and nothing of note happened. Hiraoka would have been happy to remain quiet for hours, but Hunt just couldn't hack it.

He turned to the chief inspector, just ten minutes in. 'Moves if this doesn't pan out, sir?'

'You tell me.'

'We haven't gone back to theories about a disgraced surgeon. There are still dozens we've not contacted. And the Satanist route hasn't been exhausted. This Jessica thing could be a red herring. In the wrong place at the wrong time. An accomplice?'

Hiraoka took a long drag toward the end of his cigarette and let out a long plume of smoke as if energising himself to respond to such a witless remark. 'Firstly, no surgeon worth their salt would remove someone's cerebrum in such a rash method. And nothing is connecting these murders to Satanic rituals. You know these enquiries are dead ends, sergeant. Why bring it up again?'

'Well, I hardly expect this fucking bitch of Hudson's to break open the case either. Since when are journalists from The Mail reliable leads? And there's a number of other ways she could have known the murders were linked. It might have even been a wild guess.'

Hiraoka shrugged. 'Maybe.'

'Maybe?' Hunt said in disgust. 'You aren't that sure?'

'It doesn't matter if I'm sure or not. She needs questioning, even if she knows the smallest detail. Cases have been made on less.' He chucked his cigarette and reached for another. 'Now shut up. I'm putting us live in with Hudson.'

Hiraoka flicked a switch, and Hunt sat bruised for a moment, scowling as he spoke back into his mic. 'Testing, testing. Hudders is a useless cunt, P45 in the post.'

Stood isolated in the centre of the museum's stone floor lobby, surrounded by crowds of tourists and school children, Hudson waited anxiously for Jessica. The meet had been set and coordinated by the team. Even the texts had been sent by Moreau, who was keeping tabs back at base. Hudson's only thing to do was make contact, pretend everything was fine, and slowly confront her about the journalist. That was it.

Caught in his own thoughts, the sudden static in his ear jolted him awake. It was Hunt, with a particularly nasty quip.

'Shut up, you old twat.' Was his reply, causing an elderly couple to jump back from him in shock and disgust. He'd been making a nasty habit with his expletive outbursts.

'Reign it in, you two,' said Hiraoka. 'Hudson, do you still have a view of the entrance? Any sign of your girlfriend?'

Hudson groaned at the term, dwelling more than on how it implicated him as a potential conspirator.

'Yeah, I've got eyes on the entrance, no sign of her yet. So we're sticking to script B, right?'

'That's right.'

Hudson shoved his hands into his pockets, starting to fidget nervously, feeling very exposed despite the crowd swimming around him.

'And no improvising,' Hunt chimed in.

'Obviously.'

The static in his ear quietened again, and Hudson was once more alone.

Waiting.

Some long, agonising minutes later, Jessica's tall frame appeared above the stairs and descended slowly, immediately spotting Hudson and giving him a wave. Made a note that she seemed to be dressed far more casual than usual. Some fitted jeans, a pair of sports trainers and a puffer jacket. Her smile looked innocent and sincere whilst he tried to suppress an acrid bubble of sick somewhere in the pit of his stomach. He had to keep it together, stay composed. If she was involved, she would clock if he was on to her in a heartbeat.

'Hiya! This to make up for the other day?'

He smiled, kissing her on the cheek. 'Yeah, sorry about that. I've just been busy, you know me, and I've not been prioritising the more important things in my life.'

'Oh Daniel,' she sighed, rubbing his arm and leading them into a slow crawl toward the first exhibit. 'You don't have to apologise, really.'

They steered toward a pillar running high up against the east wall, out of sight of most of the crowd. Hudson's plan had been to stay central and in the open, but looking up to spot the cameras, he realised they had just walked into a blind spot. His heart started to thud harder against his chest. She was on to him.

She fucking knows.

'I mean it. You don't have to apologise, you weren't to know. I mean, how could you?' She wordlessly reached out, pulled the tiny earpiece from his ear and dropped it on the floor.

Hudson panicked, made to sputter but she placed a finger against his lips to silence him.

'No. Now you listen. You're going to call this off. You're going to speak to your seniors back in that black car parked outside and explain everything. That you've taken my statement and it was a wild guess having seen the crime scene tents before at Hyde Park. Are we clear?

Should I need to come in, I'll happily reconfirm. But do you understand?'

Hudson pulled her hand away. His fear now replaced with anger. A deep-seated sense of betrayal. 'You've got to be fucking high if you think I'll—'

He stopped speaking. All colour leaving his face as Jessica brought up a picture on her phone. A shot of his sister crossing the street, watching for traffic. His thumping heart fell down into his stomach, and he had to breath out to stop himself from going dizzy.

'W-what the fuck are you playing at? You'll never make it out. This entire area is surrounded by armed police. It's over.'

She moved closer, enjoying herself.

'You've done very well, Danny, though I don't doubt it was a group effort. You're not nearly that smart. I suppose you're wondering what's going to happen now?'

Hudson was struggling to soak it all in. That Jess, right under his nose, had been so involved from day one. But one question still remained. 'Just tell me this,' he said, mouth going dry. 'Was it you killing those people, or were you helping someone?'

Jessica grinned, parting her lips slowly to respond, but Hudson wasn't quick enough for what happened. Her hand shot up behind his arm, spun him around effortlessly up into the wall. There, she kicked his legs out, slamming his head into the wall. A shot of pain blazed across his vision, sending him to the floor.

By the time he'd recovered himself, Jessica was already walking hurriedly toward the entrance. At that moment, he knew, without a word spoken.

It had been her all along.

With no time to digest the dizzying realisation or the excruciating pain in his forehead, Hudson scrambled up and chased after her.

Breaking out into the crisp winter air, he scanned the road to see where she had gone to. Erratically, he yelled for his team, forgetting the earpiece was gone and drew some worried looks from the crowds.

Up ahead, pulling a man in a suit from a black Audi, Hudson watched Jessica jump in and speed off. Just ahead of her, a pizza delivery guy stood behind his moped, rummaging for a few boxes. Lunging at the opportunity, Hudson broke into a full sprint, hands up.

'I need that bike!' he yelled maniacally. Before the boy had a chance to even respond, Hudson was diving forward, jumping straight on the moped and racing off, with the teenager behind him swearing and shouting angrily, pizza scattered all down the road. He didn't care. He couldn't lose her!

Accelerating hard, skidding on some slush, he raced through the traffic in the direction she'd disappeared, and soon enough, he caught sight of her taillights as she braked wildly for a red light. Seeing him in her rearview, racing wildly on a moped, she decided to go for it, jumping straight through a red, narrowly avoiding a side-on collision.

Just behind her, Hudson decided to take an equally wild gamble and shot on after her, swinging the moped on a bit of ice around the skidded car she'd avoided, up around a parked bus and on toward her unknown destination.

'Oh shit. Oh shit!'

An unseen patch of ice almost toppled him.

Hair whipping in the wind, his eyes dried out from the cold in seconds, forcing them open to stare right ahead. Keeping them locked on his target.

Screeching between rows of cars and overtaking traffic, shooting through red lights and screaming pedestrians and before long, they were breaking their way into the city of London and all its heavy traffic. A few times, with little and no regard for his own life, Hudson drove onto the pavement, partly because he had no time to brake, just to avoid his own minor crash. Amidst the screams of people falling out the way, he still had sight on Jessica.

He had to catch her, even if it killed him.

Another red light. She swerved just in time, only clipping the back end of her car but it caught Hudson straight on. The silver Mercedes Jessica avoided collided directly with him, the moped sliding clean under the five-door as he went sailing through the air. For a glorious moment the cool breeze and air was refreshing, and the sense of weightlessness was almost euphoric, until the horrific sensation of hard concrete slabs came up to meet him.

Hudson cried out as he tumbled over down the pavement and into a metal fence. His nose and head bleeding, eyes blurry, he noticed the black Audi had also gone on to crash, and from the smoking ruins

Jessica stumbled out, attempting to make her escape by foot.

Not on his fucking watch. He still had fight in him.

Pumping his legs hard, lactic acid building up, a stitch hinting at his side, Hudson raced on, charging through the crowd. Sounds of cries and yells filled the cacophony of car horns and the bustling noise of central London. Hudson could just make out the swishing hair of Jessica in the distance, less than thirty metres away and soldiered on. Arms cutting through the air. Hands carving through crowds.

The flash of blonde turned left down a side street. Hudson took note. Eyes glued to the edge of a brick wall it vanished behind. Closing in, he shoved two large men out of the way and took the same left. As he did, between a row of parked estates and vans, a glimpse of Jessica revealed her lead.

'STOP!' Hudson shouted. 'IT'S OVER!'

Through the echoing noise of slapping feet on slush and concrete, Hudson swore he heard her laugh.

Choosing riskier and more difficult ways to traverse, Jessica took a sharp right up ahead, skidding hard on a patch of black ice that almost ended it for her. Luck would fail Hudson as he too couldn't avoid it. Seeking her chance, Jessica dove toward a fire exit door halfway down the alley and disappeared inside.

Hudson, regaining his feet, followed, his chest screaming.

As the door swung open, he crashed through into a dimly lit tiled corridor. Boxes and cages lined both sides. A man at the end of the corridor, skinny, raised his hands up in protest when Jessica piled into him, knocking him clean out. Hudson screamed in protest but to no avail.

He ran after her, taking a right through a door and into the kitchen. The cooks all shouted in alarm as the pair crashed and climbed their way over the counters, diving out through another set of doors into a restaurant. Tables tipped, and food flew. But a table leg betrayed Hudson, and he fell forward, right onto his chin and drawing blood.

'Fuck!' he winced, scrambling up and vanishing into the street.

Jessica had already gained a considerable lead on the street, her tall, athletic build aiding her escape.

Taking off again, Hudson pulled out his phone and went to dial Hiraoka. Nothing worked. Eyes still on Jessica, his thumb traced a series of cracks and chips. Broken. He pocketed it and carried on. The panic of not catching her poisoned his confidence but spurred his aching legs on. Willing him to keep going.

Checking his surroundings, ignoring the bewildered looks of civilians, Hudson noticed they were near Blackfriar bridge. Then the familiar, bitter smell of the river and the long, paved walkway beside it. Tall, black, lamps rose up from the walls majestically. Architecture of a bygone era. To the right of them, office buildings, hotels and a pub.

They reached the Blackfriar, Hudson gaining some distance and sped across it, doubling back round to follow Jessica entering a short and narrow pedestrian tunnel.

'Tired, Danny?' she chided back for the first time, her shrill voice echoing mockingly.

'I won't stop! It's over, Jessica!' He paused to gulp air, trying to keep pace, his face burning up. The chill rush of air as they left the tunnel felt bliss. Sirens in the distance growing louder. 'It's fucking over!'

Only he'd not anticipated the next move.

As the pair navigated an wrought-iron gate and a narrow walk close to the river, beneath the bridge, Jessica spun around, ran straight at Hudson and slide tackled him hard.

Caught off guard, Hudson met the concrete with a crunch, his nose breaking on impact. Crying out, he turned over in time to see Jessica stood a few feet away, grinning mischievously, hands hanging by her sides.

'Oh, dear,' she said. 'That was nasty.'

Hudson pulled himself up, nursing his nose and made an attempt at standing.

Jessica came in again, raising a foot up quickly to meet his chest. Winding him immediately. Hudson met the concrete once more, gasping for breath, feeling vulnerable. Powerless.

At the mercy of a woman he thought he knew. A woman he cared for. Now a psychotic serial killer, who had manipulated him at every turn.

He felt utterly discarded. Used. Betrayed.

Hudson tried to cry out, but Jessica stepped over, gifting him a few solid punches to the face. Bloodied, damaged, out of shape, Hudson lay a ruin. He spat a globule of blood out to the left of him and shouted at her. His back sodden wet from the snow.

'Come on! Kill me!'

The answer never came. He shouted again. 'KILL ME!' And choked on the tears.

'Oh, no, it's ruined now, Danny. And you'll suffer for it. You all will. So wrapped up in your own facades. Your lies!' She stepped up close to him, kneeling down to touch his beaten face. Blood still gushing from a split on his forehead, now seeping down into his eyes. 'Pity. It would have been perfect.'

In a flash, Hudson drew out his cuffs and latched down onto Jessica's exposed wrist.

She was trapped. Her eyes bulged in horror.

'No! NO!'

Hudson grinned, hearing numerous cars screeching overhead. Doors slamming. Hurried footsteps around them. 'They're already here. Your reign of terror is over, you fucking psychopath.'

Jessica stood frozen, as if she had all but given up and soon, the tunnel filled with armed police and detectives with handguns, shouting orders and screaming for Jessica to get down on the ground.

Hudson's heavy head gave in, smacking back into the pavement. The nauseous agony suddenly took him, blotting out his vision. A strange static sweep moved across his eyes, a coldness in his hands and feet. Before the darkness took him, a peculiar word, embellished in gold, set back on a great plinth swam above and to his left.

Invicta.

Tuesday, 19th March

11:00

Stuck at home, injured and useless, the days blurred together. It was a marked improvement from his few days in hospital from the injuries sustained in his high-speed chase. Back at the flat in his own bed, with his own food and Eisa, making a late appearance. Apparently, the reason for her absence had been an unplanned date with her girlfriend, followed by a stay-over. With the stress of her bookshop and lack of sleep living with a man who suffered from violent nightmares, she'd made executive decisions to stay away.

Hudson couldn't blame her one bit.

Once the arm and his side were feeling much better, he chucked on a jacket at some time mid-morning, two weeks after the incident, grabbed his keys and left. Outside, the cold, crisp, air, kissed him sweetly. The last of the snow melting away, bringing with it a more manageable, zero degrees frost. Once he got to his car though, he winced at the thought, felt he had done enough sitting about. Hudson stuffed the keys into his jacket pocket and made his way south down the street, toward the city.

The trip took him a good two hours in total, but it was rejuvenating. Revitalising. Took his time. His lungs begging for more of it, his legs stretching out ahead of him, building a steady pace. A few gave him curious looks, some even sympathy. His face still heavily bruised.

Not long after he'd stopped at a Greggs, pastry flaking out from his mouth in rabid hunger, did he realise how far he'd come and knew that just down the road was the station. His very own. The headquarters to his demise. A firm tug in his gut warned him about what he wanted to do. To make an early appearance. He took out the envelope in his coat pocket to make sure it was all still there, then placed it back.

He tried to imagine what Hiraoka's first words would be. What the rest of the team would say when he rocked up. After the shit storm with the surgeon, who turned out to be his girlfriend Jessica, no part of town offered a crevice or hole, he could crawl away in and hide from the stories. The tales they would tell from station to station, constituency to county. He'd be forever known as the guy who slept with London's second most violent, first most brutal female serial killer.

Ended one copper. Shagged another. He closed his eyes and couldn't believe he was welling up.

'Cheer up mate, the food ain't that bad.'

A kid running past waved at him, having seen his tear stricken face. Hudson coughed, wiped his face and laughed him off. 'Yeah, I know!' Maybe he should book in another session with Dr Podelcki?

The door to Charing Cross police station looked solid. Heavy to push. He wasn't quite sure he'd be able to get it open but, he did, and the heads all but began to turn his way. One after the other. Hallways full of stares. Holding his breath, he managed to make it up to his floor and to the main office, which housed the special cases team. The murder squad. Provisionally, the team would be working out of the station for the foreseeable. A decision by Elms, apparently.

Hudson managed to slip in unnoticed, but after a few double takes, everyone had clocked on.

'Fucking hell,' said one guy in the back. Phillips, who turned in his chair and looked the other way.

Hudson saw Leigh, resting her arse on the edge of a desk, drinking a coffee. He nodded in her general direction. Got nothing in return. It felt like a blow to the stomach. Winded.

355

Back at what he presumed was his new desk, beside Leigh's, empty aside from stationary and his computer, he checked for notes and letters. Had a peek for any voice messages of which there were none.

He wanted to find Hiraoka. Had to speak with him first. It was important. As Hudson rounded the pillar, he found Hiraoka, standing up from his desk when he spotted the constable. Hudson pulled out a letter from his jacket and handed it over to him. His face solemn. Others in the room watching closely.

They all knew what it was. What it meant. A voice he could only presume was Hunt's shouted his approval. Hiraoka ignored it.

The chief inspector held up the letter. Hudson watched him. None of them saying a word. Looked into his face, searching for something. Anything that may hint at his thoughts and feelings. How he was taking it all. Maybe he wanted to punch him? Hell, he knew he had it in him. Hudson braced himself for something but watched, in astonishment, as Hiraoka slowly fed the letter into a paper shredder.

The loud buzz filled the office, drawing a few more looks.

Hudson gawked at him.

'Why?'

'You forget, DC Hudson, how long I've been doing this.' He unjammed the shredder when it stopped, got it going again. 'I'm not about to gobble down a load of shite about you fucking this case. And you can stick it to anyone in this station as well because the commander thinks otherwise. He may not be me, but he'll back you as well.'

Hudson chewed the inside of his cheek. 'Well, he's got to, hasn't he? I'm the crowning recruitment for the fucking squad. His name is all over it now.'

'No lie there. Anyway, I think the man wants a word. Keep your head. I've got you on this.'

Hudson shook his hand. Felt a sudden rush of overwhelming gratitude and another, even more shocking surge of tears in his eyes. What the hell was wrong with him? He swallowed them down and made for the commander's private, sectioned off office, knocked, went in, and shut the door behind him.

'Afternoon sir.'

'Have a seat, Daniel.'

He pulled up a chair and sat. Crossed his fingers and looked right at the man. The kingpin of it all.

'It won't come as a surprise, that following recent events, an investigation into the way you and this team handled this case will be made. I've managed to get a bit of time for you to recover, I appreciate the circumstances. I'll be very frank here, Daniel, it's quite a shit storm. I won't sit and berate you on what-ifs and the like, the investigation will pull up what we need. There's nothing you wish to tell me now off the record?'

Hudson thought about that for a moment. 'No sir. Nothing.'

'Very well. Until the investigation is closed resolutely, your movements will be limited, which means visits to the mortuary, autopsy room, evidence locker and other more classified databases at our disposal. You will be overseen by Detective Constable Leigh. She has more experience, can mentor you and Hiraoka doesn't need you tangling him up. We also want you out of the spotlight until this circus is cleared up. As a result, you will be placed on probation for the next twenty-four months, follow regular performance reviews and a final interview at the end. Does that all sound about right so far?'

'Yes sir,' he said, glad the punishment hadn't been much worse. 'One question.'

'Fire away.'

'Why aren't you... You seem very calm about this. Not that I'm conveying any guilt here, but you do seem to be taking this well.'

The commander laughed then, shaking his head. 'Whatever lets you sleep at night. I can assure you, I am not calm, despite appearances. I'm being fucked immeasurably, but I do have a code. A personal one and that's to look out for my team, whoever that may be. Which, before you came along, was extremely honourable.'

'Sir, I...'

'Don't interrupt me. I'm speaking,' he snapped. 'This team has never been spotless, but it has produced consistently excellent results, with very little hiccoughs, excluding of course a few terrorism incidences, and I refuse to let a rookie come in and shake all that up, especially after the merging of boroughs and other MITs. Tarnish all of Haskell's hard work. I will expect your full compliance and obedience with internal affairs starting next week. I don't want to hear anything about you holding anything back. When I say full compliance, I mean it. Full compliance.'

'Yes, sir.'

'Is that very clear, detective?'

He sighed, gripping the edges of the chair. 'Yes, sir.'

'Good.'

Hudson took out a yellow carton of green tea juice. Pulled a straw off the side, unwrapped it and punctured the tiny foil hole on the top. He took a long drag of it before placing it down on the railings, taking in a breath of fresh air.

Footsteps behind him and the smell of familiar smoke told him who had joined him.

'I owe you one, Hiraoka.'

The chief inspector's trademark red scarf hung loosely around his shoulders, cigarette limp between two fingers. 'You pulled it out the bag when it mattered. The coppers in this unit that matter will recognise what you did. But it's only just started, Hudson, so keep your cards to your chest. '

'What do you mean?'

'I mean, we've all, at some point, done a fucking rodeo with internal affairs. Get yourself straight. Hutchings is just the beginning.'

Hudson took another sip of his drink and shot him a puzzled look. 'Of course, I am. I don't need t— You don't believe it, do you?'

'Doesn't matter what I think, kabu, not yet, anyway.'

'Bullshit.'

Then the question he'd been nagging to ask since he'd set foot inside. 'What's the news on Jessica? Saw on the news she'd been arrested on charges of murder but no details.'

Hiraoka nodded. 'We've had enough to place her at Haskell's. We've had Bradley, the cinema owner come in just last week to confirm her identity. Now we just need to work at getting as much of a case together for CPS, to deliver a verdict on all four murders. It'll take the better part of a year, but we'll do it.'

'That's good news,' he said, relieved. 'Glad I didn't totally sour the evidence and somehow make everything inadmissible.'

'Well, we'll see. Juries still out on that.'

'Right.'

The two regarded each other silently, Hiraoka dragging methodically, puffing out small rings. Then, very gradually, a smile appeared, tugging at the corners of his eyes.

'Got a new word for ya.'

'Yeah?'

'Nemeshisu.'

'Neme… Nemesis?'

Hiraoka clapped. 'Hai! Well done, but that one was easy. I figured it fitting, bit dramatic though yeah?'

Hudson turned away and stared at a few coppers crossing the road toward the building. 'Hmm, what's the Japanese for enemies?'

'Shukuteki. Why?'

Hudson didn't answer. Instead, he drained the last of his juice, chucked it into a bin, turned and walked back toward the station, still nursing the pain in his ribs. Hiraoka watched silently, and travelled back in time to see his twenty-five-year-old self, leave him gawking in the courtyard.

And Hudson looked back at him. Saw a different man. Something else at work underneath the all the years. For now, that consoled him and would be enough to get him to go forward. His work, nor the team's, was far from done. Now they had to pull the unit back together again and tie off the rest of the case. Put Jessica behind bars for a very long time.

That was a promise, Hudson thought, as he sat back at his desk and picked up the phone. He'd make sure of it.

Message from the Author

Thank you so much for reading my first self-published novel! It's been a wild ride to get from notes on scraps of paper to here, especially now with this second edition.

If you are at all inclined to join DC Hudson on his adventures, or simply wish to support me, please visit my writing cove at www.jasonrvowles.com

DC Daniel Hudson shall return soon...

About The Author

Jason R Vowles was born and raised, well, almost everywhere in England. Born in Lincolnshire, he moved to Norfolk as a kid, then to Northamptonshire and Bristol for studies. Finally moving to Wales, he settled in Cardiff where his writing career finally took off. A veracious reader of multiple of genres, Jason plans on releasing more than just a few crime novels. A fan of all good things such as animals, good food and good booze, he finds plenty to keep himself occupied and fuelled whilst writing his next book.

If you're at all interested in any deals for free books, content or upcoming novels, you can join the VIP Reader's Club at the below:

www.JasonRVowles.com

Printed in Great Britain
by Amazon

15786425R00212